Unknowingly he brought the claw home. Beautiful, hypnotic, ancient, it was the sacred—and deadly—talisman of the fabled Leopard Men of Africa.

Unsuspected, it would crawl its way into his mind, bringing horrifying destruction into his home. And unresisted, it would demand an unbelievable sacrifice. And then—perhaps—it would move on...

Tor books by Ramsey Campbell

for Jack and Robin
(who know my secret)
and for Jack Martin
(who is one)
– friends for life

One

It took Joanna Marlowe almost an hour to cross from the mainland to Lagos. Beneath a sky the colour of sandy mud the bridge was jammed with cars and bicycles, blaring and ringing and hooting. A few canoes sprouting umbrellas glided across the lagoon, past a lone bedraggled yacht stranded in the drizzle without a hope of wind. Joanna's car was boxed in by a bus called God Save Us and a boastfully shiny black car, driven by a Yoruba man who kept leaning on his horn and chewing a cigar almost as fat as the exhaust pipe. She felt trapped by the thick, muggy heat and the traffic, yet she wasn't anxious to move. Her talk with Isaac had made her afraid to go home.

Beside her, Helen was sulking because she'd been slapped for trying to sound the horn. The little girl crossed and uncrossed her long bare legs, tugged restlessly at her shorts, rolled the window up and down. Now she was snapping the glove compartment, over and over again. Joanna was about to slap her when the bus in front lurched forward. The driver of the shiny car leaned on his horn at once, and Joanna barely restrained herself from walking back and screaming obscenities at him. She no longer felt at all like an anthropologist's wife from Oxford. She wasn't even sure whose wife she was.

Helen was jumping up and down, her seat-belt twanging. 'Look, there he is, mummy,' she pleaded. 'The boy with the toys.' He was one of the traders who plied the narrow strip between the road and the parapet, waiting for traffic jams. Joanna haggled half-heartedly with him for a set of plastic quoits, and wished she could be distracted as easily as Helen was now. She stared across at the Carter Bridge.

7

Yes, it was jammed too. At least it would mean that David couldn't be home before she was.

When she drove off the bridge at last, the traffic was still crawling. Shoppers in robes of all colours were swarming along the Marina, lorries groaned up from the quay alongside. Beyond the mass of stores, outside which women sat in makeshift shelters, selling matches or buttons or single cigarettes, cars choked the road around the hospital. A plane sailed up from Murtala Muhammed Airport on the mainland and vanished through a gap in the clouds. She felt a sudden wish to take Helen home to England, but suppressed it. She was as afraid of leaving David here as she was of staying with him.

By the time she reached the end of the Marina, the clouds had parted fully. As she drove onto Victoria Island, sun streamed over the exhibition centre and the embassies, the beach scattered with prophets in praying sheds built out of palm fronds and individually signposted for tourists. She'd left the jabber of shoppers behind, she was in the open at last, and yet if anything she felt even more boxed in.

In a few minutes she was at the bungalow. The long front lawn was steaming; beneath the trees the grass was already dry and bright. Perhaps a shower would make her feel better. Thanks to the Foundation for African Studies, they even had a shower in the house.

She drove into the open garage – and jumped, stalling the engine. David's car was already there. Seeing his new friend off at the airport hadn't taken him as long as she'd expected. Joanna cursed. She wasn't ready for a confrontation with him, with this stranger who muttered and clenched his teeth and wouldn't look at her. She dragged at the stiff door of the garage, while Helen swung on it and waved her legs as it jerked downward. Perhaps he'd left the car and gone out for a walk – she hoped so; anything, so long as it gave her time to prepare herself. But when she came round the house the front door was open, and he was waiting in the doorway.

He seemed bigger than ever. He had never looked like an anthropologist, but that hadn't used to matter; he had just been David, huge and red-bearded and gentle, who would carry baby Helen about on the palm of one hand. Now it was a stranger who stood blocking the way – except that a stranger couldn't have made her innards twist and tighten so painfully. She felt Helen draw closer to her as he stepped forward, and that was the worst of all.

But he was smiling, so widely that his lips were trembling. It was the first time in weeks that Joanna had seen him smile. 'Hello there,' he shouted at both of them, so loudly that the Alsatian began snarling next door at the Donners'. 'My God, you look roasted. I'll bet you're ready to sell your souls for air-conditioning. Where have you been?'

Before Joanna could answer – he was trying so hard to be his old self that it was as if someone was performing a parody of him – he saw Helen's quoits. 'Did mummy buy you those? Aren't you the lucky girl? Come and see what else I've bought you.'

He went into the house at once. When the little girl hesitated, Joanna found it difficult to breathe. If Helen trusted him again, perhaps the past wouldn't matter any longer . . . Helen was following him, but Joanna could tell it was only out of obedience. She followed her daughter quickly.

He was in the living-room. The sky was clouding over again, but he hadn't turned on the lights. A watery glow filtered through the windows and gathered on the carved toothy masks above the cocktail bar, the ivory Benin figurine at the centre of the Scandinavian table, the collected editions of Dickens and Trollope that came with the bungalow. David was holding up a black box. 'Here you are,' he said to Helen. 'High-Life music whenever you want it.'

It was a portable radio and cassette recorder. They'd always told Helen she could have one when she was old enough. He was holding it out to her, his smile wavering in case she wouldn't go to him. But she ran to him, pleading, 'Show me how to work it, daddy.'

He hugged her and stroked her long auburn hair as he showed her which buttons to push. But he must have felt he was trying too hard to wipe out the effects of the last few weeks, because he patted her bottom and sent her away as soon as he'd finished demonstrating. 'And what can I give mummy? You look as though you could do with a long cool alcoholic drink. In fact, let's both have one.'

Was that a good sign? In these last few weeks – in fact ever since he'd managed to track down a survivor of the old outlawed secret society – he'd hardly touched alcohol, as if he was afraid of losing control. He came back from the kitchen, shaking ice in tall glasses in time with Helen's Nigerian cassette. As he brought Joanna her Bacardi and Coke he squeezed her shoulder and gave her an apologetic, hopeful smile. She managed to smile in return, and clasped his great hand on her shoulder.

When he moved away to his chair – he moved as if he was sore inside, in his mind, perhaps – she said 'Was your friend in time for his plane?'

'In time? Joanna, you know you've got to be at least a day late to miss a plane in Lagos. He wasn't really what you'd call a friend, anyway. Though I suppose almost anyone's a friend at a party when you've had enough to drink. I just gave him a lift to save him from having to pay the earth for a taxi, that's all.'

So he *had* been drinking at the party. Early this morning when he'd fallen into bed and had gone straight to sleep, she'd been so relieved that she had slept soundly herself. It was the first night for weeks that he hadn't started pacing the room in the dark or stumbled out for a walk. Both of them had slept until late morning, when he'd woken crying, 'Oh God – Alan Knight! I've got to run him to the airport,' and had driven away, half-dressed and unshaven. Had he been drinking last night because his problems were over, or in a desperate attempt to forget them, whatever they were?

Now he seemed anxious to explain away Alan Knight and change the subject, as if it made him feel guilty somehow. 'Where did you go today?' he asked for the second time.

Before Joanna could think of an appropriate lie, Helen told him: she loved saying the name, which always made her giggle. 'To see Mr Banjo,' she cried.

'Dropped in on old Isaac, did you?' He went quickly to the bar, and Joanna couldn't see his face, only the dark grinning masks around him. 'What did he have to say for himself?'

'Not much,' Joanna said.

'What, our favourite Yoruba from Oxford with nothing to say? Not even a proverb or two? I'll have to have words with him.' His jollity was shrill, almost hysterical. All at once she knew she had been right: the reason Isaac had been so unforthcoming was that he knew what was wrong with David. He'd sat beneath the creaking electric fan in his office at the University, smiling his piano-key smile and telling her that David must be having difficulties in his research. If that was true, why hadn't David told her, his assistant since before they were married?

Now David seemed to realize that she felt cut off from him by his false gaiety. 'I meant to tell you – I've a bit of rewriting to do,' he said, 'and then I'll give you a pile of work. Some of it wasn't worth keeping. Just hysterical.'

She always typed out his work – nobody else could read his handwriting – but he hadn't let her see anything for weeks; he had even taken to locking his notes away. Could the problem really have been nothing but a snag in his research, which had preyed on his nerves but which he'd had to work out for himself? Had he just become trapped in self-doubt? She wanted to think so, but she mustn't ask until Helen was safely in bed.

He refilled her glass and closed his hand gently over hers. 'I've made dinner,' he said. 'Cold meats and salad – it's in the fridge.'

Helen had to be persuaded to join them at the table, for

she was dancing around the room to the beat of her cassette. David had regained his appetite and was making up for these last weeks, which was encouraging. Joanna was wolfing down her meal despite the fluttering of her stomach, so that she could finish, bathe Helen and put her to bed, and be able to ask him at last to tell her what had been wrong. She was beginning to sense that his gentleness was a plea for reassurance, and surely that meant he wanted her to ask.

As soon as Helen had finished, she jumped down from her chair and grabbed her radio. In a moment she was disco-dancing beneath the gaze of the masks. 'Don't get too excited,' Joanna warned her. She was enjoying the chance to sit and feel comfortable with David, even though the sky and the room were darkening; it had been so long. 'Bathtime soon,' she said.

David stood up. 'You sit and rest. I've been letting you do everything lately. I'll get her ready for bed.'

All at once the sky was very dark. Raindrops that sounded big as flies spattered the windows. Joanna couldn't see his face, only the looming masks. When she switched on the lights – they flickered a little, threatening a power-cut – she felt apprehensive once again, for Helen was looking to her for guidance. The little girl still wasn't sure of her father.

Joanna glanced nervously at him, but she couldn't refuse him. Being accepted again by his child might be just the reassurance he needed. Surely Helen had never been in real danger from him? She'd been wary of him only because he'd turned into someone she didn't know, like the victim of a spell in a fairy tale. 'All right, David, if you like,' Joanna said, and was inexpressibly relieved that Helen went to him at once.

She sat for a while, listening to Helen running about the bathroom and squealing. Now there was the hollow rumble of the bath, like thunder in the midst of the sizzle of rain. The lights flickered again, the masks twitched. Then she realized that she was listening in case anything was wrong, and made herself clear the table and go into the kitchen.

Beyond the window the lawn looked drowned, and the black sky was crawling, lowering toward her, as if it couldn't bear the weight of rain. Its looming presence, breathlessly oppressive, made her feel how near the jungle was. She washed the dishes slowly, aware that she was trying not to make too much noise, just in case. Next door the Alsatian was snuffling. Perhaps it had a cold; she had been hearing the sound for days. Just in case of what? she demanded angrily of herself. That started the litany of fears all over again: another woman, cancer, a crime of some kind – but if any of those was David's problem, it couldn't harm Helen. The important point was that Helen trusted him again. That showed there was nothing to fear.

The rain was slackening. The sound of the downpour faded like tuned-out static. Now she could hear Helen splashing, and she clattered the cutlery so as not to eavesdrop. She could still hear the snuffling – in fact, it sounded as if the dog was just below the kitchen window. Had it strayed into the garden? As the lights dimmed sharply for a moment – it made her think of a heart missing a beat – she craned forward over the sink, to see.

At first all she could see was the brooding green of the lawn and the reflection of her own face, a pale mask set in sodden velvet. Then without warning her face vanished, and the dog began to bark. All at once her chest felt too tight to breathe. She knew why her reflection had been wiped out – the power had failed. That was why the dog was barking – but though the barking came from the house next door, the snuffling was still below her window.

Could something have come out of the jungle, all the way to the island? Ever since she'd come to Lagos, that had been one of her secret fears. She could only thank God that David was with Helen. The black sky pressed down, the lurid garden was closing in like jungle, and it seemed forever before the lights flared up again.

She backed away, limp with relief. Now the kitchen was

lit she felt almost secure, walled off from whatever was outside. Perhaps David ought to find out what had strayed into the garden, while she kept Helen safe. She was wondering if it would be dangerous for him to go out there when the child began to scream.

Joanna ran through the living-room and into the hall. The lights were flickering again – the wooden lips of the masks were writhing, their empty eyes glaring dully – but she knew instinctively that it wasn't the dark the child was afraid of; something far worse. Before she reached the bathroom Joanna was crying out for David. But he didn't reply, though she could hear him muttering in there, and the bathroom door was locked.

Her fears rushed back, a shapeless mass of them blotting out her thoughts and leaving her nothing but instinct. Beyond the door Helen was thrashing about in the bath, and screaming. Joanna's senses were feverishly heightened, for she could hear the child scrabbling at the slippery bath, water sloshing across the linoleum. She lifted one leg, and with all her desperate strength, kicked the door just beneath the handle. The door flew inward, ripping the socket of the bolt away from the frame.

The first thing she saw as she staggered into the room was the colour of the water that had spilled across the floor to her feet. It was pink. In a moment she saw what had coloured it – saw the trickles of blood that were mingled with the water. Blood was trickling down the side of the bath. She had to force herself to look beyond that, to where Helen was cowering against the taps.

The child was struggling in the pinkish water. She was screaming so loudly that the tiled walls seemed to shriek, and her limbs seemed useless. The discolouration of the water made it difficult for Joanna to see the child's body. Her eyes were aching with strain before she made out that the child was unmarked. Once she was sure of that, she was able to look at David. She saw the razor-blade in his left hand at once.

He seemed hardly aware of her. Certainly his muttering

wasn't intended for her. 'It didn't work,' he was repeating lifelessly. 'It won't stop.' Perhaps he was as drained of feeling as his voice, for he was slashing mechanically at his right hand with the razor. Though its fingers were twitching, it was scarcely more than rags of raw flesh now.

He was turning toward Helen. Up went his left hand with the razor-blade. 'Won't stop,' he moaned. Before Joanna could move, he had shoved the blade into his open mouth, and swallowed. The next moment he lurched forward at Helen. It was a convulsion, not an attack. As he slumped to his knees, nothing reached her but an enormous rush of blood.

Two

Ten hours earlier, Alan Knight was thinking: My God, he's crazy. I'm being driven by a madman.

Though the expressway to the airport was slippery with rain, everyone was driving as if they couldn't leave Lagos behind soon enough. They still had miles to go, for here on the mainland Lagos sent its housing and industrial estates swarming toward the north. They'd passed the over-crowded bungalows of Ebute-Metta, but Mushin and Oshodi were still to come — if Alan ever got there, if the car hadn't left the road by then.

'I think we've got plenty of time before check-in,' he said, as casually as he could.

When Marlowe glanced at him, the car swerved. This is it, Alan thought numbly. I've done it now, I've made him crash. But Marlowe guided them back into the wake of the car ahead. 'Better let me judge the speed. We're liable to cause an accident if I try to go slow.'

True, many of the drivers were unused to high-speed roads. Alan had already seen three cars off the road today, one attended by an ambulance and two already rusting. All the same, he could see no reason for Marlowe to drive like this, glaring fiercely through the watery fan of the wind-screen wiper, overtaking whenever he saw the hint of a gap. In his great red-haired hands the wheel looked like a toy, and Alan was afraid that Marlowe regarded it as such. He was beginning to wish he had taken a taxi, even though, after Frankfurt, Lagos had the most expensive taxis in the world.

How had he ended up with this lift at all? He remem-bered being invited to last night's party ('Mr Knight, you *must* come, *everyone* knows your books, they're *dying* to meet you') but very little of the party itself: a blur of people in pale thin suits or dresses or Yoruba robes, Nigerians laughing and shaking his hand for minutes, expatriates dark as mahogany, full of all the questions you were supposed to ask a writer. They might know of his books, but it seemed that nobody had read them. After hours of this sort of thing he'd found himself talking to Marlowe, the red-bearded giant he had noticed drinking and brooding all by himself in a corner. He couldn't recall what Marlowe had said – something about the hidden dangers of anthropology? – until suddenly Marlowe's eyes had brightened, for no reason that Alan could see. 'You're going to need a lift tomorrow,' Marlowe had said, and here it was.

The downpour was worsening. As they sped through Mushin – cheap houses crammed together fifteen to the acre, four people or more to a room – the rain made grey auras just above the roofs of cars, sloshed over windshields faster than wipers could wipe. Apart from craning forward to peer through the rain, Marlowe made no concession to the weather, even though once the back wheels began to slew.

All at once he began to talk, or at least to mutter to himself. 'I shouldn't have brought my family out here. You never know anything until it's too late.'

What had he said last night about families? Marlowe swerved the car into another gap, and Alan could only sit on his prickling hands and pray that the wheels held the road. He had a horrid suspicion that if Marlowe were distracted in any way, he might forget that he wasn't in England and relapse into driving on the left.

'It's like any other science,' Marlowe said – anthropology, Alan assumed. 'We have to learn that research isn't everything. We ought to stop sometimes and ask whether what we're finding out is likely to be beneficial. But we can't stop, we have to go on, it's a compulsion. We're no more in control of ourselves than the animals are.'

His hands were trembling on the wheel; the wheel itself

was shaking. Alan turned away quickly and stared out as the stunted dense houses of Oshodi shot past, tin roofs steaming in a sudden lull in the rain. Just a few minutes to the airport, he thought desperately. Just a few minutes, and then in a few hours I'll be with Liz and Anna and we'll laugh about this. Though not about him, poor sod, whatever's the matter with him.

'Did I show you a photograph of Helen and my wife last night?' Marlowe was mumbling. 'I have to get her back to England, both of them. This country's no good for us.'

Alan could see the textile mills of Ikeja ahead. An airliner rose from the airport, slow as treacle. Though the car was rushing onward, spattering itself with mud, the airport seemed to be receding. But here was the approach road, thank God. Marlowe drove onto it without slowing, the back wheels screeching as he braked at last. It's a miracle, Alan thought. We've made it. He had never imagined he could be so grateful to see the perimeter fence and the guards.

The last raindrops were scurrying like insects down the wire mesh of the fence; the concrete pillars were piebald with drying. Though the guard's holster appeared to be sweating, he scarcely glanced into the cars before waving them on. Now that they had to proceed more slowly, Alan could relax; but it was odd that Marlowe seemed to be growing more tense. Perhaps it was a reaction after driving.

Metal roofs glittered in the car park. Marlowe eased the car into a space, turned off the engine, and sat gripping the wheel. All at once, as though he'd reached a decision, he opened the door and squeezed out. For the first time the large car felt spacious. 'We'd better get your luggage,' he said.

When Alan climbed out, Marlowe was standing by the boot to let a black car pass. As the car glided into a nearby space, he unlocked the boot and lifted out Alan's suitcase as though it weighed less than a handbag. Then he stood staring into the boot. 'Oh, good God, no,' he said.

'What's wrong?'

'I forgot to post a package. It had to go to London today. I'll never get to the post office in time.'

Alan had an idea of what he was expected to say, but after the drive he was wary. 'What is it?' he said.

'Just an artefact. I would have remembered except for meeting you and giving you a lift.'

However appalling the drive had been, it was over now, and Alan was sure he could write it into a story. 'I'll take it for you, if you like.'

'Oh, would you? That's extremely good of you. It would be a great weight off my mind.' Marlowe's voice was hollow, for he'd stooped to rummage around in the boot. As he emerged with the package, he unbent too soon and scraped the back of his neck on the metal edge of the lid of the boot. He seemed too preoccupied even to notice. 'Here you are,' he said.

It was a rectangular box sealed in brown paper, a package almost the length of a hand and a forearm, though it didn't look so large in Marlowe's hands. 'I should put it in your suitcase, just in case the Customs people think it looks odd,' Marlowe said. 'You know, the postal monopoly, that sort of thing. You can see it's all right from the label, can't you? The Foundation is highly respected, any anthropologist would tell you so.'

The Foundation for African Studies sounded perfectly legitimate – it was all this explanation that was making Alan nervous. He hid the package under his shirts and snapped the catches. Then he started. Someone was watching him: a tall man in a white suit, who was closing the boot of the black car that had passed a few minutes ago.

Before Alan could speak, Marlowe grabbed his suitcase. 'Let me take that,' he said, and strode toward the airport building, long stacks of concrete sprouting the stone blossom of the control tower. The tall man had turned away; no doubt he hadn't been watching at all. Alan had written so much spy fiction that he sometimes felt he was living a spy story himself.

Marlowe didn't slow down until he reached the check-in desk. By the time Alan caught up with him he had already dumped the suitcase on the weighing platform. Breathlessly, Alan panted that he wanted to sit in the no-smoking area, before his case sailed away behind the scenes.

There was at least an hour to wait before boarding. Marlowe was mopping his forehead. 'Fancy a drink?' Alan said.

'No, I have to get back.' Marlowe was stuffing his handkerchief back into his pocket; in his huge hand it looked as if he'd picked up a woman's handkerchief by mistake. 'I need to get back to my family,' he said, with an expression so apologetic it looked guilty. He shook hands, then strode away without a backward glance.

Alan went through into the departure hall and wandered toward the bar, looking for details he might use in his novel and trying to think of a title. They had streamlined the terminal and called it Murtala Muhammed Airport – another airport named after an assassin's victim. A priest came down an escalator, his skin black as his cloth, his collar gleaming fluorescently. A group of Yorubas in robes and caps stood by the duty-free shop, greeting each other effusively. A Hausa family strode by in search of someone, the wives chattering behind their husband, all of them in dazzling white robes like the newly baptized. A Yoruba mother sailed along a walkway, her baby slung on her back. It reminded Alan of a koala cub, alert gleaming eyes and all.

He sat in the bar and sipped a glass of the potent Nigerian beer. He had the scenes he'd come to Nigeria for, but what was the book to be called? The lack of a title made him edgy, especially when he was so near to writing the book. His mind seemed fixed on the Nigerian episode; the narrator came here in search of a birth certificate, but after much travelling and bribery, went away empty-handed, unaware that the man whose double-dealing had lured him halfway across the world, along a trail of torture and murder, was his own father. So far all the titles he could think of revolved round that theme too: *Family Plot* and *Family Circle* were too obvious; *Familiarity* sounded like a Victorian novel, and would sell just about as many copies nowadays. Shrugging irritably, he went to the window to check the departure board. Then he was coughing into his beer, and had to restrain himself from dodging back out of sight at once. Out there in the departure hall, the man who had watched him in the car park was talking into a pay telephone and gazing straight at him.

Alan finished his beer as quickly as he could and emerged into the bright spacious hall. The man in white was no longer to be seen. Of course, it was just a coincidence – the man had had to look somewhere while he was talking; and anyway, why should he have known that Alan was in the bar? If he let himself, Alan could imagine that Marlowe's package was a bomb, that Marlowe's dislike of his job was so uncontrollable that he meant to wipe out the Foundation in London. That was nonsense. All the same, he was relieved that the number of his flight had come up on the screen.

The enclosed ramp to the plane was narrow. The aisle of the plane was narrower, and blocked by shuffling passengers, yet all at once Alan was easier in his mind. It was absurd, but somehow the British Airways plane felt like British territory. He hadn't realized how secretly vulnerable he felt in foreign places. As soon as the plane lifted off and rainclouds wiped out the landscape, he forgot about the package in his suitcase, and the man, who surely hadn't been watching him after all. Perhaps he would call them to mind if he needed them. Writing had that advantage – you could always use your experiences eventually, however unpleasant they seemed at the time.

In the cramped toilet he splashed cold water on his face. When he raised the plug the water was sucked down the plughole with a shrill rush of air. He resumed his seat as the stewardesses came round with meals on moulded plastic trays. Alan ate ravenously, though his red-faced neighbour was bending forward over a sick bag and staring lugubriously into its depths. *Hangman's Dance*, *To Visit The Queen*, *The Sunday Assassin*: he was pretty good with titles as a rule – why couldn't he think of one now? It reminded him of his early days of struggle, of going to his desk in the corner of the London flat without a thought in his head. He remembered sitting beneath the patch of damp that looked like a sneering face and grinding out paragraphs purely in order to get the story over with, the story that had excited him so much – until he'd actually sat down to write it. He had never felt the least involvement with the characters as he'd struggled to make them seem real. His pen and his brain had felt scratchy, Liz had been pregnant with Anna, the damp had crept over the walls, he'd been desperate to buy a house before she had the child – and he'd finished the book with no sense of achievement at all, without ever reaching that magical point where the characters take over and dictate their story to the writer. He'd already had two novels stuck in a drawer with bunches of rejection slips, and when he'd started he'd been convinced that *this* was the one that would sell. The end-product had depressed him so much that he hadn't even let Liz read the typescript before he sent it away. Yet that book *The Sunday Assassin* had been his first major success – 'all plot, and not a wasted word,' one review had said.

Now the days of struggle were over, more or less; now he only had to struggle for a title.

How about *Out of the Past*? It sounded like a film, but he didn't think it was; perhaps it sounded like the film it might be made into. He couldn't resist it; it seemed too good an omen. He lay back in his seat, relaxing at last, and closed his eyes. The plane was bumping gently, rhythmically. He thought a hammock might feel like that, rocking in a breeze.

The hammock was in Africa, and so was he, trying to run home. He had been running for a very long time. Now the looming vegetation was too vague for him to make out where he was. He was trying to catch up with someone in the foggy dark, while something red loped alongside him, urging him on. He managed to turn aside at the last moment, into a clearing. A thin old figure leapt to its feet as it saw him, and Alan was stumbling, unable to keep his balance, falling into the fleshless arms of the figure, which had the smallest eyes and the longest nails he had ever seen. The ground had thrown him forward into its arms, because the ground was tilting, the plane was. He woke to find that the plane was landing at Heathrow.

He was bewildered to find he'd slept so long, and he was still trying to blink himself awake as he shuffled forward with the rest of the passengers, past the captain standing by the exit like a priest after a mass. What was it that he couldn't quite remember? Perhaps he would know when he woke up fully.

Chimes rang, amplified voices boomed high up in the airport hall. Suitcases appeared at the top of a ramp, slid down to the roundabout where their owners were waiting. It all had the unresolved quality of a dream; in a moment the scene might be transformed into parents watching their children on slides and roundabouts, invisible giants ringing bells overhead. He was nearly awake now. He grabbed his suitcase as it sailed by and staggered with it toward the Customs area. SOMETHING TO DECLARE, NOTHING TO DECLARE. 'Nothing' seemed easier, and the sign was green for go.

As soon as he reached the counter he knew that he'd made a mistake. The officer behind the desk was young, and eager to show he was doing his job. You could tell he would relish body searches, even though he would never have admitted it, even to himself. He stood straight-backed as a dummy, eyes gleaming impersonally in the smooth scrubbed face, his hair and moustache clipped short, his manner precise. 'Have you read the notice?' he said, like a policeman cautioning a criminal.

'Yes, I have.' Alan was sure he had nothing on the list: jewellery, wines, spirits . . . Nevertheless the Customs officer read out the items one by one. 'You're quite sure you're not carrying anything on that list?' he said.

'Yes, I am.'

A determined blankness spread over the officer's face. 'Will you open your case, please?'

Alan opened it readily enough. It wasn't even locked – that would only have risked someone breaking into it while it was behind the scenes. He should have felt smug, because he knew that the Customs man would find nothing, except that he could almost hear a warning deep in his mind. The young man was turning over shirts and under-wear like an overseer in a laundry, searching primly for stains. Suddenly he poked a rectangular bulge under the towels. 'What's this?' he said.

It was the package that Marlowe had given him. How could he have forgotten? He must still be half asleep. 'It's a parcel for these people,' he said, pointing to the address. 'They need it urgently, and so I said I'd bring it over.'

'That's against regulations.' The Customs man's face was blanker than ever. 'Please open it,' he said.

As Alan fumbled with the wrapping, almost breaking one of his nails, sweat stung his palms, as if the package were covered with cinders. Christ, why hadn't he refused to hide it in his luggage, to bring it at all? He hardly even *knew* Marlowe . . .

At last the heavy tape came away, tearing the wrapper. Inside was a cardboard box which proved, when he parted the halves of the lid, to be stuffed with cotton wool. The packing squeaked beneath his nails as he began to push it apart – but the Customs officer took the box from him and lifted out the top layer of packing. He stared into the box, then he lowered it slowly so that Alan could see within. 'I think you've got some explaining to do,' he said.

Three

Liz and Anna were waiting at Norwich. Liz was at the barrier as the train rolled in. When she saw Alan, picking his way through the Saturday shoppers back from London and the families of holidaymakers searching for luggage trolleys, she waved, and Anna came running over from the station bookstall. 'Look, daddy,' Anna cried, as he fumbled with his ticket and his luggage at the barrier, 'they've got some of your books.'

'Have they? Well, good for them.' He hugged Liz and Anna until he realized he was holding up the queue at the barrier. A man with a briefcase glanced at them as he squeezed by, and Alan could see he thought they were as beautiful as he did himself. Anna looked more and more like her mother: the same red hair and blue eyes, oval face, small pert nose, and long slim limbs. She was tall and lithe for her age – there again she took after Liz – and the pair of them had grown as tanned in Norfolk as Alan had in Nigeria. No wonder the man with the briefcase looked envious.

The car was parked on the station forecourt. They emerged beneath a bright July sky patched with dazzling clouds, into a light shower. The warm rain was refreshing, just what he needed right now. Anna danced along beside him, clutching his hand. 'Was Africa lovely? Did you see any native dancers? Did you meet a tiger? I'd love to meet one . . .'

'Now, Anna, leave daddy alone for a few minutes. You know he likes to unwind after he's been away.'

'It's all right,' Alan said. 'I don't mind.' He put an arm round each of them as they reached the car, and felt secure.

He hadn't realized how much he needed this – to feel that some things could be trusted not to change.

As they drove out of Norwich toward the coast, the clouds drew back to the edge of the sky, an iris as wide as the horizon. The rain had stopped, leaving the gentle landscape even greener. They passed villages among the sparkling fields, a few streets of houses white as sugar cubes, gone almost as soon as they appeared. Waterways glittered beside the roads, leading cruisers into the network of the Broads. Once Alan glimpsed the towers of Liquid Gases, where he'd researched *The Cold Cold War*.

For a while Anna chatted to him while Liz concentrated on driving. As she turned off the main road onto the first of the winding lanes that led to their part of the coast, Liz said, 'Was your trip a success, then?'

'I think so. Until I got to Heathrow, anyway.'

His tone made her glance at him. 'Why, did something go wrong?'

'I don't know if I'd put it quite like that.' Again he felt queasy with nervousness. 'It was my own fault. I should have known better,' he said. 'Only in a reckless moment I agreed to bring over a parcel for some anthropological foundation in London. You won't believe it, but I didn't think to ask what was in the parcel, even though I hardly knew the man who wanted me to take it. Well, of course this had to be the only time I've ever had my luggage searched at Customs, and you should have seen this character's eyes light up when he found the parcel.'

Liz grimaced sympathetically. 'One of those, was he?'

'One of the best. Mr Hitler Youth of 1980.'

Anna was growing impatient. 'What was in the parcel?'

He thought it best to tone down the truth for her. 'It was what anthropologists call an artefact,' he said, hoping she would be more easily satisfied than the Customs youth had been. Alan would have been happy to leave the parcel for the Foundation to collect, but the uniformed youth hadn't allowed that – a regulation had been contravened, nothing and nobody was going anywhere until the situation had been resolved according to the book. Eventually the argument had attracted the attention of a Customs officer old and wise enough to know when to bend the rules.

Anna wasn't satisfied. 'What's an artefact?'

He leaned menacingly over her in the back seat. 'The opposite of an artichoke,' he said, and tickled her until she begged him to stop. The danger was past; she'd forgotten her question. Nevertheless he said quickly to Liz, 'What's new with you?'

'Well, let's see. I looked in at the hotel nursery today. They've got a little boy called Hilary who's so polite he doesn't like to ask where the toilet is. Leaves little piles about the place when nobody's looking. The Phantom Crapper Strikes Again.' She grew more serious. 'No improvement between Derek and Jane. Tell you later,' she said, meaning after Anna had gone to bed.

The lane was winding downhill toward the coast now. Before long they saw the sea above the hedges, the steely water trembling with white fire all the way to the horizon. Beside the coast road, trees downtrodden by the constant wind stooped close to the ground. Liz drove along the coast road, past huddles of caravans in fields at the top of the cliffs, tents set out like wedges of cheese on a board, a village with a lighthouse. As the car sped through the village, two jet planes tore overhead from the RAF station nearby.

Soon they were home. Alan always felt a shock of pleasure at the sight of the tall white house overlooking the sea. Sea breezes rippled the lawns, flowers nodded in the flowerbeds. Liz eased the car into the left-hand garage and switched off the engine, and suddenly the only sound was the soughing of the waves.

While Alan lugged his case upstairs and dumped it in the master bedroom, Anna went out to talk to the goats that were grazing on the cliff-top, waiting to be milked by Pam from the dairy. The bedrooms were on the middle floor, below Alan's workroom and a room full of books. Not only the rooms but the landings had large windows.

Daylight was everywhere in the house, and views of the sea.

Alan was opening the suitcase when Anna came running upstairs. 'I started writing a book while you were away. Do you want to read it?'

'Well, not right now.' She looked so crestfallen that he said, 'All right, darling, I'll read it now.'

The first page of the exercise book was painstakingly inscribed *The Castle People*. The next few pages were covered with careful straight lines of handwriting, which looked determined to be neat, to please him. The title had made him expect a historical story, but she had written about little people who came onto a beach at night after the children had gone and who lived in the sandcastles, shoring them up with bits of driftwood, until the sea washed the castles away. He especially liked a description of the little people wearing shells for hats and daring one another to stand at the edge of the waves. 'It's good. You ought to see if you can carry it on,' he said, as Liz called them down to dinner.

Wine and Liz's lamb kebabs made him more talkative. Before long he'd convinced Anna that Africa was as mysterious as she wanted it to be: secret paths through giant forests, echoing with the shrieks of parrots that repeated your every call, the great eyes of tigers glowing green from the bush . . . Could he use some of this in his novel? He was beginning to wonder if his trip had given him enough of a sense of West Africa as it really was.

After the meal Anna scampered away to tidy her playroom and get ready for bed. By the time Liz and Alan had washed up the dinner things, she'd had her bath and was waiting to be cuddled and put to bed. She was proud to be left alone to bath herself. Alan sat by her bed and told her an impromptu fairy story. He had no idea how to end it, but fortunately before he reached that problem, she was asleep.

He sat for a while and gazed at her. Her long eyelashes shadowed her closed eyes softly, her hair spread out on the pillow, each filament smouldering redly in the curtained light. He had never seen anything more peaceful than her face.

He was closing the door quietly when he heard Liz gasp. She was in the master bedroom, at the far end of the hall. As he hurried to her he was seeing the sea in two windows at once, and he had the unsettling impression that the house was drifting like a ship. As he reached the bedroom, Liz was standing at the open suitcase with her back to him. She had found Marlowe's box.

She turned at once. 'What is it? Is it for me? It's beautiful.'

'You should have been with me at Customs – maybe you could have persuaded him.'

'Oh, is this the artefact?' She looked disappointed. 'I assumed you would have posted it by now.'

'The post offices were shut by the time I got through Customs. Besides, you can see it needs wrapping up. I could have taken it to the Foundation when I got to London, but nobody was answering the phone. Presumably they don't work Saturdays.'

She had lifted the metal claw out of the box and was gazing at it rather wistfully. 'What is it exactly? I thought it was a sculpture of some kind.'

'I suppose it does look rather like that.' It was strange: at Customs he'd had to agree that it looked like an especially vicious weapon. You could imagine someone holding it by the long handle and using the four curved claws to tear flesh, to gouge – but Liz must have communicated her sense of it to him, for now it looked abstract and graceful, elegant in its simplicity. Only the dullness of the grey metal suggested how old it must be.

Liz replaced it reluctantly in the cotton wool. 'I expect it's very valuable.'

'I'm sure it is.' That had been one of the problems at Customs: the young man had wanted to know why, if this was such a valuable item, there was no return address on the wrapping – perhaps because Marlowe was coming back to England? 'Anyway,' he said, 'we'll have it to ourselves until next week. I'll give this Foundation a call first thing Monday morning.'

She still looked wistful. 'I'm sorry I didn't bring you back a present,' he said.

She smiled at once. 'Just so long as you brought yourself back, that's all that matters.'

'Couldn't do without me, eh? You didn't join Derek's harem while I was away?'

'Alan, that's a terrible thing to say!' She threw a balled-up shirt at him, hard enough to hurt. Quick as a flash he'd dragged the suitcase off the bed and flung her onto the sheets. 'Want a fight, eh?' he growled. 'Want a fight?'

'No, listen, be serious for a moment,' she said breathlessly. 'That situation really is getting out of hand. Jane's desperate. Someone ought to speak to Derek about it, for her sake.'

'All right, we'll talk about it.' He was struggling with the zipper of her skirt. 'But not just now, all right?'

She smiled at his erection, which was pressing against her. 'Well, maybe not just now.'

In a minute they were frantic for each other. They had no need of foreplay, and no time. As he raised himself to go deeper into her, she wrapped her legs around him. They came almost at once. It felt as though their bodies were exploding in mid-air, a long, shuddering explosion.

They subsided limply on the bed, side by side in each other's arms. After a while she wriggled her shoulders ruefully. 'It's about time you cut your nails.'

'They help me turn pages,' he joked. He was half-asleep now, hardly aware of what he was saying. He just wanted to lie here peacefully, holding her, hearing the long subtle chords of the sea. All at once he got up irritably; Anna was whimpering. Couldn't she leave them alone for five minutes? But soon the child was quiet, and Liz relaxed in his arms again. Just a nightmare, that was all.

Four

Alan sat at his desk and gazed out of the window. A steamy whitish sky pressed down on the sea, trapping the heat in his room. From up here the sea appeared to start at the very edge of the cliff, a sea like a semicircle of mercury miles in diameter, rippling sleepily. Half a mile away he could see a strip of beach, and on it what was either a reddish piece of driftwood or someone badly sunburnt. The stereo speakers on either side of his desk were playing the Goldberg Variations, but despite the glittering stream of music, he felt restless. He couldn't write.

Perhaps it was the heat. Usually music and the seascape kept him at his desk while he was searching for words, but now the distant object on the beach was distracting him. It looked like a reclining figure whose raw face was turned to him, but why should that make him feel watched? It couldn't be anyone, for although it was redder than sunburn, it was certainly wearing no clothes. Nevertheless he was waiting for it to move, and when he had stared at it for long enough, of course it seemed to stir. Eventually the smell of coffee lured him downstairs.

Anna's playroom and the living-room were on opposite sides of the ground-floor hall. Since her door was open, he tiptoed in to see what she was doing, but the room was empty except for the multitude of her things: soft toys, games, fairy-tale records in other records' sleeves, wheeled animals she had outgrown but refused to part with. Comics were scattered across her little table, a teddy-bear slumped on her bicycle by the open window as though faint for the lack of a breeze. Small dolls peered out of a Lego house beneath wall-shelves heaped with books. For all its crowding, the large room felt lonely with the sound of the sea.

31

Anna was in the dining-room, reading Enid Blyton and kicking the legs of her chair. He gave her a hug as Liz came in from the adjoining kitchen with mugs of coffee.

'How's it coming?' Liz said.

He gazed at the whirligig of bubbles in his coffee. It looked like a hypnotist's aid: your eyelids are growing heavy, you cannot move . . . 'Not too well,' he said. 'I was trying to write a Nigerian chapter to get the feel of it, but it won't come alive. I feel as if I haven't got enough material.'

'You don't think you'll have to go back there, do you?'

'You won't go away again, will you?' Anna set down her mug with a thump that spilled coffee over the table. 'Please don't. Please say you won't.'

'I shouldn't think so, darling. Hurry up now, get a cloth.'

But Anna wasn't satisfied. As she mopped the table she pleaded, 'Promise you won't go away again.'

'Now, Anna, daddy's said that he probably won't. Why don't you go out and play while it isn't raining? Let mummy and daddy have a bit of peace.'

'Can't I just stay and listen to you?' But they didn't answer. 'I suppose I'll have to go and see the goats.'

'I expect she'll tell the goats we've thrown her out,' Liz sighed, when Anna had gone at last, pouting. 'I must find her a few more activities before we all go mad. I think I'll continue in the nursery while she's off school. She likes helping there.'

'All right, fine,' he said, trying to assemble the chapter in his mind.

She patted his hand. 'It'll come right. You'll see.'

No doubt that was true, but her assurance annoyed him a little; he'd reached the stage of writing where nobody could help – the stage where you fumble for the shape of the material and feel you'll never grasp it. Upstairs the Bach had ended, and the sea sounded like a trapped needle hissing in the central groove. 'I think I'll give it one more try,' he said.

He went into the living-room, the longest room in the house. Windows overlooked the coast road; patio doors opened onto the back garden. Two of Liz's beachscapes hung above the mantelpiece: one by moonlight, one at midsummer noon, the sea like crinkled tinfoil. It always struck him as strange to hear the restless sea while he could see it frozen up there on the wall. From the shelves by the downstairs hi-fi he selected a recording of Louis Armstrong with the Hot Five – hoping it would liven him up, and was almost out of the room again before he saw the claw.

It was standing on the mantelpiece, resting on its points. Since he'd had to keep it for the weekend, he hadn't been able to resist putting it on show. Sunlight through the patio doors turned it into a claw of silver fire, hovering above the polished wooden top of the stone mantelpiece. He'd meant to phone about it first thing this morning, but his struggles to write must have driven it out of his mind.

He hurried upstairs and stared from his window while he waited for Directory Enquiries to respond. Anna had left the goats and was performing headstands in the back garden, her long brown legs waving above the drooping flower of her skirt. The goats were cropping grass on the cliff top near the pillbox, a whitish concrete structure built for defence during the last war and guarded now by a few bushes. The glimpse of beach half a mile away was bare. Perhaps someone had carried away the red piece of driftwood.

'Directory Enquiries, which town?'

He gave the brisk female voice the details, and was glad he wasn't in Lagos; on this last trip he'd once spent more than an hour trying to place a call to Liz. The voice read him the number almost at once, and he scribbled it down. He had an odd irritable suspicion that he might forget again to phone if he didn't dial immediately.

The phone didn't ring for long at the other end before a soft, efficient voice said, 'Foundation for African Studies?'

'I'm calling on behalf of David Marlowe?'

There was a short pause. 'Putting you through to

someone who can help you.' He heard a single loud buzz, more like the noise of a football rattle than the ringing of a phone, and then the switchboard girl was replaced by a quick precise asexual voice. 'Hetherington here.'

'Good morning,' Alan said – it still was, just about – and repeated his original approach. 'I'm calling on behalf of David Marlowe.'

'Where are you speaking from?'

'Norfolk.'

'What is your name?'

The voice was beginning to sound like a policeman. 'Alan Knight. I'm a writer,' Alan said.

Now the voice was audibly suspicious. 'And what's your connection with David Marlowe?'

'I met him last week in Lagos,' Alan said. He now wished more than ever that he hadn't got involved: he could feel his Nigerian chapter slipping further out of reach. 'He had something which he said you needed urgently, and I said I'd deliver it to you. By the time I reached London on Saturday your offices were closed. I'm calling to find out how you want me to get it to you,' he said, and described the claw.

'I see.' In silence that followed, Alan couldn't resist picturing Hetherington: a tall stooped professor, white-haired and fussy. 'You'll forgive me if I sounded . . . wary when I first spoke to you,' Hetherington said. 'I thought you might be a reporter. You see, David died over the weekend, very tragically.'

'I'm sorry to hear that.' Had the crash he'd dreaded on the expressway happened after all? 'How did it happen?' he said.

'One doesn't like to presume,' Hetherington said eventually, 'but to judge from his wife's statement, there seems no doubt that he killed himself.'

Suddenly Alan felt very cold. He had been right, after all: he'd let himself be driven by a madman. He could have been killed – he might never have seen Liz and Anna again. He wanted to ask how Marlowe had died, but Hetherington obviously regretted having said so much. 'Now we must decide what is to be done about the artefact,' Hetherington said, and it sounded like a reproof. 'Do you often come to town?'

'Pretty often.'

'Excellent. May I ask you to bring the item here rather than risking the post? Please don't come down specially. There's no urgency, in spite of what David may have said. I fear he must already have been mentally disturbed when he gave it to you. Normally he would never have entrusted an item of value to someone he hardly knew.'

Alan felt he was hearing all this in a dream. He gave Hetherington his address and phone number automatically, then he let the receiver drop into its cradle. Perhaps there was a story in all this, if only he could stand back far enough to see it. Just now he felt too close. Liz would be glad that they could keep the claw for a while. There was no need to trouble her with Marlowe's suicide.

He put the Armstrong record aside unplayed. The conversation had drained him of all his creative energy – it was easy enough to lose. Now he felt as he always did after returning home from a journey: irritable, exhausted, unable to reach above the walls of his mental state. For a while he listened to the wind snuffling about the house, then he dumped the phone book on his desk and called the library in Norwich. No, they couldn't trace any film by the name of *Out of the Past*, which meant he at least had a title; all he needed now was a book to go with it. He leaned back in his seat, groaning and stretching his arms with a click that seemed to resonate through his bones; then he twisted around to look behind him. Anna was in the doorway.

Surprise made his voice sharp. 'What's wrong?' he demanded, and felt ashamed at once when he saw her flinch. 'It's all right, darling,' he said, holding out his hands. 'Come here.' But still she lingered nervously at the door. 'What did you want?' he said gently. She was twisting her hands together as if she hardly dared to speak.

Good God, he couldn't have spoken *that* sharply. 'Come on, Anna. I'm trying to work.'

'I thought I heard something. I only came up to see.'

'What sort of thing?'

'I don't know.' His abruptness had made her defiant. 'I wanted to see if you were all right.'

'Well, you can see I am. Let me do some work now, and then maybe we'll go down to the beach. Ask mummy to find you something to do, all right?'

When she'd gone, dragging her heels over the carpet to let him know she was unhappy, Alan closed his eyes; if only he could pretend to himself that he didn't care whether or not he wrote the chapter. But it was no good. An indefinable weight lay on his mind, as if there was something he had to do before he felt right again.

After a few minutes he strode angrily onto the landing. Was Anna loitering on the stairs? Maybe she was starting a summer cold; perhaps that was why she seemed so restless today. But the stairs were deserted. It couldn't have been her; it must have been the wind – yet he could have sworn that the snuffling sound came from inside the house.

Five

Anna chewed the end of her pencil and stared at the rain. She still felt wet from helping mummy rescue the garden chairs. She'd only been outside for a few seconds, but it had felt as if she'd turned the bathroom shower full on herself by mistake. The rain had pasted her dress to her and tugged at her hair, making it trail down her back like wet old rope. It made her feel squirmy and grubby just to think about it. She couldn't go out, and today was going to last forever. There was nowhere to go, nobody to play with, nothing to do.

She knew what she wanted to do. She wanted to write a story for daddy's publisher to publish. Daddy kept telling her to finish her stories, kept saying they were almost as good as his. Did it matter that they weren't as long? She didn't think so, because once she'd heard him say that the fewer words a writer used the better. He'd said so that first time he was on television. She couldn't imagine writing a story as long as one of his; it would be like walking all round the world. But it didn't matter how long it was, so long as she finished it properly. She wanted daddy to see that she could finish a story, just like him.

'*Once upon a time there were goats who lived in a feild by the sea, a Billy goat and a nanny goat and their kids Mitten and Hitten, they all lived happily in a feild by the sea except Mitten and Hitten who wanted to sale on a ship to a far away land . . .*'

She chewed her pencil, which tasted a bit like a stick of liquorice, and tried to think what came next. How did daddy always know? He must do, to be able to write so much.

She stared out of her playroom and tried to think. Out

37

on the road a car sped by, looking like one of the paintings she'd done when she was little and couldn't keep the paint inside the drawing. Rain wriggled on the window. If she stared at it long enough she felt she was underwater, especially when she let her eyes go out of focus. Or perhaps it looked more like transparent spaghetti. She shook herself impatiently – daddy wouldn't be wasting his time like this, he would be getting on with his writing. She decided to give the nanny goat a capital N. That didn't look right either, none of it did. She wished she could ask daddy to help.

Why couldn't she? She knew she mustn't interrupt him when he was working, but surely this was special? This was for him. Besides, he'd once told her that she'd helped him with a story before she could even talk, when he'd had to write about a baby. Surely he wouldn't mind if she asked him to help now? She wanted to finish this story, she wanted him to be proud of her. His editor – that was the man at the publishers who helped him write – said they might publish her one day: Knight Junior, he called her. Maybe she'd be on television for all her schoolfriends to see, and all the friends she'd had in London. Daddy would be proud of her then, mummy would be too – they'd record her programme for her to watch whenever she wanted to.

She had written 'and', and was staring at her exercise book, when all at once it was too dark to see. The sky was suddenly almost as dark as a cinema when you went in after the film had started. She got up at once: now she had an excuse. Besides, she had another reason to go upstairs to see him. She couldn't help it, she was still worried about him.

She didn't know why. She would have told mummy if she'd been able to put it into words. As she went into the hall she could hear mummy in the kitchen, the mixer growling as it buried its nose in whatever she was making. Anna would have to look after him all by herself. She used to think she could, but by now she had some idea how unpredictable and mysterious grown-ups could be. Some things about them were too big for her to grasp. It made her feel small and lost sometimes, like a mouse in someone else's house. She ran up the stairs two at a time, to see that daddy was all right.

On the stairs to the top floor she hesitated. Perhaps she *did* know why she was worried. She remembered now that she'd had the same feeling yesterday – that someone had got into the house, into daddy's room. How could she tell mummy that? It would sound silly, the kind of thing grown-ups only pretended to listen to. She couldn't hear daddy's typewriter. She hurried up the last flight and across the landing to his room.

He was sitting at his desk in front of the window. He was hunched over the electric typewriter, which was humming loudly. Rain danced on the sill of the open window. Never touch anything electric while your hands are wet, never let water anywhere near anything electric. She was afraid to speak in case he didn't answer.

No, he was all right, for he'd hunched closer to the window. She went forward to see what he was looking at. She heard the waves rumbling like an earthquake; on the horizon the grey sky looked as if it was pouring into the sea. There seemed to be nothing else to watch, except the bedraggled goats that were huddling in the shelter of the pillbox. Or was he watching her reflection? She could see his face on the glass against the sea, but not his eyes, which were out there in the foaming waves.

All at once he growled, 'Well, what is it now?'

'Are you busy?'

'What does it look like?'

'No.'

He turned to glare at her. 'Well then, I can't be, can I?'

He was being so fierce that she couldn't help laughing. He was always like this when he was working, even if she brought him a cup of coffee that mummy made. He tried to look more fierce, then he smiled ruefully. 'I can't pretend I was thinking anything worth thinking. What's up?'

'I wanted you to help me with my story.'

'That's a laugh,' he said, not laughing. 'I can't even manage my own.'

'Shall I help you?'

He hugged her, tousling her hair. 'I wish you could, little one, believe me.'

'You said I did once.'

'That's right, you did. Well then, let's see if I can repay the favour.'

When she brought him her exercise book he switched off the typewriter and sat her on his knee while he read what she'd written. She couldn't look, she was so ashamed of having changed the N and making the page messy; when she'd started she'd tried to write as neatly as typing. She snuggled her face against his bare arm so that she wouldn't have to look.

'Well, that's a good start,' he said. 'What happens next?'

'I don't know.'

'Yes, you do. Do the kids go away?'

She pondered. 'I think so.'

'So you send them off and see what happens. Where do you think they end up?'

'Africa.'

'See, you did know after all. You get them there and see what happens next.'

She was comfortable on his lap; she felt warm and safe as the rain clawed at the house. 'Tell me about Africa again.'

'Look, darling, I'm having enough trouble writing about it myself. I can't squander the little I've got.' He held her away from him so that he could gaze into her eyes. 'You don't want me not to be able to write, do you?'

'No.' She'd wanted to please him, but all she seemed to have done was to get in his way. She would have left him before if he'd told her to go. She carried her book down to her playroom, but she didn't feel like writing any more.

She looked for something else to do to make the dull day start moving.

There was nothing. She'd done all her jigsaws already, except for the Little Red Riding Hood one that was too old for her – which really meant *she* was too young. She was too young to have a pet, too, mummy had said so. If she'd had a puppy she could have played with it on days like this. There was nobody to play with, that was the trouble. It wasn't like London, where she could have played in her friends' houses up the street; all her schoolfriends in Norfolk were miles away. She knew she oughtn't to wish it, because mummy and daddy loved it here so much, but sometimes she wished they hadn't come to live here at all.

She mustn't be selfish. She liked it here really, except on days like this. She wandered into the kitchen, but there was nothing to help mummy with. She went up to her bedroom, where her shelves were piled with her Read It Yourself books and Enid Blytons, but she didn't feel like reading, not even to show daddy how much she could read. She jumped downstairs two stairs at a time for want of anything else to do, then ran up two at a time to see how many times she could do it. She'd thumped up and down the stairs six times before daddy came out of his room to glare at her.

This time he wasn't just pretending to be fierce. All at once she felt very small. She would have gone up to say she was sorry, except that she felt too ashamed. She went into the kitchen, to be with mummy. Mummy was making bread; she was wearing lumpy gloves of flour. Anna wanted to tell mummy that she was afraid she'd done something naughty, and she was just opening her mouth when mummy said, 'What on earth have you been doing to yourself, young lady?'

Anna didn't know what she meant until mummy washed her hands at the sink and got a mirror out of her handbag to show Anna her tongue. It was almost black from chewing the pencil. 'Parrots are supposed to have black tongues, not little girls. The way you chatter on sometimes, maybe you're turning into a parrot,' mummy said, then she frowned. 'Don't put pencils in your mouth, Anna. We don't want you poisoning yourself, do we?'

The world seemed full of things you mustn't put in your mouth, but that wasn't why Anna felt miserable. 'I was making a noise on the stairs and I stopped daddy writing. Do you think he won't be able to write any more, ever again?'

'Oh, I think he'll manage.' Mummy was smiling, but *she* hadn't seen how he'd looked . . . 'Now look, I'm busy just now. Would you like to watch something on the video?'

Anna followed her into the long room, where the video cassettes were lined up like books on shelves above the recorder. Most of them were too old for her – mummy said so, though sometimes daddy said she could watch. She was allowed to watch Laurel and Hardy and programmes about animals and insects. 'How about *The Wizard of Oz*?' mummy said, then frowned for a moment. 'You know it's only a story. The witch isn't real.'

But it wasn't the witch with her bright-green pantomime face that bothered Anna; it was the Cowardly Lion. She knew he wasn't real, he was only a man dressed up, but somehow that made it worse. When he peered out of the trees, making his noise that wasn't like an animal or like a person, she looked away. She didn't like him at all.

But looking away didn't help, because she could still hear his voice. She wished she'd switched the light on. The rainy windows looked as if they were melting, and the room jerked whenever the light from the television changed. Usually she didn't mind that, but now it made the claw on the mantelpiece seem to move, to creep forward when she glanced away. Why had daddy brought such a horrible thing home? It made her think of the torture chamber in the waxworks she'd been to once in London. She didn't like being in the same room with the claw, or even in the same house.

The Cowardly Lion was trying to roar again. He didn't

look like a man dressed up, he looked like a man whom a spell had turned into a kind of animal. She thought she could smell an animal in the room. Either she was imagining the smell, or the soggy goats must have moved nearer the house. She left the recorder running, because she wasn't supposed to touch it, and took refuge in her playroom.

She could still hear the Cowardly Lion. So could mummy when she came out of the kitchen to call Anna to lunch. Mummy told her off for leaving the recorder on when she wasn't watching, which seemed unfair to Anna. Grown-ups often were. At least lunch was something to do.

Daddy had lunch in his workroom. Anna had hoped he would come down and talk to her. She hoped he was working, not failing to work because of her. She must have looked miserable, because after lunch mummy played Ludo with her all afternoon, to cheer her up. It was such a long game that Anna was tempted to cheat so as to end it, but luckily mummy went into the kitchen to start dinner.

Daddy came downstairs for dinner, and was cheerful once he'd had some wine to drink. He and mummy talked about people they'd known before they got married. Anna felt left out and bored, until she thought of playing I Spy; they had to talk to her then. She grew excited with the game and her glass of wine. She was going to enjoy today after all. But almost as soon as dinner was over, they told her it was time for bed.

She had been looking forward to staying up late and playing with daddy. She'd hoped to be with him more now that he was home again, but so far she'd hardly seen him at all. And now they were packing her off to bed so that they could be together, as if *she* didn't matter. When she was ready for bed she turned her face away and wouldn't let either of them kiss her.

She lay in bed, but couldn't stop seeing the Cowardly Lion peering out of the forest, couldn't stop remembering the torture claw that was in her home, the wax faces screaming silently in the torture chamber. The worst thing had been that the wax victims weren't being tortured; they had been screaming because they knew what was going to be done to them, screaming with no chance of being heard. Perhaps they'd had no tongues, she thought, and wished she hadn't thought it. Her room was growing dark.

She slept at last, only to dream that the Cowardly Lion had crept into her room. He was reaching for her with the metal claw, since he had none of his own. She cried out as she woke. The dark in her room, and the sound of the waves, were as strange and frightening as they had been the first night she'd slept here. Someone was coming upstairs to see why she had cried out, padding upstairs. His footsteps sounded very soft. It was the Cowardly Lion.

When the door opened and he came into the room, she could see his long soft monstrous face, like the face of a soft toy that ought not to be moving. By the time she saw that it was daddy with daddy's face, it was too late: she had already cried, 'I want mummy.'

'Just wait a minute, then.' He sounded peevish, as he always did when she asked for mummy instead. It was only that mummy looked after her, and he was always too busy writing. Now she was afraid she might have driven him away. As soon as mummy came to her, Anna said, 'Daddy won't go away again, will he?'

'Was that what was wrong? No, I'm sure he won't, darling. He has no reason to.' Mummy cuddled her and stroked her head, and before Anna knew it she was asleep.

When she woke it was morning, and the rain had stopped. That was one of the good things about living here: it never rained for long. At breakfast time the sea was pale with haze, which meant a scorching day to come. As she helped mummy wash up the breakfast things, Anna heard children shouting and laughing on the beach below the Britannia Hotel.

Daddy wasn't in a good mood. He had his breakfast at his desk and didn't want to be spoken to, not a word.

'We'll go into the village, and then I'll make a special dinner,' mummy said. 'Perhaps that'll help daddy to relax.'

They were ready to go – mummy wouldn't let her cycle on the road to the village – when they heard the slam of the phone in daddy's workroom. The other phones rang in sympathy. He came downstairs as if he was looking for something but didn't know what it was. 'Problems?' mummy said.

'That was Teddy Shaw.'

He was daddy's editor. Teddy the Editor, Anna began to sing to the tune of Nelly the Elephant, until they both frowned at her. 'What did he want?' mummy said.

'Only to piss on my fucking title. It was a Robert Mitchum film. They changed the title in Britain.'

Anna shoved her fist against her mouth to keep in her giggles. She could see he was being serious, but he never said those words in front of her. Mummy was trying to calm him down. 'But you can still use it, can't you?'

'That's what Teddy said. You're both wrong. It doesn't feel right, and that means it's no fucking good.'

Mummy decided that the best thing was to leave him alone. 'We're going into the village and then we might look in at the hotel.'

'Fine, do whatever you like.' But he was staring at Anna. She felt small and guilty and defenceless even before he said, 'Just so long as I get some peace.'

Six

Anna seemed to forget the incident once they were out of the house. Perhaps she knew by now that Alan was sometimes unreasonable, or perhaps it was just that it was impossible to be unhappy for long beneath the open Norfolk sky, so blue it seemed to whiten when you looked at it. Liz thought it best not to refer to what Alan had said. She hoped Anna would forget if she wasn't reminded.

In every direction you could see for miles. To their right, past the turn-off to the village, the coast road wandered between low grassy slopes, bare except for the occasional house, a disused windmill, a gathering of caravans two miles away. To their left was a church, its graveyard slowly crumbling onto the beach two hundred feet below, the Britannia Hotel beyond it, and then the village came curving round toward the cliff top, bringing small hotels and amusement arcades and shops full of buckets and spades. Already kites were tugging at their leashes, naked children splashing in the sea beyond the bathing huts.

Anna went running on ahead along the coast road, toward the sign which warned that Seaview was closed. Most of that road had fallen onto the beach years ago. 'Chase me,' Anna cried.

'Not here, Anna.' The little girl knew to stay away from Seaview, but the road to the village was full of blind curves. 'When we come back along the beach,' Liz promised.

Along the village road, lush verges rippled in the breeze and sparrows squabbled in the hedges, darting back and forth across the tarmac. A scarecrow stood flapping its sleeves in a field; Anna waved back. Cars packed with holidaymakers roared around the bends, and Liz kept a tight hold on Anna's arm. Still, she didn't mind the holiday crowds; sometimes, in the winter, when the vicious east wind froze the air, this coast could seem very bleak and lonely. Not that she was ever tempted back to London, with its dirtiness and violence. No – it was worth suffering the winters to get away from that.

The houses of the village shone with whitewash; the walls of a terrace of cottages were cobbled with stones from the beach. Grandfathers sat in cottage gardens or on the bench in the village square, waiting for the pub to open. Most of the village folk were retired.

Beyond the pub was the open bus-shed, which sounded like an aviary much larger than the building was, and then the station, a single platform visited reluctantly by two trains a day. Sometimes the trains were on time, occasionally one failed to arrive at all.

'Look, mummy, what's Mrs Walters doing?' Anna said.

Liz wondered. Jane was standing on the pavement by the station entrance, holding a clipboard and a ballpoint pen away from her baby, who hung between her breasts from a sling. The street was so narrow that she was able to stop everyone who passed. 'You'll sign this, Liz, won't you?' she called.

'I should think so. What's it about, Jane?'

'It's a petition against closing the branch line. They want to cut us off – they don't care what damage they do to the village. Half the shops would have to close down.'

Liz doubted it, but there seemed no harm in signing. She smiled at Jane in her shapeless T-shirt and faded crumpled slacks, her baby Georgie sleeping to the sound of her heartbeats. 'You look very organized,' she said.

'I look very fat, you mean,' Jane said, which was true enough – she looked like an oversized replica of herself made out of dough. 'Were you like this when you had Anna?'

'Oh, worse – really terrible,' Liz lied, to comfort her. 'It goes away after a while, Jane, you'll see. You won't know yourself.'

'I don't know myself now, that's the whole trouble. Do

you think I've changed? Do you think I should see someone about it?'

It wasn't Jane's fault, and perhaps Liz ought to say so – but Jane was looking beyond her now, and smiling like a mask.

'Can anyone join the mothers' meeting?' It was Alex.

'Of course you can,' Jane said. 'We don't mind you showing us up.' Her tone was bantering, but Liz sensed the pain beneath it. Men glanced at Alex admiringly: her nipples, standing out through the halter top, her long brown legs, her tight round-bottomed shorts . . . 'I see you're helping keep the dairy open,' Jane said.

Alex was carrying a bottle of goat's milk. 'I wouldn't be without it. Nothing like it for the complexion. You should try it yourself, Jane.'

Liz wondered how they were supposed to know, since Alex's complexion was invariably buried under make-up, but Alex was chattering on. 'How's the little one?' she said sweetly.

'I think he's all right.' Jane stroked the golden fuzz on her baby's sleeping head. 'I hope he is. He's been waking rather a lot at night.'

'So I gathered,' Alex said. Already Liz was wondering how much more she could take: her head was thumping. Perhaps she ought to leave them to it and hope Jane turned on Alex – except that Jane never would. 'Maybe you should try him with goat's milk,' Alex said. 'Didn't I read that's good for sickly babies?'

'Oh, I think I'll carry on feeding him, thanks. It's not as if my tits are worth preserving any more.'

'Now, Jane, you shouldn't underrate yourself. I'm sure you're an excellent mother.'

Anna was demanding 'Mummy, mummy,' and tugging at Liz's hand. Perhaps she could sense the thinly-veiled hatred as the two women talked.

'And how's *your* career?' Jane said to Alex.

'Well, I'm resting just now while my agent lines up some work. There's a new horror film and some underwear modelling. I do get so bored sometimes down here – I don't suppose you'd know how that feels. I wish I could keep myself occupied like you do.'

'I thought you did, in your own way,' Liz said, unable to contain herself. At once she wished she hadn't spoken; she had only succeeded in making Jane wince, she hadn't touched Alex at all. She turned to Jane. 'Anyway, let me sign your petition. And then,' she said with heavy emphasis, 'I think we should all leave you to get on with the good work.' As she scribbled her name she added, 'You and Derek must come to us soon for dinner,' and had the awful thought that she might have been addressing either of the two women. She could hardly look up for fear of finding that the same thought had occurred to Jane too.

She left Jane as soon as she could, hurrying Anna away and staring back to make sure Alex left as well. 'See you next week at Liz's,' Alex said to Jane, which made Liz feel even worse.

She battled through the sticky crowd of pensioners and holidaymakers, past the mobile library parked on the green, the post office, whose window displayed Alan's books beneath a hand-painted 'Local Author' arrow, the hairdresser's where old ladies sat with their heads in egg-shaped helmets like the victims of a mad scientist on an old pulp magazine cover. Her headache was worsening – it felt as if a metal band was jerking tighter around her head – and she was desperate to talk. She went into The Stone Shop to see Rebecca.

The shop was full of creatures made of shells and pebbles, carved boxes containing polished stones, multi-coloured arrays selected from the beach, larger stones made into ashtrays, candle-holders, cruet-stands. Rebecca was trotting about, fussing over her creations with a feather duster. She was a small square woman who wore voluminous clothes as grey as her hair, and was Liz's best friend in the village. 'That's a pretty dress you're almost wearing,' she said to Anna. 'I wish I could dress for the weather.

Would you like to go in the back and see if you can make me a creature? I'll give you some shells.'

As soon as Anna was out of the way, carefully gluing shells together in the workshop, Rebecca said, 'What's up? You look like I feel.'

Liz threw herself into the rickety chair behind the counter. 'I've just seen Jane,' she said.

'Oh? She was in here before with her latest petition. I suppose she needs to feel she can still organize. Apparently she had quite a well-paid secretarial job before she had Georgie. Why, what was she saying to you?'

'It wasn't Jane, it was Alex Amis. She came tarting along, telling Jane how to look after Georgie and virtually saying outright that Derek tells her all the family problems. And you know Jane – she just stood there blaming herself and getting into an even worse state.'

'They make me sick, all three of them. You saw Alex here that day when she came bursting in with the news that she'd seen Derek in London with another woman. You could see how it excited her, little bitch – for all her drivelling on about poor pregnant Jane and how wicked it was of him to treat her that way. I suppose it must have made her want some herself.'

'Well, I'm inviting the Walterses for dinner, though God knows what good that'll do.' Nevertheless she felt somewhat better for talking. 'And what was your problem?'

'Oh, that.' Rebecca was apologetic. 'There's a thief about, that's all. A couple of things have gone missing in the last few weeks, just small things. I think I know who it is, but I want to be sure before I do anything. Now let's talk about something else. Stay and have coffee with me while Anna finishes her masterpiece.'

They sat sipping coffee and talking summer talk: how Rebecca's shop was doing well, how Liz needed to find Anna more to do during the holidays. 'That's lovely, Anna,' Rebecca said, as she washed up the cups, and Liz agreed: Anna had created a tortoise with pebbly head and feet poking from beneath its seashell. 'Do you want to leave it while the glue dries and collect it next time? Maybe you could come in sometimes and help me make them.'

Liz hurried to the village's only supermarket for meat, vegetables and wine, Anna pushing the shopping trolley and plaguing her with questions. 'What are tits, mummy? What will Mrs Amis do in her underwear? What did Rebecca mean when she said that Mrs Amis wanted some herself? Can I really help Rebecca in the shop?'

That at least was easily answered. 'I think she meant it, Anna. We'll have to see.' When she'd loaded her shoulder-bag they followed the curve of the village toward the sea front, past the hotels and raucous arcades. Seagulls wheeled above supine deckchairs and sunbathers on the narrow beach. Eventually, when Anna had been persuaded away from the deafening electronic pinball tables, they reached the Britannia Hotel.

It was a long three-storey castellated building, a fortress with a teddy-bear in one window. Gail Marshall, the manageress, was at the desk in the foyer, by the potted plants and the goldfish pool. Children screamed happily in the playground behind the hotel, while parents and pensioners sat in the bar. Gail was delighted that Liz had decided to help in the nursery during the holidays, and Liz was tempted to stay for a drink, but Anna was restless. Hefting her shoulder-bag, Liz made for the beach.

The sea came pouring down from the horizon, parting into slower waves where it reached the groynes. Down here, the sea always looked higher than you were. Sand dotted with pebbles led from the water's edge to the larger stones, which formed a strip against the sea wall. Beyond the wall, nine feet or so above the beach, some of the rocks were big as boulders.

At first Anna raced along the stones, crying 'Chase me.' Then as soon as she saw that Liz was following, she dodged across the soft sand to the dark hard strip of beach at the water's edge. Liz struggled along the soft strip and clambering over the timber groynes, marvelled at Anna's agility. Just now she looked as unselfconscious as some young leggy animal, yet when she went to the hotel dressed up for the occasional special dinner, Liz felt moved to see how quickly she was growing up.

By the time Liz passed the church up there on the cliff, Anna was a hundred yards ahead. A couple of gravestones leaned precipitously over the edge of the cliff; Liz was always a little afraid that one day a grave and its contents might come sliding down. 'Slow down a bit, Anna!' she called breathlessly, but the little girl had already halted, seeing a figure ahead. 'Here's Joseph,' she cried.

They often saw Joseph on the beach – Joseph, who wore his long grubby raincoat whatever the weather, its pockets bulging with stones. He lived on the far side of the village with his father, who looked after the grounds of the Britannia Hotel and gave donkey-rides along the beach. Now and then he would take his stones to Rebecca, who usually selected a few and made him accept money for them. He was about thirty – Liz wasn't sure exactly how old – and quite harmless.

He came running up to Anna, his bow-legged, stumbling gait unmistakable even from half a mile away. He was pointing eagerly at the horizon. 'Can you see the ship? Someone stuck it up there, didn't they? I had a farm in a box where you stuck in the animals to make them stand up. And I had a book where the animals jumped up when you opened it. *Boo!*' he shouted, leaping up clumsily in front of her and waving his arms.

Anna laughed and held his hand as they made for the path to the top of the cliff. To begin with, Liz had been afraid that Anna might giggle at him, but she accepted him quite happily – in fact, sometimes she was more tolerant of him than Liz managed to be, since he couldn't stop talking. Now he was fumbling in his pocket for stones. 'Look, here's a hole where something hatched out. Here's one with glittery stuff inside – that's sugar, isn't it? And here's a humbug,' he said, putting the striped stone into his mouth and spitting it out at once.

'You shouldn't put stones in your mouth,' Anna said. 'And I don't think things hatch out of stones.'

Joseph was too busy crawling about in search of his stone to heed her. He pocketed it carefully and went stooping off in search of more. 'Look where the sea burns the sand,' he said, pointing at the patterns the waves had left, dark flames in the sand at the edge of the sea.

Liz and Anna climbed the winding path toward the pillbox. As they reached the cliff top Joseph overtook them and sauntered toward the goats. 'Here, goat. Here, goaty-goaty-goat.' The female came to him first and then, as he dropped on all fours to nuzzle their faces, the kids.

Liz and Anna made for home. 'Bye-bye, Joseph,' they called.

'I'm coming now.' He struggled to his feet at once and ran to catch up. Anna grabbed his hand and ran with him toward the house. 'Joseph can have a glass of milk, can't he?' she said.

'I suppose so.' Liz didn't mind having Joseph in the house, but Alan might object to hearing him while he was writing. By the time she reached the back door he was already in the living-room, where Anna was showing him Liz's paintings. 'Don't touch anything,' Liz said, looking at Anna but meaning him as well, and was heading upstairs to warn Alan he was here when he picked up the claw from the mantelpiece.

He must have scratched himself, for he didn't just drop it but flung it away, onto a chair. 'Oh no, Joseph mustn't,' he said in a strange shaky voice.

At least he hadn't damaged the claw. Liz would have felt it served him right, except that he was upsetting Anna. He backed away as Anna went to see what he'd done to himself. 'Mustn't,' he said to himself, and floundered away from her into the hall, where after a panicky struggle he managed to open the front door.

Anna looked puzzled and hurt as she followed him. Liz went after her in case Joseph might upset her further. He was out of the garden now, dancing agitatedly back and forth, stretching his hands out to Anna, flinching back from the gate. 'Don't stay there,' he cried. 'Don't you let them.'

When Liz touched her arm, Anna flinched. 'It's all right,' Liz murmured. 'You know he's a bit odd sometimes.' She steered Anna back toward the house, more firmly when the child seemed to be resisting. She tried to gesture Joseph away as she elbowed the sunlit door open and pushed Anna screaming into the arms of the figure in the hall.

It was Alan. Anna must have screamed from shock, not from fear. Nevertheless Liz's heart was pounding, her vision was darkening; she had to hold onto the doorframe while she calmed down. She smiled reassuringly at Alan, for Anna had run to her. 'It was Joseph,' she told him. 'He was in some kind of peculiar mood, scaring her.' She glanced back in case he was still at the gate, but he had fled. There was only the bright gentle landscape, nothing at all to fear.

Seven

By noon on Friday, Liz was exhausted. Though the sun was so harsh that you could almost see the grass bleaching, it seemed not to slow the children down at all. Anna was pushing two-year-old Faye in the baby's swing, Beryl and Deirdre were racing tricycles around the hotel playground, Julian and Thom and Esther were splashing one another in the pool beyond the wire fence, and several children were scrambling up the fifteen-foot slide, toddlers included. One of the toddlers began dancing on the top rung of the metal ladder and Liz had to dash over to persuade him to get onto the slide. Then, since the two girls who worked fulltime in the nursery were busy in the dining-room, she had to prevent another toddler from climbing the wire fence that kept unsupervised children away from the pool, and disentangle Beryl and Deirdre, who had collided and were fighting. At least Hilary the Phantom Crapper had gone home, leaving a hotel legend behind him.

It wasn't only the children Liz found exhausting: it was their parents, too. Not all of them, by any means. Some were enjoying themselves as much as, and because, their children were. But Deirdre's mother was a teacher, and wouldn't leave the children alone; the moment she saw a child inactive for a moment, she would pounce. It was all that Liz and the girls could do to dissuade her from organizing games. Julian's mother couldn't find anything right with the hotel. 'Can't you give the children a choice of meals? They managed to where we stayed last year. And they organized outings for the children – surely that shouldn't be too much trouble . . .'

But the worst of them was Spike's father. Spike was a thin seven-year-old with a long, dull face and pinkish, peeling skin, and everyone could see how much his father disliked him. Yesterday his father had shamed him into braving the pool and had stood looking disgusted while Spike froze calf-deep in water, refusing to venture away from the side. 'Go on, you big baby. Look how everyone's laughing at you.' Eventually he had dragged Spike out and shoved him away as though he couldn't bear to touch him. 'Go on, you useless lump. Nobody wants to know you.'

This morning he'd virtually ignored his son, and seeing Liz trying to cheer Spike up, had shrugged and strolled away to read a magazine. Spike was in the sandpit now, picking up handfuls of sand and letting them trickle away without looking at them. Liz was about to climb down and propose a sandcastle competition for just the two of them, when his father reappeared.

'Don't bother with him. He doesn't like enjoying himself. I'm paying the earth to give him and his mother a holiday, but he doesn't care about that.'

Liz was biting her tongue, when Maggie came out of the nursery to call the children for their meal. She gave Liz a wink that said she would look after Spike, and Liz gladly left her to it.

Now that the slide was free, Anna made for it. 'I'm just going to have a drink before we go home,' Liz called. Nobody else was in sight except a reddish man at the edge of the cliff, a hundred yards beyond the playground wall. If he was as sunburnt as he looked, why on earth wasn't he in the shade? Against the glitter of the waves she couldn't make him out at all. She took refuge in the cool of the bar.

Jimmy was serving, a student teacher who worked in the hotel during the holidays. 'Here you go,' he said, drawing a lager without waiting for her order. 'And where's the little mother? I hope I get a few like her when I start teaching. When I look at some of them I wonder what I've let myself in for. Young Julian was skulking outside the window last night until someone left a drink close enough for him to grab. And how old is Faye – seven? She was saying she'd give me a kiss if I gave her a drink. Lolitas get younger and younger. Still, I'd rather have kids like that than Spike, poor little bugger.' Suddenly he ducked his head and began polishing glasses. 'Enough said. Here comes the fond father.'

Liz turned to see that Anna was still on the slide, and hoped Spike's father wouldn't come into the bar. He was striding past the pool enclosure, swinging his metal-tipped stick and fluffing up his curly black sideboards between finger and thumb. When he pushed open the windows and stepped into the bar she turned away. She didn't trust herself to be polite.

But he came straight to her. 'What's this, drinking alone? We can't have that. A Scotch for me, Jimmy, and give this lady whatever she wants.'

'I don't want anything just now, thanks.'

'Well, give me a shout when you do. I don't like to see ladies drinking alone. Mine's upstairs resting in case you wondered. No wonder, with what she has to put up with. I'm not surprised you came straight in here.'

Liz could only walk away without replying and sit in the window. Eventually he flung his corduroy jacket over a chair next to an old couple and began to hold forth to them. Liz squinted at the cliff-top. The reddened man was still there, but she couldn't make him out from this angle either, couldn't even decide if he was watching the sea or the hotel.

Anna was even less self-conscious now that she was alone, standing on the platform at the top of the slide like a sailor in a crow's nest, then letting herself slide down head-first, before running around to climb the ladder again. Liz watched until she realized she was risking more attention from Spike's father. She was downing the last of her drink when the door from the foyer opened. She'd never be able to slip away now, for here was Alan's mother.

She was a tall pale dry woman in her early sixties. Today she wore a silky blue ankle-length dress. She surveyed the bar as if she found nobody worth greeting, then she strode over to Liz. 'Hello, Elizabeth. Alan told me you were here, so I came to see my grandchild.'

'She's outside. Would you like a drink first?'

'Yes, but let me pay for it. Please, I insist. Yours is a lager, I take it.'

Liz felt as she'd meant Spike's father to feel. She and Isobel had never been friends – they seemed to have nothing in common except Alan – but Liz did her best, for Alan's sake and Anna's. Isobel returned with the drinks and stood waiting for Liz to open the windows Spike's father had closed. 'I think we ought to sit outside so that the child needn't come into the bar.'

A few round metal tables shadowed the lawn outside the bar. A breeze tried to flip over the beermats, like a baby doing its best to imitate its father. Liz meant to remark on the sunburnt man, but Isobel seemed not to notice him. Instead she stared at Anna. 'Surely you aren't letting the child go on the slide unsupervised?'

'She'll be all right, Isobel. She's been used to it for years.'

'Yes, I seem to remember your letting her on it before she was two years old.'

'That's why she's so confident now.' Liz recalled that holiday all too well; for a short time they'd stayed with Isobel, five miles inland, but there had been so much friction between the two women that in the end Alan had had to bring Liz and Anna to the Britannia Hotel instead. Isobel had paid most of the bill – they couldn't have continued their holiday otherwise. Liz hated feeling obliged to people she didn't like.

'Well, I can't bear to watch.' Isobel turned her back on the playground, as if Liz were forcing her to do so. For a few minutes she was silent, sipping her gin and tonic; from her expression it might have been vinegar. Something else had annoyed her. 'Alan didn't seem very glad to see me today,' she said.

'I expect he just didn't want to be interrupted. Did you let him know you were coming?'

Isobel stared affrontedly at her. 'It's a pity if I have to make an appointment to see my own son.'

'Oh, sometimes I virtually have to make an appointment to speak to him, and I'm in the same house.' Liz was trying her hardest, but evidently Isobel was offended at being compared to a mere wife. 'He's having problems with his writing just now,' Liz said.

'I wonder why that is? Has he anything to worry him at home?' When Liz shook her head, less angrily than she might have, Isobel stood up. 'Well, I can't wait all day for the child to come to me,' she said, and strode toward the playground.

Anna jumped off the slide and ran to her. She sat for a while with her grandmother at one of the parents' tables in the playground and chattered to her, while Liz tried to relax with her drink. She must get in touch with her own parents; they were supposed to be coming to stay. She hoped they were, because she'd just put off Barbara Mason, an old friend who'd written asking if she could take up an open invitation.

Anna was back at the slide now, crying 'Watch me, Granny!' as she ran up the ladder two rungs at a time, pushing away Isobel's hand as she tried to help her up the first rungs, and shouting '*Beep-beep*' when Isobel waited anxiously to catch her at the bottom of the slide.

Shortly, the children crowded out of the nursery, having finished their meal, and Isobel returned to her gin. Spike's father emerged from the bar, Scotch in hand. 'They haven't let them out already, have they?' he complained.

Anna was trying patiently to show Spike how to ride a tricycle, and for once he didn't look quite so morose; he was pushing the pedals and realizing he was in control. 'He's fine. He's enjoying himself,' Liz said.

'That'll be the day.' His father strode irritably toward the playground. 'What's he up to now? He'll be running the babies over, he's that clumsy.'

Liz jumped up and grabbed his arm. 'It's all right, leave

him alone. Anna's looking after him. And Maggie's there – she'll make sure there are no accidents.'

He looked amused by her vehemence; she could have hit him. 'True enough, that's her job. If anything happens, it's her responsibility.' Having found someone else to blame for his son's failings, he strolled back to the bar.

Liz wouldn't have minded another drink, but Isobel was leaning confidentially across the table, gesturing her to sit down. 'Elizabeth, I hope you won't mind my saying this, but I wonder if you oughtn't to care less for other people's children and more for your own.'

Liz controlled herself. 'What makes you think I don't care for her?'

'Well, since you ask, letting her play nursemaid, for one thing. She's too young – and besides, it's such a temptation. Children have dreadful things done to them these days, you've only to read the papers. I'm not saying that Anna would do anything like that, not if she's brought up correctly. But even she could copy things she's heard about or read.'

Anna was running toward them now, having entrusted Spike to Maggie, and seeing her, Liz felt her anger fade. If Isobel regarded Anna as she seemed to, then that was Isobel's loss. Anna scampered past them and into the bar. 'Hit me with an orange juice, Jimmy,' she cried, in imitation of some film.

'My God, another Lolita.' He uncapped the bottle and poured with a flourish. 'Are you going to pay me as well?'

'Certainly not,' Isobel said. Before Liz knew what she intended, Isobel had marched into the bar, thrust a coin at Jimmy and taken Anna by the arm. 'You shouldn't be in here at all, nor speaking to grown-ups like that.'

Jimmy's face betrayed his feelings. 'And I'll have no dumb insolence from you,' Isobel said. 'Did I hear you were studying to be a teacher? God help *your* class.'

Liz followed her angrily into the bar, on the verge of losing control. 'That's enough, Isobel. Anna's with me. Drink up, Anna, and then we must be going.'

Isobel turned her back on them. 'Well, of course she isn't *my* child.' That annoyed Liz less than the sympathetic grimace Isobel earned from the old couple in one corner of the bar. 'Goodbye then, Anna,' Isobel said, and to nobody in particular, 'Next time I shall ring up in advance to make sure I'm welcome.'

'Oh, for God's sake, Isobel,' Liz hissed, following her into the deserted foyer, 'don't be so bloody stupid,' but Isobel stalked off to her car and drove away.

Liz had another lager, and after a while her hands stopped twitching with frustration. If Alan was in as bad a mood as she assumed, there'd be no point in hurrying home. Still, she had said they'd be home for lunch. She finished her drink and winking at Jimmy, hurried Anna down to the beach. It was the quickest route, since the coast road was so winding.

Just now the beach was almost deserted. Bare strips of sand and pebbles stretched away for miles in both directions, walled in by sea and cliffs. The enormous sky was empty except for the white-hot sun. 'Do try not to show off in front of Granny Knight so much,' Liz said, but Anna was already chasing off along the beach.

Liz felt edgy, trying to keep pace with the child, and before long her feet were aching on the pebbles. As she passed beneath the churchyard, she found herself glancing up nervously at the precarious graves. She was glad when she reached the path to the top of the cliff, a quarter of a mile before the scar where Seaview had once been.

Anna went scrambling up ahead of her toward the pillbox. Beyond the cliff-edge, Liz could hear the bleating of the goats. When she reached the top she saw that they were beyond the pillbox, huddled just outside the hedge at the end of her garden. Anna was among them, chatting to them as usual, no doubt.

It was the way Anna was standing so still that told Liz something was wrong. She was staring into the grass at the foot of the hedge. Now she was backing away, almost falling over one of the kids as she went. Both she and the kid cried out, and Liz could hardly tell which cry was which. She ran to the child and hugged her, but that didn't stop Anna trembling. As the child clutched her mother's dress, burying her face in it, Liz stared into the undergrowth, afraid to see.

In the glaring sunlight everything was so intense that at first she could make out only an explosion of colours and textures beneath the spiky green grass: white, glistening red, and hectic swarming black. Someone had dumped an old rug there, ruined by tomato ketchup and covered with flies. It must be a rug, for she could see the legs at the corners: a rug that someone had used to carry offal to dump beneath the hedge – *her* hedge. But one of the kids was missing, and Liz knew what that meant even before she saw its head, still attached to the disembowelled body by what remained of the neck. A bluebottle was crawling over one bulging eye.

Anna fled crying toward the house, and Liz watched her go. As for herself, she thought she would be sick. She stumbled toward the gate, trying not to breathe until she was well away from the hedge, and saw Alan staring down at Anna from his workroom. The next moment he had vanished, presumably to open the back door. In the midst of her horror, Liz felt inexplicably uneasy because she hadn't had time to see his face.

Eight

The rain came hissing toward the house as though the sea itself were breaking over the top of the cliff. As the grass of the lawn whipped back and forth, the whole of the garden seemed to be shuddering. Rain lashed the kitchen window, but Liz could see the hedge at the end of the garden all too well. The blackened hedge was tossing like an animal in pain, and she could hardly bear to look. As the black stain of a thundercloud sped towards her, engulfing the sky, she felt somehow as if a darker stain had seeped into the fabric of the house.

The mutilated animal had been so *close*; it might just as well have been inside the house. No wonder the house felt soiled and all at once a good deal smaller – though perhaps it felt so only to Liz. Last night Anna had sobbed for hours and insisted on sleeping with Liz, while Alan slept in the spare bedroom on the top floor, but at least that seemed to be the end of it; today she was just rainy-day restless, as far as Liz could tell, except that she refused to be on her own for any length of time.

As for Alan, the incident had made him more withdrawn. He seemed unable to work. Instead he'd been wandering about the house all day, looking for thoughts. She could hear his slow footsteps on the stairs. Anna had been helping make coffee, but now she hurried into her playroom, the only room on the ground floor that didn't overlook the back garden. Liz was staring out at the hedge again as Alan came into the kitchen.

'I wish you'd seen who did it,' she couldn't help saying.

'Don't you think I do too, for Christ's sake? It would make life a lot easier. You make it sound as if I didn't want to see.'

'It's only that you must have been so close when it happened. It just seems strange that you didn't hear anything.'

'Do you know what the most boring thing in the world is? Telling the same story twice. You heard what I told the police. Anyway, you know I like music when I'm working – or even,' he added bitterly, 'when I can't work. I don't see that there's anything terribly suspicious about that.'

The policeman who'd called yesterday had seemed to think there was. He was a large, stout, red-faced man who looked as if he ought to open a pub when he retired. It clearly disturbed him to have to interrogate a writer, because he'd made Alan repeat half his answers as if to show who was in charge. When he'd told Alan for the third time to think if he had seen anything suspicious, Liz had sensed Alan's growing fury, and it had frightened her. The policeman had left at last, promising vaguely that someone would keep an eye on things. Since then, Liz had kept feeling that the house was being watched, but she had yet to see the watcher. It wasn't in the least bit reassuring.

Nor was Alan – not while she knew that there was something he was holding back. Perhaps he sensed that; perhaps that was what was making him linger now that she had poured the coffee. He was clasping his mug and staring at the thin weaving steam. At last he said, 'Well, maybe I wasn't listening to music when it happened. It's just that I didn't want to say that to the police.'

He seemed to hope she would be satisfied with that. Of course she wasn't, but before she could question him, Anna came in. 'I don't know what to do,' she complained.

'Just a minute, Anna. I think I know something you'll like,' Liz said, and hurried to the living-room. Yes, there was a wild-life programme on television, the kind Anna loved: birds unfurling in slow motion, enormous alien close-ups of insects, worlds you could tread on without knowing they were there. She'd meant to draw the curtains unobtrusively over the patio doors, so that the sight of the hedge wouldn't remind Anna of yesterday, but the child had already followed her. Couldn't she have stayed with her father for just a few more moments? To make matters worse, as Liz drew the curtains Anna said, 'I don't want to be in here, mummy.'

'Oh, why not, darling?'

Anna pointed at the mantelpiece. 'I don't like that.'

'What, the claw?' On top of everything else, this seemed wilfully irritating. 'Why ever not?'

'I just don't. It's nasty. I don't like to go near it,' Anna said defiantly, as if Liz should understand a good deal more that she couldn't put into words.

'Well, don't worry. It won't be here much longer.' As far as Liz was concerned, that would have been the end of it. But just then Alan marched in.

'What's the matter now?' he said irritably to Anna.

'She doesn't like your claw.'

'Good God, Anna, it won't hurt you. Daddy's looking after it for someone.'

Anna trudged away to her playroom, looking lonely and vulnerable. Liz's heart suddenly went out to her. She must still need comforting. At least the rain was keeping her inside the house, out of danger. Last night Liz had imagined finding the child laid open beneath the hedge. They were all nervous. No wonder Anna found her father's irritability alarming.

Liz switched off the television, not least because its light made the claw appear to jerk. She still found it beautiful, too perfectly shaped to seem vicious, but the illusion of movement made her think of a restless severed limb. 'What were you going to tell me?' she said.

'Oh, nothing terribly significant,' he said reluctantly. 'It was only that my mother rang up yesterday afternoon, not long before you came home.'

'That would have been after she came to the hotel. What did she have to say?'

'Nothing much. Anyway, it's not what she said. It's just that I might have been talking to her when what happened out there happened.'

His hand was resting on the mantelpiece, leading her gaze to the claw, and she had to look away, for the claw still appeared to be flickering. 'But what *was* she saying?'

'All sorts of things. Not just about you.'

Perhaps he couldn't see how tense she was growing. 'Such as?'

'Oh, that I behave as if I don't care for Anna, that kind of thing. Just words. They don't mean a thing. She's probably forgotten what she said by now. Look, I came down here for coffee, not to be distracted. I'm still trying to write this fucking book.'

'That's all you care about, isn't it? Nothing matters but your work. As long as that's all right, everyone else can go to hell.'

'It's a good job I do feel like that, or we'd soon be bloody starving. Aside from which, I've just told you that it isn't all right. Try listening for a change. You certainly aren't helping, or that wretched child.'

That seemed so unfair – good God, their entire life was built around his work schedule! For a moment she was too furious to speak.

'Christ, I'm sorry,' he said at once and taking hold of her shoulders, tried to pull her to him. But she was too stiff with fury to respond, even if she'd wanted to.

'I'm sorry,' he said again. 'I didn't mean what I said. I hardly know what I'm saying. All this business has got me down too, you know. I suppose I just try to keep my feelings to myself.'

'Then you should either try harder or not try at all.' Still, she was softening toward him; presumably, he'd been trying to seem strong for her sake. 'You shouldn't try to hide things from me. I always know when you do.'

'There's no point in worrying you when you can't help, is there?' He must be talking about his work – she couldn't think of anything else that would make him sound so savage. 'Anyway, there is something we ought to talk about, since you insist, and that's my mother.'

'Well, she certainly has enough to say about me.'

'Liz, you're being paranoid. Whatever makes you say that?'

'Because you know damn well she called you up yesterday to talk about *me*. Don't tell me she accused *you* of not caring for Anna. She thinks the sun shines out of your arse.'

'Well, does it matter what she says? We know you're a hell of a mother. She only says these things because she feels left out. Maybe we should involve her more in Anna's upbringing. After all, she *is* my mother.'

'Alan – I've tried to involve her. But do you really want her telling Anna the opposite of everything we say?'

'Well, if it'll keep the peace—'

'I won't have Anna confused or worse, even to keep the peace.'

'Well, it's up to you,' he said irritably. 'Anyway, I've wasted enough time down here. Not that I think I'll be able to work after all this.'

Was that another dig? As he let go of the mantelpiece his hand brushed the metal claw, which rose for a moment, scratching at the air. 'By the way,' Liz said, 'weren't you supposed to be taking that to London?'

'Yes, I will be.' He seemed to want to change the subject. 'No point in making a special journey. Anyway, I thought you liked it.'

'Yes, I do, but Anna doesn't seem to. I don't want her disturbed for no reason, especially now.'

'I've told you, I'll take it next time I go.'

With that, he left her and tramped upstairs.

She stayed for a while in the long room, feeling dissatisfied. By now it was so dark outside the drenched windows that it looked as if the black sky were drowning the house. She had a vague feeling that Alan had deliberately used the argument to avoid explaining something to her. If there was no urgency about delivering the claw to London, why had he needed to bring it from Nigeria? But she found she couldn't think for any length of time about the claw; her thoughts grew blurred and repetitive, frustrating her.

Anyway, she didn't feel that was the explanation she was seeking.

Eventually she tiptoed out and peeked into the playroom. Anna was writing a story, gnawing her pencil and glancing up nervously when the rain tapped at the window. Liz withdrew quietly so as not to disturb her, and went up to her workroom on the floor above, next to Anna's bedroom. Here she could be alone when she wanted to be, with her large old desk, her sewing machine, her shelves of well-thumbed paperbacks, some of them dating back to her childhood. More important, from up here she could satisfy herself that the cliff-top and the beach were deserted. Somehow, though, that wasn't as reassuring as she'd hoped. Perhaps speaking to her parents would be.

It was no use. At first all she got was, 'All lines to Carlisle are engaged, please try later,' and then, when at last the robotic voice vacated the line, her parents weren't answering. She only hoped they were still coming to stay, now that she had put off Barbara Mason. She would have loved to see Barbara again, jolly optimistic Barbara and her ancient capacious shoulder-bag that she refused to part with. She must call her parents later. If for any reason they weren't coming, perhaps she could still invite Barbara.

Suddenly she craned across the desk. The garden had been out of sight while she was on the phone and Anna had been alone downstairs. The garden looked half-drowned, the sky blackened everything. She shoved herself back from the window and hurried downstairs.

Anna was still writing. Nothing else moved on the ground floor except faint blurred shadows of rain, and even those vanished once Liz switched on the lights in the long room. All at once she was irritated by her fears; would even a maniac who disembowelled animals venture out on a day like this? Yet the curtains hiding the patio doors made her feel irrationally afraid. Keeping them closed in the daytime shrank the room. She strode forward and opened them wide with a tug on the cord.

Then she stumbled backward, choking on a cry. A

crimson face was pressed against the glass, peering in at her.

The next moment she saw what it really was: the glistening movements in the empty sockets were of rain, not eyes – but that only made it worse. She ran up to Alan's room, almost falling, and dragged him down to look. She would have screamed for him, except that screaming would have brought Anna as well. By the time she got him downstairs, she was sobbing as much with frustration as with fear, because the face had gone; the rain had scoured it away. But she knew what she had seen: the imprint of a face that had been pressed against the window, trying to peer through the crack between the curtains – a face that must have been covered with blood.

Nine

When Anna heard mummy and daddy arguing, she felt shaky inside. It must be something very serious, because mummy had closed the playroom door and the door of the long room as well, so that she wouldn't hear. It must have something to do with the long room, because she'd heard mummy cry out in there and then bring daddy downstairs. She wished she could hear what they were saying. That might tell her why she no longer liked to go in there.

Rain staggered down the window in waves that kept washing away the roads and the fields. Teddy-bears sat forlornly in corners of her playroom, and she felt as they looked. The sounds of mummy and daddy arguing made her feel helpless, trapped in her room. Their muffled sounds were like the first rumbles of a storm.

She tiptoed across her playroom and pressed her ear against the door. Daddy was keeping his voice down, mummy's voice was rising. It sounded as if he was trying to convince her she was wrong about something. His voice seemed monotonous and overbearing; it made Anna's tummy tighten just to hear it. She still couldn't make out a word, but she could hear that mummy had lost her temper. All at once, with a violence that made her jump back, the door of the long room slammed open and she heard mummy hurrying upstairs.

Mummy had gone to her workroom to phone – Anna realized that when she heard the downstairs extension ringing as mummy replaced the receiver. Who had mummy called? She wished she could ask her, but she didn't want to go out of her playroom in case mummy and daddy hadn't made up. Being near them when they weren't speaking to each other, or barely speaking, always made her feel uncomfortable and useless.

She tried to play, so as not to think. She got out her Little Red Riding Hood jigsaw and emptied the pieces onto her table. Separating the edges from the rest occupied her mind for a while, but in the end she just stared at them, defeated. There were too many edge pieces for her even to count, and she couldn't see two that looked as if they fitted together. Besides, she didn't like the picture on the box, the grinning wolf dressed up in an old woman's bonnet, his bright red tongue lolling. She didn't want to make that picture. She swept the pieces into the box.

She was replacing the box in her cupboard full of toys, when a car drew up outside. She peered through the rain, but the car was a humpy blur. The driver was almost at the house before she saw that it was a policeman, the red-faced policeman who had been to the house already.

She went and sat down, feeling dizzy and sick. Mummy must have called him. Soon she heard the three of them talking in the long room. Daddy's voice was loudest and angriest, but still she couldn't make out a word. What had happened now? She remembered the poor goat lying in the grass like an old torn doll, a doll whose insides were sticky and wet. Things had been crawling over its insides and over its eye. She used to stroke the goat and talk to it, but nothing could have made her touch it then.

Mummy was talking now, her voice was shrill and desperate. Suddenly Anna couldn't stand not knowing. She pulled open the doors and ran through. 'Mummy, what's wrong?' she cried.

The three of them stared at her as if she ought not to be there. 'Not just now, Anna,' daddy said sharply.

They must be talking about something so horrible that they didn't want her to know. She began to cry. 'The poor goats,' she sobbed.

Mummy squatted down beside her. 'Don't fret, darling. It was only—' She was hugging her tight, but Anna knew it was only to give herself time to think of a story; when she spoke she didn't sound very convincing. 'It was just that I thought I saw someone hanging about near the house.'

Daddy was nodding his head, looking smug. The red-faced policeman spoke while he had a chance. 'I was just saying, Mrs Knight, we did have a man keeping an eye on things. He says the only one he saw getting soaked around here this afternoon was himself.'

Mummy looked as if she wanted to be reassured but couldn't quite believe it. Daddy showed the policeman out and came back smiling. 'Pompous old bugger. Good riddance. Still, that's a relief, isn't it?' he said.

Mummy was nodding, rather dubiously. Anna felt as if they'd forgotten about her, and about the poor goat. She couldn't help it, she began to cry again. This time daddy put his arm around her. 'What's the matter now?'

'I was thinking about the poor goat,' she said, between sobs. 'He never hurt anyone. Why did someone want to hurt him? I loved playing with him. He was my friend.'

Daddy hugged her and swallowed and seemed to find it hard to speak.

'Sometimes people do very bad things,' mummy said. 'Not all people, just a few. Even in a place like this.'

'But why?'

'Maybe they don't know themselves,' daddy said. 'Something makes them do it. Maybe they can't stop themselves.'

Anna knew that mummy and daddy were doing their best to explain to her, as they always did when she asked questions. It made her feel happier to know they were anxious to comfort her, that she was no longer excluded, but even so their answers weren't very comforting. If nobody knew who had killed the goat or why, how could anyone stop him from hurting the others?

For the rest of the day she could think of nothing else; she couldn't play, she had to keep peering out through the rain to make sure the goats were still there. That night, she dreamed that someone was creeping up on the goats, out of the pillbox on the cliff: at first she thought it was the

Cowardly Lion, or the wolf in the old lady's bonnet, but then she knew she was too afraid to see his face.

When she woke next day, the room was blinding, even with the curtains drawn. Out on the cliff the grass was sparkling beneath a cloudless sky. The goats stood placidly, cropping the grass. She'd be able to keep an eye on them all day – but then she remembered it was Sunday, when daddy always took her and mummy for outings. She thought of asking to stay at home, but her parents seemed anxious to get her out of the house.

Today daddy took them to Cromer. Butterflies flickered like flames full of colours above the fields as they followed the coast road, jets swooped overhead with a sound like tearing. In Cromer, daddy inched the car through the clutter of tourists, shielding his eyes against the glare of white buildings while he looked for somewhere to park. Some of the maze of narrow streets led nowhere at all.

'We all need a ride on your favourite bus,' he said, and they caught the bus to Sheringham. It was an open-topped bus, which Anna loved. Mummy hung onto her as she craned out to see the heathery heath above West Runton, the glimpse through trees of the ruins of Beeston Priory, which always made her feel mysteriously expectant at the same time as it made her think about bees. In Sheringham she played hide-and-seek through the trains in the railway museum, a station with posters that were older than daddy or mummy, and wandered along the promenade that ran, twisty as a stream, beneath the fishermen's white cottages. Mummy and daddy walked hand in hand behind her. She thought it was the nicest day they'd had together for ages. At least, it was until they returned to Cromer.

Daddy stopped outside the car park, blocking the footpath. 'Jesus Christ,' he said, so loud that people turned to look. 'Look what some bastard's done to my car.'

Someone had dented his door; scraped metal glared through the paint. 'Who was parked next to me?' he said, as if mummy should know. 'I can't remember, can you?'

'I think the space was empty,' mummy said, and Anna

thought so too. 'Never mind, it doesn't look as if it'll take much repairing.'

'Well, it wouldn't to you, would it? It isn't your car.' He turned on Anna. 'This wouldn't have happened if we hadn't gone on your stupid bus.'

That seemed so unfair that Anna couldn't speak. Her mouth was trembling, her face was growing hot; she thought everyone was looking at her. Mummy put her arm round her. 'For goodness' sake, Alan. There's no need to take it out on her.'

Daddy stalked to the car and glared at the dent. He seemed to calm down eventually, and opened the door. 'Why don't you sit in the back?' he said, as mummy stepped forward. 'Let her ride with me for a change.'

Mummy hesitated; she didn't like Anna to ride in the front. 'Oh, please let me, mummy,' Anna begged. 'I'll put the seat-belt on.' Mummy must have realized she wanted to sit in the front as much to be with daddy and feel that he loved her as for the ride, because she said reluctantly, 'I suppose you're big enough.'

But before Anna had had time to fasten her seat-belt, daddy suddenly drove in a wide angry swoop around the car park and into the road. He had to brake sharply, and she lurched forward, grabbing at the belt.

'Watch what you're doing!' mummy said, in a shocked voice. 'Do you want to kill the child?'

He glared at her in his mirror. 'What the hell is that supposed to mean?'

They were frightening Anna; it was as if it was all *her* fault somehow. She scrambled over the back of the seat to mummy, accidentally kicking the glove compartment open and spilling a handful of maps. 'That's right,' daddy snarled, 'do some more damage, why don't you?'

'Perhaps I'd better drive,' mummy said, hugging her and giving her a secret look which meant *Never mind, he doesn't mean it really.*

'Fuck off.' He pulled out in front of a car that just managed to brake in time, and went swerving through the traffic toward the coast road. This time Anna didn't feel like giggling at what he'd said. She was too aware how worried mummy was about his driving.

He slowed down once they reached the coast road, and drove without speaking. Anna was afraid to speak too, both during the drive and at dinner afterwards; all the little noises she made while eating made her nervous – she was afraid he would shout at her again. Mummy talked to her, perhaps to tell her that she needn't keep quiet, but Anna had never been so glad to go to bed.

That night she dreamed of the Cowardly Lion again, but managed not to cry out when she woke, in case daddy came to her. She didn't think she would sleep again, but when she woke she was surprised to find it was morning. Today she was going to the hotel with mummy. She was glad that daddy was too busy to come down for breakfast – if he was finding it hard to work, he would blame her.

She didn't enjoy the nursery as much as she hoped she would. It was so muggy and hot under the whitish sky. The toddlers pushed her away and whined for their mummies, and wouldn't play with her or be looked after. The older children didn't want her either, and she just felt in the way. She was glad when mummy came out of the bar to get her at lunchtime.

But mummy wasn't taking her in the bar. 'I've just spoken to daddy on the phone. He wants us to meet him on the beach for lunch.'

Her face told Anna that everything was all right now. She went on: 'He's been writing all morning. He was just ratty yesterday. You know how he can be. He wouldn't hurt you on purpose.'

As they went down the sandy path to the beach, they could see him, a tiny figure in the distance beside a dab of green paint that was the thermos bag. The sea came rushing to meet them, louder and louder. Anna began to run, because she could see Joseph with his back to daddy – Joseph stooping about the beach, bow-legged, in search of pebbles.

She hadn't quite reached Joseph when he looked up. She saw him gape, drop a handful of pebbles that squealed as they fell on the beach, then look behind him. Suddenly he was stumbling away from her and daddy, so clumsily that he splashed into the sea and almost fell. He didn't stop until he was beyond Seaview, the falling road, and had scrambled up the next cliff path.

Anna felt like crying. Why had he run away? She had only wanted to say hello and find him a special pebble. But then daddy grabbed her and threw her in the air, until she couldn't think for giggling and screaming. 'Never mind,' he shouted. 'We don't need that silly bugger, do we? Let's see what we've got for our picnic.'

He'd packed the thermos bag full: cold chicken, cheese, salad, half a bottle of lemonade for Anna, a bottle of wine for him and mummy and maybe, though mummy didn't really approve, a little bit for Anna too. He kept standing behind Anna and saying, 'Here you are, madam,' like a waiter when he poured her wine. She was cheering up, but she wished she knew why Joseph had run away, wished she could bring him back to ask him . . .

When they'd finished eating, daddy chased her up and down the beach. Mummy joined in for a while, then she lay down in the sun. Daddy kept chasing, and Anna dodged him, onto the sea wall or onto the wooden groynes, but she wasn't really enjoying herself any more; daddy's nails were so long that he scratched her whenever he caught her. She was glad when mummy called, 'That's enough now.'

Daddy lay down with the Sunday papers. Mummy was already nodding with the heat. Restless, Anna began to hunt for shells and stones for Rebecca. 'Don't go out of sight,' mummy called.

Anna tired of the pebbles after a while. She went to the edge of the sea and watched a water-skier racing by on his V of water. She was tempted to see if she could walk along one of the groynes above the waves, try to walk as far as one of the breakwaters – giant iron arrows, orange with rust and green with weed – but the seaweed that trailed from the groynes made the timber look as if it was swaying, and she knew it would be slippery. She watched the shadow of the nearest breakwater for a while, drawing itself in over the waves like the shadow of a sundial, and listened to the sea; she thought she could hear pebbles rattling back into the sea with each wave.

A movement made her look at the top of the cliff. Several big boys with haversacks and red knees had been picnicking near the pillbox; now they tramped away. She glanced at her parents: mummy was asleep, daddy was fanning himself with the colour supplement – then she shaded her eyes and gazed up the cliff. She couldn't see the goats anywhere.

She went back to her parents, and stumbled on the stones as she watched the cliff. The only movement up there was a glimpse of red by the pillbox. It looked wet, but it was gone before she could make it out. 'Daddy, I can't see the goats,' she said.

'Can't you?' He seemed half-asleep, and annoyed that she had disturbed him. 'Well, never mind.'

He was no use. If she asked him to go up and look, he'd only be ratty. If she told him why she wanted to go up, he might tell her not to – grown-ups were like that sometimes, they didn't understand how important things could be. 'Please may I have some more lemonade?' she said.

'You've drunk it all.'

'Can I go and get some more?'

'Yes, if you like,' he said wearily. 'Just be quick.'

He seemed glad to get rid of her. She clambered over the sea wall and ran to the path up the cliff before he could change his mind. She kept staring upward as she climbed. Grass shivered in the wind, a few wispy clouds drifted by above the edge; she felt as if the cliff were shifting. She glanced down at the beach as it fell away beneath her. Mummy and daddy were small as dolls now, and very far away. The wind blustered in her ears until she couldn't hear anything else. Would daddy hear her if she called out? She was beginning to wish that she hadn't come up by herself, that she'd woken mummy and asked her to come with her, but she had to go on now, to make sure the goats were all right. She toiled up the path, fighting the wind from the sea. She was nearly at the top now. Perhaps the goats were safe after all; perhaps she'd see them as soon as she reached the top, for as the wind caught its breath, she thought she could hear them. Yes, she could. Just beyond the edge, over by the pillbox, she could hear snuffling.

Ten

A scream woke Liz. It sounded as if the sky were splitting. Perhaps it was part of her dream, in which someone had been chasing someone else, but it was also above her. She saw the jets screaming away over the horizon as she opened her eyes, but at first she couldn't distinguish much else; the sun had got into her eyes while she was asleep, and everything looked bleached, over-exposed, difficult to interpret. Then she was on her feet and staring about. 'Where's Anna?' she cried.

Alan glanced up from a colour supplement; on the glossy cover a primitive mask bared pointed teeth. 'She went to get some more lemonade.'

'Went where? You didn't let her go up to the house, did you?'

'Why not? Where else would she get it from?' He was staring irritably at the supplement, as if he couldn't meet her eyes. 'She'll be all right,' he mumbled. 'It isn't far.'

'You let her go up there alone? After what happened?' Liz felt sick, her legs were rubbery. 'How long has she been up there?'

'Oh, not long. I don't know exactly.' He heaved himself wearily to his feet. 'All right, for God's sake, I'll go up if it makes you feel better.'

He strode up the cliff path. She was meant to see how he was driving himself, exerting himself for her peace of mind. All at once Liz wondered if there was some other reason why Anna had gone up to the house. Maybe she hadn't wanted to stay with him while Liz was asleep. Had something happened between the two of them? She made herself climb faster. Sand trickled from the ragged edge of the path.

By the time she reached the top, Alan was almost at the house. The windows were blank with sunlight and she couldn't see through them. Apart from the goats, the cliff-top seemed deserted; the flattened grass looked dusty with sand and harsh light, the coast road shimmered away toward the Britannia Hotel, the fields were giant samples of paint, green and yellow. The only thing that struck her as unusual was a glint of glass by the entrance to the pillbox. It was a bottle, a broken bottle of lemonade.

It was a popular brand. Millions of people besides Anna must drink it. Nevertheless Liz craned into the dim entrance to the long low concrete building and called, 'Anna' down the crumbling steps. She held her breath, so as to hear better and so as to avoid inhaling the stale animal smell that wafted up from the depths of the pillbox. Nobody answered her, but before she could call again, she heard a faint movement from somewhere within.

She glanced toward the house. Alan had reached the garden path. If she called him, she might be taking him away from Anna – and besides, she was furious with him. Suppose the movement in the pillbox wasn't Anna but whoever had killed the goat? She was dithering while Anna might be in danger. Taking a deep breath of fresh air, she went quickly down the steps.

When she reached the bottom, at first she couldn't see. Her eyes were full of the dazzle outside. She had to stand there for a moment, one hand on the cold sweaty wall, and close her eyes. In the underground dimness with its rank smell of mould and concrete dust and something else, she heard movement again. Perhaps a goat had strayed down here; she couldn't recall how many she had seen outside. That would explain the bestial smell.

She opened her eyes as soon as she could and stepped forward, calling, 'Anna.' To her left was a bare room the width of the pillbox. Sunlight blazed in through two small square apertures high up in the wall – gunports, presumably – but it only blurred the edges of the apertures and made the rest of the room more difficult to see. Still, it was clear the room was empty, except for a couple of beer-cans and a crumpled paper handkerchief.

She turned away, down the dim corridor. Small cells opened off it on both sides, each one lit by one of the square apertures. Sometimes she had to halt and close her dazzled eyes, and then she began shivering as the chill of the place settled over her like fog. Her footsteps and the empty echoes of her voice were shrill. Wouldn't Anna have answered by now? Perhaps she was afraid to admit she was down here after being warned so many times to stay away from it. Surely it couldn't be that she was unable to answer?

Liz halted again, gripping the edge of the doorway, and squeezed her eyes shut to drive away a flock of overlapping after-images. Concrete dust whispered down from beneath her hand, and in the silence she heard another sound ahead. It couldn't be Anna. Please, let it be one of the goats . . . She opened her eyes and groped her way forward, though her vision was crowded with vague pale blotches. All at once she was desperate to find the source of the snuffling.

The next cell on the left was empty, and so was the one on the right. The squares of blue sky looked unreal, part of a different world. As she stepped into the dark area between the sets of doorways, she realized that the corridor ahead wasn't only dim: it was flooded. She must be smelling the stagnant water as well as the goat, for it smelled worse than any animal she had ever encountered. There was something about the smell that she didn't even want to consider.

She was sick with apprehension now. The goat must be injured; that was why it was snuffling. She forced herself forward, to get it over with. Empty cells, blurred squares of distant sky, shrill echoes of herself that she couldn't hush. Now she was at the edge of the water that covered the floor, and now she could see why it was darker here: a clump of bushes outside prevented daylight from reaching into some of the cells. At the edge of the darkness, she realized something else. The stench that she had tried not to define reminded her very much of blood.

Before she knew what she was doing, she was groping forward along the left-hand wall. The water was shallowest at the edges, but even so it soaked her sandals at once. Reflections doubled the doorways, which looked drowned and wavering. Each cell was darker, each step toward the snuffling took her further into the dark.

She flinched and almost cried out when she glimpsed movement in the next cell opposite, a dark shape creeping away from the entrance. It was only ripples in the water that had spread into the cell. The water made her feet drag – as if her fear wasn't enough to slow her down. There was a dim shape in the next cell across the corridor, but that was just a stain on the concrete floor. So was the dark huddle on the floor of the cell beyond that.

She was sloshing onward now, pressing on because she'd almost lost her footing. No, it couldn't be a stain. It was an object, a glistening object lying on the dank floor. Surely it must be dim reflections of the ripples that had made it seem to stir. There was no need for her fists and her stomach to clench like this.

But it had eyes, and they were watching her.

She stumbled backward, fighting to keep her balance on the slippery floor. It was only some tramp sleeping rough, she told herself desperately: a tramp – that was why he was so thin. So he was naked – why not, on a day like this? But even then she didn't believe herself, not when she could see how his entire body was glistening. The liquid that covered him from head to foot was too dark for water. She had smelled it all the way along the corridor. His bared teeth were glistening with blood too.

He was rising slowly on all fours, exactly like an animal in its lair. Around him she thought she glimpsed scattered bones, ragged with flesh. His eyes gleamed yellow, his teeth bared further in a grin or a snarl – and then she was running wildly down the corridor, almost falling at the water's edge, one outstretched hand scraped raw by the rough concrete wall. She might have screamed for Alan, but her throat was choked by fear and the smell of blood. She was sure that any moment the thin bloody figure would leap on her back, drag her down on the floor of the dark corridor.

When she reached the steps she stared back, trembling. The corridor was deserted. She fled up the steps, so clumsily that she fell, bruising her knees. She stumbled into the daylight, away from the pillbox, toward the house.

Alan was striding toward her, half-dragging Anna. 'She was waiting for the lemonade to chill,' he said angrily. 'I had to go searching for her. She was waiting by the road – she wouldn't wait in the house.'

He saw Liz's expression and came quickly over to her. 'My God, what's wrong?'

It would take too long to describe what she'd seen. 'There's someone down there,' she said, pointing to the steps, though her hand was shaking almost as much as her mouth. 'I think he's the one who killed the goat.'

'Is he, by Christ? Well, we'll soon find out.' Before she realized what he meant to do, he disappeared into the pillbox.

She hadn't wanted him to go down. There was only one way in or out, and he could have guarded that while she called the police. He'd strode into the pillbox as if he was eager for violence, and now she was afraid of what might happen, down there in the dark. Suppose he couldn't see the creature until it was too late? Suppose it was ready for him – waiting for him? Wind tugged at the grass, sand hissed at the edge of the cliff, the cries of children drifted along from the Britannia Hotel. It was only half a mile away, and so was Jane's house in the other direction, but somehow that only made her feel all the more alone.

She told Anna to wait where she was, a hundred yards away, then she hurried alongside the pillbox, trying to see through the gunports. But she could see nothing, and worse still, she couldn't hear Alan; her ears were full of the ominous roar of the sea. She wavered between the gunports, afraid to cry out a warning in case it distracted him. What had she sent him down there to confront? She couldn't even reach the gunport of the cell where she had seen the figure crouching in the dark, for the bushes were too thick.

She was still wavering outside the pillbox and straining her ears when she heard movement on the steps. She glanced nervously at Anna to make sure the child was far enough away to be in no danger. But it was Alan on the steps. He stood shaking his feet dry, and gazed oddly at Liz. 'Come on, let's go down and finish the wine if it hasn't been pinched,' he said. 'There's nobody in there. Nobody at all.'

Eleven

Coming home from the hotel on Tuesday, Liz stayed on the road, away from the beach, and made Anna hold her hand round the succession of blind corners. Grasshoppers buzzed like static in the untrimmed verges, cows plodded after one another through the fields; a procession of clouds passed along the horizon, so slowly that they looked pasted on the blue sky. It was the kind of day when Liz normally liked to go exploring with her family, to villages that only the locals seemed to know, or to drive through the Broads, to cruise through the changing landscape, woodland and marshes, herons and windmills and lone houses among the trees; she often wished she could bear to travel by water. But she didn't want to see Alan, nor to go home.

After leaving the pillbox, he'd spent hours trying to persuade her that she'd imagined what she'd seen. She would have been only too glad to believe that herself. She had been on edge, admittedly; after seeing the dead goat under the hedge, it was no wonder she'd been expecting something even worse. Could she really have distinguished so much in the dark? Alan had found nothing, and that was enough to make her agree not to call the police yet again. The trouble was that everything he said only succeeded in making her feel more alarmed – because he seemed to blame Anna.

She couldn't understand him. Did he blame the child for what Liz had seen in the pillbox? For the bloody face she'd seen on the window? For her nervousness? Perhaps he didn't know himself; perhaps he was trying to conceal what he felt. But that didn't make it any less unpleasant. Just now Liz felt she didn't want to know him.

At least he was likely to stay out of her way while she

made cakes for tomorrow's afternoon tea. Jane was coming, Rebecca, Gail, if she could get away from the hotel – and Alex, heaven help them all. Every second Wednesday they met in a different house. Rebecca's was untidy and welcoming, no doubt just as it would have been if it were full of the children she could never have; Alex's was spotless as a show house, and as cold – no wonder her photographer husband went away so often, and for so long. Gail's cottage was like an annexe to the hotel, the phone always calling her back to the desk. And Jane's was even untidier than Rebecca's, strewn with bits of food and Georgie's nappies, a house out of control. The last tea had been at Jane's, and Jane had invited Alex, which was the only reason Liz had invited her now.

They were home now. In the sunlight, the hedge and the pillbox looked as innocent as everything else – which meant that nothing seemed innocent at all. Alan was in the long room, replaying his cassette of the Nigerian documentary. At least Anna wouldn't go pestering him, not while the claw was there – when *was* he going to take it to London? – and no doubt he would leave them alone, as he was busy. 'We're home,' Liz called, and ushered Anna through to the kitchen. 'Would you like to play in the back garden?' she said to the child.

'No, I don't want to. I don't like it.'

'Don't you, darling?' Liz did her best to sound casual. 'Why not?'

'There's a man out there.'

'Oh, I don't think there is.' The garden was as it should be – paths, flower borders, grass – and she could see nobody beyond the hedge. She opened the back door. 'There isn't, look. There's nobody.'

'He's lying down where you can't see him.'

Liz hoped that the child hadn't seen her clench her fists. She stared along the side of the house, then strolled carelessly to a point on the lawn from which she could see through the hedge. She could see nobody, but that was no longer reassuring. 'I can't see anyone,' she said, 'but you can stay in and help me, if you'd rather.'

For a while they made cakes. Anna chopped up fruit carefully, proud that her mother let her use the big knife. Liz smiled to herself as she watched the child, but she was also watching the garden. Everything seemed too intense: flowers bobbed and shook their heads at her, the hedge shuddered in the breeze. She wished she could see beyond the hedge.

She had just put a batch of scones in the oven when Alan came in. 'Have you nearly finished?' he said. 'I've got something to show you.'

He led her to the long room, after she'd made sure that Anna went into her playroom. 'Sit down and watch this,' Alan said. 'You'll see why in a bit.'

It was the Nigerian documentary. Theatre groups performed in dusty car parks, singers toured shops made out of corrugated metal and tried to sell their records; crowds poured into a mosque and as many gathered outside; camels lined up in a market, women balancing gourds on their heads marched by. After a while Liz had to break off watching to take out the scones, and that was a relief; the way she felt now, the film seemed a jumble of images, too much to take in, especially when she didn't know what Alan meant her to see. As she sat down again, he restarted the cassette. 'What am I supposed to be looking for?' she said.

'You'll know when you see it.' Nevertheless he was frowning. The cassette ran on – priests and card games in market-places, women with gorgon hair, hundreds of fishermen plunging into a river to net a multitude of fish – and then it was over. 'Just let me run it again,' he said.

'What exactly are you trying to find?'

'I wanted you to see without me having to tell you. Well, all right,' he said reluctantly, 'you can look for it too. I remembered I'd seen a shot of a kind of bright red man. I thought it was near the beginning, but I could have been mistaken. I'm sure he's what you thought you saw in the pillbox. You must have got the idea from the film.'

She could have glimpsed it on Sunday, while she was trying to read. It was the kind of peripheral glimpse her imagination might have seized upon and produced when she was searching the pillbox. She wanted to believe that, she *wanted* to be reassured, but as he ran the tape back and forth, muttering to himself, she was simply becoming more nervous. Crowds scampered into the mosque then scurried out backwards, fishermen were flung out of the river as though the fish were fighting back. On the mantelpiece the metal claw jerked as the light caught it. Why couldn't he find what he'd seen? What if it wasn't on the tape after all? She was peering desperately at the screen, wanting to plead with him to stop the parade of images, when the doorbell rang.

Before Liz could get up, Anna had run to the door. 'Hello, Anna,' Liz heard. 'Is your father in?'

It was Isobel. Today she wore a tailor-made mauve suit: jacket, blouse and slacks. She strode into the long room and nodded briefly to Liz, then she saw that Alan was running the cassette. 'I hope I haven't interrupted you at work,' she said.

He turned off the sound. 'No, not really. Don't worry.'

'I was on my way home from Hemsby, so I thought I might drop in. I didn't phone in case that disturbed you. You're searching for something, are you? Is it to do with your work?'

'No, nothing like that. It's something we thought Liz saw.'

'I see.' In two words Isobel managed to imply that if he felt obliged to waste his time, he was too old for her to stop him. 'Something on the television?' she said.

'Well, no, not exactly. Out on the cliff. She thought she saw a man hiding in the pillbox.'

'But in fact he was on the television?' She turned to Liz. 'I suppose you were overtired.'

'We've both been a bit on edge,' Alan said defensively. 'Someone killed a goat on the cliff the other day.'

For God's sake, Liz cried silently, don't tell her that! Some hangover from his childhood always made him blurt out the truth to his mother, whatever the consequences. 'What do you mean, killed it?' Isobel demanded. 'Ran it over?'

'Nastier than that,' Alan said, while Liz cringed inwardly. 'It looked as if they used a knife.'

'But good heavens, you shouldn't let the child stay here while that kind of thing is going on. I'll take her, by all means. I'm sure Elizabeth would welcome a rest.'

'Thank you very much, Isobel, but I'm sure I can cope.' Liz's mouth was growing unwieldy with resentment. 'Anna's a sensible girl. She knows to stay with me. She's in no danger.'

'Well, I can't force you. Or the child, if she prefers not to come.'

Perhaps hearing that they were talking about her, Anna wandered in from the playroom. 'Would you like to come and stay with me for a while and give your mother a rest?' Isobel said.

Anna must have felt accused, for she looked at Liz for reassurance. 'I want to stay with mummy,' she said, almost pleading.

'Oh well, that's that. There's obviously nothing I can do.' She turned her back on both of them. 'I came to invite you all to dinner next week,' she said to Alan, making it sound like a challenge.

'We'd love to come. Wouldn't we, Liz?'

'Of course we would.' She found it easier to be dishonest while Isobel had her back to her. 'Would you like a cup of tea, Isobel?'

'I don't think so, thank you. I think it'll be best if I go.' Halfway down the path she turned and gazed at Liz. 'My offer is still open if you should change your mind.'

As soon as she had driven away, Alan said, 'I wish you wouldn't resent her so much. She's only trying to help.'

'Yes, at my expense.'

'Oh, that's nonsense. Why do you say that? If she's difficult sometimes, it's only because she'd like to see more of her grandchild.'

'She sees as much of her as my parents do.'

'Well, it isn't my mother's fault if your parents live so far away, is it? It isn't her fault your father has a weak heart and won't drive.'

She stared at him. 'I can't talk to you at all,' she said, and went into the house, half-blind with nerves and anger. In the long room the cassette was still running; great crude masks were dancing. She made for the kitchen, trying to think, through the jumble of her emotions, if there was anything she'd forgotten to do.

She had barely reached the kitchen when Anna came trailing after her. 'Anna, will you please go out and play or find something to do so you don't get under my feet,' she cried.

'I don't want to go out. The man's there.'

'Don't be so childish.' Often the little girl behaved as if she was older than six; right now, for some reason, she was acting as if she was considerably younger. Liz strode into the garden to show her there was nothing there. A breeze tousled her hair, flowers stooped like ballerinas, the hedge shook. Amid the roaring of the sea she heard children shouting and an unpleasant high-pitched sound she couldn't place. She was almost at the point where she could see through the hedge when she faltered. Anna had been right. There *was* a man beyond the hedge.

The next moment Liz relaxed. It was only Joseph; she would have known that grubby raincoat anywhere, especially on a hot day like this. He was bending over something in the grass, and he had his back to her. His raincoat blocked her view. But she could still hear that high-pitched sound, and it made her apprehensive. Joseph's right arm was rising and falling, the torn sleeve of his coat was flapping. Liz hurried to the hedge to see what he had found.

But she stumbled away before she reached the hedge, one hand over her mouth to stop herself from crying out. That might bring Anna, and the child mustn't see. Liz hadn't seen a great deal herself: only far too much – only the sharp stone in Joseph's right hand, which came up redder every time it rose into the air. Now she knew what the high-pitched noise was. There couldn't be much left of what lay at his feet, but whatever was left was screaming.

Twelve

Alan thought: Christ, what's wrong now? Everything seemed to be going wrong since he'd come back from Nigeria: his work, his home life, his surroundings. Both he and Liz were seeing things – she at the window and in the pillbox, he on the cassette. And that was yet another problem to undermine his work. He had been so busy trying to find the man he thought he'd seen on the cassette that he'd completely lost the inspiration the documentary had originally given him. Now his mother and Liz were at each other's throats, which made him feel helpless and edgy, and he was being drawn into silly, time-wasting arguments. Worst of all, there was Anna, moping about the place as if she expected someone to pounce on her, behaving as if she was afraid to be alone with her father or even to have him touch her, making a ridiculous fuss about the weapon he'd brought home from Nigeria, doing everything she could to make it difficult for him to work, even upsetting his mother.

And now, on top of everything else, here was Liz with the latest bad news.

For a moment he thought she wanted to reopen the argument – about his mother, or her parents, or whatever the devil the matter had been. Then he saw how white her face was, and he was furious: nothing was going to make her look like that if he had anything to do with it. 'What's wrong?' he said, suddenly gentle.

'Go and see.' Whatever the matter was, she clearly didn't want to say in front of Anna. 'Go quickly. Just beyond the hedge. I'll call the police.'

She didn't sound at all hysterical. She was hurrying Anna into her playroom – 'Just find yourself something to do for a few minutes' – as he made for the back door. Though he felt apprehensive, she had also raised his spirits; perhaps at last there would be something to confront.

As soon as he had let himself out of the side gate he saw Joseph, his coat flapping like a scarecrow's. For a moment he wondered if Liz had been hysterical after all; there was nobody but Joseph on the cliff. Then he saw how Joseph was tearing at an object in the grass – tearing with his bare hands. Both the object and his hands were crimson. Alan went forward quietly, gritting his teeth.

The noise of the wind and the sea must have drowned the sound of Alan's approach, unless Joseph was too preoccupied to look up. Alan was able to creep within arm's length of him, close enough to gaze down at the body of the goat. It was torn wide open, and Joseph was dragging out the small intestine, a glistening rope that seemed endless. His nails were biting into it; Alan had never seen his nails so long. With a kind of horrible banality, he made a mental note that his own nails needed cutting too.

Joseph stumbled backward without warning – surely the goat was twitching only because he was dragging at it, not because it was still alive? – and Alan saw his face. His eyes were blank, as if they couldn't bear to see what he was doing. He was chewing; a trickle of blood ran down his chin from whatever was in his mouth.

The next moment he saw Alan. His eyes widened with horror – with realization of what he had done? He gave a shrill inarticulate snarl and stumbled away, running bow-legged toward the path down to the beach. He slithered down a few feet, then whirled around and came stumbling upward, slipping on drifts of sand. A family – a podgy man in Bermuda shorts, a plump woman squeezed into an imitation leopard-skin swimsuit, two bright pink children wrapped in bath towels – were climbing the path, blocking his way.

They had seen his crimson hands and his wild eyes. The man came after him, shouting '*Hey!*' Joseph dodged between Alan and the edge of the cliff. For a moment Alan thought he'd trapped him – Joseph was forced to teeter on the very edge, which began at once to crumble – then Joseph fled crabwise toward the house. Let him get there, let Anna see what he'd become, then perhaps she'd appreciate her father . . . Horrified by his own thoughts, Alan raced after Joseph, trying to head him off.

The plump woman had seen the carcass in the grass. 'Oh, the swine!' she cried, thrusting her shoulder-bag at the elder of the children and giving them a shove toward the family car. Then she joined the chase. Though her flesh quivered wherever it bulged out of her swimsuit, she was as fast as any of them and a good deal more furious.

Alan had managed to keep Joseph away from the house. Joseph went lurching toward the pillbox, waving his hands frantically, scattering drops of blood. Alan noticed he was wiping his hands down his coat. Perhaps he felt he would be rid of his guilt if he got rid of the blood. Now he was struggling out of the smeared coat, tearing off the buttons. For the first time Alan saw what he wore underneath: trousers and braces, but nothing else.

Joseph was nearly at the pillbox. Perhaps they could trap him in there. Alan's gesture to the couple said as much. The man dodged behind the building to head Joseph off, Alan ran straight at him. The woman was running at him too, her face red with exertion and fury. They would almost certainly have caught him if she hadn't turned fastidiously aside to avoid treading on the smeared coat. Joseph fled toward the road, stretching out his hands on either side of him as far as they would go, as if he wished they would vanish, as if he could forget they were there.

He stopped before he reached the road. The police were waiting for him, the red-faced policeman and a younger man with a crew-cut. The sight of them seemed to paralyse Joseph, for they almost reached him before he turned and tried to flee. The young man brought him down with a rugby tackle. The dry earth beneath the parched grass must have knocked all the breath out of him. Even so, the young policeman grabbed his arms and twisted them viciously up his naked back.

Alan found the capture rather sordid and unpleasant. No doubt in reality such things always were. The older policeman seemed embarrassed too. 'All right, lad, we've got him now. Go easy on him.'

'Go easy on him?' the plump woman cried. 'Have you seen what he did to that poor dumb animal? Give him to me, I'll show you how to treat him.'

'It's all right, Freda,' her husband said, glancing warily at the police. 'They know their job. We'd best be getting back to the children.'

After a while she allowed herself to be coaxed away. Alan led the older policeman to the remains of the goat, where flies were already gathering. To his surprise he'd begun to like the man, who had proved to be human after all. 'My wife won't have to see this, will she?' he said.

'She was the one who called us, you know.' But he looked sickened himself. 'Did you see him in the act? Well, then I think we can let her off.'

Alan had to retreat from the smell of blood before he could describe what he had seen. The young policeman was hauling Joseph to his feet, still with his arms twisted behind him, and Alan's testimony seemed redundant; the evidence was there on Joseph's hands, and dribbling from his mouth. The young policeman marched him forward and forced him to stoop to the carcass, into the stench of blood. 'Did you do this?' he shouted.

Joseph's moan was wordless, but there was no mistaking the sound of guilt. The young policeman dragged him backward, wrenching his arms further up between his shoulders. Alan felt sorry for Joseph, but helpless to intervene. Joseph surely couldn't have known what he was doing. But what could have changed him so much and so suddenly, to make him act that way?

All at once Joseph gazed into his eyes with an expression both pleading and accusing. Alan felt inexplicably afraid of what he might say. Nothing, probably, for he was spitting out blood, and the young policeman had already begun to drag him off to the police van. But Joseph struggled back toward Alan. 'He made Joseph do it,' he said thickly. 'He brought it here.'

'Don't you be telling lies,' the young policeman said, jerking Joseph's arms. 'Nobody made you do it but yourself. And this gentleman never brought the goat here, either. You're loony, that's what you are, but that won't help you.'

He forced Joseph to stumble toward the road. Joseph stared back over his shoulder, crying, 'He brought it here!' until his captor shoved him into the back of the van.

Alan felt dizzy with guilt, but the red-faced policeman was apologetic. 'I may have to bother you again,' he said, 'but I hope there won't be any need.'

When the police had taken Joseph away, Alan stood for a while at the edge of the cliff. The sea glittered jaggedly, the pebbles on the beach looked like stubble in brown flesh. Another police van arrived to collect the carcass. It was undoubtedly their most sensational case for years. Suddenly he didn't want to be alone, though he wasn't sure if he should tell Liz what he felt, or even if he could. He hurried back to the house.

Liz was waiting for him in the back doorway. She must have persuaded Anna to stay alone in the playroom for a while. 'I'm sorry I behaved as if you were imagining things,' he said at once. 'It must have been Joseph all the time. At least it's over now.'

'I suppose so.' She seemed understandably depressed, yet relieved. He held her for a while, but that reminded him that he wasn't telling her the whole story. Telling her might upset her for no reason; and anyway, he knew what he had to do. Eventually she said, 'Maybe I shouldn't leave Anna by herself too long,' and he was able to go up to his workroom.

He sat staring out of the window at the cliff-top, at the reddened patch of grass where the goat had lain. He was right, he knew. He'd known what Joseph was going to say even before he spoke. It explained so much – Anna's apparently irrational fear, his own glimpse on the video-cassette, perhaps even the things Liz had seen: he no longer knew how real they'd been, and it didn't seem to matter. Above all, it explained the change in Joseph, and that showed how serious the situation was. Thank God, he knew what to do.

He made three phone calls quickly. His agent was booked up for the rest of the week, but Teddy the Editor was free. It wouldn't have mattered if he hadn't been, but he was a good excuse, a means of making things look more natural to Liz. Alan made one more call, then he went downstairs to her. 'Shall we take Anna to the hotel for dinner?' he said.

'To celebrate, you mean?'

'Not quite that.' Liz had immediately regretted her sarcasm. 'I just thought it would take the pressure off you a bit,' he said.

'God knows I need that. All right, let's.' Then she looked suspiciously at him. 'Are you trying to soften me up for something?'

He was glad she thought so; that way she wouldn't realize that what he really wanted was to get all three of them out of the house for a while, away from whatever was there. 'Well, Teddy wants me to go into London and have lunch with him tomorrow. You don't mind, do you? You've got your at-home with the girls in the afternoon.'

'Do you have to go? Yes, all right, I know you do. I only hope I can persuade Anna that everything's all right without mentioning Joseph.'

'I'm sure you will. I'll try not to be back too late.'

Seeing that she'd accepted the excuse, he was able to say, casually, 'And I'll take that African thing with me.'

Thirteen

That night Alan couldn't sleep. Either the heat was tropical, or he'd had too much to drink at the hotel. Long after Liz had fallen asleep he lay awake beside her, sweating and prickly, bothered by the vague idea that there was something he had to do. 'All right,' he found himself muttering at the dark, 'I'll do it, I'm going to do it tomorrow.' But still his compulsion wasn't satisfied; it kept jerking him back from the edge of sleep, stranding him in the rumbling seaside dark with fragments of the day – Joseph stumbling backward as the raw intestine unravelled; Joseph helpless on the ground with the policeman on top of him, himself carrying Anna asleep in his arms, out of the hotel to the car. Why did all these memories make him feel uneasy?

He slept at last, and woke late, feeling as if he'd run for miles. By the time he'd rushed through washing, shaving and dressing, Anna was sitting by Liz on the bed, and Liz was blinking herself awake. He kissed them both, then grabbed his briefcase and hurried out to the car. As he passed the living-room he glimpsed the empty space on the mantelpiece where the claw had been before he had packed it in his briefcase, and felt intensely relieved.

He backed his dented car out of the garage and drove to Norwich. Soon the sea fell behind. Golfers and hikers wandered over the green landscape, barges roamed the waterways. Luckily there wasn't much traffic on the roads – for he was driving before he was fully awake – and he drove through the villages without mishap. A postman cycled from house to house, women with wicker baskets chatted outside shops – but Alan barely noticed them, intent on his driving.

He reached Norwich earlier than he had expected. The train reminded him of the railway museum, for his carriage was faded and empty. Why did these musty old carriages always seem so dim, even on sunny days like this? He sat and gazed along the ranks of deserted seats, settees crammed together. His briefcase was on the floor beside him. He pushed it away a little with one foot, so that it wouldn't be quite so near him.

The carriage was still empty when the train jerked forward. The jerk felt like an awakening – except that he was still trying to struggle awake five minutes later. The landscape was rushing past faster now, but it hardly changed at all and wasn't enough to distract him from the contents of his briefcase, nor from the muttering of his thoughts. He wasn't sure if he believed his intuition of yesterday. Hadn't he been thinking too much like a writer, trying to make everything fit together too neatly? Could such an insignificant object really have influenced Joseph so profoundly? But if not, why had the anthropologist been so anxious to get rid of it? It didn't matter what Alan thought; whatever his reasons he had to deliver it to the Foundation.

That relieved his anxiety, a little. The train was rocking him back to sleep, and there was nothing in the landscape that his mind could seize upon to stay awake. He moved over on the seat and placed the briefcase between himself and the window. In a few moments he was nodding. There was something he had to do. His head was nodding, it seemed to agree. His body knew what he had to do; why couldn't it let him into the secret? One more nod that he was distantly aware of, and then he was lost in a dream.

Perhaps it was the answer, for he was close to home. He had to find Anna. There she was, running through the murky fields ahead. He didn't know exactly where he was, but he could hear the sea, though it sounded as he thought a rainstorm in a jungle might sound. He had to catch up with Anna, for a shape was running beside him on all fours, a naked shape with a human face, a shape that glistened red all over, even in the dark. Now he had outdistanced the shape and was running effortlessly, his feet hardly touching the ground. In a moment he would catch Anna. That was when she looked back, and he saw the terror in her eyes. He felt as if the ground beneath his feet had fallen away. She knew that he hadn't been chasing her to save her. He sprang at her, raising the claw that had been in his hand all the time.

Had he closed his eyes so that he couldn't see what he'd done? Certainly he'd had a blackout of some kind, because now he was somewhere in the jungle, stumbling through the greenish light beneath enormous dripping trees. Now he knew: the scene with Anna hadn't happened yet, and he was here to prevent it from ever happening. Here was a clearing with a few conical huts, a pot steaming over a fire, a thin leathery man with small blank eyes like a spider's, squatting with his back to a tree. Alan stumbled toward the man with the spidery eyes, for he was Alan's one chance to stop what was going to happen. Then, for a moment too brief to grasp, he realized what he would have to do in order to make sure of that chance, and it was so dreadful that he woke shrieking.

The carriage was still deserted. He wished there were someone there, even though it might have been embarrassing. Beyond the window at the end of the carriage, more seats lurched back and forth; beside him a blur of hedges raced by. He'd already forgotten what he had to do in the clearing in the jungle, and he was trying to forget his dream about Anna too, but there was one thought he couldn't avoid: the dream hadn't been entirely false to his feelings about her. He had to admit that he was relieved to get away from her.

At least, in a *sense* he was . . . But being away from her also allowed him to consider his feelings about her. He'd been uneasy whenever they were alone together, ever since he'd come back from Nigeria. All of a sudden she was getting on his nerves. Couldn't that be because his work was giving him trouble? Yes – but that wasn't the whole of it. Whenever he was alone with her, he felt that there was something he had to do, if only he could think of it. Perhaps he didn't *need* to think of it, just let his body act it out for him. For some reason he was remembering their last day on the beach, when he'd chased her and caught her, more and more roughly . . .

He found he couldn't think of that for too long. It made him feel guilty and nervous, exactly as the dream had made him feel. If only he could wake fully he might be able to deal with it, but his thoughts were blurred, like something left in an attic for years. Most frustrating was the notion that the dream should have made clear to him what the claw was.

He was still trying to grasp the impression, when the train pulled in at Liverpool Street. What was wrong with him, letting a dream bother him so much? God knows, he needed a clear mind for his meeting with Teddy, especially if he was going to break the news that the book might be late. He grabbed his briefcase and made for the taxi-rank.

By the time he arrived on Queensway it was almost lunchtime. London was crowded with tourists, and half the shoppers in Oxford Street had been wearing robes – it was almost like a continuation of one of his dreams of Africa. Yesterday he'd been fairly sure he'd know what to say to Teddy when the time came, but now he felt sure of nothing, except that he wanted to deliver the contents of his briefcase as soon as he could. He wished he'd arranged to go to the Foundation first.

Teddy was 'in a meeting'. Editors always seemed to be 'in a meeting' – when they weren't out to lunch. Alan sat on a leather sofa in the foyer, a high-ceilinged room elaborately decorated with plaster vegetation, and leafed through *Publishers Weekly*, glancing at a full-page advertisement for himself – '*Britain's leading thriller writer up there with Deighton and Le Carré.*' A few years ago he'd never have dared dream that a publisher would spend that kind of money to advertise his books. He should have felt more pleased, but the sense of something to be done was still nagging at him.

Soon Teddy came up from the basement. He was a tall Canadian with a youthful face that always looked scrubbed as a schoolboy's at a prize-giving. Though he was thirty-two, Alan had seen barmen refuse to serve him because he looked under age. Today he wore jeans and a T-shirt printed with a marihuana leaf. 'I hope you're starving,' he said.

That and the T-shirt meant they'd be lunching at the pizza parlour. 'Pretty much,' Alan said. At least a leisurely meal might help him relax and choose his words.

Small chance. The moment they sat down at their table, decorated with a large American flag, the waitress bobbed over to them, a pert girl with a stars-and-stripes apron and a Cockney accent. She brought them a carafe of white wine as soon as she saw Teddy.

Alan had just ordered his pizza and taken a mouthful of wine when Teddy said, 'How's *Out of the Past* coming?'

'Not too well,' Alan said, bracing himself for the worst.

'Yes, I had that impression last time we spoke. You don't think you can deliver on time, am I right?'

'Not without rushing it.' Alan wished he knew what Teddy thought of him, but the editor's face was bright and blank as a poster. 'I'm sorry,' Alan said. 'I don't want to seem temperamental.'

'Nobody thinks that. You're one of our most professional writers. You take it at whatever pace feels right to you. It shouldn't take you more than a couple of months past the deadline, should it?'

Just now Alan didn't know, and wondered if Teddy was flattering him in order to make him commit himself. 'I hope not,' he said.

'Well, keep me up to date on how it's going. Just don't feel too pressured, that's the main thing. Anyway, I wanted to tell you, we're giving you an excuse for delivering it late. You'll recall we're doing the first paperback of *Spy on Fire* in September, and we very much hope you'll agree to a signing tour.'

Alan should have been delighted. At the start of his writing career he'd often dreamed of one day being important enough to tour the country at his publisher's expense, signing his books. But now he felt he was agreeing only because he could think of no reason to refuse. As soon as they'd finished their pizzas and cheese-cake and coffee, he declined another drink in Teddy's office and ran for a cab to take him to the Foundation for African Studies.

The Foundation was an elegant cream stucco building near Russell Square, with a pedimented doorway flanked by round windows, portholes of gleaming white plaster, and the air of a miniature country house. Lions the size of cats perched on the gateposts between black railings, and a man was clipping the lawns in front of the building with long-handled shears. Alan wondered vaguely if he could be a plain-clothes guard, then dismissed the idea as fanciful. Perhaps he could work it into a future book: he filed the image away in his mind.

The front door was open. The man, whose shears were almost as tall as himself, glanced up as Alan went in. Beyond the door was a foyer with a graceful staircase, at the foot of which a young woman with braided hair sat at a switchboard behind a desk. A small neat man with glossy black hair that almost hid his gleaming cranium scurried out of a room near the desk and frowning abstractedly at Alan, hurried upstairs. 'May I help you?' the young woman said.

'I'm supposed to see Dr Hetherington.'

'Why, there he is. Dr Hetherington!' she called – but already the small neat man had turned and was descending the stairs.

So much for Alan's image of a tall stooped white-haired professor. At least Hetherington seemed as fussy as he sounded on the phone. He gazed at Alan, then his frown cleared. 'Ah, yes, of course,' he said. 'You're bringing me the Leopard Men's claw.'

He led the way upstairs to his office, a sunny spacious room overlooking the lawns, and lined with books in glass-fronted bookcases, out of reach of the sunlight. Through the open window came the murmur of traffic, and from closer by, the sound of clipping. Flicking a switch on his intercom, Hetherington called for tea, while Alan sank into a leather chair that sighed. Now Alan could ask the question that had nagged him all the way upstairs. 'You said the Leopard Men. The Nigerian secret society, you mean?'

'Correct.' Hetherington was obviously glad of a chance to lecture. 'At least, they were last heard of in Nigeria,' he said. 'That was in the Forties, when they were simply killers, sometimes for hire. But the Leopard tradition was found across a wide belt of Africa, from Guinea through Sierra Leone and Liberia to Nigeria and Cameroon, on through Chad and the Sudan to Uganda and even Kenya – though there were only scattered reports there. Its influence was powerful while it lasted. One wonders if it has died out completely, even now.'

A secretary came in with a teapot, mugs and milk and sugar on a tray. Hetherington poured the tea himself, giving all his attention to the task. Alan felt that if he asked a question he wouldn't be heard. There was something he needed to know, but was afraid to ask. Hetherington brought him a mug at last – 'Do tell me if the tea isn't as you like it' – and Alan took it.

'They used to dress up in leopard skins and masks, didn't they?' he said. 'They lay in wait for people and killed them with the metal claws.'

'Yes, in some areas there was a ritual robing. There were many regional variations. In the Western Congo, for example, where the tradition came from Gabon, they would tear off their victim's thumbs with their bare hands, and all the flesh between the eyes.' Suddenly he had the look of a teenage girl squirming at her first horror film.

'The important element seems to have been to tear out the heart while the victim was still alive.'

Why did Alan feel nervous? 'You mean they were cannibals?'

'So we're led to believe. Only the Leopard societies, of course, not the cultures in which they occurred. Supposedly they devoured their victims as a way of achieving power. Some cannibalism appears to be based on the belief that by consuming the victim you take on his powers, but it seems the Leopard Men were trying to reach back to some older form of magic, one that demanded human sacrifice and cannibalism. I mean, of course,' he added primly, 'that is what *they* believed.'

Alan now realized why he was nervous: because he didn't know what he was afraid to hear. Outside, the sound of the clipping continued. The blast of a horn on the road seemed so loud that he jumped, almost spilling the tea.

'The tradition seems to be traceable back to the Ju-Ju men of the nineteenth century,' Hetherington was saying. 'Before that, there is no documentation. That was David Marlowe's task, to trace it back to its origins. It seemed an impossible task to me, but he was a brilliant researcher. I wonder,' he said sadly, 'if the research affected his mind. The way he seems to have become obsessed with the claw that he gave you, for example. Heaven knows how many people it may have killed. Certainly I should never have given it house room.'

And yet he had expected Alan to do so. Still, it had been Alan's own decision to put it on display. Now, presumably, it was Hetherington's, whether he wanted it or not. Alan sipped his tea automatically, though it seemed to be making him hot and light-headed. The clipping of shears felt as if it was nipping at his brain.

'David set out to interview surviving Leopard Men, and I understand that he succeeded,' Hetherington said. 'We shan't know until we see his notes, and we'll have to wait until the Nigerian police have finished with them for that. Perhaps it was the interviews that caused his break-down – the strain of having to be polite to such men. I could never have done it myself. I don't believe in treating murderers like normal human beings – and these men were worse than murderers. Presumably each one of them must have gone through his own disgusting initiation ritual.'

'What was that?' Alan said, though he wasn't sure by any means that he wanted to know.

'Why, the killing of the child. One can only hope that some of them refused when they found that was what they were required to do – even if refusing meant being killed in their turn. You'd have thought that a man who had the courage to face those who'd chosen him would also have the courage to make them remove the compulsion. But of course these were superstitious savages. They would have been too scared to refuse.'

Alan was gripping the mug so hard he thought it might shatter, thick as it was. 'What did you mean about killing a child?'

'Each man had to give his young daughter to the cult before he could be accepted – a girl child of his own or his wife's blood. They would send the child running down a path through the bush at night. When they caught her they would tear her to pieces and eat her.'

Alan managed to set down his mug on the carpet, though he could hardly see. He was blinded by a flood of memories – the dream of chasing Anna and bringing her down with the claw, his feelings about her since he'd brought the claw home, the dream which suddenly came flooding back to him – the chase dream he'd had on the plane out of Lagos. It must have started then, the influence on him. He groped for his briefcase, snarling under his breath. He had to control himself, or when he got hold of the claw he wouldn't be able to stop himself flinging it at Hetherington, this small intolerably smug man who had let the influence gain such a hold on him.

He shuddered as he groped in the briefcase, for the

touch of cold leather made him feel for a moment as if he were groping inside a corpse. He *must* calm down, he *must* shake off his fears in order to be able to look. But he'd already felt the contents of the briefcase, and that was why his fears were worse. He wrenched the case wide open, thinking sickly of Joseph tearing open the goats, and peered in. He couldn't believe it, even when his vision cleared. He hadn't brought the claw with him at all.

Fourteen

He must have lost it somewhere between here and home: in the pizza parlour or in one of the taxis, perhaps. But that made no sense: he hadn't opened his briefcase since before he'd left the house – not even at lunch with Teddy, for he'd thought that there was nothing in the case except the claw. Could it have been stolen on the train while he was asleep? The possibility wasn't even worth considering. 'I haven't got it,' he muttered, hardly aware of Hetherington. 'It isn't here.'

'I don't understand,' Hetherington said, rather snappishly.

'Do you think I do?' He was trying desperately to recall when he'd put the claw in his briefcase. He'd been drunk last night when he'd left the hotel – he thought he'd drunk so much to celebrate being about to get rid of the claw – and Liz had had to drive. As soon as he'd reached home he'd taken the claw from the mantelpiece. No, that couldn't be right; he'd carried Anna to bed, managing to tuck her up without waking her, and then there was a vague memory of his drunken attempt to make love to Liz. *Then* he had stumbled downstairs, while Liz got into bed. He'd gone to the living-room mantelpiece and reached out for the claw. Now he had located the moment, he could no longer be deceived. He'd reached out drunkenly and knocked the claw off the mantelpiece, behind a chair. After that there was a blank, until he remembered lying in bed.

He must have dreamed he'd put the claw in his briefcase – but was there more, and worse, to it than that? He'd forgotten that he had the claw while he was approaching the Customs barrier at Heathrow; he'd forgotten to call the Foundation to begin with; he'd forgotten for a while that he had agreed to bring the claw. It felt very much as if his thoughts about the claw had been manipulated. In that case, could he have been made to think he'd brought the claw so that Liz and Anna would be left alone with it? 'It must be at home,' he said tightly. 'I'll have to phone my wife.'

'Is that really necessary?'

'You're asking me if it's necessary?' He wished he had the claw in his hand right now, to use on Hetherington. 'You let me keep that thing in my house, around my wife and child, when you knew what it was, and now you're begrudging me the cost of a phone call? How much do you want? I'll write you a fucking cheque.'

'That won't be necessary under the circumstances.' Hetherington had turned pale as an elderly virgin confronted by a piece of hard-core pornography. He pushed the phone across the desk, then withdrew his hand hastily, as if he couldn't bear the thought of touching Alan.

As soon as Alan had dialled, he turned his back on Hetherington, who he sensed was fuming, and listened. For a few seconds there was silence except for the measured clipping of shears, a sound that seemed to fill the room. Alan thought of sharp metal, and the thought made his fingers writhe. The next moment a woman's voice came on the line.

It wasn't Liz. Of course – Liz was having her at-home. One of the others – Gail, Jane, Rebecca – must have answered the phone. But why couldn't he understand what she was saying? Because she had begun at the end of a sentence. Only when she repeated her message, and then again and again, did he realize that it was a recorded voice, telling him that all lines to that part of Norfolk were engaged.

He slammed the receiver down so hard that Hetherington flinched. 'I can't get through. I'll have to go home at once.'

Hetherington held up one finger. 'Will you let me know what transpires, please?'

'Oh yes.' Though he was almost at the door, Alan turned

so that the man could see his snarl. 'I'll be letting you know about that, don't you worry.'

He ran downstairs and out, past the braided girl and the man with the shears, which were now nibbling the very edge of the lawn, by the railings. True or not, the idea of the man as a plain-clothes guard now seemed absurd, if only because it had become so trivial. Couldn't Alan have let his professional imagination run away with him about the claw as well? Maybe he should try his hand at writing horror stories. But no – that explanation was simply too tempting to be true.

He found a free taxi before he reached Russell Square. The streets were relatively clear now, between lunch and the homeward rush, and the taxi raced toward Liverpool Street with hardly a pause; yet Alan was almost contemplating asking the driver to take him straight to Norwich and his car – or even all the way home. Commonsense told him that would be crazy. How could it be quicker, with all those winding roads? Alan's fists were aching, his palms felt raw with sweat. Should he at least try to phone again, or would he miss his train?

The taxi swung down the slope at Liverpool Street a couple of minutes before a train was due to leave for Norwich. Without waiting for change, Alan thrust a five-pound note at the driver and dodged through the crowd to the ticket barrier.

There was no time to phone. But, maddeningly, once he'd stumbled panting into the nearest carriage and thrown himself and his empty briefcase on a seat, it seemed that there were minutes to spare. The train ought to be moving by now, yet two minutes, three, elapsed, and still it seemed to show no sign of moving. His body was straining to race for the phones, and he was just beginning to doubt that he was capable of holding it still, when the train suddenly lurched forward and it was too late.

Now that the train had trapped him, it seemed almost to be taunting him. It stopped at every station, even when nobody was boarding or alighting. Between stations it cruised as if it had all the time in the world. Shapeless clouds paced it along the horizon, and made Alan feel that the train was drifting slowly as clouds. His time was slowing down to a standstill, but at home time must be moving faster. It would take only a second for the first blow to fall, and then there would be raw flesh for the claw to tear . . .

He must stop imagining what might be happening at home, or he'd never be capable of driving when he reached Norwich – but how *could* he stop? He found to his dismay that he was muttering to himself; he had no idea how long he'd been doing so. An old lady who'd boarded the train at the last station with her arms full of bags of apples leaned across the aisle. 'Are you all right, my dear? What's the trouble?'

'Oh, it's nothing.' Yet saying that only made him feel more uncomfortable. He longed to tell her he'd been unkind to his wife and child and wanted to get home to make it up to them, but he was appalled by his own glibness – especially when he thought what might actually be happening. Yet surely he was worrying unnecessarily: after all, nothing very bad had happened to them yet; nobody at home had been affected like Joseph. There had never been any Leopard Women, it didn't matter that Liz was at home with the claw. But that felt like a contrivance in a story, a device he didn't believe in, but had to use to keep the plot moving.

The old lady alighted two stations before Norwich. One of her bags burst, spilling apples over the platform. Alan had jumped to his feet and was opening the door to help her until the thought of missing the train stopped him. Wasn't he too eager to believe that there was no danger at home? Didn't he feel too reassured – suspiciously so? He'd already forgotten the claw too often, and he was beginning to be on the alert for signs that his thoughts were being manipulated.

Before the train came to a halt at Norwich, he'd flung open the door and was running toward the ticket barrier. By the time he reached the station forecourt his keys were in his hand. He backed the car out in a single sweeping movement and swung it out onto the main road. Now he felt in control, no longer helpless. All his instincts were tuned at last.

He drove steadily toward the coast road. He would be in time, he *must* be. The green landscape sped past, water flashed and vanished. He was halfway home when he thought of the last time he'd driven so fast – the day he'd scared Anna so badly. Liz had accused him of trying to kill the child. Had that been what he'd wanted? He was driving faster now, no longer calm, muttering curse after curse at Marlowe, who'd given him the wretched claw in the first place.

The shadows lengthened as he drove along the coast road, darkness already fingering the landscape, reaching for his home. His readiness to manufacture images dismayed him, but so did the thought that they might be true. Overhead the clouds were thickening, hastening the twilight. Everything ahead of him looked smudged, and he would have slowed down if he'd dared. Nothing was clear any more.

Now he could see the house. It looked utterly innocent: lights in the curtained windows downstairs, the kind of sight that would look welcoming at the end of a winter drive. He slewed the car into the driveway and turned off the engine. There was silence – no sound of the women, no sound of Anna or Jane's baby, Georgie. No doubt Liz's at-home was over by now, but why was the house so still? He left the car in front of the garage and ran across the lawn to the front door.

He had the key ready. It slipped easily into the lock. The door swung inward on the hall, the darkest place in the house. Then there was Liz, coming slowly toward him. He couldn't see her face, and that made him afraid to speak.

'Everything all right?' he said, to get it over with.

'Oh, Alan,' she said. 'I'm afraid to tell you what's happened.'

Fifteen

It was Rebecca who found the claw. She and Gail had arrived together, shortly after Jane and her baby. Rebecca was placing Anna's tortoise made of shells on the mantelpiece, beneath Liz's seascapes. 'There you are,' she said, 'the start of an exhibition. Two generations of the Knights.' She stooped to tickle baby Georgie, who was laughing because everyone else was, and then she peered under the chair nearest the fireplace. 'Hello, what's hiding under here?' she said, and scooped out the claw.

'Oh, *no*. Alan was supposed to be taking that to London.' Liz couldn't understand how she'd managed to overlook it while cleaning the room this morning; she could only assume that she hadn't seen it because she'd expected it not to be there. 'I can't even phone and let him know. He'll be out lunching with his editor, but I don't know where.'

'Pigs. Well, it'll give him an excuse to go to London again, so I don't suppose he'll mind. I'll leave it here, shall I?' Rebecca said, and replaced the claw on the mantelpiece.

Anna cried out. 'Oh, don't put it next to my tortoise.'

'Why, do you think they're going to fight? It might be an unequal contest, at that.' Rebecca moved the tortoise along the mantelpiece. 'Happy now?'

Anna nodded reluctantly. Liz had done her best to persuade the child that the man who had killed the goats was locked away, but Anna still seemed unconvinced. 'Can I take Georgie in my room and show him my toys?' Anna said.

'Oh, I wish you would,' Jane said. 'Anyone who takes him out of my hair is the next best thing to a saint.'

Anna grinned as if Jane had made a silly joke, and

carried Georgie across the hall. 'Be very careful with him, Anna,' Liz called.

Jane seemed already to have forgotten about him. She was gazing at the claw. 'That's a beautiful piece. It's very old, isn't it? How long have you been hiding it from us?'

'Alan brought it back from Nigeria. It isn't ours, we're only looking after it.' Liz was feeling a hint of dislike for the claw herself now, which annoyed her because she knew it was irrational. 'Follow me,' she said. 'Long drinks are waiting in the fridge.'

They sat in the back garden, drinking and chatting idly. Jane had delivered her petition and sounded defiantly hopeful, Gail was having a party tonight in the hotel to celebrate her wedding anniversary: seventeen years with Ned, she announced – which meant she could invite her friends without making them feel they had to buy presents. Liz noticed that she'd issued the invitation before Alex came. After a while they stopped talking and just lazed in the sunlight. Warm breezes ruffled the grass, the sea murmured at the beach. All at once they heard Anna shouting. 'Oh, what's he done *now*?' Jane complained, heaving herself to her feet.

'You sit and rest, Jane. I'll sort things out.' Liz didn't like Jane's edginess at all, not when it had to do with the baby. She hurried to the playroom to find out what was wrong.

It wasn't Georgie after all; he was sitting happily in the middle of the room, hugging two of Anna's old teddy-bears. Anna was leaning out of the window, shouting at a group of teenagers on holiday, who were breaking off souvenirs of the garden hedge. When Liz went to the front door, they strolled onward. She left the door open for Alex, though by now had begun to hope that Alex's lateness meant she wasn't coming.

As Liz emerged into the back garden Gail was saying, 'I think people who hate their children need medical help. I was telling her about Spike's father,' she explained to Liz. 'One of the other parents finally told him what they thought of him. I'd been biting my tongue ever since he arrived – not that telling him off did any good. The whole family left the next day, and no doubt he made life even worse for Spike when they got home.'

Liz wondered if some of this was meant for Jane. 'Anyway, that's enough depressing news,' Gail said. 'Are we starting soon, Liz? I could do with something to eat to fend off the effects of alcohol. We can't wait for Alex all day.'

'I'm sure she's coming. She told me she was.' Jane sounded almost desperate. Liz guessed she was terrified of any kind of scene with Alex, in case it weakened her pretence that nothing was wrong. Gail looked as though she felt she had to speak, but Liz grimaced at her just in time, for here was Alex now.

She was wearing even less than last week: shorts, and a bandanna that just covered her breasts. Liz felt Jane shrink into herself. 'Sorry I'm late,' Alex said jauntily. 'I was down on the beach reading a script my agent sent me, and I lost track of the time.'

Liz went into the kitchen to get her a drink. Through the window she heard Jane ask, 'What's the script about?'

'Well, they want me to play the younger woman in this triangle. She keeps the marriage together by sleeping with the husband and helping him sort out his problems.'

There was a silence tense as wire about to snap. 'I'm sure that must appeal to you,' Gail said icily.

Jane got up so quickly that her canvas seat fell over. 'Do you want another drink, Gail?' She sounded close to hysteria. 'I'm having one, will you?'

'Let's take the drinks into the dining-room,' Liz called, glad to join in the interruption. 'I know Gail's starving.'

They stood aside for one another in the doorway, a ritual of politeness that seemed somewhat farcical under the circumstances. In the end Alex went first, and looked long-suffering; she'd only just sat down outside, after all. Jane went to check on Georgie, and came back looking relieved. 'He's happy for once,' she said.

Liz had already laid out sandwiches and cakes. Gail and Rebecca heaped their plates, and Alex took her usual token couple of sandwiches. 'I have to watch my figure when I'm going to play a part,' she said, and Liz could almost hear the four of them asking the same question: when did Alex ever do anything else? Jane was eating as if she couldn't taste the food at all, stuffing sandwiches into her mouth with a kind of grim absorption. One way or another, the food was disappearing rapidly; there wouldn't be much left for Anna.

Liz went into the hall to call her, but hesitated; wouldn't it be better to leave the children where they were, to give Jane more of a respite? She came back without calling, trying to be unobtrusive about it; but Alex had noticed and misinterpreted her actions. 'I don't wonder you're worried about her,' Alex said, 'even if they have put that madman away. It's a pity that's all they're allowed to do to him.'

'What are you talking about?' Rebecca said.

'Why, whatever his name is, the creature in the raincoat. Did he ever have a name? I'm amazed they let him roam around for so long. You could tell what he was like just by looking at him.'

'If you mean Joseph, he was just about the gentlest person I've ever met. I'm sure he never hurt a living thing until these last few weeks.'

'Never got caught at it, you mean. I'm sorry, Rebecca, but it's because of people like you that there are so many criminals at large.'

Perhaps Rebecca felt compelled to defend Joseph because it was Alex who was attacking him. 'There was nobody I was happier to have in my shop,' she said.

'Then you can't be much of a judge of character. I don't mean to be rude, but you put the rest of us at risk with your attitudes. Don't you realize the danger Anna must have been in before they caught him? Just because you haven't any children of your own it doesn't mean you can ignore their welfare.'

Liz was damned if she'd let Alex drag Anna into the argument. 'That's nonsense. I'm sure she was never in the slightest danger from Joseph.'

Rebecca interrupted. 'You're right about one thing, Alex – I try not to judge people. But there are cases where I make an exception,' she said grimly. Jane gaped and reached out to hush her, but it looked as if Rebecca was determined to go on – except that just then, up the hall, Georgie began screaming.

Liz was first into the hall. Anna was already running towards her. 'He's frightened, mummy! He saw the man looking in the window!'

'Which man?' Liz glanced into the playroom first. Georgie was sitting on the floor, paralysed by his own screams, but the window was empty. As Jane picked him up, Liz strode out of the open front door. The garden was deserted, and so was the road. 'Which man, darling?' she said.

'The man. The man who comes into the garden.'

'Now I told you, Anna, the police have taken him away. You remember I told you that, don't you? There's nothing to be frightened of any more. Anyway, come along, you can have some sandwiches before they're all gone.' The women would have to restrain their hostilities in front of Anna.

But Georgie was a problem. Jane had taken him into the dining-room, but he still continued to scream. Jane seemed unable to cope with him. 'Shut up, Georgie,' she was muttering, 'shut up, shut up,' in a voice so lifeless and monotonous that the others looked away awkwardly.

Alex stood up as soon as Liz returned. 'Would you mind very much if I go now? I've got a bit of a headache, and I don't want it to get worse. I wouldn't be much use here.'

Liz could only stare at her and wonder if she could really be so lacking in any kind of awareness. Still, she was leaving, that was the main thing. Liz didn't bother to see her out.

Alex's move seemed to release the others from their

stasis. 'Let me have him, Jane,' Gail said, and rocked Georgie quiet almost at once.

Jane bent forward in her chair as though about to be sick, and began to sob. Rebecca tried to put her arm round her, but Jane shook her off. 'Leave me alone,' she cried. 'It's only plain Jane, she's not worth bothering about. She even drives away other people's guests. Nobody wants to know her. She's no use as a mother either. You'd think she could at least be a mother with these tits.'

The women encouraged her to let go, sob it all out, in the hope that she might feel better. Liz made her a cup of tea, and Anna gravely brought her a sandwich. When Jane refused with an attempt at a smile, Anna went back to her own sandwiches and seemed to lose interest in the situation. Gail put Georgie down and tried to comfort Jane. 'Don't you worry about driving that bitch away. If you hadn't, I would have.' But that only made Jane flinch further into herself. Then they had to chat to her and change the subject, and that was how nobody noticed Georgie crawling away to the long room.

After a while Jane ceased sobbing, and sat hunched over her cup of tea, sipping it shakily. At last she looked up. Her eyes seemed to say that she felt better now, but instead she suddenly cried out and almost dropped the cup. 'Where is he? Where's Georgie?'

She leapt to her feet and hurried down the hall. Liz let her go. She mustn't go herself, however apprehensive she felt all of a sudden; that would only be taking responsibility for Georgie away from Jane. There was silence except for the rumbling of the sea, an ominous rumbling. Then Jane cried out, and Liz went running down the hall.

Her heart was pounding, her mouth suddenly parched. The front door was open; Alex must have left it that way. Beyond the doorway of the long room, the sea was rumbling; for a hallucinatory moment it sounded as if the room itself were full of thunder. She stumbled through the doorway, into the room.

Georgie was propped up by the television. Jane was in

the middle of the carpet, staring at Liz. She was holding her handbag wide open, exhibiting it, but at first Liz couldn't tell what was wrong. 'Someone was in the house,' Jane cried. 'I left my bag in here and they've taken all my money.'

Liz had to make her face into a mask, in case Jane saw how relieved she was. Whatever Liz had feared – she no longer knew what it was, if she ever had – it hadn't happened. But Jane was pointing at the mantelpiece. 'And they took that,' she said. Anna's tortoise was still there beneath the seascapes, its pebble eyes gleaming dully – but the African claw had gone.

Sixteen

Alan didn't dare believe it. It seemed too good to be true. The police had already been, Liz said – the stout policeman yet again, with an expression that suggested the joke was beginning to wear thin – but he hadn't searched the house. Alan began searching at once: first the long room, in case the claw had only fallen after all, and then the rest of the ground floor, in case Georgie might have dragged it somewhere. Suppose the thieves had kept Jane's money and thrown away the claw? Suppose it was still close to the house? He went out to look.

The sky was clearing. Twilight would take its time after all. The gardens, the hedges, the house – everything looked calm and clear, as if it were giving back some of the light of the day. He searched the gardens, then he paced back and forth along the road, a leaden strip between the glowing verges. Once he caught sight of a glimmer among the roots of a hedge, but it was only an empty bottle. If there was anything to find, in this light he should see it at once.

Eventually he went down to the beach. Above the sea the sky resembled smoked glass. Foam spread across the dying colours of pebbles and sand. Along the cliff the Britannia Hotel was lit up, and he could hear music: Gail's and Ned's party had begun. He searched until it was too dark to see, by which time he was well away from the house. Why was he still behaving as if the thieves had thrown the claw away? Whoever had stolen it must have it now, and as far as Alan was concerned, they deserved whatever it brought them.

He climbed the path toward the pillbox, and as he came in sight of home he felt like a climber who'd reached the last slope to the peak. It was an immense relief to be rid of the claw at last. It had gone as unexpectedly as it had come and, thank God, Anna was safe after all. Whoever had stolen the claw had also taken away Alan's aggressive feelings towards the child. He felt grateful to the thieves. Now he needn't admit any of those feelings about the child to Liz, and that was even more of a relief.

By the time Alan returned from his search, Liz had put Anna to bed and was sitting in the long room, trying to read a Stephen King novel. 'It looks as if it's gone for good,' Alan said happily.

She must have thought his tone was meant to cheer her up. 'I'm sorry,' she said.

'Don't worry, Liz. It wasn't your fault, and anyway it really doesn't matter.'

'Well, I don't think it was my fault myself. It was that Amis bitch, treating everything as if it's hers. Doesn't even bother closing other people's doors. All the same, I do feel responsible.'

'There's no need.' He wanted her to share his feeling of relief. 'I've told you, it doesn't matter.'

'If it doesn't matter, why did you spend so long searching?'

'Just to make sure.' She was undermining his sense that everything was all right now. 'Honestly, I'm glad it's gone. I should never have brought it home in the first place.'

'But what about the people you were supposed to give it to?'

'I'll phone them in the morning. I don't think they'll care much either. They didn't seem to think it was particularly valuable.' If Hetherington made a fuss, too bad; he could go and look for it himself, and suffer the consequences. 'Look,' Alan said, suddenly inspired, 'I tell you what. All this has been a strain on you, and no wonder. I'll stay with Anna while you go to Gail's party.'

'Oh, it's too late. I'd never be ready in time.'

'Of course you will. It won't take you long to get ready. Go on.'

'I'd rather go with you.'

'I know, but we'd never get a sitter now. You go, it'll be just what you need.'

After a while she stood up and kissed him, then she went upstairs to change, though not without a doubtful backward glance. He leafed through the television schedules: nothing worth watching. Maybe he'd play a videocassette.

She was downstairs again surprisingly quickly, wearing a glittery stole over her backless ankle-length dress. 'I'm sure it would do me just as much good to stay with you,' she said. 'We could have our own party. I bet it would be sexier than Gail's.'

'Well, I'm pretty tired. I wouldn't be good company.' He felt impatient for her to leave – tiredness, no doubt, a desire to stop talking, to be alone to enjoy his sense of relief. 'Never mind,' he said, seeing her look of disappointment. 'There'll be other nights.'

He stood at the front door and watched as she drove away, her headlights picking out the curve of the hedges beside the road. Then, almost at once, the night had swallowed her up and he couldn't even distinguish the outline of the hedges from the rest of the dark. For a moment he wanted to call her back, but why should he want to do that? It was about time he spent some time alone with Anna. Now the sound of Liz's car had merged with the roar of the sea. He closed the door.

At the foot of the stairs he halted, listening. There was no sound from Anna; the breathing was the sound of waves. All at once he was glad that Liz had gone; he felt somehow freer, less constrained. Perhaps he'd felt that she no longer trusted him enough to leave him alone with Anna. Why ever not? It wasn't as if he had actually done anything to the child, or ever would. No point in speculating about Liz's feelings; he might grow angry with her if he thought about it for too long. He tiptoed upstairs.

Anna was lying on her right side, her right hand nestling beneath her red hair. As he eased the door open, the light from the hall touched her face and her sleeping eyes flickered, her left hand opened and closed on the quilt. He froze, afraid to wake her. He wished he hadn't come to look, for the sight of her was making him uneasy. No wonder: the memories of how he'd felt about her were uncomfortably vivid, even though the cause of his feelings had now been taken away.

Suddenly, he was aware of how hungry he felt – he was ravenous. He closed the bedroom door as quickly as he could without making a noise, and crept downstairs to the kitchen.

He found cold meats and some of Liz's home-made rolls in the fridge, but the meat tasted oddly unsatisfying, no doubt because he was tired; it had been an exhausting day. He finished chewing at last, then, when he'd washed the dishes, he went into the long room to pour himself a large Jack Daniels and find something to watch.

There was nothing that could hold him. Even when he played a cassette of a Hitchcock film he felt restless, more aware of the flickering of the image than of the film itself. It felt as if a storm were building up behind the film, with distant flickers of lightning. He couldn't read either. He found that he was suffering from a neurosis he'd experienced when he had begun writing books: if he tried to read someone else's fiction, he was so aware of the effort behind every sentence that there was no flow at all to his reading. Eventually he put the book aside and put on a record of a Brahms quartet. Perhaps that would calm his nerves, still jangling after the stress and strain of the last couple of weeks.

Soon he dozed. Traces of old dreams troubled him: Anna running, the claw reaching out to fasten on her, drag her back . . . Couldn't he have dreamed that because he'd already known about the Leopard Men? He'd known *something* of them before he met Hetherington, but now it seemed impossible to recall how much. He nodded, started awake with an unpleasant taste in his mouth. He didn't want to sleep just yet, because there was something that needed explaining. In his moment of dozing he'd forgotten it again. The Brahms was twining and unravelling its complicated melodies. He turned off the sound and stood by the hi-fi, trying to remember.

His head was empty, and felt hollow with the sound of the sea; never before had it seemed so loud. He paced up and down the long room, glancing now and then at the mantelpiece. Whatever the answer was, it wasn't there. Moonlit waves were frozen in Liz's painting on the wall, while the sea roared outside in the dark. He licked his lips – the unpleasant taste was still there – and tried to retrace his thoughts. Leopard Men, Hetherington, Leopard Men . . . cups of tea, the sound of clippers on a lawn . . . He felt as if he had no control over his thoughts. Hetherington, Hetherington . . .

And then he thought of Marlowe. At once he knew. Why had Marlowe killed himself when he'd already got rid of the claw?

Alan hardly noticed he was still pacing back and forth as if the room were a cage. Surely he needn't worry about Marlowe? No doubt Hetherington had been right – Marlowe must have been put under intolerable strain by his research into the Leopard cult . . . But Alan was remembering what Marlowe had said on the way to the airport: how he shouldn't have brought his daughter to Nigeria, how he had to get her away before it was too late. How much had Marlowe hinted that he hadn't dared admit openly? Had it already been too late?

All at once Alan was afraid for Anna. Surely he needn't feel that way – and yet he had to see her. He took a last gulp of Jack Daniels in an attempt to drown the lingering taste – could it just be the taste of sleep and stale drink? – then he headed for the stairs. He hadn't reached them when he felt an inexplicable compulsion *not* to go up – not until he'd called Liz home from the hotel. Christ, hadn't he the courage to go upstairs by himself? Besides, whatever would Liz think? She was already suspicious of him.

He crept upstairs. He felt pleased by how silent he could

be; after all, he didn't want to wake Anna, did he? Outside the window, the darkness was breathing long, slow, moist breaths. At the end of the back garden the hedge looked wet with dimness; beyond that, the darkness was solid as tar.

He tiptoed along the hall to Anna's room and inched the door open. Her face was still toward him, but her posture was contorted, as if she were trying to fight off an unpleasant dream. Without warning, and for no reason he could grasp, he found himself thinking: thank God, she was asleep – he *mustn't* wake her, *mustn't* let her see him. Why not, for God's sake? He backed out of the room, afraid as much of his own feelings as of waking her. Slowly he eased the door closed, so slowly that it seemed it would never meet the frame. It had inches to go when it gave a faint creak, and she woke.

Seventeen

It was broad daylight when Anna went to bed, and she felt as if she would never fall asleep. She lay and watched her bedroom curtains darkening as the sun moved on; she listened to cars on the coast road, whirring into the distance until they sounded smaller than ants. She was waiting to hear daddy's car.

Mummy must be waiting too, downstairs. She knew mummy was nervous, waiting to tell him that the metal claw had gone. That didn't worry Anna – she was glad it was gone, she hoped it never came back – but mummy's nervousness disturbed her. It wasn't like mummy to feel that way about daddy; they had always seemed sure of each other before, and that had made Anna feel sure of them too. The idea that that could change disturbed her more than anything else she could think of. Somehow, all at once, everything seemed to have gone wrong. A thief had got into their home, and she couldn't understand how he'd managed it when she'd been in her playroom across the hall; it made her feel *she* was to blame for not seeing. Mummy and Granny Knight had been arguing about her, too, and she felt as if that was her fault: she wouldn't have minded going to see Granny Knight, she was just a bit funny sometimes – old people were. She couldn't tell daddy or even mummy how she felt, and that made it worse. She was sure there were things they weren't telling her. They hadn't told her about Joseph.

He must have been the man she'd known was hiding near the house – the man who had killed the poor goat. Yesterday, when mummy had made her stay in her playroom, she was sure they'd found out something they didn't want her to know. As soon as mummy was out of the way, Anna had run upstairs to the toilet and then crept into her bedroom. That was how she'd seen the policeman dragging Joseph to the van. She'd felt sorry for Joseph, especially when his arms were twisted up behind his back, until she'd caught sight of his nails, his long, bloody nails. He must have killed another goat, for there were only two now.

She hadn't been meant to see Joseph. She'd dodged back from her window before daddy could see her and had hidden in her playroom, feeling sick. So Joseph had been the one – that must have been why he'd behaved so strangely toward her. At least the goats were safe now. But instead of being relieved, all she felt was guilt: she hadn't been supposed to see him – she'd seen something that she wasn't meant to see. She wondered if Joseph had seen *her*, if he would come back to punish her for watching . . .

Now she felt worse. He must have done all that to the poor goat with just his nails. Mummy had told her that the police had locked up the man who'd hurt the goats – Anna wished she could have told mummy that she knew who he was, but that would have meant admitting she'd been spying. And anyway, she was still frightened, even if he was locked up. The house didn't feel the same, didn't even smell the same; she had nothing to rely on. She lay in her room, which was growing larger and more vague as it grew dark, dreading the moment when daddy would find out the claw was gone. She was listening for his car, and mistaking the sound of the waves for a car in the distance, when she fell asleep.

She dreamed that Joseph had got into the house. Mummy and daddy were arguing downstairs, so loudly that they didn't hear her when she cried out to them. She ran to her window, but it wouldn't open. She thumped it with her fists and cried for help, but none of the crowd of people strolling by could hear – not even Granny Knight, who didn't seem to want to look at her. Everything was sunny out there, everyone wore bright clothes; only her room was very dark. When she heard Joseph on the stairs, she couldn't scream. She couldn't hear her parents now; perhaps they were no longer in the house. She ran back to the bed and hid under the blankets.

She tried to lie absolutely quiet and still as he came into the room. It was no use. The longer she held her breath, the louder her gasp would have to be; she knew that from playing hide and seek. He was padding toward the bed, reaching out with his long nails, and somehow she knew that when she saw him it would be even worse than she feared. Perhaps he'd brought the goat's head, perhaps he was wearing it on his. She was dreaming; she knew it was a dream, she must wake before he reached her, before he pulled the blankets off her and she saw. If she cried out she would wake, if she could just stop holding her breath, if she could just move a muscle. Her fear had her frozen, she was trapped. She felt him reach for her, his nails dragging at the blankets like a dog's claws, and she choked and cried out and woke.

She was lying on her side in a knot of blankets. She had been dreaming, she was awake now, the dream would go away. She forced herself to open her eyes to make it go more quickly. The room was very dark, as dark as it had been in her nightmare, but that wasn't why she screamed. A figure with nails so long that the light from the landing shone through them was standing in the doorway, watching her.

She cringed back until she felt the headboard pressing against her through her pillow. The floor just inside her room creaked as the figure came in. He was going to do to her what he'd done to the goats. Apart from the creak of the board she could hear no sound in the house – no sound of mummy or daddy. They had left her alone with Joseph. Her disbelief and horror almost choked her. '*Mummy!*' she screamed.

The figure halted. Oh, please let mummy be here after all! Please let her scream have scared him away! 'It's all right, Anna,' the figure said. 'Go back to sleep.'

It was daddy. He was holding up one hand, making a

gesture that was meant to calm her down, but it only showed his nails. How could she be calm when he didn't sound calm himself? 'I want mummy,' she said.

'She isn't here just now.'

'Where is she?'

'At the hotel. You go back to sleep now. I'm here.'

He sounded as if he didn't want to be. His voice was so harsh by now that it only made her more awake. 'I want her to come home,' she pleaded.

'She won't be long.' He stepped forward. 'Here, let me tuck you up, and then you must go to sleep.'

He'd moved so suddenly that she couldn't help flinching back, toward the far edge of the bed. Why was he so anxious for her to go to sleep? The sight of his nails made her distrust his words. She remembered the way he'd scratched her on the beach. She couldn't bear that now, here in the empty house, in the dark.

'What are you doing, Anna?' He was reaching for her with those nails. 'Don't do that, don't be stupid. You'll fall out of bed.'

Perhaps he only meant to catch her before she fell, perhaps that was why he made a grab for her, but his voice was savage now, and so was his face – what she could see of it in the dark. Before he could reach her, she struggled out of bed.

'What's wrong with you, child?' He came round the foot of the bed, and the light from the landing touched his face. For a moment she was terrified that it wouldn't be his. It was, but it looked so vicious that it didn't look like him after all. 'Get back into bed at once,' he said, as if he was still daddy.

As he moved toward her, trapping her between the bed and the wall, she climbed onto the bed. Her bare feet were tangled in the pillows; she was going to fall into his arms, into his claws. She clutched the headboard and kicked herself free, then she jumped off the bed and ran out of the room.

Where could she run? The house was empty; mummy

wouldn't hear if she cried for help; nobody would. She thought of hiding until mummy came home, but where? She had just reached the downstairs hall when she heard him above her. 'Want to play hide and seek, do you? You won't like it when you're caught, by God you won't.'

She couldn't hide. It was as though he'd heard what she was thinking. She thought of hiding in the dark and waiting to be caught by those nails. She ran to the front door. She wanted mummy, she had to go to her.

The shock of her first step on the cold hard path made her realize how far she would have to run barefoot, all the way to the hotel. She might have given up, except that she heard daddy on the stairs. 'Going to tell tales to your mother, are you?' he was muttering. 'No you don't, you little fucker.' She ran down the path, biting her lip to stop herself from crying out as the stone hurt her feet, and out of the gate.

There was only one way she could run barefoot: along the beach. She could just see the cliff-top by the afterglow which hung like mist above the fields. She fled across the grass, veering away from where the poor goats had been killed. She couldn't see the remaining goats, but there was an animal smell in the air.

When she reached the path, she wavered. Did she really have to run all the way along the beach in the dark? It was so unfair. Waves made the beach seem to be expanding and contracting dimly; she could see nothing else. She glanced over her shoulder at the house, wishing desperately that she could go back. A dark shape was searching near the house, hands stretched out for her. She dodged out of sight at once, down the path.

At least the sandy path was kinder to her feet, though she had to go slowly for fear of skidding over the edge. Once the glimmer of the pillbox was out of sight she had a better view of the beach. It was dark, bleak, deserted. Only the waves shifted, hissing. Along the cliff, so distant that she couldn't imagine running all that way, were the lights and music of the Britannia Hotel.

She stumbled across the pebbles, bruising her feet, and slithered down the sea wall on her bottom. Another strip of pebbles, and then she was on soft sand, cool and soothing. She ran. At first it had been the pain in her feet that had made her cry, but now fear took over. What had *happened* to daddy to make him like this? She was sure that he wanted to harm her – that he hated her.

She turned, hearing his footsteps on the path down the cliff. Though she couldn't see him for tears, she could hear him. 'Running to mummy, are we?' he shouted. 'You don't stand a chance. You come back here right now or it'll be all the worse for you.' His voice no longer sounded like his. She fled in terror along the beach.

She heard him clattering over the pebbles and jumping down the sea wall. Pebbles ground together, a vicious sound that lodged in her head. He came thudding over the soft sand after her, cursing and snarling as his feet sank into it, becoming more savage with each step. The lights of the hotel seemed to have floated away. 'Mummy!' she screamed, and ran panting toward the receding lights.

At least he wasn't gaining on her, even when she passed beneath the graveyard. A shower of soil came raining down, and she dodged widely aside to avoid it. Now the sand underfoot was moist and chill, and she felt as if it were grabbing at her. A patch of polluted foam lay stranded yards from the edge of the sea, quivering like tripe. She flinched aside from it, and glanced back to see how far behind he was.

Then she screamed. He'd sneaked up, unheard, over the sea wall and now came clattering over the stones up there, faster than she could ever run on the sand or anywhere else. She screamed again for mummy, she turned to flee over the yielding juicy sand. She had taken only a few steps when he fell.

She faltered and looked back. His fall on the stones had been a heavy one, and she couldn't help hoping he might not get up – at least not until she'd reached the hotel. But already he was rearing up and brandishing the object that had tripped him. For a moment, as he raised it above his head and came for her, she thought he'd found the claw. But, no, it was a piece of wood. And as she turned, screaming, to flee, she saw that protruding from one end of it was a long, sharp nail.

Eighteen

Before long, the party overflowed out of the hotel bar and into the foyer. Red wine tinted the goldfish pond, cigarette stubs were gathering at the roots of the potted plants; now and then the roar of conversation and laughter made the cut-glass chandeliers jingle. Most of the hotel guests had been drawn into the party now that their children were in bed, and then there were Gail's and Ned's friends from here to Norwich – big-buttocked girls who ran a riding school, middle-aged ladies Liz had seen sitting at their easels on the cliffs, a fiery old woman called Mrs Tremayne, who had made an elaborate flower arrangement specially and was now shaking her stick at Gail: 'Don't you be saying I shouldn't have made you a present, Gail Marshall.' A pair of Labradors were chasing through the ground floor into the bar, where the chef was arm-wrestling all comers; from there into the lounge where Jimmy the barman was singing folk songs to a guitar – and finally round and round the goldfish pond, almost knocking Rebecca from her perch on the stone rim, where she sat looking pensive. No doubt she was thinking about Jane. Liz felt almost guilty for enjoying herself so much.

There was no doubt about it, she appreciated having an evening away from Anna. Of course, she and Alan could hire sitters – sulky teenage girls who seemed to regard the job as one more dull village activity – but a night like this was special. It was like not being married at all, except that at the end of it she'd be able to go home to everything she and Alan had built together. She felt ten years younger, especially now that she'd had a few drinks. To think she'd been doubtful about leaving Alan at home!

She wandered through the crowd, looking for someone

she knew well enough to flirt with. At least Alex wasn't here, though in view of the fact that Jane hadn't come Liz wouldn't have been surprised to see her escorted by Derek. Of course the theft from Jane's bag was really the last straw. She *must* have the Walterses round to dinner; surely there was a way to force Derek to face the situation before it was too late? In the lounge Jimmy was singing *We Shall Overcome* so passionately that she thought he must be quite drunk. Sidestepping the Labradors, she went into the bar.

Ned was coaxing corks out of several dusty liqueur bottles that had been here longer than the Marshalls. 'Here you are, Liz,' he shouted through the crowd. 'You don't want to miss this.' She struggled across the room, which was hot and smoky even though the windows were open, and he thrust a glass of something into her hand. She was about to take a sip when she heard a child crying; the switchboard was connected to microphones in all the rooms. 'It's Tessa,' Gail announced, and the little girl's mother hurried upstairs. Liz couldn't help smiling to herself: for once, she didn't have to listen for Anna – not tonight. She turned and chatted to Ned and some of his friends; then, when she began to feel dizzy with heat and smoke, she wormed her way out to the foyer and went to see what Jimmy was doing.

The ferocity of his last song seemed to have lost him his audience, for he was sitting alone in the lounge, among the disintegrating magazines and the cupboards full of board games, with the guitar between his knees and his chin resting above the pegs. His long face and full lips were drooping.

'I hate to think what you're going to sing now,' Liz said, in an attempt to cheer him up.

He tried to smile. 'I don't feel much like singing at all.'

Liz sat beside him on the musty settee. 'Anything I can do to help?'

'No, and I can't do anything either.' He was running his thumbnail up and down the lowest string, making a sound like a discordant saw. 'It's my girlfriend Heather. She's in trouble with the law.'

'Nothing serious, I hope.'

'Depends what you call serious.' He slapped his hand over the soundhole, suffocating the echoes of the string. 'Half a gram of cannabis,' he said, with sudden fury. 'Just about enough to make one joint. Would you say that was serious?'

'No, not really.'

'Tell that to the law. You'd think she'd assaulted a child or something. If she lived in a big city, the police probably wouldn't even care; but she's living in a small town, so she'll have to go in front of small-town magistrates.' He was sawing at the string again, so savagely that his nail was cracking. 'And that's only the start of it. She's training to be a teacher – that's how we met. Christ knows what this'll do to her career.'

Liz was sympathetic, but growing ill at ease; another child was crying out for her mother, and it sounded uncomfortably like Anna. 'She'll still be able to get a job somewhere, though, won't she?'

'What, with a police record? You reckon that's a good qualification for teaching, do you?' He looked ashamed of losing his temper with her. 'Sorry – some of the people who were in here before got on my nerves. There was one girl so pissed she could hardly stand up who was telling me all about the evils of drugs. Anyone who uses drugs should be flogged in public, and all that frigging nonsense.' He grinned mirthlessly. 'Well, no use letting people like that get through to you. That won't help Heather.'

Liz squeezed his hand. 'I'm sure it won't turn out as badly as you think. Whatever happens, she's lucky to have you to look after her.' But Jimmy didn't seem comforted. She would have stayed with him – it dismayed her to see him so downcast, and she was sure that she could raise his spirits – but the faint cries of *Mummy* were nagging at her. She knew she ought not to interfere: it *couldn't* be

Anna, however much it sounded like her. But at the same time she wanted to go and find out what was wrong.

Jimmy's long fingers were limp in her hand. Perhaps he was only suffering her touch and really wanted to be left alone. 'Let me know what happens, anyway,' Liz said, 'and you know you can count on me if there's anything I can do to help.' She was already heading for the foyer. Really, *someone* had to see to that child.

But when she reached the foyer, she could no longer hear the cries. Someone must have gone to her at last. Liz wandered around the foyer and almost fell over the romping Labradors. She couldn't see anyone she knew. She was relieved to see Mr Mullen, Joseph's father, hadn't come to the party; she wouldn't have known what to say to him. She paused by the switchboard – still no sound – then she went to see what Ned was uncorking.

She had just entered the bar when everyone suddenly went quiet. For a moment she thought it was something she had done. Conversations failed one after another, layers of sound peeled away to reveal the silence. But nobody was looking at her; they were all staring at the open windows. Was it going to be another anniversary surprise? Then Liz heard the cries again, louder and more desperate – not from the switchboard at all, but out there in the dark.

'*Anna!*' she cried, so loudly that the crowd fell back to let her reach the window. Before she reached it she was running.

Almost at once she was beyond the light of the hotel, and the bright mats of grass, rectangular and spiky, were giving way to velvety darkness. Only the roaring of the sea stopped her short of the edge of the cliff. Underfoot the grass was slippery. She went forward cautiously, furious with herself for taking so much time.

When she reached the edge, she saw Anna. The beach was a long sinuous glimmer, foam flecking the border of sea and sand, but the palest shape was a small lonely figure at the foot of the cliff. 'Anna!' Liz cried, suddenly afraid that the tiny figure wouldn't move. But Anna cried out and began to run desperately back and forth as Liz ranged along the cliff top, looking for the nearest path down.

Finding it, she ran down the steep dim narrow slope, clutching at handfuls of grass, her heart lurching as sand slithered from under her feet. Anna was scrambling toward her, and they met halfway. The child hurled herself on Liz as if she was drowning and clung to her, shaking and sobbing. Though Liz couldn't see her in any detail, she seemed physically unharmed. That was one less fear – but what had happened to Alan? 'All right, mummy's here,' she murmured, over and over. 'It's all right now. What's wrong?'

She was hugging Anna fiercely, waiting for her to speak, when she heard something fall on the beach. She peered down, screwing up her eyes. At last she made out, amidst the stones like the scales of a snake as long as the beach, a face turned up to her. For a moment she was ready to defend Anna in any way she could, and then she thought she recognized the man on the beach. 'Is that you, Alan?' she called, hardly believing.

He didn't answer, but she could see now that it was. It was Alan, even though Anna shrank against her as he came slowly up the path. 'It's all right, Anna,' she murmured. 'It's daddy.' Whatever had happened couldn't have been so bad after all. Her heart could slow down now, stop pounding.

He came and stood close to them in the dark. The wind ruffled her clothes, striking chill on her exposed shoulders. Was that why Anna was trembling? But as he reached out to touch one or both of them, Anna flinched away. At once Liz knew that whatever was wrong, she didn't want to discuss it in front of the people at the hotel, nor here on this narrow precarious path. 'Come on, both of you,' she said, her voice harsh with apprehension. 'Let's get you home.'

On the way to her car, she avoided the party by going round the nursery side of the hotel, where the swings in the playground squealed faintly in the dark. Anna refused to stay with Alan in the car while Liz said her good-byes, so Liz left him staring blankly into the driving mirror and hurried into the hotel, with Anna clinging to her hand. She was beginning to dread finding out what had happened. There was a look in Alan's eyes that she had never seen before.

Gail was in the foyer. 'Oh, you mustn't go yet, Liz. Ned's just going to open the oldest bottle. It's been such a good party that we thought we would, while all our best friends are here. You'll have to stay for that. I'll never forgive you if you go now.' The sight of Anna seemed to throw her for a moment, but she was clearly so drunk that nothing surprised her very much. 'Anna can go and listen to Jimmy. You'd like that, wouldn't you, chick?'

'I'm sorry, Gail, we absolutely have to go. I'll tell you why next time,' Liz said, privately wondering if she'd be able to.

When Anna saw that her father was in the car, she wouldn't get in. Eventually he climbed out dully, like a sleepwalker, apparently unable to look at them. 'Quickly, Anna, in the back,' Liz said. Someone had to behave as if nothing was amiss. The questions would have to wait until they were home.

As Liz drove, the road wound back and forth, lit hedges springing up in front of her like spooks in a ghost train, Alan's glimmering face riding the dark. The journey had never seemed so long. As soon as they arrived, she rushed Anna upstairs to bed, then had to sit with her, stroking her hair, for almost an hour before the child fell asleep. In all that time Anna said only, 'Don't go away, mummy. Don't leave me again.' At least she could speak; but her plea only made Liz more anxious to question Alan. Anna's eyes drooped shut at last, and remained shut when Liz stood up. She tiptoed to the door and glanced back at the small vulnerable tear-streaked face. How dare anyone try to harm Anna? She strode downstairs, feeling angry, miserable, afraid, determined.

Alan was in the long room, staring at his distorted

reflection in the dead television screen. As soon as she came in, he stood up and faced her. His expression was unreadable – deliberately so, she thought. Before she could speak, he said, 'Look, Liz, this is very important. I want you to be honest with me. Have you been feeling hostile toward Anna lately?'

She couldn't believe it. After all that had happened – whatever it was – he was accusing *her*. 'What are you trying to say?' she demanded.

'Don't ask me to explain just yet. Look, this is vital, you've got to tell me.' His eyes looked raw with frustration now. 'Have you felt as if you wanted to hurt her? Tell me, for Christ's sake. I won't blame you.'

'Just what has your mother been saying about me?'

'Oh *Christ*, don't start that now. Keep to the point.' His attempt to be calm had failed; his fingers were at his temples, as if he wanted to claw them open. 'Are you saying you haven't had any such feelings? None at all?'

'That's right,' she said, her voice sweet with fury.

'Will you swear?'

'I'll tell you, Alan, if I start swearing, I won't stop.'

'Well, I can understand how you feel. I don't blame you.'

That was the second time in a couple of minutes that he'd undertaken not to blame her, as if she ought to be grateful. Was he having a breakdown? Certainly she felt as if she no longer knew him. He looked as if he was willing her to ask him something so that he could explain, and perhaps she might have, except that just then Anna came downstairs. 'I want to sleep with you, mummy,' she pleaded. 'I can't sleep.'

It wasn't the plea that made Liz afraid, it was the way Alan looked: pitifully relieved. 'Yes, you two have the bed,' he said. 'I'll stay down here.' As Liz took the child upstairs, Anna clinging to her so hard it was clear that she wouldn't let her mother leave her alone again, she heard him say, 'I don't expect I'll sleep.'

Nineteen

It was almost dawn before he slept. He paced the long room for hours, shuddering from head to foot whenever he remembered what he'd almost done or thought of himself at all. If he couldn't be trusted with Anna he had no right to stay here, he kept thinking. More than once he found himself heading for the front door, but where could he go? Perhaps down to the beach and into the waves until they were too strong for him, until he couldn't come back. Sometimes his shuddering turned into a groan of disgust with himself, but with a consideration that seemed grotesque under the circumstances, he tried not to make any noise in case it woke Anna or Liz. He hardly knew what he was doing. When at last he huddled on the couch, it was to hide from himself.

The phone woke him. He knew he ought to answer it before the ringing of the extensions on each floor woke Liz and Anna, but he was listening to the sea, slow and distant as his breathing heard at the edge of sleep. Then he remembered why he was on the couch, knew why he didn't want to wake.

He struggled to his feet in the early morning light. He felt cold and outcast and contemptible, unrecognizable to himself. As he grabbed the phone he remembered grabbing the piece of driftwood, remembered feeling that the moment when the nail in the wood bit into flesh would be as satisfying as the drag of a fishhook buried in a prize catch. He was close to fleeing, running in the hope he could lose himself. Instead he ground the receiver into his ear as if the pain could suffice.

The voice, when it came, was distorted by jagged static

and its closeness to the mouthpiece at the other end. 'May I speak to Mr Alan Knight?'

The man's politeness seemed exaggerated, made Alan think of the police. If they had found him out, that might be the best thing for everyone. 'Knight speaking,' he said, and felt as if he were giving himself up.

'My name is Banjo.'

That sounded like a bad joke, not merely pointless but unbearably tasteless, and Alan was about to drop the receiver into its cradle when the other said, 'Dr Hetherington told me where to reach you.'

The name made Alan grind his teeth, as much to hurt himself as anything. 'You're a friend of his, are you?'

'A friend of a colleague of his.' The other hesitated. 'He called me to find out if I knew you. You seem to have shaken him up.'

There was no satisfaction in that, not now: no reason to go on talking, no point to the call. 'Well, what do you want?' Alan demanded.

Again the hesitation, and now the static and the way the man was speaking into the mouthpiece told him it was a long distance call. It sounded, he thought miserably, like Nigeria. 'Dr Hetherington told me that the talisman you took back to England was stolen from you,' the other said.

'So?'

A longer pause. 'Have you any children?'

Was he accusing Anna of stealing the claw? For a moment Alan felt protective of her, until he remembered how inappropriate that was. 'I have one daughter,' he said, appalled how guilty and hopeless saying that made him feel.

'Is she safe?'

'What do you mean?'

The voice repeated it, slowly and clearly. 'Is she safe?'

All at once Alan understood that they both knew what that meant. 'No,' he said in a voice he hardly recognized as his.

'And you've been having dreams you can't explain.'

Alan thought of the dream of hunting Anna, the fleshless man with the spidery eyes, the resolution that had been too terrible to remember when he awoke. 'How do you know all this?' he said when he could.

'Because I think I am responsible for what is happening to you.'

Alan's fist clenched until the receiver groaned. 'Where are you?'

'Lagos.'

'Called up to gloat, have you?' Alan managed not to shout, for fear of waking Liz and Anna. It wasn't consideration, he realized now: he was simply afraid to face them.

'No, Mr Knight. I want to help you. I did my best to help David Marlowe, but I was too late.'

'You helped him, did you!' Alan swallowed his bitter laughter before it carried upstairs. 'My God, you certainly have some results to show for it, don't you! And now you want to do the same to me!'

'Mr Knight, Marlowe was my good friend. I worked with him and knew him well. I saw what was happening to him and told him to get rid of the cause however he could. That is why he gave the talisman to you.'

'Getting rid of it didn't help him much, did it?' Alan hissed.

'No, not at all. I told you, I was too late.' The voice was subdued now. 'For you there is still time. Now I know better what has to be done.'

'Why should you want to help me? I don't even know who you are.'

'Isaac Banjo, translator at the University of Lagos.' He caught his breath audibly. 'I want to help because of what I have already done. I have daughters of my own.'

'How can you help me?'

'First you must come here. I give you my word that it is necessary. These are not issues that can be discussed at a distance, particularly on a line like this.'

Good God, he was talking telecommunications now! 'You're really asking me to come all the way to Nigeria?'

'Yes, on the first available flight. What else can you do?'

Dismayingly, that made sense. 'Just to talk?'

'To do what you must to regain yourself. That can only be done here.'

Alan had to believe him; he was the only person in the world who seemed to be offering hope. At least Anna couldn't be in danger from her father at that distance and besides, he wanted to come face to face with the man responsible for what had happened to him. 'All right,' he said.

He copied down the numbers where the translator could be reached, he told him he would let him know when he would be arriving at Ikeja, and felt he was doing all this in a dream. Before the end he had to shout over a crossed line. When he put down the receiver, wondering if he had any right to hope, he realized Liz and Anna were awake.

He went up at once, to get it over with. He stood outside the bedroom door and was tempted to listen to their murmured conversation, to hear what they were saying about him. That made him so frightened of himself that he knocked hastily and went in.

Anna was in the double bed. She looked small and vulnerable. Liz was standing beside her, and turned to stare at him, her eyes utterly unwelcoming. 'Look, I have to go away,' he said.

'Yes, I think you better had.'

She managed to make him sound both outcast and unreasonable to be leaving. He couldn't argue, he could tell her anything except that he was going back to Nigeria. He closed the door with a gentleness that made him want to weep. It wasn't Liz's attitude that sent him to the phone to find out how soon he could leave for Nigeria, it was the way Anna had hidden behind her mother as soon as he'd entered the room.

Twenty

Isaac Banjo was a tall Yoruba in a spotless white linen suit. His eyes were warm and sympathetic, his handshake felt like a promise of friendship and help, and Alan had to be content with that while Isaac deflected the touts who were clamouring to carry Alan's bags or find him a taxi and led him out of the airport, through the uproar of passengers squabbling with bored airline clerks and with one another. Alan was glad to be organized so efficiently, not least because it put off the time when he would have to talk.

Isaac stowed the bags in the boot of his dusty car and gave Alan an encouraging look, and then there was no talking once he manoeuvred onto the road to Lagos. Misshapen buses bounced over the potholes, battered taxis dodged through the traffic, their wing mirrors turned end up to give their drivers more room to scrape by, and that was all there was until Lagos closed in. Then they were hours in the go-slow, the city's daily eighteen-hour traffic jam. Today was an even day of the week, when only cars with even-numbered plates were allowed onto the island, yet the go-slow seemed even more sluggish. Hawkers came to the windows of the car with Swiss watches and Japanese radios, customs road blocks further on held up the traffic. By the time the car crossed the bridge to Ikeja, it was growing dark.

Isaac's house had a view of the lagoon between the larger houses. He drove his dilapidated odd-numbered car out of the garage so that it would be available tomorrow. Still they couldn't talk, for Isaac's plump motherly wife had made them a stew and insisted they get it inside them at once, his two bright-eyed daughters wanted to show Alan their schoolwork afterward and pleaded with him to read them a story in bed. He did, though he felt close to weeping. That Isaac trusted him with his daughters seemed to give him back too much of himself too soon, too painfully.

When at last they were alone in Isaac's study, which contained books in so many languages Alan gave up counting, he asked the question which had been building up inside him ever since they'd met. 'Just why do you feel so responsible for me?'

'Because of what happened to Marlowe.' Isaac handed him an imported whisky and poured one for himself. 'I saw what the talisman did to him. He wasn't always as you saw him, as he became. I don't know of a father who was more loving. I think there's no doubt that he killed himself in order to save his daughter from him.'

'After he'd taken me for a fool and given me the claw.'

'For a long time he believed he couldn't get rid of it. He must have been so drunk at the party that he gave it to you on impulse.'

'It didn't look much like a sudden decision to me.'

Isaac gazed sadly at him. 'You're right,' he said, forsaking the Yoruba deviousness. 'He must have been looking for an opportunity. I'd told him that if the talisman was preying so much on his mind, he ought to get rid of it however he could. You see why I must help you.'

Alan couldn't hate him. He almost wished he could, so as to have a tangible enemy. 'Did he know you had a daughter?' Isaac said. 'I can't believe he would have given it to you if he had thought so.'

Alan remembered Marlowe's complaint that he had to bring his family with him to Nigeria – remembered saying that he hadn't got that problem. At last he saw what all that had meant. 'No, I don't think he did,' he admitted, touched that Isaac was anxious only to defend his dead friend, not Isaac himself.

'Then I am more to blame. If you shit in the road,' he said, quoting a Yoruba proverb, 'you'll find flies when you come back.' He stood up abruptly. 'I managed to persuade the police to let me copy what's left of his notes. They may help you understand.'

That seemed unlikely, since they consisted of a few grey photocopied pages of charred fragments from notebooks. 'He burned everything else,' Isaac said, 'but I can tell you more.'

Alan wasn't sure if he wanted to know more once he had read the first fragment. '1946 police reports: victims waylaid in evening on path back from market or farm. Spikes driven into neck. Heart and lungs always taken. All flesh removed from severed heads to prevent identification, yet Leopard Men often killed before witnesses – seemed to think themselves magically invulnerable . . .' These must be later notes, the handwriting had degenerated so much. Had Marlowe been trying to regain control of himself by listing facts? They didn't seem the kind of thing that would have helped his mind.

The handwriting on the next sheet was more precise, though the notes read like speculation. ' . . . cannibalism as a source of magical power: Gilles de Rais was said to have eaten children. Sierra Leone *Weekly News* 4th April 1891 notes similarities of Jack the Ripper mutilations to those of Leopard Men. Was Ripper a magician who ceased his activities when he'd achieved his aim?'

Alan was seeking an answer, not more questions, and certainly not this description of the ritual of one group of Leopard Men: 'Girl was sent along crooked footpath. High bush either side, creepers covered any opening. Leopard Men lay in wait. Sometimes made animal sounds before they sprang.' He imagined the claw biting into flesh, and almost tore the page in turning it. 'Eisler in Hibbert Journal takes Leopard Men to be survival of primitive practice of hunting in packs. Men learned from beasts of prey, ran down prey and surrounded it, devoured it alive. Animal sounds meant to recall this? Sound of snuffling???'

Alan couldn't understand the three question marks – bad style, that was all – and the notes were growing less coherent, less objective, and even less meaningful to him.

'Witchcraft a stage through which all races pass. Attempt to regain lost powers of primitive? Every race capable of reaching back to THE SAME primitive powers. We all came from Africa . . .' THE SAME was underlined three times, so emphatically that the pen had torn the paper. He felt bewildered and irritable, he was beginning to wonder what he was doing here at all. 'Sound of snuffling,' he said jeeringly, despairingly.

'Yes, I can explain that.' Isaac's voice was gentle. 'You should know the legends of the Leopard Men.'

'Quite a few, are there?' Alan snapped, and felt ashamed. 'I'm sorry. You must think me very ungrateful. I do appreciate your letting me come here, looking after me like this. It's just that all that's happened . . .'

His voice was trembling, he couldn't go on. Isaac grasped his hand while he closed his eyes and took deep shuddering breaths. Eventually Alan was able to say 'Tell me what you were going to tell me.'

'There are two legends you should know.' He seemed to be debating with himself which to tell first. Eventually he said 'The origin of the Leopard cult is itself a legend.'

The tone of his voice made it clear that legend was a kind of truth. 'Marlowe believed they were trying to reach back to powers they felt man had lost when he ceased to hunt in packs.'

Alan found himself staring at the last fragment: 'Every race capable of reaching back . . .' He wasn't sure that he wanted to know. 'Reach back how?' he said.

'The oldest version David traced was that a Ju-Ju man had the first claw made by an artisan whom he then killed. It isn't clear if that was to prevent the secrets of the making from being revealed or to blood the claw. In any case, it seems that the powers he invoked were too strong for him. There's a suggestion in the legend that he encouraged the cult to be formed in the hope that it would dissipate the hold the claw had over him. Presumably it didn't, because he ran with the Leopard Men even when he was too old to hunt. He had to be fed every time they made their kill.

The legend says he cannot die. He is doomed to wait to be fed every time the talisman makes a kill.'

'Which talisman?'

'The one Marlowe gave you.'

Night pressed against the windows, black and moist as the earth Alan could smell. It felt almost like being buried alive, though he could hear some animal snarling in the distance. 'You're saying that was the original?'

'So he believed.'

'But how could a piece of metal do all this?'

'Do you believe things have souls? We believe everything has. The talisman has an evil soul.' As Alan looked skeptical, Isaac went on, 'David came to believe that the originator of the talisman would try to influence whoever held it to use it. The legend says that he would appear in the form of a naked man covered with the blood of all his feasts.'

Alan felt as if he was on the edge of a precipice of belief where nothing was familiar, yet everything was. 'What can I do?' he cried.

'That is the other legend. It must be as true for you as David thought it would be for him.'

His voice was grave. 'Tell me the worst,' Alan said.

'Simply this. There is a legend told throughout Africa that the last Leopard Man will come from a far land and destroy the power of the claw.'

Alan couldn't quite shrug that off, as all his Englishness demanded he should; it was as though he had already known. 'That's all?'

'Not at all. David traced variations as far as Kenya. They must have been among the papers he destroyed, but he told me most of them, I think. All the legends say that he will confront the giver of the claw and take his power to destroy it for ever. Once they come face to face in the jungle the legend will tell itself.'

Alan thought of his dream of the jungle, of the scrawny feral figure that rose to meet him. 'My God,' he said, shuddering less with terror than with realization, and then he thought he perceived a flaw. 'Why wasn't it Marlowe? Why didn't it work for him?'

'Because he was no longer capable of doing what had to be done by the time he found out what it was.' Isaac gave him a long sympathetic look. 'You have one great advantage. You've put an ocean between yourself and your child.'

So that was why he'd insisted that Alan come to Nigeria to learn what he must do. If this was reassurance it was appalling, and yet it made Alan so furious with himself he could hardly sit still. 'What am I supposed to do?' he demanded.

'Most versions say that the giver of the claw must die in order for the power to be consumed. David was convinced that meant the giver must be killed.' He sat forward and looked ready to clasp Alan's hands. 'Whatever happens, I shall be with you. You won't have to do this by yourself.'

Alan blurted out his question in order to deal with his flood of emotion: gratitude, fury with himself, anticipatory fear. 'Why are you doing all this for me?'

'Because of what I wished upon you.' He held up one pink palm as Alan made to speak. 'No matter that I didn't realize I was doing so. I want to help destroy what destroyed my friend David Marlowe.'

Alan reached out impulsively and grasped Isaac's hands. 'We will. By God, we will.'

'Now we must try to retrace David's steps,' Isaac said, 'to the man who gave him the claw.'

Twenty-one

They seemed to have been trudging through the shanty town for hours, peering out from beneath their umbrellas as they picked their way through the narrow makeshift random lanes, when Isaac halted suddenly. Rain shrilled on the corrugated tin roofs and awnings, water rushed down the open sewer channel which cut through the mud of the lane, and he had to shout to be heard. 'You ought to know this,' he said, and took Alan's hand. 'It may help.'

For a moment Alan thought he was going to give him a charm. But Isaac was shaking his hand, running a second finger across Alan's palm as he did so, and rolling his eyes. Here they were, standing in the maze of rickety shacks and propped-up shelters of tin and cloth, ankle-deep in the sucking mud and shaking hands like freemasons, blocking the way of three women with sodden cartons balanced on their heads. Beyond the shacks, palm trees nodded in the rain. Alan wondered if both he and Isaac were mad. But Isaac leaned his head close to Alan's beneath the umbrellas while the women grumbled past. 'That is the secret sign of the Leopard Men,' he said.

One handshake and the Leopard Men would take him for one of them, Alan thought sardonically – at least, if he hadn't died of pneumonia by then. Warm mud squeezed between his toes as he stumbled after Isaac, shoes in one hand, umbrella in the other. Each leaning shelter seemed more ramshackle than the last. An overpowering smell of marijuana drifted through the rain. He didn't blame them for smoking, whoever they were. How on earth could people live like this? They had crowded onto Lagos Island from the farms, lured by the big city, only to be cleared onto the mainland. It was their choice to live here, and

God knows, he had worries enough of his own – but then he saw the child. She was gazing out of a shelter through a gap in the hanging canvas that served as a front door, which was so sodden that it was impossible to see what colour it had originally been. She was brushing away flies automatically, as a horse flicks its tail, and gazing at him with great brown eyes. She couldn't have been more than eight years old. All at once he felt his eyes moisten and he was unable to move.

'Nearly there,' Isaac said, then he saw where Alan was looking. 'Don't worry,' he said. 'We'll have you back with your family if it's within my power.'

Isaac obviously assumed that he was just homesick and yearning for his own child. Nevertheless, as they squelched onward, Alan heard the child coughing, dryly and painfully, and his own muddy discomfort suddenly seemed shamefully trivial, especially now that Isaac seemed to feel the need to state a limit on how much he could help.

Just then Isaac stepped delicately aside into yet another lane of mud, and halted almost at once. 'Ah, I thought I'd come the right way,' he said. 'Here we are.'

At least the building in front of which he'd halted had four walls and a front door, though the door had obviously been made for a larger frame. The window-panes were cellophane, billowing in the downpour. 'Perhaps it will be best if you wait while I speak to them,' Isaac said, and stepped onto the plank which served as a bridge across the overflowing channel.

Before Isaac pounded on the front door, Alan saw a black smudge peer out through cellophane. Isaac knocked several times and eventually the door was opened by a large woman in a dress and matching head-dress, bright as parrots. Alan could see that she recognized Isaac from when Marlowe had brought him along to translate. Was that why she stood in his way and wouldn't let him inside?

Finally, after a prolonged discussion, a man appeared in the doorway and gestured Isaac within. Alan watched the door being heaved back into place, and then he waited in the rain, with the water and waste streaming past his feet. He stared dully into the channel, watching the edges crumble.

Suddenly the door of the house laboured open, and Isaac stood there. 'All right,' he said, with a grimace that meant it had been a struggle. Alan strode across the plank, which bowed in the middle until it was touching the miniature flood, its ends sinking in the mud and threatening to make him slip – and into the house. One step inside, and he halted, dismayed.

There was only one room, and it was full of children and basins and crippled furniture. He had to peer, because the room was dim with steaming clothes, spread over ropes strung between the walls. Basins were everywhere, catching drips from the roof, ringing like beggars' cups – one dud coin after another. The few chairs looked as if they had been rescued from a dump and repaired with bent nails. At the foot of the large lumpy bed stood several wooden boxes containing scraps of blankets. For pets, Alan thought – but how could there be room for animals? With a shock he realized that the boxes served as beds for some of the children. All the children, five of them, were staring at him.

He couldn't meet their eyes. He felt accused, as though it was Anna who was staring. So he'd thought he could write about Nigeria on the basis of a tourist's visit, had he? He felt utterly fake. If he ever returned home, he would tear his Nigerian plot to bits. But the children's father blocked his view and stretched out his upturned hand.

Alan pulled out a wad of brown ten-naira notes. Ten, twenty, thirty, fifty – divide by two and you had pounds. Thirty pounds, forty, and the hand was still outstretched. By the time it closed on the notes, Alan felt he had paid a good deal, but wasn't Anna's safety worth infinitely more? The man was stuffing the notes into a Coca-Cola bottle, which already looked almost full. Perhaps in time he'd be able to buy his family's way out of all this. Alan hoped so.

He screwed the cap into the bottle and dragged the bed

aside, then he lifted a floorboard and hid the bottle in the mud beneath the floor. Still frowning, he beckoned Alan and Isaac to follow him out of the house. One of the children scampered after them, but he gestured her back, shouting, 'I told you to stay away from him.'

He led them around the house to the back, walking with exaggerated dignity, ignoring the mud and the downpour, even though his outsize multicoloured shirt immediately grew darker with rain. Behind the house was a hut like a large privy, fashioned out of corrugated metal. There were a few footprints in the mud outside the door, but not many. The man wrenched back the bolt, and Alan saw the old man who was shut in there, lying on a camp bed.

He oughtn't to be shocked. If it weren't for the Nigerian respect for the family, the old man would probably be dead. The frowning man could hardly be blamed for locking his father away from the grandchildren, under the circumstances – and anyway he was housing him as close to the family as he possibly could. At least the hut looked watertight, and the old man had a flashlight by the bed and a couple of basins for washing and relieving himself. Alan forced himself to step into the hut, to see exactly what a Leopard Man looked like.

He looked very much like a withered old black man who was waiting to die. He couldn't have been active for years. He was stirring, gripping both sides of the mattress with his skinny hands and sitting himself up in a series of jerks, tiny timid movements that showed how fragile he felt. His face and bald head were covered with wrinkles, like fingertips that had been soaking for hours. Isaac stepped forward to question him.

The son followed, and there no longer seemed to be room in the hut for light. The old man groped for the flashlight and switched it on, but its glow was so feeble that it merely outlined a few glimpses: the old man's broken yellow nails, his fleshless arm, his glistening toothless gums, his dimming eyes. If he meant to direct the glow at his visitors, he was too weak; the flashlight rolled out of his hand, onto the blanket. Alan wished he had let Isaac come here by himself: their only purpose in coming was to find out the name the old man had given Marlowe, which Isaac had forgotten. But he mustn't allow himself to feel qualms at this early stage, for there would be worse than the old man to be faced. All the same, nothing could have induced Alan to give the handshake to the old man; nothing could have made him touch him.

Isaac was speaking. The old man's son stood close to him, a warder at visiting time. The old eyes glimmered at Isaac, the dry lips gaped and closed and gaped. Alan could hear flies buzzing in the hut; they were either large or numerous, or both. He felt lost and helpless; he couldn't understand a word Isaac was saying.

He mustn't feel like that. Isaac was helping him, he could trust Isaac; Isaac knew what he was doing. All the same, standing there uselessly gave Alan far too much time to think, to realize how far he was from Liz and Anna, how long it had been since he'd spoken to them, let alone seen them. His eyes were growing used to the dimness; he could see the flies, or some of them. They were crawling on the old man, whose son made no move to brush them off.

Isaac was asking a question; that much was clear from the tone of his voice. That must mean he was nearly finished – there was only one question he needed to ask. But the old man gazed emptily at him and pressed his lips together. Perhaps he felt that having answered once was enough. The buzzing of flies seemed so loud that Alan felt as if they were crawling inside his skull.

Isaac stooped to the old man and repeated his question. He looked ready to pick up the old man and shake him. The son stepped forward, and Alan wondered if he was going to drag Isaac away from his father. Certainly violence was in the air. The toothless mouth was opening, down there in the dark. Perhaps the old man would answer after all.

Then Alan shuddered and turned away. Isaac or the son

must have jarred the bed, for the flashlight moved and flared. The light glistened on a large fly swelling like a boil on the old man's cheek. But that wasn't why Alan stumbled out of the hut. As the flashlight beam lit up the old man's eyes, they had been gazing straight at him.

He stood in the downpour, mud hissing all around him, as if it were full of snakes. Rain flooded down corrugated walls, clattered on roofs. Isaac emerged from the hut almost at once, and Alan hurried toward the marshy street. As he glanced back at the hut, he saw the son ramming the bolt into its socket with immense force, as if to make sure the door would never open again. Alan turned his face up to the rain. After the suffocating hut, even the downpour seemed refreshing.

'We must go to Port Harcourt,' Isaac said. 'I know where now.' Of course, he'd only needed reminding. He sounded triumphant, Alan wished he could share his optimism, but he was still seeing the eyes of the old man in the hut and remembering what lay ahead. As the old man had gazed at him, Alan had glimpsed in those eyes something hungry and inhuman, something that was far older and more dangerous than the old man himself. They had looked very much like the spidery eyes in his dream.

Twenty-two

Port Harcourt was a ghost town surrounded by flames. There wasn't a soul in the streets down by the docks. Alan felt as if he were walking through residential streets that had become deserted overnight, an urban *Marie Celeste*. Those windows that weren't bricked up gleamed darkly, lifelessly. Long straight streets, glossy with rain, led into the town, where presumably there was life, but nothing moved on them except the flames of the oil refineries beyond the town. Giant cranes laboured up and down the nearby wharf, carrying crates and sacks and steel drums from the dazzling, floodlit ships, but they were the only sign of activity in the maze of docks and warehouses.

The houses had used to be lived in before the trading companies took them over, that was all. He was exhausted and shaken up by the journey – three hundred miles or so from Lagos, and forty miles inland. His whole body felt parched, thirsty even for the tropical rain, his eyes prickly and hot. No wonder he felt on edge – except that he knew that these weren't the reasons at all.

Isaac had brought a flashlight and a map, neither of which seemed much help in the shadowy streets. As he peered at the map, the flames of the refineries sent huge vague shadows of the warehouses staggering toward the two men. 'Don't worry,' Isaac said, his voice low as if he, too, was affected by the strangeness of the place, 'we'll find it.'

Alan was hardly reassured. They'd have more to worry about when they did find it. So far he'd let Isaac lead, but sooner or later he wouldn't be able to hide behind him any longer. Isaac was invaluable because he could speak all the languages and for many other reasons, yet by helping, he was putting off the moment when Alan would have to act for himself. The eyes of the old man in the hut had told Alan that his nightmare of the jungle glade was real, and waiting for him.

Isaac sensed his mood, but mistook its cause. 'We'll find out what we want to know,' he said. 'We mustn't take no for an answer, that's all.'

'I can't see what we can do if he refuses to help. It's not as if he was ever a Leopard Man.'

'His father was.'

'That's no reason why he should know anything, though, is it?'

'I think he does. I'm convinced that David learned something from him.'

A shadow as tall as the warehouses crept over a building, and it took Alan a moment before he was sure it was the shadow of a crane. 'But you said he sounded scared when you told him we were coming.'

'Then we should be able to scare him into talking.'

It seemed grotesque to Alan – himself and a University man, stalking along the rain-blackened crime-movie street like cops or private eyes. Cranes lumbered about the wharf, darkened buildings dripped loudly and shrilly. He wondered if Isaac was as apprehensive as he was. Or didn't Isaac suspect what lay ahead? 'But it isn't *us* he's scared of,' Alan said.

'True,' Isaac admitted. 'He's scared of the Leopard Men, of what they might do to him if he talks. I think he has nothing to fear – but it may be in our interest to behave as if he has. If there are any Leopard Men left in a place like this, I think they'll be anxious to disown their past, for fear of the police.'

Alan wished he could feel as confident. Hadn't Isaac seen the eyes of the old man in the hut? If the power of the Leopard Men could still possess someone as senile as that, how could any others deny what they were? Warehouses loomed over him, shadows roamed the lifeless streets. Suddenly Isaac halted. 'This is it, I think.'

He was pointing at yet another tall house. The upper

windows were glazed and blank, but the windows on either side of the front door were bricked up. The name of a tyre manufacturer clung to the wall above the door; some of the letters were losing their grip, leaning on one another. When Isaac knocked on the door, Alan thought he saw one of them shake.

After a while Isaac knocked again. The house must be full of rubber, and Alan could hear how the knocks were swallowed up at once. He heard several huge mechanical gasps on the wharf, and the rattle of an enormous chain. Isaac knocked once more, long and hard, then he gazed at Alan in the silence. 'Perhaps there may be a side door,' he said.

There was. When they found the way to it through the remains of a garden suffocated by grit and dust, they discovered that it was open. Presumably, since Isaac had written to prepare him for their visit, the night-watchman had left the door ajar for them. As Isaac pushed open the door and raised his flashlight, an overpowering smell of rubber greeted them.

Following the beam of light through the doorway, Alan could see nothing but tyres: tyres lined up on the racks or piled on the floor, rank upon rank of them, extending in every direction until they merged with the darkness. Narrow aisles led between them. The stench of rubber was so thick that it seemed to darken the air, as if the rubber was soaking up the light. It also seemed to prevent sound from travelling far, so that as Isaac advanced, calling 'Mr Ogunbe', it sounded as if he were calling into fog.

Alan hoped they'd find him soon. Now that he was inside, the warehouse didn't seem at all like a house; he suspected there were no longer any rooms. The rubber aisles closed in on him, and he was afraid of upsetting the piles of tyres, bringing them crashing down on him. Much like a ghost train, the interior of the building seemed considerably larger than the exterior. The narrow aisles might go on for ever; the dark made it impossible to see where they ended.

Suddenly Isaac halted. A light was flickering in the

distance, illuminating an intersection of aisles. In the shaky glow, the segmented piles of tyres looked as if they were stirring, like grey worms rearing up. 'That must be our man,' Isaac said, and hurried forward. 'Mr Ogunbe!'

If it was, then it seemed he'd changed his mind about helping. The light darted to the left, and they glimpsed a man with a flashlight crossing their aisle; then he disappeared and the intersection was dark again. Isaac strode toward the point where they'd glimpsed him. Alan hurried in pursuit, more afraid than ever of bringing down the rubber walls; he could smell how it would feel to suffocate under them. The jerky light kept making them seem to wobble, an unnerving joke. Had the man at the intersection been white? Surely Ogunbe wasn't a white man's name? Really, whoever it was had crossed too quickly for Alan to see.

When they reached the intersection, there was no sign of the other man's light. Isaac shone his beam along the left-hand aisle, where hundreds of grey segments squirmed with shadows. There were several intersections, and no way of knowing which route the man had taken. Isaac put his finger to his lip for quiet. He looked determined but bewildered.

In a moment they heard two things. Far off in the dark – perhaps it would have seemed closer in the daytime – a door closed. Alan recognized the sound from having heard it a few minutes ago. It was the side door. Had the watchman left the building? No, for to their right, where the man with the flashlight had come from, they heard someone moaning.

Isaac swung his light that way. Tyres came swelling out of the dark, looking fattened. It was an aisle of larger tyres, that was all. Isaac went forward, taking the light away as he searched for the source of the moaning. Why did it sound so muffled? Alan kept pace with him, so as not to be left behind by the light. He wasn't sure by any means that he wanted to find whoever or whatever was giving out those agonized moans.

They had reached the second intersection when he saw

light down the left-hand aisle. In a moment he made out an office door. Of course, it was the night-watchman's office; the maze had brought them to the front of the building. 'Mr Ogunbe,' Isaac called, and started toward the lit door.

He stopped almost at once. Someone was crashing about in the office. They heard a chair fall, and a tin mug; then the light beyond the frosted glass began to sway as someone's hand collided with the shade. They saw the hand, a huge blotch that loomed on the frosted glass of the door. In a moment they saw the silhouette of a man as he stumbled against the door. His face was a dark blur pressed against the glass, which vibrated with his desperate moaning.

Suddenly he fumbled the door open. Had his face left dark stains on the glass? Before Isaac could turn the light full on him, he reeled forward into a pile of tyres. They toppled, blocking the aisle, rolling and swerving. Some rolled toward Isaac, who retreated, bumping into Alan, shoving him against a rack of tyres. For a moment he thought the whole place was about to fall on them.

Isaac had dropped the flashlight. It rolled in a circle, its beam stuttering over tyres, slowing. In the light from the doorway they saw that the man from the office had fallen. He was crawling toward them over the tyres, still moaning. Isaac retrieved the flashlight and shone the beam into the man's face.

At first Alan thought he was wearing a mask and that perhaps that was why his moaning was so muffled. Looking at his face, he found that he was thinking – so incongruously it was horrible even before he understood why – of a rag doll with stitches for mouth and eyes. Then the man crawled closer to the light, and Alan stumbled backward, retching. The mask was the man's face. He would tell them nothing, even if he could see them. Someone had sewn up his eyes and his mouth.

Twenty-three

Anna was sitting at a table in the room behind the counter at The Stone Shop. She was making a bird, trying to glue the halves of a shell onto the back of a stone for wings. The wings kept falling off, or sticking lopsidedly, and her fingers were sticky and peeling; they unglued themselves every time she moved them. There wasn't much room on the table for her to work, what with Rebecca's half-finished stone creatures, Rebecca's handbag spilling its load of handkerchiefs and lipsticks and make-up, and the 'doctor and nurse' love story that Rebecca was reading, which was folded in half, its pages glued together like a book daddy had once shown her that he'd had to cut open with a knife. She was fed up with gluing, she wanted to paint her bird – that was the part she enjoyed most. She looked longingly at the pots and brushes on the shelf, but it was no good, she had to make the bird first. She mustn't give up. She longed to feel she was some use to someone.

She had managed to line up the shell wings at last and was waiting for the glue to dry when someone at the counter said, 'Isn't that sweet.' An old lady had picked up Anna's caterpillar, several pebbles with a grin painted on the front one. Anna had stuck them on a large stone, which she'd painted green for grass. 'By Anna, aged 6', the cardboard notice said. While Anna watched, the old lady called Rebecca over and bought the caterpillar. 'That little girl in there made it, did she? What a clever child,' the old lady said. 'She'll go far.'

Anna smiled at her, then turned away. She felt like crying. Selling her work didn't matter any more, and nothing else seemed to. All she wanted was to know what she'd done to make daddy hate her so much.

He'd gone away without even saying goodbye to her. That showed how much he hated her, even more than what happened the night mummy had gone to the party. She didn't want to think about that, she wasn't even sure by now what *had* really happened, but she couldn't forget waking up the next morning to find he'd gone away. He always said goodbye to her, and 'Look after each other' – and he always gave her a kiss to keep safe for him until he came back. This time he hadn't even spoken to her. That showed how much he blamed her for what had happened.

She went to the shelves for brushes and pots, to give herself something to do: yellow for the bird's body, blue for the wings. She carried them back to the table and sat there, trying to want to paint. But all she could think of was daddy. She was nearly sure that he'd gone away because of her. She *had* stopped him writing, whatever mummy said. There was only one other thing she could think of that he could blame her for, that would have worried him so much: she'd let the metal claw be stolen, the claw he'd brought home from Africa.

She ought to have seen who'd taken it. She would have done if she'd been in her playroom opposite the long room when the claw had been stolen – only she'd left her playroom because the man had been looking in the window. She was sure the man *had* been there – baby Georgie had seen him and started crying. She had almost seen him dodging out of sight, even if mummy didn't believe in him. But at the same time, she knew he was no excuse. If she hadn't left her playroom she would have seen who had come into the house.

She tried to remember hearing someone sneak in – she had been trying ever since that afternoon – but try as she might, she couldn't remember anything of the kind. She'd been sitting near the kitchen door. She was almost certain that *no* stranger had come into the house, but what would that mean? She felt she was trying to excuse herself. She'd let the claw be stolen, daddy had been looking after it for someone, it was far worse if you lost something that belonged to someone else. It was nearly enough of a reason for daddy to hate her, but knowing that still didn't help. Even supposing the claw could be found, she couldn't bear the idea that it might come back.

She didn't know why, she didn't want to think. She was *glad* it had been stolen; that was why she felt so guilty. She opened the yellow paint and dipped in a brush, to stop herself thinking. The glue should be dry by now. The claw *mustn't* come back, the idea terrified her, made her feel as if the stuffy room that smelled of glue and paints had turned into a freezer. It was worth being hated by daddy if it meant the claw had gone for good. The bargain shocked and dismayed her. She pulled the bird of shells toward her, and the wings came off again.

She was sitting miserably, feeling as if she'd pulled the wings off a butterfly by mistake, when Rebecca came in. 'That's a nice surprise, isn't it?' she said, which seemed a cruel joke, until Anna realized that she was talking about selling the caterpillar to the old lady. 'Since it's your first sale, I won't take a percentage.'

When Anna didn't smile, Rebecca came to see what was wrong. 'Never mind,' she said, spotting the broken bird. 'Shall I mend it for you? It won't take a minute.'

Anna nodded, but she didn't care, and that must have shown in her face. Rebecca sat down by her. 'What's the matter, love?'

Anna couldn't tell her. There seemed to be so many things she couldn't talk about now. She hadn't been able to tell mummy what had happened that night on the beach – even thinking about it made her feel somehow ashamed. But mummy had asked her only once, she seemed not to want to know. 'Is everything all right at home?' Rebecca said.

'Grandad isn't very well,' Anna said, just for something to say. 'Grandma and him were coming to stay with us, but now they can't.'

'So I believe.' Rebecca wasn't satisfied. 'Have you heard when your daddy's coming home?'

Anna had to look away. She didn't know if mummy had even spoken to him since he went away. Except to ask her about that night on the beach, mummy hadn't mentioned him at all, didn't want to talk about him. That showed how much was going wrong, and it frightened her. She was afraid to ask when he was coming home, in case mummy said 'never'.

Rebecca took her hand. 'If you ever need a friend to talk to, remember I'm here.'

Anna knew Rebecca wished she was her little girl, and for a moment she wanted to tell her some of what she felt – tell her how afraid she was of the claw, and how she didn't think that anyone had sneaked into the house to steal it. Rebecca had been there; perhaps she might have noticed something Anna had missed. Before Anna could think what to say, Rebecca looked back toward the shop. 'Here's your mummy now,' she said.

Anna felt a surge of relief. She didn't need to speak after all. Mummy was here, mummy would protect her. But protect her from what? All at once she felt uneasy. She couldn't think why, but she didn't want to go home.

Twenty-four

Halfway through the village, Liz began to hurry. Beneath the cloudless August sky the houses shone like chalk. Parents were urging children back to hotels for lunch and trying to persuade them to part with bucketfuls of crabs and pebbles, souvenirs of the beach. Fishermen bristling with rods tramped through the crowds, lunchtime coachloads of tourists piled into the pubs. The sun stood over all of them, baking Liz's bare arms, but she felt cut off from everything, trapped in her own world, surrounded by strangers. In the whole street there wasn't a face that she knew, and Anna had been out of her sight for too long.

Eventually she struggled as far as the post office, through the crowd that halted bodily to watch a hang-glider every time he sailed by above the village. Sunlight was peeling the 'Local Author' sign away from the window above Alan's books. The sight of his name, repeated again and again like an admonition, made her feel depressed and helpless, and as she noticed how the sunlight was fading his name, she wanted to weep. She had never been able to reach the part of him that created his stories: she hadn't wanted to, she'd known that he must keep it secret and untouched. Now it was as if she'd never known him at all. She made to hurry past, and collided with Jane's husband Derek.

'Just the person I wanted to see,' he said.

'I'm rather in a hurry, Derek.'

'I'll be quick.' Momentarily, hysterically, she wondered if he said that to his women in bed. She could imagine him as being slightly apologetic as a lover. Was it his politeness, or his faint air of needing to be mothered, that appealed to his female conquests? He looked and carried himself rather

165

like Leslie Howard: at nine years old, when she'd seen *Gone with the Wind*, she'd preferred Ashley Wilkes to Rhett Butler. Now she found it difficult to understand what she'd seen in either of them.

'I was wondering if it would be convenient for us to take up your dinner invitation soon,' Derek was saying, as if he were in his office in Norwich, dictating a solicitor's letter. Some of his obsessive correctness was at Jane's insistence. At least he was in his shirt-sleeves today, though he still wore a tie with a gold pin and carried his jacket folded neatly over his arm. 'Or would you rather wait until Alan comes home?' he said.

'I don't know when that'll be.'

She could feel him recoiling from the hint of wrongness, much like Jane. You bloody hypocrite, she thought, and almost said it out loud. 'I think it would do Jane good to get out of the house more than she does,' he said. 'I really don't know what's wrong with her just now.'

The only reason he was taking Jane out was that Alex was away filming. Perhaps Liz's thoughts showed on her face, for he said, 'You don't care for me very much, Liz, do you?'

'I don't care for what you're doing to Jane.'

'Perhaps if you could see the situation from my side . . .'

'Yes, well, this is hardly the place to discuss that. Look, I've invited you both to dinner, and that invitation still stands. This week's no good, but how about Monday?'

'Monday will be fine. I'm very grateful to you, Liz.'

He made it sound as if she was undertaking a duty. Of course she was, but all the same, just now she'd be glad of company at home. She hurried away, shaking her head, to The Stone Shop.

Rebecca came out of the room behind the counter. 'Anna just made her first sale. I'll have to take her on as an apprentice. How was your morning?'

'Oh, you know,' Liz said, hoping that Rebecca didn't.

'Like that, eh? Well, never mind.' She looked sympathetic. 'Any news of your father?'

'No change. I suppose he's as well as can be expected.' He'd had a coronary. Last time she'd seen her parents her mother had been vainly trying to cut down his intake of food and drink and cigarettes; Liz ought to have seen what was going on, but she must have felt that her father would never change, would always be this stout jolly untroubled figure – Father Christmas all the year round. No doubt his air of seeming to have no troubles had made their effect on him worse. Her mother refused to let Liz go to help; the doctor said he'd be all right if he took things easy . . . She could cope . . . Liz must have problems of her own . . . If only she knew! Liz mustn't worry, her mother had said – an impossible piece of advice.

She beckoned Anna out of the room full of shells. 'I think we'd better leave Rebecca to it now.'

'Oh, do I have to go home, mummy?'

'You certainly do if you want any lunch. Come on,' she said more gently, 'we'll have rollmops with salad. You like those. Rebecca doesn't want to put up with you all day.'

'Not a bit of it, Liz. I'd happily keep her until closing time.'

'Well, it's very nice of you to say so, Rebecca, but we really must be going.' Rebecca's motives were kind, but she was rapidly undermining her authority. 'I've things to do at home.'

Rebecca must think she could see through that – perhaps she could – for she said, 'Have you heard from Alan?'

'Yes, he's been keeping in touch.'

'How is he?'

'Very well.' Liz wasn't sure if she sounded bitter or ironic. How much did Rebecca suspect? All she should know was that Alan had gone away again – Liz couldn't bring herself to talk about the situation, even to her. As Liz hurried Anna out of the shop, Rebecca watched them dubiously.

The sunlight outside made them blink like moles. At first Liz could see nothing at all. Strangers closed around them, and she kept hold of Anna's arm until they reached the village green, where the crowd was less dense. Anna didn't run ahead as she usually did when Liz let go of her. Instead she gazed up at Liz, looking heartbreakingly old. 'When will daddy come home?' she said.

Liz hurried her toward the coast road to avoid being overheard. 'Do you want him to?' she said, and suddenly felt tactless.

'Yes, I think I do.'

'You aren't sure.'

'Yes, I am.' Anna sounded defiant. 'He just frightened me before he went away, that's all. I thought he wanted to hurt me. He didn't seem like daddy at all. But I do want him to come back, I *do*.' Suddenly she was near to weeping. 'He hasn't gone away because of me, has he?'

'Of course not, darling. You mustn't think that. You know it's always his work that takes him away.'

'But what made him like that? He did frighten me.'

'Perhaps problems with his work. You know how he can be sometimes.' She hoped that convinced Anna – because it didn't convince her. If anything, Anna had been closer to the truth: Alan no longer seemed like anyone she knew or wanted to know. When he'd called her from Lagos a few days ago she'd felt that she was talking to a stranger – except that no stranger could have made her feel such a mixture of emotions: anger, grief, nervousness, defensiveness . . . It had been a bad line, hardly the best medium for confession or explanations, but all the same, she'd been appalled by the way he chatted on to her as if nothing had happened. She could tell that he *knew* how false he sounded, but what comfort was that? She'd wondered if he'd called for reassurance. If he'd only admitted that, or asked for her help, she would have told him to come back, that together they would deal with whatever was affecting him – but he wouldn't even give her a hint, nothing to hold onto at all. She'd known her father was ill by then, but she hadn't told Alan. He was no longer someone she wanted to tell.

Now that they were in sight of home, Anna was running

on ahead. Goats were cropping the grass near the hedge. At least they were safe now that Joseph had been put away. Outside the garden, the parched grass was turning the colour of straw. Above the sea, on which glinting ripples swarmed to the horizon, a few gulls circled, repeating elaborate patterns of grey and white. The white house looked starkly isolated in the flat landscape, the windows blank with sunlight, preventing her from seeing inside. As she drew near she heard that the phone was ringing.

Her mouth tasted sour, her stomach tightened. Was it Alan or her mother? She fumbled in her handbag for her key as she ran toward the house. No time for distractions: nobody was watching her from the field across the road – nobody could be as red as that. The crimson glimpse at the edge of her vision must have been sunlight through her eyelids.

She ran through the hot stuffy house, trying to blink away the dimness, and grabbed the downstairs phone. 'Hello?' she gabbled, afraid that whoever it was might have given up.

'May I speak to Mr Knight?' The voice was sharp, asexual.

'I'm afraid he isn't here.' She was rather annoyed to have been made nervous for no reason – just another business call. 'Can I help?'

'Are you his secretary?'

'If I am, someone owes me a lot of wages. I'm his wife.'

'Oh, I beg your pardon.' The joke had gone down like a lead balloon. 'I take it he's keeping in touch with you?'

'To some extent. Why?'

'I'm sorry, you must wonder who I am. My name is Hetherington, of the Foundation for African Studies. Presumably you know that your husband returned to Nigeria to find out more about the artefact he brought home – the artefact that was stolen from your house. He was supposed to convey it to us. I wonder if you have any news of it?'

Now she knew who he was. Alan had mentioned him.

But she was still bewildered: was *that* why Alan had gone back to Nigeria? 'No, the police are still looking,' she said.

'If you'd like to take my number, you can keep me informed, if you will. I'm sure you understand that the artefact is the property of the Foundation. If it is retrieved, it should be delivered to us at once.'

She scribbled his number on the pad beside the phone, then replaced the receiver and stood there, pencil in one hand, receiver in the other. So Alan had been so worried about the loss of the African claw that it had taken him back to Nigeria? He'd already had problems with his work, and then she'd allowed the claw to be stolen . . . She couldn't condone the way he'd behaved toward Anna, but it seemed that she had to take some of the blame herself. Perhaps she needn't feel so helpless any longer. At least now she could see how she might help.

Anna was in the long room, playing with the remote control, making television channels interrupt one another, giggling. As she remembered how nervous Anna had been of that room while the claw was there, Liz felt a momentary qualm. But there was more at stake than the child's moods. Liz had no idea how she would do it, but if it was within her power, she was going to find the claw – and if Anna didn't like it, that was just too bad.

Twenty-five

In a couple of days both Liz and her ideas were exhausted. How did people in novels always know where to search? Because the author always left them a clue – there was always something the police had overlooked. But if the police hadn't searched where Liz was searching, she suspected that it was simply because it was useless.

She drove along the coast, stopping at every antique shop to poke through the musty clutter: books with rickety faded covers, chipped furniture, dusty glass and copper and porcelain – until Anna grew bored and wandered out into the sunlight, and Liz had to keep running to the door like a nervous shoplifter to make sure she was still there. She knew Anna was basically sensible and wouldn't just wander off, so why was Liz so nervous? She didn't want Anna out of her sight, that was all.

The whole thing seemed hopeless. Why would even a teenage thief sell stolen property in shops like these? Liz drove inland to Norwich and bought all the collectors' journals she could find, then felt compelled to search the shops there too. The streets were full of cars, coasting by or waiting at the kerb, and she refused to let Anna stay outside. When the child said, 'What are you looking for, mummy?' she had to mutter vaguely about a present. She wasn't sure if Anna believed her.

Back home she pored over the journals. Anna offered to help, and so Liz had to watch television with her instead. When the child had gone to bed, Liz searched the columns of items for sale until the tiny print began to writhe before her eyes like dancing snakes and ceased to look like words. Why should thieves advertise? Why should they be less intelligent than she was? In a world that contained so many unsolved crimes, it was ridiculous to look for clues. At last she stumbled upstairs to bed and dreamed she was searching for goats.

Sunlight woke her. Anna had drawn the curtains and was sitting next to her, waiting patiently for her to wake. 'Shall we go on the beach today, mummy?' she said.

The day was too bright to waste. 'Yes, let's have a picnic – just the two of us.'

She hadn't been awake enough to choose her words. On the beach she found they'd lodged in her mind like the memory of a disturbing dream. Anna seemed happy to search for stones for Rebecca, but Liz was unable to relax, even when she started on a half-bottle of Chianti. The sky was cloudless, the sand sparkled minutely, the sea was calm except for an enormous impersonal whispering. Everything felt as flat as it looked, and accentuated how far she was from anyone else on the beach. She used to like the feeling of not being crowded, but just now she would have welcomed company. She wondered if Barbara Mason still wanted to stay. Probably Barbara had made other plans by now.

Liz was glad when a family set up camp nearby, windbreak and folding chairs and a hamper. Their two children were throwing a striped ball that kept peppering her wine with sand, but she was pleased when Anna progressed from returning the ball to playing with the other children. Really, she ought to have the chance to play with children of her own age more often; no wonder she was frustrated sometimes. Of course there was always the hotel nursery, but it wasn't the same. If only her school and her friends weren't miles away along the coast! Liz could have driven her there to visit, except that the drive would take her away from the phone, and she wanted to be near it – even though she had no idea what she was waiting for.

When the children came hungrily back to their parents, bare feet glittering with sand, the family invited Liz and Anna to share their picnic. Liz had brought plenty, but accepted a token hard-boiled egg and chatted to them as she surreptitiously picked fragments of eggshell out of the soft white flesh. Yes, she lived here. Yes, her husband worked here. He was a writer, a writer of crime fiction. Yes, it did get lonely round here in the winter sometimes. She offered them some wine, but the woman's long face stiffened beneath the dyed hair, and the bull-necked man's lips pursed. Before long they were packing their hamper and shifting camp along the beach. As they left, the woman opened her handbag. 'I think you should have this,' she told Liz.

It was a pamphlet from the Evangelical Tract Society of Hinckley: a testimony of religious conversion written by a schoolboy shortly before he was knocked down and killed by a car. It didn't seem much of an argument for getting religion. Had the woman given her the pamphlet because she was drinking or because her husband wrote crime stories? No doubt both activities were frowned upon.

Anna went back to searching for the best stones. A water-skier raced by on his leash, feathering the water; otherwise there was nobody for half a mile. Liz wished she could close her eyes for a little – she felt as though the beach and the sea were pressing against them, burning them – but she kept nodding and waking, thinking she could hear a phone, or that someone was spying on her from the cliff, or that Anna had run away. She mustn't doze in case Anna wandered too far. Joseph was locked up, yet the day of the pillbox was still fresh in her memory, and with it the figure she'd seen in the dark. She narrowed her eyes to keep out some of the light, and watched Anna search.

Then her eyes widened. Suppose Alan had been right to search down here? Suppose he hadn't looked far enough? All at once, to Anna's surprise, Liz was searching too. Anna looked pleased that her mother was helping her.

It didn't seem a good idea for very long. There were grey gleams everywhere, and it was impossible to tell whether or not they were stones until she went to look.

Suppose the claw was *under* the stones? Then a hundred people might never find it, let alone one woman and a child.

'You haven't seen anything of your father's down here, have you?' Liz said, suddenly wondering if Anna could have seen the claw down here, and, if she already had, whether she would say so.

Eventually Liz gave up. She kept thinking she could hear a phone. Besides, she couldn't shake off the notion that someone was pacing her along the top of the cliff, peering down at her. Every reddish glimpse up there looked like a figure, though whenever she glanced upward there was no sign of anyone, nor of anything red. Why did she feel as if it were Anna's fault? She must have had too much to drink. 'I think I need to get out of the sun for a while,' she said. 'Come home while I have a lie-down.'

She knew nobody would be waiting at the top of the path. The snuffling sound was only the wind. Or perhaps it had been a goat. When she reached the top, the goats were quite near, until they fled to another patch of relatively green grass. They were all that she could see; the sun was in her eyes, eating away the outline of her house. She must be drunk, for in some way the goats seemed an answer. But what on earth was the question? Head down, she hurried blindly toward the house.

As she entered the shadow of the house, she faltered. The plunge into shade was too sudden – the grass looked almost black – and so she couldn't really be seeing a red trail that led across the garden to the house. She hurried to the front door and scraped the key into the lock. 'Hurry up, child,' she said to Anna, pushing her inside.

In the hall she found that she was virtually blind. No wonder she almost tripped over Anna, who had halted. 'It's all right,' Liz said harshly. The low blurred voice coming from the long room must be the television or the radio. Anna had left one or the other switched on, that was all. Half-blind, Liz strode to the door of the room and threw it open. Yes, it was the television. Anna really must learn to be less careless and untidy; she'd left some article of clothing on a chair in front of the set, a dark blur against the screen. But as Liz stumbled forward, dizzy with drink and sunlight and needing to sit down, the blur rose up in front of her. She screamed.

'I'm sorry, I didn't mean to alarm you,' Isobel said.

Anna was giggling uncontrollably, perhaps from shock. 'You stop that right now, miss,' Liz said furiously, 'or I'll give you something to make you stop.' She turned on Isobel. 'How did you get in?'

'Why, the front door was open. I assumed you'd stepped out for a moment. Weren't you aware that it was?'

'No, I wasn't,' Liz said, and thought that she sounded accusing. That would do no good, even though she hated the idea of Isobel prying into her home. 'I've been a bit distracted lately,' she said.

'Yes, quite. I hope you don't mind, I made coffee while I was waiting. Let me get you some.'

Liz sat down while the blackened room paled and swam back into focus. She had to close her eyes before she could get rid of some of the dollops of blackness. Now she could see Anna, who looked upset by the way she'd snapped at her. Before Liz could apologize, the child followed Isobel to the kitchen. Wonderful, Liz thought. Just the way to make Isobel think that the child wouldn't even stay with her mother.

When Isobel brought in the coffee, Anna returned with a glass of lemonade for herself. Liz smiled at her, but she wasn't looking. 'Would you like to find yourself something to do in your playroom, Anna?' Isobel said. 'Your mother and I would like to talk privately.'

Did Isobel want to take over the running of the house? Once Anna had gone, Isobel said, 'Well, dear, what seems to be the trouble?'

'I don't know that anything is.'

'Oh, really, dear, you mustn't try to keep things from me. What's the trouble between Alan and yourself? Why did he go away so suddenly?'

'Because he needs to do more research.'

'Is that your story? I see.' Isobel shook her head sadly. 'Don't you think it's strange that he went away without telling me?'

'No, not particularly,' Liz said, and almost added: Not when he married me for his freedom.

'Well, I do. We always used to be close. It isn't like him to leave me worrying like that.' Now she was offended. 'And how long is he supposed to be staying away?'

'I really couldn't tell you, Isobel.'

'Well then, there's something wrong there, don't you think?' She seemed to be debating which approach to take. 'I wonder,' she said, as if performing a duty, 'if he'd stay away if he could hear some of the talk.'

'What talk? What on earth do you mean?'

'I don't like spreading gossip. Still, it's best you should know what's being said.' She frowned like a headmistress conducting an unpleasant interview. 'I put you on your honour, Elizabeth. Is it true that after Alan had gone away, you left the child alone in the house while you went to a party at the hotel?'

'You put me on what? Who the *hell* do you think you are? No, it certainly isn't true, and you'd better tell me who said it.'

'I'm sure you understand that I can't do that. I was told it in confidence. In fact, I can't remember who it was. Anyway, that's rather beside the point. You won't deny that the child came crying to you at the hotel?'

'No,' Liz said dangerously, 'I won't deny that.'

'Then you can appreciate why people are talking. They're worried about you.'

'Worried how?'

'Really, dear, you force me to say these things. They're worried about your behaviour lately.'

Liz remembered the night that Alan had virtually accused her of wanting to ill-treat Anna – the night before he'd left her. 'Let me make something clear to you. Alan was still here the night she came running to the hotel. Here with her, do you understand that? That's why she came running to me. Maybe you should start worrying about *his* behaviour.'

Isobel held up one hand. 'I really think that's rather cheap, accusing him in order to defend yourself. I should have expected better of you. He would never harm the child. At least, he wouldn't have when I knew him,' she said with a kind of bitter triumph, 'when he lived with me.'

'But he wouldn't have been able to have a child then, would he? That would have been taking things a bit too far.'

'I don't know what you mean, and I don't want to know. You can be very coarse sometimes.' She shook off her disgust. 'In any case, dear, we shouldn't be quarrelling. Don't feel that you have to defend yourself to me. I know how much of a strain it can be to bring up a child single-handed. That's really all I came to say. I'll take the child off your hands for a while whenever you need a rest from her.'

Just now, despite all that had been said, it seemed a tempting offer. 'All right, Isobel, I'll tell her you've invited her.'

'I hope you'll allow her to decide for herself whether she wants to come.'

'Of course I will. What are you trying to say? I don't keep her locked up, you know.' She was tired of the argument; she wanted to be alone to think, if she could. At least, she thought she wanted to be alone, but now she wasn't even sure of that; her head was pounding. 'I'd like to be quiet now, Isobel. I'll be in touch if I need you.'

At the front door – rather grotesquely under the circumstances, Liz thought – Isobel said, 'I hope you'll both still come for dinner,' and wouldn't leave until they'd agreed a date. Liz stood gazing at the flat landscape long after Isobel had driven away. Who was spreading stories about her? How dare they suggest that she wasn't looking after the child as well as she possibly could, considering all that she had to put up with?

But there was another problem, more immediate and perhaps more disturbing. How had Isobel got into the house? The more she thought about it, the more Liz was convinced that she hadn't left the door open at all.

Twenty-six

By lunchtime on Monday, Anna was intolerable. Sunday had been an unforecasted rainy day, and she'd hardly left Liz alone for a moment, pestering her to read her latest story every time she finished a paragraph, refusing to watch television unless Liz watched it too, constantly complaining that she had nothing to read, and asking Liz to find her things to do. The house had become overrun with her toys that had strayed out of the playroom: bears in armchairs, dolls on the carpets, even her bicycle in the hall.

Eventually Liz had lost patience. 'You know perfectly well not to ride in the house. How old are you supposed to be? I thought you were a big girl.' But then Anna had started whining – she didn't like living here any more, she had nobody to play with, when was daddy coming home – and that had been more than Liz could stand. She'd made a hasty dinner and had sent Anna to bed early, despite her protests. She'd restrained herself from going up to look until she was sure that the child was asleep. Had Anna cried herself to sleep? Liz had thought for a while that she heard snuffling upstairs.

Eventually she'd gone to check. Anna had been peacefully asleep, though her eyelids looked sticky with dried tears. Downstairs, Liz had fetched her story from the playroom to re-read; something about it was nagging her, something she'd almost noticed.

After two more readings she still couldn't define the cause of her unease, the story was just what it seemed to be, a series of harmless anecdotes about a family of goats who lived in a field. Liz had watched television to take her mind off Alan and the rumours that someone was spreading about her, only to wake up to the doodling of light after the programmes had ended. It had made her feel utterly alone, that and the sound of the sea and the snuffling of the moist wind around the house. She'd gone to bed and dreamed that she was watching goats, staring at them for hours or perhaps for days before she gave up and wandered away. She'd woken up before she knew where she was going.

On Monday she was determined to be kinder to the child. She let her make prawn cocktails for tonight's first course, and tried to conceal her growing despondency at the thought of an evening with Derek and Jane. Perhaps they could tell her who was spreading the rumours – perhaps she could rid herself of at least that problem. She'd thought that once Alan had gone away there'd be less tension around the home, but instead it was worsening. She felt very much as if she were lying in bed at four in the morning, restless and jaggedly nervous, incapable of peace.

After finishing making the prawn cocktails, Anna wandered away, but soon came back. 'I don't know what to do,' she complained.

'Why don't you take your bike out now that it's stopped raining?'

'I don't want to go out. I don't like it.'

'What don't you like?'

'Someone keeps looking at me over the cliff.'

'Now that's silly, Anna. Why would anyone do that?' Liz ignored her own leaping pulse. 'Where did you think you saw something?'

'I don't have to see him. I know he's there.' To Liz, she sounded more obstinate than nervous. 'Just out there. Beyond the hedge.'

'Well, you can see there's nothing. Here, I'll lift you up.' She did so, for as long as she could manage it; slim though she was, Anna was no lightweight. The hedge had broken out in diamonds, the parched grass looked drowned in cider. 'There couldn't have been anyone,' Liz said. 'There's nowhere they could stand.'

'I don't care. He's still there. He's hiding.'

'Oh, Anna, for heaven's sake. I'm too busy to take you out to show you there's nothing. All right – don't go out if you don't want to. Since you've got such an imagination, why don't you get on with writing your story.'

'I don't want to.'

Liz remembered her undertaking to be kinder. What was she thinking of, mocking the child's story? You'd think she was jealous of Anna for taking after her father. 'I'm sorry, darling,' she said. 'I know I wasn't very encouraging yesterday, but I read it properly after you went to bed, and I really like it. I'm anxious to find out what happens next.'

'I still don't want to. I don't like it any more.'

'Good God, Anna, is there anything you *do* like?' She felt helplessly frustrated, desperate to vent her rage on something. Just as she was setting out ingredients for this evening's main course she found the perfect excuse. 'Oh, *shit!*'

Anna started giggling at that, but stopped when she saw Liz's face. 'What's wrong?'

'I've got no sherry for the bloody marinade. Now I'll have to go into the village.'

'I'll go if you like.'

'Would you mind?' It seemed odd that she was proposing to go out now, but perhaps the village was far enough from the cliff. 'All right, I'll make the sweet while I'm waiting. Just be careful, and hurry back.'

As Anna cycled away, Liz called, 'Remember, ask for the dryest sherry they have,' and watched until Anna was out of sight, long brown legs pumping easily, red hair streaming like inexhaustible fire. Suddenly she felt intensely proud of her. Of course she was irritating at times, but so were all children. For a moment she seemed too precious to let go, but Liz couldn't cling to her for ever.

In the kitchen she switched on the mixer and made the meringue topping, then on an impulse she went out to the cliff. Anna wouldn't be home for fifteen minutes at least, however fast she cycled on the winding road. Liz hoped she would take her time on the bends and began to wish she hadn't made so much of hurrying back.

There was hardly a breeze on the cliff-top. Fat clouds basked on the horizon, the sea glittered sleepily; her garden was almost still. Of course there was no red trail in the garden; there hadn't been on Friday evening, before the rain. Was it any wonder that she kept seeing red?

She went to the edge of the cliff and leaned over. As the sea swayed at the edge of her vision, she felt she was falling. Nevertheless she leaned as far as she could, until she was sure there was no hidden foothold. If anyone tried to climb up here, the cliff face would simply crumble away, and there wasn't a path for another hundred yards. A family – parents, two children, a dog and a large inflatable duck – stared up at her from the beach. Let them stare. At least now she could prove to Anna that there was nothing to fear.

She strolled back to the house. Anna should be home any minute. Liz made her a lager and lime, her beer-garden treat, and put it in the refrigerator to chill. She dawdled over the marinade, wishing Anna would hurry up. What could she do while she was waiting?

A quick call to her mother, in the hope that her father was better. She carried the phone into the long room, and sat with it on her lap, the lead stretching back into the hall. Anna should be home by now, but perhaps she'd had to queue. Suppose Liz's father was worse? She was cradling the phone as if it were a child she was trying to lull to sleep, when all at once it twitched and rang.

She almost dropped it. It was more like a bomb than a phone. She managed to grab the receiver while she kneed the extension back into her lap. 'Yes, who is it?' she demanded.

'Is that Mrs Knight?' said a woman's voice that she didn't recognize.

'Yes, yes, who's that?'

'One moment please, I have a call for you.'

Perhaps it was Alan – but the line sounded too clear for Nigeria. Could it be Hetherington, asking about the claw? Suddenly Liz wondered if it was about Anna – *why* wasn't she home by now? She pressed the receiver against her face as if that would force the caller to speak.

Eventually he did. 'Hi, it's Liz, isn't it? How are you?'

She knew the voice, but couldn't remember from where. 'I'm all right. Who's that?'

'It's Teddy Shaw here. Alan's editor. We met once, if you recall.'

'Of course, yes. I'm sorry, I've rather a lot on my mind.'

'I guess you must have, with Alan leaving you on your own again. I was just wondering, are you likely to be in touch with him in the next day or so?'

'I don't know.' She'd had enough of lying and pretending.

His pause was almost imperceptible. 'Well, if you happen to be in touch, could you ask him to give me a call? It's about his signing tour. Or maybe you could get his number for me to call.'

'I'll do my best.' She was willing him to go away; where *was* Anna? 'I can't promise.'

'Right, I know it's difficult to keep in touch with Nigeria. Has he found what he was after, do you know?'

How could she answer that when she didn't know what it was? 'I expect so,' she said.

'So things aren't looking too bad.'

'No,' she said, 'they couldn't be worse,' but her hand was over the mouthpiece. 'I suppose not,' she told him.

'Well, maybe I'll give you a call in a couple of days to see if he's been in touch.'

'All right,' she said, to get rid of him. She was already making for the hall as she replaced the receiver, and almost tripped over the lead. Why wasn't Anna home yet? Then she fought down the panic. Good God, she was only a few minutes late – no doubt she'd been sensible and had taken her time on the curves. Once Liz reached the road, she'd be able to see Anna's little red head bobbing above the hedges.

But when she opened her gate and stared across the fields, there was no sign of her.

Something had happened. The landscape was too flat to hide her. She wouldn't have dawdled or stopped to talk or play when Liz had specifically told her to hurry. Oh, why had she sent her at all? Because she'd wanted to get rid of her for a while. No wonder people said she was neglecting the child.

Liz ran for her key and slammed the front door, then hurried towards the turn-off for the village. Now she couldn't see beyond the first curve, and she began to run. The hedges and the tarmac seemed to drift by as if they had all the time in the world. Her sandals stuck to the road, the burning tarmac dragging at her feet. Was that Anna beyond the next curve? No, the glimpse had been too red for Anna's hair.

She was running in the middle of the road now, praying that she'd hear any cars, though the chirring of grass-hoppers seemed almost deafening and seemed to be tangled among her nerves. Every curve was another reason to hope, another disappointment when she arrived there, panting. The heat was like a great weight on her shoulders, slowing her down. The red glimpses were of a scarecrow, a red figure standing in one of the fields – she couldn't quite see which.

Her chest was hurting, her legs ached. These days she was driving too much and walking too little, but her discomfort didn't matter so long as she found Anna, so long as nothing had happened to the child. She *must* be safe – what could possibly happen to her in a place like this? It was only the glimpses of the scarecrow that were making Liz nervous. It must be the heat-haze that made it seem to glisten – an unpleasant effect, given that it was dressed, or painted, from head to foot in red. She hadn't time to locate it and look at it directly. It might scare crows, but it seemed unable to scare the animals out of its field; from its direction she could hear snuffling.

When she came abreast of a stile, she clambered onto the top bar and perched there as long as she could, supporting herself with trembling wrists. Fields surrounded her, blocks of yellow in green frames. She could see almost to the village. There was no sign of a red scarecrow, and no sign of Anna.

She had to go back, she must call the police. The thought of calling the police yet again was no longer a bad joke; it made the situation real. There was no more room for hope. She should have known the child was in danger – whatever the danger was. She jumped down from the stile, jarring her ankles, and ran for home.

She came in sight of the house at last, and saw her car. Panic had wiped it from her mind as she'd started toward the village. No doubt Alan's car was still parked in Norwich, or would they have towed it away by now? She couldn't believe how long it took her to cross the road, open the gate, stumble down the path as her ankles throbbed, unlock the front door, grope along the hall while her eyes adjusted. At the back of her mind was a desperate hope that Anna would be waiting for her – but Anna had no key.

She grabbed the phone and carried it into the long room, where there was more light. As she fell into the nearest chair, she was already dialling. Shouldn't she check with the wine shop before she called the police? But it was too late. Though she could hardly see what she was dialling – a blotch on her vision made it seem that someone was looming outside the back window – she had reached the police. 'Police station,' said a voice she knew by now. She turned toward the window to dispel the illusion of a figure, but as she did so, the figure began to knock on the glass. It was Anna.

'Wrong number,' Liz said, cursing herself for not hanging up at once; they must be able to recognize her voice. She threw the phone on the chair and ran to unbolt the back door. 'Where on earth have you been?' she cried.

'They wouldn't serve me in the wine shop.' Anna looked nervous and resentful. 'They said I was too young. I had to go to Jimmy at the hotel.'

How could Liz have forgotten that the child was under age? It was Alan's fault that she was so confused. No doubt now there'd be gossip about her sending Anna to buy alcohol – Liz, the alcoholic mother. She ought to feel sympathetic to Anna, but for the moment she felt nothing but helpless rage.

'They all looked at me in the wine shop as if I'd done something wrong,' Anna said tearfully. 'And Jimmy looked as if he didn't want to serve me either. And then I came home and you weren't here, and I came round the back to see if you were there, and you know I don't like it at the back. Why couldn't you know what was going to happen?'

Liz didn't hit her very hard, but she had to do something before her rage became uncontrollable. She slapped Anna's bare arm. She'd forgotten how long her nails had grown. In the moment before Anna fled sobbing into the house, Liz saw the scratches she'd made on the small tanned arm.

She stared after her. Beside the house the sherry bottle shone like amber, a parody of worth. She must go to Anna, say she was sorry, calm her down – but she was a little afraid to go after her. As her nails had scratched the child, she'd had the strangest feeling, so strange that she couldn't define it. And she didn't like it at all.

Twenty-seven

Before dinner was over, Derek had seen off three large Scotches and more than half the wine, and Liz had never known him so drunk. Perhaps he'd been drinking before he and Jane had arrived, for in almost no time at all he'd reached the stage of knocking over ornaments, blushing as he muttered an apology. By now, as they lingered over apple meringue in the pool of shaded light while the afterglow crystallized beyond the window, he was expansively relaxed. When he dropped his spoon and smeared his fingers, or dislodged his jacket, which he'd slung over the back of his chair, he laughed as if it was his night off – as if he hadn't had one for years.

During dinner he'd told anecdotes about his job, and seemed not to care that they could guess who he was talking about. 'That's enough. Don't tell any more,' Jane kept pleading, but Derek was unabashed. 'It's all right, we're all friends here. You aren't bored, are you, Liz?' Liz had to admit she preferred him like this, even though his jollity seemed shrill, defensive. At least it gave her no chance to talk about their problems, which she felt she ought to be doing. At the moment she had more than enough of her own.

As Jane went to phone the baby-sitter for the second time, Derek launched into another anecdote. 'Then there was the old dear who popped off recently and left two wills, one with her daughter, one with her son. That was just the start of the trouble. You see, the children couldn't stand each other. Really – they'd come to blows in front of their mother more than once, and I don't mean when they were kids, either. It was getting her down so much that she'd made these two wills with different solicitors on the same day. She left everything to the son in the will she gave him, and everything to the daughter in the other one. It wasn't until she popped off that they found out there was more than one will. So they both obliterated the date on theirs, so they could claim theirs was the first . . .'

'But the solicitors would have a record of the dates, wouldn't they?'

'You'd think so, but that was where the fun really started. Both the solicitors had lost their copies, would you believe, and so they had to swear to the dates. I tried to tell the children that the result would be the same in the end – they'd each get half – but they're bound to insist on fighting to the end, so half their legacies will go in costs. Sometimes I just don't understand people. In fact I don't know if I ever do. What makes us strange creatures tick, Liz, do *you* know? I expect if Alan were here he'd have a go at telling us.'

There was an awkward silence. Jane had returned, and looked timidly reproving. 'That's all. No more stories,' Derek said.

'Is Anna upset?' Jane said to Liz.

'She may be. Why?'

'I thought I heard her snuffling in her room.'

Liz went up to listen. Through the windows on the stairs and the landing she saw the sky darkening, closing in. She stood outside Anna's door until she could hear the child's breathing. It was quick and shallow. Perhaps Jane had heard her in the middle of a bad dream. Being able to hear her breathing so clearly through the door made Liz feel strange, as if all her senses were unnaturally keen. She was tempted to open the door, but then she might see the scratches she had made on the child's arm . . . She went downstairs.

Derek had unbuttoned his shirt collar and pulled open the knot of his tie. 'Oh, don't do that, it looks so sloppy,' Jane was wailing. 'Just because I am, it doesn't mean you have to be.'

'Now, now, you look splendid.' He was being kind; Jane

looked as if halfway through putting on her make-up she'd lost interest and never finished. 'You'd be a lot better if you weren't forever denigrating yourself.'

'I can't make myself sound any worse than I am.'

'Now, what nonsense. Why do you say these things?'

'Because I thought I might be a good mother, and I can't even be that. There's nothing of me left, and I've got nothing left of you either. I thought children were supposed to save marriages. What a joke! I wish we'd never had a child.'

'You mustn't say that, Jane.' He sounded desperate. 'You know you don't mean it. It isn't like you at all.'

'How do you know? You don't know what I'm like. You haven't cared about me for years.'

Liz wondered if she should leave them to it; it might help them to talk things out, assuming that when they sobered up they remembered what they'd said. But Jane turned gratefully to her. 'Was Anna all right? I shouldn't have made you go up. You don't need me to tell you what to do. I don't know anyone who cares more for their child.'

That was too much for Liz. 'I wish you were right, Jane. I don't like the way I've been behaving toward her at all. She's been getting on my nerves so much, I wonder if there's something wrong with me. I've been acting as if I hate her.'

'Now don't you start, Liz,' Derek said, with forced joviality. 'Everyone feels like that about their children sometimes. They wouldn't be human if they didn't. Don't worry about having those feelings, it's only going to make them worse. Ignore them and they'll go away.'

That didn't seem very helpful to Liz, nor apparently to Jane, who looked bright-eyed with despair. Perhaps Liz hadn't made herself clear; perhaps Derek thought she was simply talking out her feelings in order to cope with them. No doubt he thought she was far too stable to need help. But how could she be stable, after all that had happened to her? She ought to make that clear – but Jane was nodding at the door behind Liz, a warning gesture. Liz turned and saw Anna leaning sleepily against the frame.

'What are you doing down here, Anna? You should be

in bed.' The scratches on the child's arm were livid; Liz's face grew hot with shame. 'Come on, tell me what's wrong, and then I'll take you up.'

The child was hardly awake. 'Want to sleep in your bed,' she mumbled.

'All right, hurry up and I'll tuck you in.' Liz guided her upstairs, holding her elbow gently so that she wouldn't stumble and wake. Nevertheless Anna opened her eyes as she slipped between the sheets. 'Are you coming up soon?' she said.

'Not just yet, no. You try and go back to sleep.' Couldn't Liz even have dinner with friends without the child making demands on her? She stroked Anna's forehead, as much to quieten her own resentment as to soothe Anna. As soon as the child's eyes closed, Liz tiptoed out of the room.

Derek had lowered his voice, but Liz could hear him as she went downstairs. 'Look, I'm sorry I've left you to cope with Georgie all the time. I'll try and concentrate more on local clients, then I won't be away so much. I know Georgie's precious to you, whatever you say. And you know he is to me. We have to take care of him, he's all we've got.'

Jane must be pushing him away. 'All right, I heard you. Don't make me any messier than I already am.'

They were sitting apart and looking away from each other when Liz went in. 'There, you see how much you care for her,' Jane said anxiously. 'You don't hate her at all.'

'You're only seeing how I behave in company. I'm worse when I'm on my own. Surely you've heard the rumours about me,' she added, out of desperation.

'Rumours? Good heavens no! I'm sure there are no rumours.' Derek's quick response made Liz suspicious, especially since Jane had withdrawn into herself. Wasn't there only one person who could make Derek and Jane so devious? But Derek had thought of another anecdote, changing the subject at once.

After that the evening seemed to peter out. They chatted, but avoided half the subjects they thought of. Jane kept asking what time it was and telling Derek that they should be going. Eventually she turned on him. 'I want to get back to Georgie, I don't like leaving him. I wish you wouldn't drink so much, then we wouldn't have to walk back in the dark. I've told you I've seen someone loitering.'

'Loitering where?' Liz demanded, but Derek frowned at her and shook his head. 'Nothing to worry about,' he murmured.

It was all very well for him to assume that Jane was being paranoid; *he* didn't have to stay here at home by himself. Had he forgotten Joseph, and the robbery? That reminded Liz to ask Jane, 'Did they ever recover your money?'

For a moment Jane seemed not to know what she was talking about. 'Oh, you mean the money that was stolen from my bag? No, they never did.'

Even if they had, it wouldn't necessarily have meant that they'd recovered the claw as well. Liz waved to Derek and Jane, until she found that she was waving at the dark. The brooding thunder of the sea followed her into the house. She didn't feel she'd helped Derek and Jane, nor did she know how she could have. Something about their visit had made her deeply uneasy.

She washed up the dinner service, which she'd left in the sink to soak. The Fairy Liquid bottle squirted out a few green bubbles, and she had to suck up water with it before she had enough lather. It wasn't like her to forget to stock up, but then a good many things weren't like her recently. By God, if it *was* Alex who was spreading the rumours about her . . . But there was nothing she could do for now, since Alex was away. She left the plates in the drainer and wandered through the empty house.

It didn't take her long to decide to go to bed. She didn't want to read or watch television, and she especially didn't want to think. She was tempted to wait a little in case there was a phone call – but from whom? If she gave in to that, she'd end up falling asleep in her chair. She didn't want to wake alone.

She crept upstairs to the bathroom, switching off lights as she went. As she reached the landing, she heard a sound in her room. Was Anna still awake? Jane must have been right after all, for Liz could hear snuffling. Perhaps Anna was making the sound in her sleep. Rather than risk waking her, Liz kept on to the bathroom.

She was halfway through brushing her teeth when she turned off the taps in order to listen. Anna must be awake, for Liz could hear, faintly but clearly, the padding of bare feet on the polished floorboards of the bedroom. Liz took her time over washing, in order to give the child a chance to return to bed. By the time she'd finished drying herself, the footsteps had ceased.

Liz eased open the bedroom door and a shaft of light from the hall fell across Anna's face. She looked as if she'd been asleep for hours. Liz tiptoed to switch on the lamp on the bedside table. There was an unpleasant smell in the room – presumably a whiff of some kind of effluent, drifting up from the sea, although, curiously enough, it made her think of a zoo. She would have closed the window, except that then Anna would probably be unable to sleep for the heat.

She switched off the hall light and closed the door, then she slid gently into bed. Anna stirred a little, but didn't wake. Liz must have imagined the sound of bare feet after all. She turned off the bedside lamp, and then she lay there, not moving. She was holding herself still so as not to wake Anna, not because she felt that she and the child weren't alone in the room. She'd felt that as soon as she'd turned off the lamp, which showed how irrational it was. She mustn't switch on the lamp again, in case she woke the child. Nevertheless it was a long time before she fell asleep, and the impression persisted into her dreams that something was lying near her in the dark, lying absolutely still and waiting for her to act. In her dreams she felt that soon she would know what to do.

Twenty-eight

Dear Barbara,
I'm afraid you will think this is a very strange letter, but
what else are friends for? Besides, I expect you remember
when we agreed that if one of us was ever in trouble she
could always count on the other one. Do you think we really
thought we would have to? Anyway, you did want to come
and stay, so I don't feel quite so awful for making you keep
your promise, but I needn't tell you that I wouldn't have if
things weren't very serious. Everything seems to be going
wrong at once, and the worst of it is that it's making me lose
all my patience with Anna. I really need someone to talk to,
and there's only you. I'm hoping that when I see you I'll be
able to describe

Liz read what she'd written, her pen hovering above the
space where the next word should go, then she tore the
page jaggedly from the pad. That was just about what it
deserved. It was a ridiculous letter, so melodramatic at the
outset, so unable to deliver at the end. Surely she was
exaggerating. Really, would anyone feel or behave differently under the circumstances?

She stared out of her workroom window. From up here
she could see where the village curved round to the Hotel
Britannia. On the cliff-top the grass looked ready to burst
into flame – one match would do it. Here and there she
could see spots of colour: striped balls bouncing on the
crowded sand, a green bikini and a purple one, something
glistening in the dark of the pillbox entrance. Pam from
the dairy was milking the goats. Liz had heard her say that
she wished she could take a knife to Joseph, to peel off his
skin very slowly. Everyone felt violent sometimes, not just
Liz.

All the same, she wanted Barbara to come. If someone else were here, perhaps Anna wouldn't mind staying at home so much. She couldn't go on keeping her caged in the house – but even so, she'd felt a qualm as she'd driven home after leaving her at The Stone Shop. She shouldn't have given in to the child, shouldn't have let her out of her sight if it was going to make her feel this way. Now she was growing resentful, blaming Anna for worrying her. Surely that alone was a good enough reason to want someone to talk to. Perhaps she was too close to the situation; Barbara might see at once what had to be done. She picked her first attempt at a letter out of the wastebasket, from among scraps of cloth.

Dear Barbara,
Yes, it's old scatterbrained Liz, and you're right – having put you off, I now want you to come. At least I remember to fill up the petrol tank these days, so we'll be able to go out sightseeing. I do hope you haven't made other arrangements or can cancel them if you have, because I'd love to see you. Alan's had to go away, so it will be just like old times. We can sit up half the night and tell each other everything. So bring yourself and your world-famous bag . . .

That was all the false heartiness she'd been able to manage. Even so, she preferred it to her second try. She might have copied it – it was too crumpled to send – but the thought of copying so much jollity made her feel rather sick. She'd have to write another letter, and that reminded her of Alan at his desk, writing and rewriting. She swallowed before the lump in her throat made her start to weep. If she hadn't lost that wretched claw for him he might be here with her now. She could only hope the police brought it back; she'd keep it here until he phoned, until she could tell him to come back. Couldn't he even let her know where he was? Did he think she no longer cared what happened to him? She couldn't blame him for frightening Anna, for losing his temper with the child. She was beginning to know how he'd felt.

Dear Barbara,
I do hope you haven't gone ahead and made arrangements
for your holiday, because I'd very much like to have you stay
after all. I'll explain why when I see you. Do please come,
because I need to talk to you. Give me a call and let me know
when you can make it, and I'll meet you from the bus – the
train isn't worth much these days. I'm dying to see you!
Much love,

Liz

That would have to do. At least it gave her an excuse to
drive into the village, to the post office, and go and see
Anna while she was there, buy her lunch if she wasn't
ready to come home.

Was she making unreasonable demands on Barbara? She
was sure that Barbara wouldn't think so, not if she
remembered her vow that Liz could always count on her.
It dated back to the time Barbara had failed her nursing
finals because her doctor fiancé had died of malaria in
Kenya. Liz had just bought her first car, a rusty can-
tankerous Mini, and she'd persuaded Barbara away to
Cornwall, to help her through the worst of her loss. Once
she'd forgotten to fill the tank and they'd ended up
stranded in a storm miles from the nearest petrol station,
after trying vainly to find lodgings in a town that was
locked up for the night. In the end they'd had to sleep in
the smelly car, which, for the last three days of their tour,
had refused to travel more than fifty miles a day. It had
been all they could do to crawl on board a train at Penzance.
Liz must have looked as woebegone as she felt when they
staggered into the stuffy carriage, because Barbara had
burst out laughing. 'Don't look so destroyed, Liz. It's
cheered me up no end, really it has. It's the funniest
holiday I've ever had.' And then, more seriously, 'Nobody
else would have gone to all that trouble for me. If you
should ever need me, you've only to let me know.'

Now Liz had – or would have as soon as she reached the
post office. She was certain Barbara would come, even if she
had to cancel other plans. The thought of Barbara, digging

in her bulging bag for yet another photograph or thank-you letter from a patient, or misprint from a newspaper, made Liz feel optimistic. Surely Barbara would cure her of her impatience with Anna? Of course, if Alan came home while Barbara was there, that would be best of all.

She strolled downstairs, swinging her keys. She'd take Anna to lunch in the beer-garden or at the hotel. It made Anna feel proud of herself, and why not? Blue sky shone in all the windows, light filled the house; in the hall the telephone was bright as a ripe tomato. She was almost downstairs when it rang.

She couldn't help starting. She mustn't react as if every call was a threat; it would only make her nerves worse. Anyway, it might be good news. Perhaps it might even be Barbara. She lifted the receiver.

'Mrs Knight? Mrs Alan Knight?' a woman said.

Liz wasn't fond of that usage. 'I'm Alan Knight's wife, yes.'

'He's still away, isn't he?'

'Yes, I'm afraid he is. Who's speaking, please?'

'Don't let him come home.'

Liz must have misheard her. 'I'm sorry, what was that you said?'

'If you love your child, don't let your husband come home.' The woman's voice had already been shrill, but now it was rising. 'Go away – take her far away, and don't let him know where you are. You mustn't stay there, it's too dangerous.'

'Look, I don't know who you are,' Liz said, her throat suddenly so dry that it was threatening her voice, 'but I'm going to put this phone down right now unless you tell me who you are and what you want.'

'It doesn't matter who I am.' The woman's voice came scraping through the earpiece, until Liz felt as though a piece of metal was deep in her ear. 'Don't you understand what I'm saying? Your child is in danger. For God's sake go away.'

Twenty-nine

Anna sat in the room behind Rebecca's counter and gazed at a stain of red paint on the table. Out in the sunlight beyond the counter, painted stones and glass shelves gleamed, people strolled chatting among the shelves or brought things to the counter, everything was bright and cheerful. She didn't like sitting alone in the room; there were too many shadows, the red stain looked too much like a monster, the stones waiting to be made into things reminded her of Joseph, who might well have collected some of them. She was doing nothing in here, she didn't want to glue or even to paint. But if she went out, she'd want to speak to Rebecca, want to speak so much that she mightn't be able to stop herself, and she was afraid to think what she wanted to say.

Mummy was worried, that was all. Mummy was still mummy, whatever she did. Anna told herself that fiercely, over and over. Mummy was worried because she didn't know when daddy was coming home – Anna was sure of that now. Perhaps she was also worried about having lost the claw; perhaps that was the something of daddy's she'd been looking for on the beach; she must blame herself, just as Anna did. Those were the reasons why mummy was on edge, why Anna couldn't be sure any longer what mummy would do.

Rebecca came behind the counter, and Anna put her hand over the scratches on her arm. She couldn't tell Rebecca what had happened, she would feel too disloyal. It was between her and mummy. Everything would be all right once mummy stopped being worried. But the scratches on her arm were throbbing, the stones on the dim shelves looked like blank eyes watching her, the jingle

197

of the bell above the shop door made her jump. When Rebecca said, 'Hi Liz,' she couldn't help growing tense.

'Where's Anna?' Mummy sounded almost as if she was accusing Rebecca of hiding her.

'Why, here she is.'

In a moment mummy was at the counter, peering beneath her thick frown into the room. Suddenly Anna felt as if the dimness of the room was her friend, saying that she didn't have to go. 'Come on then, don't keep me waiting,' mummy said.

Perhaps it was because mummy sounded so impatient that Rebecca said, 'You're just in time. I'll take you both for lunch and then Anna can stay for the afternoon if she likes.'

'Thanks very much, Rebecca,' mummy said without looking at her, 'but I don't feel like going to a pub just now.'

'I wasn't thinking of a pub.'

'Thanks anyway, but we really can't stay.' Mummy's voice was colder, as if she thought Rebecca had meant to tell her off. 'We're going straight into Yarmouth.'

'I didn't know you were going anywhere this afternoon.'

Anna hadn't known either, but the way mummy was behaving, she thought she'd better not say so. 'Well, now you do,' mummy said. 'I'll speak to you again, Rebecca.'

She hurried Anna out to the car and tipped the driver's seat forward so that Anna could climb in the back. Anna had hardly settled herself when mummy slammed the door and drove into the crowd. Why was she so anxious to get to Great Yarmouth? Calling it Yarmouth always seemed to Anna like not calling a grown-up 'Mr' or 'Mrs'. Or was mummy just anxious to get out of the village? Somehow that seemed right, though Anna couldn't tell why and knew she shouldn't ask – not the way mummy was now.

Mummy drove fast once they were out of the village. Usually Anna liked going fast, but now she remembered the day daddy had driven home from Cromer after someone had banged his car. She looked at mummy's eyes in the driving mirror, mummy's eyes hanging above the speeding road, and wasn't sure if she liked what she saw. Perhaps you were supposed to stare like that when you were driving. She looked away from the mirror and caught sight of the letter propped above the dashboard, a letter to mummy's friend Barbara. 'Is Auntie Barbara coming to stay?'

'Why? Do you want someone else interfering as well?' Mummy seemed to mean 'as well as Rebecca', and Anna was dismayed. Mummy seemed a bit ashamed of herself. 'Yes, I've asked her,' she said more gently. 'We'll have to see.'

Her voice was gentler, but not her driving. The road swung back and forth between sandhills and glimpses of flat water, toward the sea, then inland to villages. Some of the villages were hardly even streets. Lonely birds hovered over fields. Anna couldn't help it: the letter to Barbara made her feel safer – though why she should need to feel safe she didn't know. Mummy wouldn't harm her, she knew how to drive. Eventually she managed to enjoy the ride, the twists and surprises of the road, and by the time they reached Yarmouth she was hungry.

She ought to have waited instead of saying she was hungry as soon as she saw a place to eat. Mummy stopped the car at once, even though the pizza parlour was so crowded that they couldn't have a table to themselves. Anna hadn't really meant here, but she felt she'd better not say anything.

The place was full of screaming babies and smeary trays and spilled ketchup. They had to share their plastic table with two little boys, one of whom kept spitting out his food onto his plate while the other tried to tell their parents, who were busy with more children at the next table. Anna's patch of table was sticky with a mixture of sugar and ketchup, and she wiped it as best she could. She sensed that mummy was growing tense with all the heat and noise and cigarette smoke.

When the pizzas arrived, Anna's was lukewarm on top

and soggy underneath. Cutting it felt like cutting a bathroom sponge. 'Poo pie, mummy,' she joked, to help herself eat.

'Nobody's forcing you to eat it,' mummy said, so savagely that people turned to look and laugh.

Anna ate the rest of it in silence, though now she didn't feel like eating. She and mummy could always share jokes – mummy never lost her temper over them like that, especially not in public. Anna always used to say poo pie when she was little and didn't like her food. Now mummy had made her feel like the boy across the table who kept spitting on his plate. Her ears were burning, and each mouthful of pizza tasted nastier. 'I've finished, mummy,' she said at last, and mummy threw a penny into the mess on the table for a tip and stalked to the cashier's glass cage.

Anna felt depressed and hurt. She couldn't enjoy anything now. Mummy held her arm like a policeman as they strolled through the crowds on the promenade. She knew mummy was waiting for her to say what she wanted to do, but there was nothing. The beach here was full of people, she preferred the beach at home. The boating lake was like going for a sail in the bath once you'd been on the Broads. The Crazy Golf was crowded and anyway stupid, and the Kiddies' Cars were full of babies, except for the ones stuffed with big kids, their knees and elbows poking out on both sides. She found a pinball machine that she liked, that shouted at you in a monster voice when you were winning, but when she made to squeeze through the crowd at the fruit machines to look for another game, mummy shouted, *Stay with me,* over the uproar of the machines, as if Anna were trying to escape. Anna felt depressed again. 'I don't want to go on anything else,' she said miserably.

Mummy's lips went thin, and she didn't speak until they were outside. 'Well, what *do* you want to do?'

Anna heard the warning note in her voice, but she didn't care. 'I wanted to make things for Rebecca.'

Mummy glared at her as if she'd been forbidden to

mention Rebecca. 'We're here now. What do you want to do here?'

'I don't know.' The way mummy was, Anna was too depressed to care what she said. 'Nothing.'

'Then you'll just have to do what *I* want to do,' mummy said – but she seemed not to know what that was. She stared about at the beach and the piers, the model village, the Maritime Museum. 'For a start, let's get away from all these people.'

It took them a long time to struggle through the crowds, and she could feel that mummy was growing more tense. At last they reached the river quays, where there were fewer holidaymakers. Barges rocked gently in front of the Town Hall, the smell of fish drifted along the river wharf. Now that there was room to stroll along the broad quay, mummy was relaxing, so much so that she let go of Anna's arm. As far as Anna was concerned, it was too late. She felt depressed and bewildered and bored. She didn't understand mummy at all.

That was how she felt when they came to Haven Bridge, and that was why she thought of something naughty to do. A ship was coming down the river, and she knew that the bridge would have to lift up its halves to let the ship through. If she timed it right, she could be on the other side and mummy wouldn't be able to get to her. She wasn't going to run away, she only wanted those few minutes away from mummy. Mummy was making her feel like a dog on a leash.

As the ship sailed toward the point at which they would lift the bridge, she quickened her pace, ready to run – but then mummy grabbed her arm. Just because she no longer knew what mummy was thinking, she shouldn't have assumed that the opposite was true. 'Oh no, you don't,' mummy said, in a voice like a saw. 'That's enough for one day, miss.'

'You're hurting me.' Anna began to cry. 'You're hurting my arm.' But mummy didn't let go until she'd dragged her back to the car, all that way through the crowds. Anna's arm hurt dreadfully, worse than when she'd fallen off the top of the climbing frame at the nursery. The worst thing was the way people laughed as they saw mummy dragging her along, as if that was the proper way to treat her. They didn't know that mummy was never like this.

Mummy held on to her while she unlocked the door. She threw the driver's seat forward and shoved Anna into the gap. Anna baulked, for she'd seen the letter still propped on the dashboard. Just now it seemed her only friend. She reached for it with her throbbing arm; she'd seen a postbox at the corner of the car park. 'I'll post your letter, mummy,' she said.

'No, you won't.' Mummy leaned in, still holding onto her, and snatched the letter. She must think Anna was going to play another trick, though nothing could have been further from Anna's mind. She ran to keep up with mummy – she wanted to anyway, though the grip on her arm gave her no choice – as mummy hurried toward the postbox. Auntie Barbara would come to stay, she would help mummy stop worrying, help her get better. She was mummy's best friend.

As mummy stepped out of the car park, tugging Anna's arm even though she was hurrying, she turned away from the postbox. For a moment Anna thought she hadn't seen it, then she realized what mummy was going to do. She could only stand there feeling sick as mummy let go of her for long enough to tear up the letter to Barbara and throw the pieces in the nearest wastebin.

Thirty

Liz drove home from Yarmouth feeling surer of herself
than she'd felt for days. Dark clouds were crawling above
the fields, toward the sea, but the darkness couldn't touch
her. She could hardly believe how much destroying the
letter had helped. When she thought of the letters, that
one as much as the ones she'd rejected, she cringed
inwardly. How could she have allowed herself to become
so hysterical? She couldn't even recall now why she'd been
so desperate to invite Barbara. She'd let everything get on
top of her, that was all. No, not everything – just Anna.

That made her feel calmer, as if her problems were
capable of being solved. Of course Anna was disturbed by
all that had been happening, but there was a limit to the
allowances that could be made for her, the liberties she
could take. What had she been doing the night Alan had
chased her along the beach? Perhaps Liz had been looking
at that incident the wrong way. When she glanced at Anna
in the mirror, at her untypically secretive eyes, she was
almost sure she had.

The blackened road veered back and forth like smoke
beneath the crawling sky, the verges glowed luridly. A
phone box stood beside a deserted stretch of road – a red
oblong rooted in the streaming supine grass. As the door
of the empty box creaked open in the wind, Liz heard the
phone ringing, ringing. It reminded her of the anonymous
call, but that didn't bother her so much now; the voice
must have been disguised – it must have been one of the
people who were spreading rumours about her; perhaps
the caller was the source of all the gossip. Now she was
trying to scare Liz away for whatever warped reason an
anonymous caller might have. She must have heard that

Alan had been with Anna the night the child had fled to the hotel – that was why she'd accused him. The call was another reason to doubt that he had done anything to Anna. Anna was rubbing her arm where Liz had held it, rubbing as if the pain would never fade. Liz was sure she hadn't held her that hard. If Anna was exaggerating that, why not Alan's behaviour that night as well?

The house was catching the last of the sunlight before the sky closed up. It looked unreal against the gathering dark. As Liz dragged the garage door into place, she wondered if the child would try to flee from her as she'd run away from Alan. But Anna went reluctantly into the house, into her playroom. That wouldn't save her from answering the questions Liz was determined to ask.

Anna stayed out of the way while Liz made dinner. Didn't that prove she had something to hide? When she ventured into the kitchen to pour herself an orange juice, wincing as she used the arm she wanted Liz to think was injured, her movements sounded clumsy, intrusive, far too loud. That was because the house was empty – empty of Alan. Liz had to make an effort to restrain herself from blurting out her questions.

As soon as they sat down to dinner, she said, 'Anna, I'm going to ask you something, and I want you to tell me the truth.'

'All right,' Anna mumbled through a mouthful of salad.

Liz waited until the child had finished her mouthful; she wasn't about to give her an excuse not to answer. 'What did you do that night I went to the party at the hotel?'

Anna stared blankly at her. 'Nothing,' she said, forking up another mouthful.

'It won't go cold. Leave it until we've finished talking,' Liz said, and the echo told her how loud her voice was. 'What did you do to make daddy chase you out of the house?'

'I didn't do anything.'

Her blank stare, and the forkful of food she was still holding, infuriated Liz. 'Put that down and answer me.

Anyone would think you were starving as well as everything else I'm supposed to be doing to you.' She glared at Anna until the fork dropped onto her plate. 'Don't ask me to believe that daddy chased you all the way to the hotel for no reason. What had you been doing?'

'I was asleep. He woke me up.'

She looked tearful and hurt, but Liz wasn't to be put off. 'And then what happened?'

'He frightened me.'

'How?'

Anna gaped at her as if the question were meaningless. Liz felt her fury growing. 'I'm asking you a question, Anna. What did he do to frighten you?'

Anna's eyes were blank again. She was silent for a while, then she said, 'He just did.'

Liz felt as if she should have known it all along: Anna had fled for no reason, Alan had only been trying to bring her back. He'd gone away because Liz had lost the claw, not because of Anna at all. Even if he had lost his temper with the child that night, who could blame him? Liz had – perhaps that had been another reason why he'd gone away. She stared at Anna, then looked away quickly. If she lost her temper now, she didn't know what she might do to the child.

Anna was behaving as if Liz had already mistreated her. She winced whenever she reached for the salt or the pickles. 'Stop your play-acting,' Liz said. 'I didn't hurt you that much.' The bruises weren't very marked – less so than the scratches on the child's other arm. The sound of Anna crunching lettuce grated on her nerves.

After they'd washed up the dinner things – Anna taking plates mutely, holding herself aloof – Liz decided she couldn't stand any more. 'If you're going to sulk, young lady, you can take yourself off to bed.' It was a relief when Anna did so. Coming out of the bathroom, she hesitated over which bedroom to enter. Eventually she went into Liz's room as though she were doing Liz a favour. Liz tucked her up and made herself stoop to give her a token kiss, but the child turned away under the sheets.

For a while Liz sat in the long room with the telephone by her side and wished that Alan would call. She didn't blame him any more and would have hated him to feel that he couldn't come home. She would have called him if she'd known where he was. Eventually she moved the phone into the hall and made herself watch television, though she hardly knew what she was watching. Here were television cops, beating up someone as usual; here was a play that might be a horror story or a comedy, she couldn't tell which.

She'd moved the phone into the hall, yet she kept glimpsing red at the edge of her vision. As she glanced at the empty space on the mantelpiece, she realized that *that* was why the house felt empty – because she'd lost the claw. The sound of the sea made it feel even emptier, the sea that separated her from Alan, the sea that she could never cross.

Eventually she called her parents. Her father said he was glad of the rest – just what the doctor ordered; she could only pray that it was the line that made his voice so weak. Then she went to bed. Anna was asleep, otherwise she might have drawn away from her mother. Liz could hug the small warm body to her, purge her mind of other feelings, believe that they would be friends again tomorrow, reach inward to the untroubled centre of herself and sleep.

She'd forgotten her strange feelings of the night before until she switched off the bedside lamp. It was as though she'd wakened something in the dark by switching off the lamp – as though she'd wakened the dark itself. It was crouching by the bed, watching her, licking its lips. How could waves sound so much like slobbery breathing? She hugged Anna to her, to cling to reality, but the child was hot and restless. Liz inched away for fear of waking her, and felt as if she were trying to be inconspicuous. She lay stiffly on her back, trying to think of nothing.

She must have slept, for she woke in the night, halfway

through a dream of lying in wait for someone. There was a taste in her mouth, so unpleasant that she stumbled to the bathroom without thinking of the dark, and gargled with cold water. The taste was gone before she had a chance to decide what it was. She switched off the bathroom light and groped back to her room.

The dark was darker after the bright room. She was tiptoeing barefoot through the dark, and she wouldn't see the crouching figure until she fell over it, or until her bare foot touched its face . . . She stumbled loudly back to the door and grabbed the light-switch.

The room was empty but for Anna, and the light had wakened her. 'What's wrong, mummy?' she whimpered, half-asleep. 'Where did you go?'

'Just for a drink. I'm coming back now. Snuggle down and go to sleep.'

'I want a drink too.'

'You would.' Liz brought her a glass of water, which she drained in two gulps. In bed Liz hugged the child until Anna pushed her away, complaining she was too hot. Liz lay awake as the child tossed and turned restlessly, and tried to control her thoughts – forced herself not to tell Anna to be still. Why should Anna's restlessness matter when there was nothing in the dark?

At last Liz slept, only to dream that something was dragging her down into darkness – darkness that was hot and sticky and capable of suffocating her with its stench. She hacked and sliced at her captor, but the small fingers wouldn't let go. At last she woke, still in the grip of the dream, and found that Anna was staring at her along the pillow. For a moment Liz thought the child knew what she'd dreamed. But at least it was daylight now, and they could get up.

After such a restless night, no doubt arguments were inevitable. When they sat down to breakfast Anna said, 'I want to go to the shop today.'

'No, not today. You were there all yesterday morning.'

'Rebecca doesn't mind. She says I can go every day if I want to.'

'Does she indeed. Well, I don't want you to. Not for a while at least.'

'But I want to go. I like being with her.'

'But you don't like being with me.'

'Of course I do,' Anna said – too quickly, Liz thought. 'But I like making things in the shop.'

'You just try staying at home with me for a while instead of running off all the time.'

'I don't want to. There's nothing to do.'

'So you have to go to Rebecca's to make things, do you?' Liz was losing her temper. 'I'm sure you'll find plenty to do if you put your mind to it. If you can't, it's your own fault.'

Anna sulked for a few minutes, clanking her spoon against her eggcup until Liz was ready to grab it from her.

'But I *want* to go to the shop,' Anna said at last. '*Why* can't I go?'

'Because I say so, and you're not too big to have your bottom smacked if you can't do as you're told.' In the past she always used to explain things to Anna; what had happened to their closeness? 'Because I think Rebecca has used you as an unpaid worker long enough,' she said, 'and because I want you near me.'

She hadn't known until she said it how true that was. She remembered how she'd felt when she saw that Anna was going to run across Haven Bridge, she remembered the anonymous phone call, and there were other reasons, too deep in her mind to define. She couldn't help it if she was being irrational: she didn't want Anna to be out of her sight again.

'I don't like staying at home,' Anna was complaining. 'There's nobody to play with. You never have the time.'

'My God, I spend half my life making time to be with you.'

'We never go to the nursery any more. I used to be able to play there and look after the babies.'

'All right,' Liz cried, 'we'll go there today.' For a moment it seemed like the answer: Anna would be kept busy, Liz would be able to keep watch unobtrusively.

They hadn't been to the hotel since the night Anna had fled there. At first there'd seemed to be too much to explain, and then each day Liz had stayed away had made it harder for her to go back. Now Liz realized that by staying away she was only helping the rumours to thrive. It was about time she put in an appearance, if only to show that nothing was wrong.

They walked along the beach to the hotel. The morning haze subdued the heat and gilded the sunlight on the waves. Families were already staking their claims on the beach; children were digging eagerly as terriers, spraying sand all around them. Anna chased ahead over the clattering stones, and Liz grew tight inside. Must the child be forever making her feel this way?

She left Anna in the nursery while she went to tell Gail they were here. Joseph's father was reinforcing the posts that held up the wire netting around the tennis court. He stared out at Liz through the wire. Surely it must be the sun in his eyes that made him look so fierce?

Gail was calculating bills in the office behind the reception desk, her pocket calculator chirping each time she touched its keys. 'Hello, Liz,' she said with an abstracted smile. 'What brings you here?'

'I just came to tell you we'll be in the nursery today.'

'Oh, are you coming back?' All at once Gail's face was blank. 'I thought you'd given up.'

'Things have been a bit complicated lately. I'd like to come back, and Anna would, if you still want us.'

'You know we're always glad to see you.' Suddenly Gail was sounding more like a manageress than a friend. 'I'm always here if you want to talk. I just have to finish my sums first.'

'Go ahead, don't let me disturb you.' Liz went out of the hotel, the relentlessly cheerful chirps of Gail's calculator slowly fading behind her.

Anna was waiting by the gate of the nursery playground. 'They won't let me help.'

Were they going to make life difficult for Anna too? Liz's fist clenched on the gate as she dragged it open. 'Who won't, darling?'

'The big girls. They say they're looking after the little ones.'

'Well, let's see if we can't sort it out.' Dismayed by her own paranoia, she made to take Anna's arm as they headed for the nursery, then her fingers shrank back from the bruise.

There was nothing for Anna to do. The few children who were younger than her were being looked after by their older sisters, Vanessa and Thelma and Germaine and Kate. Kate, an eleven-year-old with large unrestrained breasts, was driving away anyone who tried to play with her baby brother Simon, and the other girls wouldn't let anyone touch their little sisters when they fell down or cried for mummy or wet themselves. 'They've been like that with us too,' Maggie confided to Liz. 'You'd think they'd prefer to go in the pool or look for boys or something.'

Perhaps they did want to, and that was why they kept picking on Anna, pushing in front of her at the slide, ignoring her when she tried to talk to them. Eventually Maggie let her help sort paints and building toys, but Liz knew how useless and frustrated she must feel; that was how she felt herself.

When the children were called in for lunch, Anna went out to the slide and Liz took refuge in the bar. Jimmy was polishing glasses. 'Isn't this your day off?' Liz said.

'Trish rang to say she'd be late.' He was already pulling a lager for Liz. 'I don't mind filling in,' he said. 'Better than being on my own.'

'Your girlfriend?'

'They fined her. Could have been worse. But the college principal had her in – said he'll have to let the schools know about it wherever she applies to teach. I don't know why he didn't just kick her out of college. It'd be a quicker way of ending her career.'

'Perhaps by the time she starts teaching it won't matter so much.'

'Sure, they'll all be smoking in the staffroom.'

'I meant she might find somewhere with a liberal head teacher.'

'They'd have to be pretty damn liberal. And there's the governors too.' He glanced toward the windows. 'Here we are, Anna,' he called. 'Come and cheer me up.'

Liz didn't want the child to stray, but all the same, couldn't she have even a moment to herself? Anna was stepping in through the open windows. 'Why don't you make the most of the playground while the other children aren't there?' Liz said.

'I don't want to. Someone's watching me.'

'Who?' Liz shoved her chair back. 'Where?'

'I know he's there, but you won't be able to see him.'

'Oh, Anna, if you start that again . . .' Well, what *would* she do? There were marks to show what she'd already done. 'Can't you just play by yourself for a while and let me have a rest?'

'Hang on a moment,' Jimmy said, as Anna trudged morosely toward the windows. 'Here's Trish now. I'll give you a game of something if you like, Anna. Is it all right if I take her along to the Space Invaders?'

It sounded fine to Liz. Now that she thought about it, he was just about the only person here whom she felt like trusting with Anna. Plump denimed Trish took his place behind the bar, and gave Liz another lager as he and Anna headed for the seaward end of the village. Thank God there was someone to take Anna off her hands for a while! She only hoped they didn't meet anyone she knew. She wished she had dressed the child in long sleeves. Someone was bound to wonder about the marks on the child's arms.

Thirty-one

As soon as the train stopped, the jungle began to close in. It towered over the railway line and the makeshift station, a platform without a signboard. Perhaps it had never had one, or perhaps the board was being put to use in a village somewhere. In the distance the jungle was being cleared for a road, and Alan could see the yellow machines lumbering about, caterpillar treads churning the earth; he could even hear the faint scream of giant saws over the noise of the crowd on the train. But the jungle felt even closer than the crowd: a dark, relentlessly green profusion that glistened in the steamy sunlight and overhung the railway, its unrelieved luxuriance matting the landscape all the way to the horizon, where it swallowed or was swallowed by the low thick clouds. The jungle surrounded him, it blotted out everything familiar; he felt as if it had overgrown his mind. He was trapped by the jungle and the dawdling train, in a crowd of people who spoke languages he didn't understand. It was no good telling himself that Isaac understood them. Isaac had no more idea than he had if anyone had followed them from Port Harcourt.

He would rather have been in the jeep, jouncing over the potholed roads. At least then they would have been alone, except for the occasional battered flashy car that roared like a mad beast through the jungle.

He and Isaac had driven from village to village, following every stage of Marlowe's route that Isaac knew or could deduce. In one village they'd had to spend all day participating in a funeral ceremony where the corpse lay in state on a shaky four-poster bed; in another they'd waited overnight to consult the chief, whose only emblem of chieftainship had seemed to be a battered portable radio.

They had learned nothing anywhere. Marlowe had had to visit all these places, Isaac kept saying; eventually they would find what he had found. But Marlowe hadn't found a man with his face sewn up. Alan tried not to think about what else might be waiting.

Now it seemed that Marlowe had taken the train to places where there were no roads, and so they'd caught this ageing train, whose carriages announced they'd been Made In Sheffield. Even though they had reservations, they had to bribe their way aboard the train, and bribe their way into this carriage packed with people and livestock. The carriage smelled of cheese and goats and chickens and sweat, a mass of smells that gathered in Alan's throat and thickened in his stomach. He was facing a fat man who held a goat between his knees, his own legs were shoved against Isaac's by a basket of live chickens, which the enormous woman next to him was using as a shelf for her breasts. The enormous woman kept grinning at him like a shark; the fat man had eyelids so heavy that Alan could never be sure if he was watching or asleep. The woman couldn't be a Leopard Man, but what about the man? Alan found, not for the first time even in this heat, that he was shivering. He tried to think of Liz and Anna, to cling to some memory that promised him a future, but all he could see in his mind was the face with the sewn-up mouth and eyes, inching towards him along the flashlight beam.

The train was making restless noises. A line of men was urinating over the edge of the rickety platform, since there were never any toilets. Now the men shook themselves off and ambled back towards their seats. Salesmen were still tramping the aisles of the carriages, shouting over the excited chatter of the crowd, the squawking of chickens and bleating of goats. Singers stood in the aisles, beggars grumbled past them; a leper thrust a fingerless hand at Alan for alms. He was almost used to sights like that by now and they hardly bothered him. It was the men who looked normal who made him uneasy.

The train was groaning forward now. As it jerked suddenly, two men on the seat facing him leaned forward, coming at him and Isaac in a single movement. Alan managed not to flinch back, except inside himself, but Isaac must have sensed his fear. 'Be calm, be calm,' he murmured. 'Nobody here is anything to worry about.'

'How can you tell just by looking at them?' Alan muttered. 'They must have gone unnoticed in Port Harcourt, whoever they were.'

'Exactly. None of the people here could have.'

Alan had to accept that; Isaac should know. 'And it is my sincere belief that nobody has followed us,' Isaac said.

'Not even the police?'

'Especially not.'

There was just a hint of sharpness in Isaac's voice. The man with the sewn-up face had died before their eyes in minutes; they'd had no time to help or to get help. Alan had backed away until he'd felt the rubbery darkness looming behind him. He'd felt like rubber himself, perished rubber. 'We mustn't go on,' he'd babbled, closing his eyes as though that could blot out the sight of the sewn-up face, the sewn lips that had sunken inwards because the jaw couldn't drop, even in death. 'I'll stay here in Africa. Anna will be safe then.'

Isaac had led him out of the dark, out of the warehouse and back to Isaac's home. It wasn't until they were on the edge of Port Harcourt that Isaac had put in an anonymous call to the police, in a dialect that wasn't his. He'd done that for Alan, to make sure their search wasn't hindered. 'You mustn't give up,' he'd told Alan. 'You must fight their influence or it will destroy you. It will never wear off of its own accord.' That had been Alan's secret hope, so secret he hadn't admitted it to himself: that the influence would leave him in time, that he would be able to go home, himself again – but Isaac must know what was best, however unwelcome it was. Alan had been too stunned by Ogunbe's death in the warehouse to do anything but follow Isaac. He hadn't realized how shaken Isaac was until they were nearly home and Isaac had stumbled to a tree and held on, shaking and retching, getting it over with so that his wife and daughters wouldn't see.

Looking back and watching the jungle swallow up the station, Alan remembered the first time he'd ridden a roller coaster, that moment when he'd realized that he couldn't get off, that he had to ride the nightmare all the way. This train ride felt like that – except that the station wouldn't have saved him from the nightmare. He looked away from the jungle as it thickened around him, trees shutting out the horizon and most of the sky. He looked at the goat which was gazing up at him with large moist scared eyes – but not for long; the sight reminded him too much of Joseph, of what Joseph had done. Thinking of Liz and Anna couldn't wipe out those memories; the memories merged in ways he didn't dare to face. He could only think of the days he'd spent at Isaac's home, the last time he had felt at all peaceful.

He'd stayed while Isaac pored over maps, planning their route. The house was bright and spotless, and the gentle waves and the yachts on the lagoon had soothed him. Isaac's pretty wife and their two bright-eyed teenage daughters had looked after him, though Isaac had told them nothing. It showed how deeply Isaac trusted him or believed he would be cured that he'd let him in the same house as his daughters. Yet all this had only filled him with grief that he couldn't go home, go back to his home that had once been like this. He'd yearned to phone Liz, but what could he have said? He could only gaze at the lagoon – that at least had spared him the agony of thinking.

One evening he'd been sitting on a garden chair, brooding, watching the water grow dark, when the younger daughter had taken his hand to lead him in to dinner, and all at once he'd started sobbing, wordlessly and uncontrollably. He couldn't tell how long the child had stayed with him, squeezing his hand, but eventually Isaac's wife had been gripping his shoulders too, and the two girls had held his hands while he wept there in the sudden night. That time had given him back some sense of worth. Someone had cared for him, even as he was now.

'It is a waste of time worrying over what is behind us,' Isaac said, over the uproar of the train and its passengers, bringing Alan back to himself with a lurch, to the inexorable journey into the engulfing jungle. 'If anyone had meant to harm us they would have done so in the warehouse.'

That seemed reasonable. Ogunbe had already been reluctant to talk to them; perhaps he'd asked the advice of someone who'd known his father – someone who'd sewn him up to silence him and as a warning to them. 'I'll be all right,' Alan said, remembering the children clinging to his hands, Isaac's wife gripping his shoulders as if by doing so she could literally hold him together.

'You're willing to go on?'

'Yes, we must.' Alan couldn't see any way to turn back now, but in any case, he was regaining strength. Remembering Isaac's family, he'd realized something else, too: in a sense, Isaac was risking his own home and family in order to help. If Isaac was prepared to go on, how could Alan hesitate? He'd come so far from home that he had nothing to lose and his own family to gain. He'd go wherever Isaac led; he wouldn't be turned back by horrors, even by the face in the flashlight beam, the hands recoiling in agony as they groped to pick out the stitches . . .

'Perhaps this'll be the lead we're looking for,' he said, as much to encourage Isaac as himself. He could hardly believe they'd find whoever had given the claw to Marlowe; they'd need some other break. But as the train groaned onward into the jungle, twilight closing about him like steam, he was growing more determined; he *would* face whatever he had to face. If Isaac could on his behalf, then he must too. Yet it wasn't long before he was remembering that journey as the last chance he'd had to turn back.

Thirty-two

It was no dream. Bright green lizards were scuttling over a clump of tree-roots twice as tall as Alan, and he was wide awake. The jungle dimness closed in like green steam; his forehead was streaming, his clothes were sodden, the giant trunks were dripping rain. Parrots and enormous butterflies, vivid as hallucinations, darted through the greenish air; monkeys swung screaming from branch to branch two hundred feet overhead. Ahead of him, the forest ceiling dropped to the level of the oil-palms, which rattled and jerked with the rain.

A flash of lightning sent bars of shadow slicing through the undergrowth, toward the village of conical huts, green beehives three times the height of a man. Four tribesmen waited at the edge of the village, spears in their hands, their loinclothed bodies slick with rain, their skin the colour of tar. As he followed Isaac, the air felt almost as hindering as the insect-ridden vegetation underfoot. Perhaps that was his own reluctance to go on.

They'd found the lead they had been so desperate for. Leaving the train at last, they'd trudged for miles through forest, beyond the settlement the station had served, such as the settlement was. It had taken them hours of wandering, during which they realized they'd been misdirected from the settlement, before they found the village, a handful of squat square huts where tribesmen sat in the dusty compound as if they hadn't moved for years. Alan had no idea what race they belonged to. They and their chief had sat, growing dusty, while Isaac spoke to them, and Alan had wondered – rather horribly, at that – if this would be as much of a blind alley as Port Harcourt. But the chief had remembered Marlowe, and had sent them where he'd sent the anthropologist: back to the coast, east of Lagos – where the police had told Isaac that the Leopard murders were continuing. All at once the trail was coming clear, taking Alan further into the jungle, further into his dream. Now that something was happening at last, their progress seemed almost too swift. Already they were at this village on the coast, where a tribesman had been murdered by the Leopard Men.

One of the tribesmen in the rain stepped forward and held up his spear. At least this was nothing like Alan's dream of the glade, of the spidery figure and the cooking-pot, Alan thought as Isaac began to parley. He had almost to shout to make himself heard above the clamour of rain on palm-leaves and the rumble of thunder. Rain broke on the points of the spears, crawled glistening in the tribes-men's cropped black curls; Alan felt rain crawling on his own scalp like lice. In the village, the only woman he had seen was hurrying a small boy dressed in enormous baggy shorts into one of the beehive huts.

Isaac was still talking – Alan had lost all sense of time; he could have been standing in the mud for hours – when the other tribesmen stepped forward to stare at Alan's long cracked nails. They stood so close to him that he could smell their breath and see their decaying gappy teeth. Before, they'd looked stern and suspicious, their faces giving noth-ing away, but now they were altogether more distrustful.

They walked around him, prodding and pinching him, and then they stared into his face. The tallest of them addressed him. When he turned his head to ask Isaac what the man had said, his neck felt stiff, painfully tense. 'They want to look at your teeth,' Isaac said.

Alan could only do as he was told. He bared his teeth and tried not to look afraid; above all, they mustn't sense his fear. It was only like being at the dentist's, after all; certainly he felt as helpless. The tribesmen were thrusting their fingers into his mouth, pulling his lips wider until the skin that attached them to his gums felt as if it would tear. The man who had been parleying with Isaac came to look. He stared expressionlessly for a while, then he nodded and turned away. As Isaac followed him, Alan stumbled after them. His legs felt so weak he was afraid of falling. No doubt the three tribesmen close behind would catch him if he did.

The village was more or less circular. Interlocking rings of huts surrounded a central compound. The thatched pyramid roofs reached almost to the ground and rose to points twenty feet overhead. They looked freshly painted with the rain that streamed down them, layer after layer. Beyond one open doorway Alan heard children whispering in the dark – many children. He wondered if they were being hidden from him.

He wasn't sure what made him peer more sharply at a hut on the other side of the compound: perhaps an inkling that the men were turning him away. The interior was dark, and a leaf that dangled from the thatch above the doorway hindered his view, but he glimpsed someone lying in the hut. As he squinted, he saw that the supine figure was glistening. It couldn't be with the rain. He had the impression that there wasn't much left of the still figure in the dark.

Though he quailed inwardly, he managed not to flinch. The Leopard Men must have done that to the corpse in the hut, and that meant he was on their trail at last. Perhaps soon his helplessness would be over. The thought made him halt, forgetting where he was, until his shoulders began to sting. The tribesmen were prodding him with their spears, steering him towards the chief's hut – he could tell it was the chief's by its size. He lurched forward involuntarily through the entrance, and almost fell at the feet of the chief. Perhaps he'd been meant to fall.

The chief sat in a tall chair carved with masks and symbols. He might have been an ebony statue, larger than life, his hands gripping the arms of the chair. He looked old and fiercely proud, as far as Alan could make out his expression beneath the drooping eyelids. An animal's pelt covered his scalp, its empty legs dangling beside his ears, yet it seemed not at all absurd. Old shields and spears leaned against the walls and a rusty notched blade lay at his feet.

Isaac stepped forward to stand beside Alan, and began to speak. Alan felt helpless again, standing there stiff-faced while Isaac spoke on his behalf – all the more so because the chief was staring straight at him. Time passed, until he could no longer tell if he was actively holding his face stiff or was just unable to move it; Isaac's speech seemed as unlikely to stop as the roaring downpour. Alan's legs were shaking with the effort of standing still, but he couldn't shift his feet – he was too aware of the points of the spears, hovering almost negligently at his back. For all he knew, Isaac was still going through the formalities of addressing the chief.

After what seemed like hours, the chief leaned forward, necklaces rattling like dice on his bare chest. He was staring fiercely at Alan and pointing through the doorway. As his mouth opened, Alan saw the gaps in his teeth, but his voice and his movements seemed unchallengeable. Alan found that he was turning to leave even before the spearmen ushered him outside. Without asking Isaac, he knew where he'd been told to go. At least he could go without being prodded; at least he could steel himself against what he must see.

Outside, the rain leapt in the compound, pitting the mud, surrounding each hut with a watery aura, pouring down his face until he could hardly breathe. The spearpoints touched him almost gently as he hesitated, blinking in order to see. Yes, they were driving him toward the hut where the Leopard Men's victim lay.

His stomach tightened as he reached the doorway. He had to see this; it was the first real step of his search. He wouldn't flinch, he mustn't show fear. That was his only clue as to how to deal with the situation in which he found himself – you didn't show fear in front of primitives or mad people or wild beasts.

He blinked the rain out of his eyes, wishing that they could stay blurred. Now he could see that the shape in the hut lay on a mattress. Old though it was, the mattress must indicate respect for the victim. He forced himself to peer into the dark, to see without going closer. The spears were pricking him, he was going to have to stumble in, but suddenly there was no need, for a flash of lightning showed him everything.

He thought he'd managed to steel himself. But it was one thing to be told what the Leopard Men did to their victims, quite another to see for oneself – albeit briefly – the red, ragged hole that the heart had left, the raw stumps where fingers had been torn off, the eyes that had seemed to glare at him. They looked far too big for their sockets now that the skin had gone from around them.

He'd seen all that, but it was only a memory now. He could turn away before the next flash; what else could the spearmen expect him to do? The lightning flashed again, but he was turning; the mutilated corpse was at the edge of his vision. The splintered hole in the chest, the fingerless hands, the eyes bulging from their raw sockets . . . Then he realized that the Leopard Men did this to children, their own children. It was too much. His torso jerked forward convulsively, and he vomited into the mud and the rain.

When he straightened up at last, so weakened now that he didn't care what the spearmen were doing, he saw that they were all staring ambiguously at him. Even if he'd been able to, he wouldn't have dared to move, not even to brush the dribbles of rain from his eyebrows out of his eyes. Had he shown disrespect to their dead? What would they do now?

They stepped forward, and his muscles stiffened until they felt like bone. But the men gazed approvingly at his vomit, poked it with their spears. Gradually, with a wave of relief that made him afraid his legs might give way, he realized that he'd done the right thing. He'd proved he was human, free enough of the taint of the Leopard Men to be appalled by what they'd done. For a moment – only a moment – he felt he could go home.

No, that was a false hope. He had to go on, and now he felt he could. Though he was shuddering, he felt cleansed; the rain was almost refreshing. When they indicated that he should return to the chief's hut, he managed to control his legs enough to walk without stumbling.

Once the men had spoken to the chief, he made a sign for Isaac to address him. Again, Isaac seemed to speak for hours before the chief replied. Sometimes the heavy lids drooped further, and Alan wondered, as his legs twitched with the strain of standing, if the old man was dozing. He wouldn't have blamed him. The endless incomprehensible stream of language was sending Alan to sleep on his feet.

He started awake when the chief suddenly spoke. The old man was sitting even straighter in his chair, his throne. He was gazing expressionlessly at Alan as he spoke to Isaac. Whatever he was saying, Isaac had reluctantly to agree, though not without a glance at Alan that looked apprehensive, or worse. Alan restrained himself from demanding what was wrong. He'd soon know; the chief had raised one hand in a gesture of dismissal. The audience was over.

The tribesmen led Isaac and Alan back to the edge of the forest. The din of rain and screams of birds and animals sounded gigantic as the trees. When he blinked rain from his eyes, Alan could just see the trail that led back to the jeep. Beyond the tribesmen, children were venturing out of their hut to splash in the mud, rushing in again to take refuge as the lightning flashed. As Alan turned to follow Isaac, one of the tribesmen lifted his spear. Alan thought he was wishing him victory.

Once Isaac was sure of the trail, he began to talk, shouting to make himself heard above the downpour. 'I had to tell him you were under the curse of the Leopard Men, otherwise he would have told us nothing.'

'What did he say?'

Isaac hesitated. 'He seemed to know already.'

Alan shook his head, impatiently and nervously. Water sprayed from his hair. 'I don't mean that. What did you learn?'

'Well, they saw the men who did it. They were too far away to be stopped. From the description they sound like the old Ju-Ju men, but I don't understand how they could have survived all these years. They were very thin, not like men at all, so I was told. You saw what they did to their victim. I was told they used only their teeth and nails.'

The forest was growing darker, except where the lightning glared down, and even that blackened the shadows. Screams greeted every flash. 'Does he know where they are?' Alan demanded.

'His men pursued them into the forest to the east, but then they lost them. I had to be careful what I asked. Ordinarily he wouldn't admit that to outsiders – certainly he wouldn't tell the police. It's a matter of pride that his warriors should deal with the culprits themselves.'

Suddenly he was avoiding Alan's eyes. 'He told you something else, didn't he?' Alan said.

Isaac didn't look at him. 'You're sure the claw is lost.'

'Stolen.'

'Gone, at any rate. It's probably all to the good. There's no reason to suppose you're meant to give it back, and besides, one wouldn't like to think that it was anywhere near your wife and child. The Leopard society was exclusive to men, but that needn't mean that its influence is.'

His reluctance was almost palpable. 'Is that all?' Alan demanded, and when Isaac didn't answer, 'What else?'

'I am afraid I may have been wrong about the legend – about what must be done for the power to be consumed.'

'I'll do anything if it works.'

'I ought to have known,' Isaac said to himself, as if he could still avoid telling Alan. 'I should have known what might be necessary to consume the power of a cannibal society.'

'I'll do anything that's necessary.' The look in Isaac's eyes had made him quail. 'Anything,' he repeated, but most of his fierceness was directed at himself, for he felt sick and fearful. He was close to recalling what he had had to do in his dream.

Thirty-Three

'Isobel,' Liz said suddenly, 'have you a key to my house?'

They were washing up after dinner at Isobel's. Outside the open kitchen window, the wind groped over the twilit fields. Though they were too far inland to hear the sea, the grasses sounded like waves. It was that time of day when everything is vaguest, when one's eyes are no longer to be trusted, and Liz couldn't convince herself that the fields weren't full of crouching figures, or perhaps just one figure that was ranging back and forth. At least the house itself was brightly lit. It ought to have felt like a refuge, but, instead, it always made Liz think of a ceramics showroom – hardly lived in at all, each room a display of pottery and porcelain and glass, everything neatly and tastefully in its place: a lonely woman's house. Whenever they visited, Liz was always terrified that Anna would break something, which was why she was nervous as she washed up, passing the child the plates to wipe. Suppose Anna dropped a piece of the best china? It was partly nervousness that had made her blurt out her question.

'Why, whatever makes you think that?' Isobel said.

'That day you were waiting – I honestly don't think I left the door open. Did you let yourself in?'

'Well, dear, what did I say to you at the time?'

'I'm not talking about what you said.' Isobel had been patronizing her ever since they'd arrived, treating her as if she was ill in some way, and Liz had had enough. 'I asked you a straight question. Have you got a key?'

'Yes, of course I have. Alan gave it to me when the three of you went to Scotland, so that I could look in now and then. He didn't ask me to return it, so I assumed he wanted me to keep it.'

'He must have forgotten. I'd like to have it back, please.'

Anna had finished at the draining-board now and was reaching for the jacket of her white suit. 'Good heavens, how did you hurt your arm?' Isobel cried.

The scratches and the bruise were fading. Even so, Anna had kept her jacket on until it was time to wash up, despite the heat, as though she was ashamed of the marks or anxious to hide them. Now she gazed at Isobel as if she dared not answer. 'What's the matter, child,' Isobel demanded shrilly, 'can't you speak?'

'Don't go on at her, Isobel. Did you ever see a child who wasn't covered with bruises?'

'Yes, certainly. Alan never was.'

Only because you never let him play like a normal child, Liz retorted silently. Only because having lost your husband, you were taking no chances with him. 'And those aren't just bruises,' Isobel said.

Feeling accused, Liz hit back. 'We were talking about the key that you kept. Have you been in my house when nobody was there, apart from that one time?'

'Good heavens, what am I being accused of now?'

Liz was tempted to answer directly – to say that she was finding it increasingly unlikely that a common thief would have stolen the claw: surely it hadn't looked gaudy enough.

'You wouldn't say these things to me if Alan were here,' Isobel said.

'A lot of things might be different if he were here.'

'And whose fault is it that he's gone away, I wonder?' She held up one hand before Liz could respond. 'You can't tell me that nothing's wrong. He didn't tell me he was going – he hasn't called me since he went away, not a single call. Have you told him not to?'

'Why on earth should I want to do that?'

'Oh, I can think of some very good reasons why you wouldn't like me to talk to him. Maybe they're the reasons why you don't want me to have access to your house.'

'I don't know what you're talking about, Isobel.' The skirmish had moved to the lounge, where Liz sank onto the rich leather settee. She was growing tired of the argument; she wanted the key to her house, that was all – she felt insecure enough at home as it was. 'I haven't been saying anything to Alan about you. Believe me, I've very little control over what he does.'

'Oh? I should have said it was the other way round.'

'What are you getting at, Isobel?' Liz felt Anna growing tense beside her on the settee, but she was too furious to stop. 'If you've something to say, spit it out.'

'I shall. It's my duty.' Isobel took a deep breath. 'To begin with, just look at the state of that child. Half the time she looks scared to death. You're deliberately keeping me away from her – and if you ask me, that tells a story in itself. Not only do you let her go into bars, you let her be on familiar terms with that barman, who certainly uses drugs if his woman friend does. God knows what else he gets up to.'

Liz decided that was more than enough for Anna to hear, but Isobel held up one hand when she tried to interrupt. 'Ah, I thought you'd rather not talk about him. He's the reason why you spend so much time at the hotel, isn't he? I gather that you don't do much to help at the nursery any more.'

'I get on very well with Jimmy.' Liz was choking back her anger in case it made her weep. Thank God for him; thank God for someone who could take Anna off her hands for a while. 'Who's been gossiping to you about me?' she demanded.

'You know perfectly well that I can't tell you that. Someone has to keep an eye on things.'

'For whom?' Her fingernails were scratching at the swollen leather; Anna drew away from her to the far end of the settee. 'For you?'

'For Alan, I should think.'

'And just what are they going to tell him?' Liz barely restrained herself from adding, 'If he comes back.' Then she wondered why she'd left it unsaid.

'If he could see his child at this moment, nobody would

need to tell him anything. Look at her. She's scared out of her wits.'

'I hardly think so, Isobel,' Liz said, and was unable to look. 'If she's upset it's no wonder, considering what she's heard from you.'

'Oh, you're very skilled at blaming other people. It's never Elizabeth's fault.'

'Do you know, Isobel, I still haven't the faintest idea what *is* supposed to be my fault. All I've heard are a lonely woman's prejudices and fantasies. No two things you've said fit together.'

'Well, let me fit them together in words even you will understand. I think you're maltreating the child because you feel guilty about carrying on with your gentleman friend at the hotel. You're taking it out on her.'

'All right, Isobel, that's the finish.' Liz stood up, feeling less enraged than exhausted. 'We're going home, but first I want that key.'

'I don't know where it is.'

'Then I'll help you find it. I'll tear your house apart if I have to.'

'Yes, I believe you would. And you want me to think you're fit to look after a child.' Isobel glanced sadly at Anna, and Liz had to look. The child's face was pale and stiff, her eyes bright and blank. She looked ready to cry or to run away.

Isobel snapped open her ornate handbag, which glittered like a chandelier. 'There you are,' she said, and dropped the key into Liz's hand. The movement was so quick that Liz was instantly suspicious. Perhaps she'd had it copied. 'Is this the only one you have?'

Isobel stared stonily at her. After a while she spoke. 'Well, you've achieved what you set out to achieve. You've made sure there's a reason not to let the child come to visit me.'

'Do you know, Isobel, I think you're right.' Liz took Anna by the elbow, making her flinch, and hurried her to the front door. The wind had dropped; the air felt plushy, suffocating. The slam of the car door was the only sound in the night. Liz drove away without a backward glance.

Hedges swung back and forth in the light of her headlamps, beyond the unchanging patch of lit road. It was like being on a ghost train, except that there was no crouching figure behind the hedges, nothing that would spring out and frighten her. All at once Anna said wistfully, 'Can't I go to see Granny Knight any more?'

'Anna, if you do one more thing to annoy me . . .' Whose side was the child on? Liz drove faster, glaring at the speeding patch of road. Would Anna rather be with Isobel than with her? What would the rumour-mongers say about her then? She'd make sure they never had the chance.

The garage door loomed up against the enormous dark beyond the cliff. The headlights seemed to foreshorten perspective, to bring the edge nearer. She could hear the sea thrashing about in the dark; for a moment the darkness looked as if it was shifting too. She parked the car, pulled down the garage door and almost collided with Anna. 'There's someone in the house,' the child whispered.

Could it be Alan? 'Where?' Liz demanded.

'He looked out at me.'

That was all she would say. Liz unlocked the front door and called 'Alan' once, before the child whispered, 'No, it isn't daddy.' The lit hall led to darkness and closed doors. Liz eased the door shut and stood listening, but all she could hear was the sea, the constant undertone of the house. Eventually she made herself go forward, switching on lights as soon as she could reach them. The ground floor was deserted, which meant that she had to go up, and up again. Each empty room made the next door yet more threatening.

The house was empty, silent except for the sea and the wind, snuffling somewhere she couldn't quite locate. Had Anna really thought she'd glimpsed someone, or was she just getting her own back on Liz for refusing to let her visit Isobel? Perhaps she'd pretended to see an intruder because of the argument about the key. Just about everything had been her fault – letting Isobel see the marks on her arm, making Isobel think she was frightened of Liz. She'd played up enough for one night. 'Come on, quickly,' Liz said harshly. 'I want to get to bed.'

'I want to sleep in my own room.'

'No, you don't, and you're not going to.' If the child was frightened of her, she'd better do as she was told. Liz's face must have said so, for Anna undressed in the master bedroom and climbed into bed. She looked meek and submissive now – or was that fear? Just now Liz didn't care. She went through the house, switching off the lights, and was sure as soon as she turned off the bedside lamp that they weren't alone in the dark. The snuffling which she hadn't been able to locate sounded closer now; it made her think of an animal, lying there in the dark beyond the bed. Her nervousness was Anna's fault too. She dragged a sheet over her ear to shut out the moist snuffling, and tried to sleep. It was Anna who was making all this happen. Once again, as she hovered on the edge of sleep, she felt that somehow her dreams would tell her what to do.

Thirty-four

Sunlight woke Liz. It filled the room and glowed in Anna's hair as the child lay asleep, face buried in the pillow. Liz lay and gazed at her, at the small, still face, and wished they could stay like this for ever. Anna's mouth was pouting slightly, her left cheek was flushed by resting against the pillow, her hair was a stream of auburn fire. Liz remembered how she'd felt when she had first held her in her arms, remembered the first time she had seen Anna asleep, all the peace in the world in that tiny face. She was growing hot with sunlight and a kind of protective fury. Anna was still her child, Liz wouldn't let anyone harm her. *Nobody* was going to take her away.

She gazed until Anna began to stir, as if Liz's gaze was making her uneasy. Liz inched herself out of bed so as not to wake the child, and then she noticed that Anna was lying at the very edge of the mattress. Had she moved as far from Liz as she could manage? Liz suppressed her annoyance before it could take hold. She didn't like feeling that way about Anna, she mustn't let herself do so.

But she had to struggle with her feelings as she showered in the bathroom. She was remembering yesterday evening; the argument with Isobel, Anna siding with her against Liz. It was no wonder the child was nervous, after all that had happened, but why should that make her disloyal? She simply had no excuse. Liz towelled herself roughly, without knowing how much of her roughness was meant for herself, then she stared at herself in the mirror until she realized that she had no idea what she was looking for - some sign in her eyes of what she felt about Anna, perhaps? She hurried downstairs to make breakfast, to give herself less time to feel.

The smell of frying bacon must have woken Anna. Liz heard the toilet flushing, the gurgle of the washbowl, and eventually Anna came down. She went straight into her playroom. Couldn't she even say good morning? She was behaving as if she were afraid to come near her. She was making Liz tense, which was the last thing Liz wanted. The situation between them had to be sorted out. Liz called 'Breakfast's ready' before it was.

Anna trudged in as if she expected to be punished, sat down and stared at the table, hardly glancing at Liz. All right, then – if that was what she expected, that was what she'd get. No, that wasn't the way to sort things out. But Anna seemed determined to annoy her, picking babyishly at her toast and bacon as if she needed Liz to cut up her food for her.

'Don't you want any more?' Liz said at last, and when Anna shook her head, she ate the child's food herself. 'Have some cereal,' she said.

Anna emptied cornflakes out of the packet until her bowl was piled high, sprinkled the pile with sugar and doused it in milk, then sat staring at it while the sugar dissolved and the cornflakes drooped. Wasn't she going to eat at all? Was she going to starve herself so that people could accuse Liz of that as well? Liz forgot her decision to keep calm. 'Anna, what on earth is the matter with you?'

Anna stared at her as if she were a stranger. If anything had destroyed their closeness, it was her and her disloyalty. At last Anna said, 'Why won't you let me go anywhere any more?'

Liz controlled herself. 'Now, Anna, that isn't fair. Why, we went to Yarmouth just the other day.'

The child stared more blankly than ever at that, but it wasn't Liz's fault that Anna had gone to Yarmouth determined not to enjoy herself. 'You never let me go anywhere I want to go,' Anna said, poking at her soggy cereal until milk spilled onto the table and a drowned plastic whistle poked up from the mound, a hidden gift.

'I can't go to Granny Knight's or make things at the shop – I can't do anything I want to.'

'I didn't realize you were so fond of your grandmother.' Sarcasm wouldn't help. 'And I've explained why I don't want you to go to the shop. Look, we'll go to the nursery today.'

'I don't want to.'

'Oh, Anna, don't be difficult. I can't go far.' But now she'd said that, she wasn't sure why. Suppose Alan rang? 'If there are any calls for me and they can't get through, they'll probably try the hotel.'

'I don't want to go. I don't like the children there.'

'Will you leave that alone!' Anna was still poking at her cereal, spilling milk out of the bowl. 'I don't think much of them either. But there's Jimmy, you know he'll play with you if he's free. I think it's very nice of him.'

'But I want to go to Rebecca's.'

'Look, we've been through this before.' Tension was dragging at the skin above her eyes, tightening on her forehead. 'I want you to stay where I can see you.'

'But I'm not little any more,' Anna complained.

'Then why are you whining? Anyway, it isn't that. I'm nervous, that's all. I don't want you going off where I can't see you – not for a while at least.' But evidently Anna didn't believe her. All at once she had a disturbing notion that Anna might be right not to trust her – that she was lying to her without realizing it. 'If you must know,' she said in an attempt to retrieve the truth, 'I want to go to the hotel because I won't have people thinking I don't dare show my face there.'

'Oh, mummy, why are you being like this? You sound so horrible. You're behaving as if you don't like anyone. Soon we won't have any friends at all.'

Liz had to close her eyes and clench her fists to control herself. Her head was pounding, her hands wanted to be claws. Inside her eyelids everything was red. If Anna made one more remark like that, she'd be sorry – and Liz didn't care who saw the marks. Was this all the thanks she got for protecting her – suspicion, disloyalty, insults? Her nails were scratching her palms, and that made her even more furious: it wasn't she who should be hurting. Her eyes were burning, she didn't think she would be able to keep them closed much longer, even though if she opened them she would almost certainly let fly. She ground her fists against her temples in an attempt to rub away the tension, the tension that felt like a storm about to break, and then she jerked, eyes wide, head pounding as if there was a pneumatic drill in her brain. The phone was ringing.

She lurched down the hall and grabbed the receiver. Barbara, Alan, another anonymous call – the possibilities were multiplying. 'Yes?' she cried.

'Liz?' It was a woman's voice that she couldn't identify. 'Is that you?'

'Yes.' Perhaps it was a bad line – long distance? 'Is that Barbara?'

'Barbara who?' There was a long pause, then the voice said, 'Are you sure you're Liz? It doesn't sound like you.'

'Yes, I'm sure.' Liz was pressing her forehead against the door of the long room; the glossy paint seemed to soothe her, a little. 'Who is this?'

'It's Jane. I should have thought you could tell. I wanted to talk to you.'

Liz closed her eyes and opened them again; the red was fading. She'd never heard Jane so shrill. She had a sudden unpleasant idea that it was the voice of someone who couldn't hear herself, who was beyond listening. 'Well, go on,' she said.

This time the pause was so long that she wondered if they had been cut off. 'I wanted to talk about . . . I wanted to talk about what we were talking about,' Jane said.

Her head was starting to throb again. 'What was that, Jane?'

'You know.' It hadn't seemed possible for Jane to speak more shrilly, but she was doing so. '*You* know,' she pleaded.

'I've really no idea. Give me a hint,' Liz said, feeling as if she were being forced to play some kind of insane game.

'You must know. You brought it up. You do know. You *do*.'

'Look, Jane, I don't mean to be rude, but I've problems of my own.' Her headache was threatening to blind her. 'What is it? What do you want to say?'

Jane muttered something. Whatever it was, it sounded like a cry of despair. Perhaps Liz wasn't meant to hear, because the next moment Jane had broken the connection, and Liz was left staring at the buzzing receiver. Good God, was this yet another worry? She couldn't take on Jane's problems as well, not now. All the same, as she replaced the receiver, part of her mind hoped that Jane would call her back.

She strode into the kitchen and shot a warning look at Anna. 'It's a good thing for you that Jane called.'

'Why? Can I go and see her?'

'Anna, you really don't know when you've said enough, do you? No, you can't go and see her. I probably ought to go myself – she sounds as if she needs help. Maybe I could have helped her just now if you hadn't made me so angry.'

'I didn't mean you to be angry, but don't you think it's true? Granny Knight said you made a reason so I couldn't go to see her.'

'*Anna!*' Liz couldn't stop herself, nor did she want to. She darted forward, raising her hand, her nails tingling. Before she could reach Anna, the child flinched back, so violently that she almost fell out of her chair. That was better; Liz had to stop herself from grinning. 'One more word out of you,' she said, 'and by God, you'll be sorry.'

She stood over the child, hand raised. Anna looked terrified, and so she ought to be. When the child began to tremble, first her lower lip and then her body, Liz had the uneasy notion that she wouldn't be able to turn away. Why was Anna staring at her as if she were a monster? The child was just like the rest of them. 'I want daddy to come home,' Anna whimpered.

'You don't think he'd treat you any differently, do you?' It was Anna's fault that he'd felt obliged to go away. She wished she had the claw – that would shut Anna up, once and for all. The thought made her raise her hand again. 'Just you sit there and don't dare move. I'm going to call Jane, and then we're going to the nursery. Any objections? There'd better not be, for your sake.'

She had to make herself turn away before she could lower her hand. Why should that disturb her? There was nothing abnormal about her behaviour; anyone would do the same if they had to deal with a child as maddening as Anna. Maybe Jane might have wanted to discuss her feelings about her own child. She went back down the hall and dialled Jane's number. There was no reply.

Perhaps Jane had found her own solution, or perhaps Jane had guessed it was Liz calling back and was refusing to answer because of the way Liz had spoken before. The bell made Liz think of a small heart pulsing, a parody of a heart. As she stood there, willing Jane to answer, she heard the back door close stealthily. Anna must be afraid that Liz would hear she was going outside. Liz couldn't begrudge her that. She surely couldn't come to any harm out there.

Jane's phone rang, rang. Liz was thumping the wall with her fist, softly but achingly. Damn the child for making her so curt with Jane! Now Liz felt she wouldn't be able to go to the hotel until she knew what was wrong. But why not drive to Jane's and then to the hotel? That made her feel decisive at least. She hung up the receiver and went to the back door to call Anna.

Her head began to throb at once. She stared about, then she ran out beneath the sky that looked faded by the heat. Her head was so painful that she hardly knew what she was seeing, except that there could be no doubt of it. Goats stared indifferently at her from where they lay on the parched broken grass; nothing else moved on the top of the cliff. Anna had gone.

Thirty-five

To begin with, Anna didn't mean to run away. It was only that she couldn't stay in the house while mummy was being so horrible. Mummy was making the house feel nasty, a small dark grubby place that hated Anna, that wanted to lock her in. As soon as mummy went to phone Jane, Anna crept to the back door, tiptoeing all the way in case mummy might hear her and drag her back.

She closed the door as if it might shatter and stood outside the house. The pillbox was too bright to look at, the grass was as faded as daddy's books in the post office window. The air was rippling with heat above the goats, as if they were cooking. She was still in the small dark place. It wasn't the house after all, it was her feelings – her feeling that mummy hated her more than she would have believed anyone could.

She wanted to cry, but it was too horrible for crying. Mummy wasn't mummy any more. She couldn't be mistaken; other people were noticing too. Sometimes children were taken away from their homes when their parents hurt them, they were put in a kind of prison so that they'd be safe. Anna didn't want that, she didn't want to be taken away, she didn't know what she wanted. Yes, she did: she wanted daddy to come home. If they were all together again, perhaps everything could be the same as it used to be.

She didn't believe that, she wasn't sure why not. She had no time to think. The feeling of darkness and danger was stronger out here, as if something was near her, watching and waiting. Was it the man she could never quite see, the man she thought was too red to be a person? She hadn't told mummy that, mummy would never believe her, she'd only lose her temper; and besides, Anna couldn't say that she'd ever seen him, not *seen* him exactly. She wanted to go back in the house, but she was afraid that mummy would hurt her again for no reason. Before she knew where she was going, she'd wandered to the road.

The road was striped with water, as though the verges were leaking. She walked toward the thin streams and tried to guess when they would disappear. She could see flowers reflected in the nearest strip; it looked so real that for a moment she thought it was, and then, as she took one more step, it vanished. It had never been there. There it was again, or one like it, a hundred yards further on. She wasn't particularly enjoying her game, but at least it was something to do. At least it took her away from the house and the feeling of danger.

When she reached the turn-off to the village, she looked back at the house. Her heart jumped. Mummy was in the back garden, staring toward the edge of the cliff. Anna wavered; she couldn't go on, she had nowhere to go, she didn't dare go to The Stone Shop without permission. She ought to go back. Mummy wouldn't hit her for just going for a little walk. She'd just taken one hesitant step toward home when mummy turned and saw her.

'*Anna, come back here to me at once!*'

It didn't sound at all like mummy. It wasn't a shout so much as a scream. Anna couldn't make out mummy's face, but she knew what it must look like: a mask as cruel and threatening as the voice, as unlike mummy. She faltered – she didn't dare to go back while mummy was like that, but if she didn't, mummy would be worse – and then she ran.

She'd passed the turn-off to the village before she could think where to go. She was running, that was all – running as if she could run away from all the horrible things that had happened. Why had mummy and daddy ever come here, away from all Anna's friends? There was nobody to play with here, nobody to tell about the things that were happening, nothing but the dried-up fields and the dust in

the air and the sunlight that hurt her eyes. There wasn't
even mummy any more, and that was worst of all.

She ran past Seaview, the road that was falling off the
cliff, and then she started to wonder where she *was* going.
Could she hide along there, in the long grass that overhung
both sides of the disused road and was beginning to tear
the road apart? She thought of hiding for a while and then
going home in the hope that mummy would be herself
again, but then she heard the rattle of the garage door.
Mummy was going to come after her in the car.

Anna fled toward the edge of the cliff. Her thoughts
were so jumbled that they could only drive her onward.
The longer she stayed out of mummy's reach, the worse
mummy would be when she caught her, but Anna couldn't
bear the idea of being caught even now. She remembered
how daddy had chased her toward the hotel, and had the
horrible thought that whatever had made daddy like that
had got into mummy too. That made her run with no idea
at all where she was heading.

Eventually she reached a path along the edge of the cliff,
where mounds overgrown with sandy blackberries hid her
from the road. As she stumbled along the path, she began
to sob. She might just as well go back to the road; mummy
would find her sooner or later. She heard the car stop on
the road, the slam of the car door and mummy shouting
her name in a voice she might have used to call a bad dog,
then the engine snarling as mummy drove on. She could
hear how much mummy would hurt her when she caught
her. She stumbled onward, hardly seeing.

Grasshoppers leapt out of her way, seagulls screamed
above her as if they were trying to guide mummy to where
she was. The sandy twisting path and the gathering heat
were slowing her down until she felt there was no point in
going on, and then, as the path turned outward toward the
edge of the cliff, she saw the disused windmill. From
where she was standing, it looked the size of a bollard, a
blinding white bollard with tattered toy vanes stuck onto
one side. The sight of it made her begin to run in earnest,

not to reach it but to get to the house beside it, Jane's house.

The slam of the car door sounded as if it was just the other side of the blackberry mounds. '*Anna!*' mummy shouted, so close that Anna had to hold her mouth shut with her fingers so that she didn't cry out. She stood still, though trembling, until the car moved off, and then she fled toward Jane's. Surely everything would be all right once she got there: mummy had said she wanted to see Jane, and Anna could look after baby Georgie while the grown-ups talked.

She was hundreds of yards from the cottage when she ducked down, panting. The path turned here, toward the edge of the cliff, and the blackberry mounds gave way to a field of long grass that surrounded Jane's hedgeless garden and the windmill. The grass was dry and thick; she'd never be able to run through it without making a lot of noise. Mummy would hear her long before she got to Jane's. She wished she could scream for Jane, but she couldn't do that to mummy, even mummy as she was now. As she kept her head down and peered between the blades of grass, she felt as if she were trapped in a tunnel too low for her to stand up – the small dark grubby place again.

Mummy's car was still moving, though it had reached Jane's cottage now. It hesitated a few moments while mummy craned out, then it went on. Anna dashed into the field at once, desperate to reach the cottage before mummy stopped the car again and was able to hear. Grass-blades clashed around her, a bird of some kind clattered up. She tried to bend as low as she could while she ran, and for most of the way she could see only grass – grass that slashed at her arms and legs. She felt she was bleeding all over, but she hadn't time to look.

When she broke out of the field she found that she had only a few scratches, hardly big enough to see. She was still running, because she couldn't hear the car. Had it stopped, or was it too far away to be heard? Perhaps she couldn't hear it because of baby Georgie, who was screaming upstairs – screaming as if he'd never stop. Maybe she could help Jane look after him. Jane didn't seem to be very good at calming him down.

She ran across the lawn, past the unkempt rock-garden that looked like mouldy bread and rotting wood. The thirsty fields quivered in the heat, the vanes of the windmill looked as if they were straining to turn. She was heading for the back door of the cottage, so that mummy couldn't see her from the road. She wanted to get to Jane as quickly as she could, not only because of mummy – she wanted to stop Georgie screaming. She'd never heard him cry like that before.

The cottage blocked out the sunlight, seeming to fall over her like a pale shadow. The windmill loomed at the edge of her eye and made her feel nervous, as if something else were near. She was straining to hear the car, but all she could hear was Georgie. Now she saw that the back door was shut. She'd have to make herself heard over Georgie's screaming, and mummy might hear her too.

She was almost at the back door when several things happened, all of them in Georgie's room. She heard a thump like a ball thrown against a wall, or perhaps it was more like a fruit. Georgie stopped screaming. She was glancing up at the window of his room – the sudden silence frightened her, she didn't know why – when someone looked out at her.

The silence seemed to swell in her ears. She could hear nothing but her own gasp of horror. The figure at the window was the man she could never quite see, the man who was too red. She could see him now, grinning down at her with his sticky crimson teeth. She could see now that he wasn't a person after all, not with that face as long as an animal's, not with those eyes and teeth.

She had no idea how long he stood there before moving away. She stood trembling, staring at the blank window, feeling smaller than a baby. She wanted to run home, away from her terror, away from the thought of him up there with Georgie, Georgie who had stopped screaming, too suddenly. She wanted to scream until mummy heard her and went in to find out what was wrong. She wanted to find mummy before mummy went in there, wanted to scream at her not to go in. She didn't know what she wanted, and so she couldn't move, not even her mouth.

She was staring up at the empty silent window when mummy came round the house and dragged her roughly away to the car.

Thirty-six

The car wouldn't start at first. It sat coughing dryly in the garage while Liz pumped the accelerator and turned the ignition key again, again. It was giving Anna time to get away, but it wouldn't help her in the long run; Liz would only be more furious when she caught her. Her throat was ragged with her one shout to the child. As she shifted the lever back into neutral, her nails scratched at the knob, sliding off the plastic. The stubborn car and the impossible child were driving her into a frenzy. She was grinding her teeth, until the taste of blood made her stop.

Eventually the car lurched backward onto the drive. She slammed the garage door into its slot and sent the car screeching into the road. Had Anna had time to reach Jane's? It would serve her right if she ran into Jane while Jane was in such a state – but Liz didn't mean to let her. She'd deal with the child herself, by God she would.

The car felt swift as a big cat now, chasing effortlessly round the curves. Fields shot by, pale with speed. If she didn't catch Anna before she reached Jane's it would be the worse for her. She'd teach her to give Jane gossip to spread – how Anna had run away from her mother, how she'd looked scared to death. Liz would make sure she had reason to be.

She stopped the car and craned out of the window, trying to see over the blackberry thicket that stretched for half a mile along the cliff-top. She couldn't see Anna, and the glitter of the sea lodged in her eyes like broken glass. If the child was in the thicket, Liz hoped she was caught among the thorns. It was nothing to what she deserved.

When Jane's house sailed into view, a blob of dazzling white that expanded as the windmill sidled out from behind it, Liz wondered if Anna meant to take refuge with Jane after all. She stopped the car by the house. She could hear Georgie carrying on – at least that ought to keep Jane busy and would give Anna no chance to tell tales. But suppose the child was already past the cottage? Liz drove on, peering at the fields.

A few yards on she halted. Anna couldn't have had time to run so far. She must be hiding somewhere along the way. She wanted to play hide and seek, did she? She'd find Liz wasn't in the mood for games. Liz turned the car, and as she did so she caught sight of Anna. She was at the back of the cottage, gazing up at Georgie's window.

Liz closed her door without making a noise and padded toward the child. She was delighted to find how quickly and quietly she could move. Jane must be in Georgie's room, no doubt Anna had called up to her. Georgie was quiet now, which presumably meant that Jane was too busy dealing with him to come down to Anna. Another hundred yards and Anna would never be able to outrun her, even if she turned and spotted her. Liz would have sprinted, except that she didn't want Anna to notice her. In fact, Anna was so intent on the window that she was almost within arm's reach before she noticed Liz.

Her look of horror made Liz so furious that she had to restrain herself from knocking the child down outside Jane's cottage. But had the child meant that look for her? Hadn't she looked like that *before* she'd seen Liz? Liz couldn't see how; she was just trying to find excuses for Anna, which was more than the child deserved. She grabbed Anna's arm, her fingers sinking into the flesh, and began to drag her toward the car.

Anna was hanging back and trying to open her mouth. Was she struggling to scream for Jane? If she was, it would be the worse for her. Liz yanked at her arm, and she stumbled a few steps, digging in her heels. Liz was about to slap her, whether or not Jane could hear, when Anna managed to stammer 'Mummy'.

'Don't you mummy me.' But it seemed the child had

something to tell her, and it would only irritate her not to know. 'Well, what is it?' she said, calmly if not gently.

'I saw the man.' Anna looked desperate enough to say anything. 'He's in Georgie's room.'

'Which man?'

'I've told you about him.' Anna was almost crying with frustration. 'The man who hides near our house.'

Liz could hardly speak, it was so pathetic. Did Anna really expect her to go into the house to look for her imaginary man, just so that she could run off and take refuge with Jane? She must think her mother very stupid. That made Liz even angrier – too angry to go and see Jane. She'd been considering locking Anna in the car and going back to make sure that Jane was all right, to find out what had been wrong with Jane when she'd called, but now she was too angry to talk to anyone. Was there no end to the trouble the child could cause her? She yanked Anna toward the car and didn't stop even when the child stumbled and almost fell. 'Now you get in there,' she said savagely, 'and don't you say another word.'

Anna was about to open her mouth when she saw Liz's eyes. As Liz shoved her into the back seat she seemed to curl up into herself, only her eyes showing. Liz thought of an insect playing dead. If Anna was as frightened as that, she deserved to be. It wouldn't hurt her to stay like that for a while.

Liz drove home, wrenching the car around the curves, stamping on the brake as they pulled up outside the house. She flung Anna inside and slammed the front door so hard she was afraid for a moment that the glass would break. 'Get up to your room,' she snarled, 'and stay there until I come for you.'

When the child had fled upstairs, Liz sat for a while to try and calm down. She didn't know how long she sat – quite a time, certainly. Whenever she thought of Anna she grew furious. She ought to be thinking of Jane; she shouldn't have let Anna distract her from Jane. She carried the phone to her chair and dialled, dialled several times, though it was clear the first time that Jane wasn't going to reply.

She sat with the unresponsive phone in her lap. Damn the child for everything she'd done today, for days, for weeks! She couldn't bear to be alone in the house with her; it angered her too much. She wished she could talk to someone about Jane. Couldn't she talk to Rebecca? But The Stone Shop wasn't on the phone. She could go there, of course – the shop would keep Anna out of the way while they talked – but that seemed too much like giving in to the child.

Eventually she went upstairs. Anna was lying on her bed, her face buried in the pillow. She didn't look up until Liz began to speak. If her eyes were puffy from crying, so they damn well ought to be. 'We're going to The Stone Shop,' Liz said, 'because I want to talk to Rebecca. Don't think we're going for your benefit, miss.'

She walked one step behind Anna as they went to the car. She didn't have to hold Anna's arm now, she could tell that the child wouldn't dare to run. Just now the child didn't look capable of doing anything except what she was told.

Liz swung the car onto the road and drove toward the village. Hedges raced by, rustling like paper; the occasional car was a brief insect buzz. She had to slow down to a crawl when she reached the village, where holidaymakers were spilling off the pavements of the narrow streets. They seemed to regard her as more of an intruder than they were; when she touched her horn, they stared at her as if she were mad. At least it made the crowd part, parents snatching children out of her way. If they'd had any idea how she felt, they'd all have stayed on the pavements.

Eventually she found a place to park, beyond the post office. The 'Local Author' arrow had fallen in the dust inside the window, and Alan's name had faded like sky-writing. She had a sudden piercing fear that her memories of him were fading as well, but she couldn't dwell on it now; she had to think about Jane, with Rebecca's help.

She pushed through the dawdling crowd to The Stone Shop. It was locked.

Had she mistaken the time? No, it was past lunchtime, and this wasn't early closing day. Rebecca never closed for more than an hour at lunchtime – she always said she couldn't afford to. Yet there was the CLOSED sign, hanging against the glass. Liz knocked on the window, though she didn't expect an answer, and none came. She was standing there in the oppressive murmuring street, feeling helpless and aimless, when Anna said, 'What's Rebecca doing?'

That seemed the kind of childish question that was best ignored, chatter for the sake of chatter, until Liz realized that Anna was peering toward the back of the shop. She screwed her own eyes up, squinting through the glare of sunlight on the window and the maze of display shelves. There was Rebecca, sitting in the dim back room. She appeared to be gazing straight at Liz without seeing her. Liz banged on the window and waved until Rebecca moved.

When Rebecca emerged into the sunlight, it was clear that something was badly wrong. She looked stunned, almost like a sleepwalker. She saw Anna, and was visibly struggling to compose herself as she came to the door. Liz cursed the child silently. How could she ever find out what was wrong in front of Anna?

But Rebecca had already thought of that. 'Hello, Anna,' she said, too brightly. 'Are you going to finish painting your bird while your mummy and I have a talk? I've stuck it together for you.'

Anna looked unhappy, but went to the back room quickly enough. She didn't mind doing what Rebecca told her, Liz thought bitterly. 'Close the door, Anna,' Liz said as the child made to sit down at the table. She watched until Anna did so. 'What's wrong?' she said, though Rebecca's expression made her afraid to know.

'It's Jane.' Rebecca stared at her for what seemed a very long time. 'She's killed Georgie.'

'Oh, no.' Liz felt sick and in danger of losing her

balance; she would have held onto something for support, but everything around her was too fragile. 'When?'

'Today. This morning.' Rebecca was staring at her, but perhaps not seeing. 'She called the police herself.'

Somehow that added to the horror; Liz shrank from imagining how Jane must have felt. 'How do you know all this?' she said, almost accusingly.

'The police came to see me about some of my things at Jane's house.'

Liz didn't understand. She wanted to hug Rebecca and weep, she could tell that Rebecca wanted to give way too, but they couldn't. It wasn't the crowds gazing in the window and trying the door that prevented them, it was the thought that Anna might come out of the back room.

Rebecca seemed to be talking in order to control herself. 'She must have been out of her mind, Liz. They finally drove her to it, that bitch and Jane's swine of a husband. The police said she didn't seem to know what she'd done. All she could talk about when they got there was how she'd been stealing from me.'

Liz stared at her. 'I don't know what you mean.'

'Haven't you been listening? I told you once that someone had been stealing from the shop. Well, it was Jane.' Her face was beginning to crumple. 'I knew it was, but I could never bring myself to tackle her about it. Maybe I should have, maybe she was scared I would. Maybe that was one of the things that made her kill Georgie,' she said, and despite the crowd gaping through the window less than a yard from her, she clung to Liz and wept.

Thirty-seven

Liz sat in the playground outside the Hotel Britannia. It was one of the hottest days of the year. The sun looked as if it had burned a round hole in the metal sky. Children raced one another in the pool, splashed out and shook their sparkling hair; younger children were pleading with their parents for ice creams. Anna was in the playground, looking after the youngest ones. Liz watched her, trying not to hate the child.

It was all Anna's fault. If she hadn't annoyed Liz so much, Liz might have been some help when Jane had phoned. If Anna hadn't run away, Liz could have gone straight to Jane's; she might have been in time, she might have . . . She was in an agony of guilt. Worst of all, if Anna hadn't started her nonsense about the man who was hiding, Liz might have gone in to Jane anyway. If it hadn't been for Anna, Georgie might still be alive. How could Liz not hate her?

She was doing her best, telling herself that Anna couldn't have known, being determinedly gentle with the child, to compensate. Couldn't Anna tell that she ought to take care? Apparently not, for now she was gazing longingly at the pool, then at Liz. Liz shook her head, but still the child came over to her. 'Can't I have just a little swim?' she pleaded.

'Not now. Not while the big ones are in the pool.' Not while a swimsuit would expose the marks on her shoulder from the day Liz had caught her outside Jane's, scratches and a swollen purple bruise. 'Anyway,' Liz said triumphantly, 'you haven't got a swimsuit with you.'

'Can I take my blouse off, then? I'm so hot.'

Was the child determined to let people see her injuries?

248

'Keep it on,' Liz said. 'I haven't taken mine off, have I? We'll both be elegant. We hardly ever wear these blouses Granny Knight bought us.'

Anna looked sulky. 'Go on, Anna,' Liz said; Maggie the nursery girl was approaching, and Liz didn't want to lose her temper in front of her. 'Look, the little ones don't know what to do with themselves. You go and look after them.' Not the way you looked after Georgie, she thought before she could stop herself.

For a while she sat and talked to Maggie, then she kept an eye on the children while Maggie went in to lay the nursery tables for lunch. A seven-year-old brought her twin to Liz for first aid. Both little girls were silent, pale and tight-lipped while Liz tended to the gash, caused by a falling tricycle. Why couldn't Anna be like them? Had she ever been? She was copying Liz now, giving first aid to a reluctant toddler – 'I'll be nurse because you've hurt yourself,' she said. For the first time Liz wondered if the toddlers wanted Anna to look after them.

She was brooding about that when Ned came to her. 'Gail would like a word with you.'

The foyer was stifling, and smelled of dusty plants and carpet shampoo. Gail was fanning herself with a bunch of receipts; she glanced sharply at the long sleeves. 'We're both a bit sunburned,' Liz said glibly.

Gail shrugged that off. 'Derek has managed to get Jane into a private ward near Norwich,' she said. 'Rebecca and I are going to see her. Will you come?'

'I should come, Gail, I know I should, but I don't think I can, not yet. You do understand, don't you? Maybe when Alan comes back, when I'm not on my own.'

Gail raised her eyebrows, though she was obviously trying to understand. 'And I don't want to leave Anna,' Liz said desperately. 'We couldn't very well take her with us.'

Why had she said that? She felt she was saying too much in an attempt to hide the truth.

'You could leave her in the nursery,' Gail suggested. 'It would only be for the afternoon.'

'Well, as I say, Anna isn't really the problem.' She wished she hadn't mentioned the child at all; Gail had seemed altogether too eager to take Anna off her hands. 'It's just me, Gail. I can't help how I feel. Tell Jane I'm thinking of her,' she said, which sounded so feeble that she wished she hadn't said it at all.

She wandered through the ground floor of the hotel, trying to think before she went back to Anna. Children were clambering on armchairs in the lounge until their father chased them out; in the games room opposite, a pair of table-tennis bats formed a round-winged insect on the table. She couldn't go to see Jane, not yet – not until she knew what to do about the claw.

She was sure that Jane had taken it. Rebecca had virtually told her so: she'd said she didn't believe that any money had been stolen from Jane's bag that day at Liz's house. The claw must be somewhere at Jane's, too well hidden for the police to find. She couldn't raise the subject in front of anyone else, she didn't know why. The more she thought about the claw, the more urgent it seemed to retrieve it, yet thinking about it seemed to snag her thoughts, preventing her from planning coherently. When she heard the rattle of the grille she went to talk to Jimmy in the bar.

He wanted to talk about Jane; everybody did. 'You can't assume any kids are safe, whatever their parents are like in public,' he said morosely. 'You never know what goes on in their homes. You can't know what they do to their kids when nobody else is watching.'

He was making her uncomfortable, not least because she wasn't sure that he was talking solely about Jane. What did he know about it? He hadn't even started teaching, and even when he did he'd have no idea what it was like to have to put up with a child all the time, without being able to send it home at the end of the day, or take a holiday from it at all. He was just like the rest of them, trying to make her think there was something wrong with her. Since he didn't seem disposed to change the subject until he'd finished lecturing, she took her drink out of the bar.

The sun made her eyes ache. Why should it worry her that she couldn't see her surroundings straight away? Now she could: Anna was helping a toddler up the steps to the slide, though he didn't look entirely convinced that he wanted to go; nobody was in sight who shouldn't be. Liz sat down at a table on the grass to watch, the plastic chair burning her thighs and back for a moment, before the heat faded. Then she made to dodge into the bar, but restrained herself. It was too late. Alex had already seen her.

'Hello, Alex,' Liz said, as coldly as she could. 'Finished your filming?'

'I've finished that one. I've some more glamour ads to do.' She sat opposite Liz and stretched her long polished legs into the sunlight, to show them off or to add to their tan. 'I heard about Jane. I wish I hadn't been away.'

'Why?'

'Well, what a question! She had nobody to turn to, had she? Derek was away. She couldn't cope on her own. Things finally proved too much for her.'

Liz stared at her. 'Something certainly did.'

'I don't know why you're looking at me like that. What do you mean?'

Liz hadn't the patience to reply to that. 'What do *you* mean, spreading rumours about me? It was you who told people that I'd left Anna alone the night I came to Gail's party, wasn't it?'

'Oh, Liz, I really can't remember. I may have passed on some story of the kind. I'm sorry if it wasn't true – I wasn't at the party, after all. Don't let's fall out. Hasn't there been enough viciousness without our starting too? We ought to rally round.'

Liz almost laughed out loud, though without a trace of humour. 'Surely you can't believe that Jane would want to see you.'

'Well, why not? I'm her friend too, aren't I? I should have thought we could forget our differences under the circumstances. I'll do everything I can to help.'

Liz punched the table-top to restrain herself from lashing

out. The noise was so loud that parents glanced across from the nursery. 'Are you really as stupid as you make out, Alex? Haven't you done enough?'

'If you're trying to imply that what happened was my fault, I think you're very cruel.' She looked as if she were trying to suppress the moisture in her eyes. 'In any case, I don't agree with you. I really think I relieved some of the strain on their marriage. Derek came to me for things he couldn't get from Jane.'

'I'm sure he did.'

'It's true, however awful you try and make it sound. Do you know that she hadn't let Derek touch her since she was pregnant? Jane didn't kill Georgie because of me, she did it because she should never have had a child. I know we don't like to think of it happening to someone we know, but it happens all the time. You can hardly pick up a newspaper these days without reading of another case.'

Liz hid her fists under the table; her nails were tingling again. 'Do you honestly think it was just another case of a mother losing patience – another battered baby? Have you any idea what Jane did?'

'I know she killed him, and that's all I want to know. I should think that's all you know, as well. You weren't there, were you?'

'No, but I've heard what happened. Someone who was there was so appalled he couldn't keep from talking.' No, but she'd been as near as made no difference, and she'd talked to Jane on the night of their dinner about wanting to harm one's child; she might as well have been at Jane's side, egging her on. 'She didn't just kill him; she tore him to pieces. You made her do that by giving her too much to cope with.'

Alex stood up, overturning her chair. 'I think you're the cruellest person I've ever met. I never want to speak to you again.' She stumbled away, one hand at her eyes, and vanished around the side of the hotel. The parents who had been watching turned away.

But, curiously, speaking her mind hadn't made Liz feel

any better, however much Rebecca and Gail would have applauded her; instead she felt exhausted and depressed. Accusing Alex had simply been a way of avoiding her own guilt and Anna's, bloody Anna's. She decided to go back and talk to Jimmy. It was easy to coax him into talking about pleasant things, that was part of his job. Anyway she felt sorry for him; this wasn't much of a preparation for having to deal with a roomful of children. One was more than enough.

She talked to him until the bar closed, then she collected Anna from the nursery, where she and another girl were playing tennis with plastic bats and a sponge ball. Anna looked bored and resentful. At least Maggie had given her lunch; Liz realized that she'd eaten lunch herself at some time during her stay in the bar, and that she was quite drunk. It was a good job she hadn't brought the car. Being drunk didn't make her feel any less guilty about Jane, though.

Her guilt followed her home. The sun swelled as it sank toward the hazy fields; families trudged up from the beach, slow as a herd of cattle in search of water. Anna was tired, and beginning to whine: 'My shoulder hurts. It hurts, mummy. It *hurts*.' She sounded as if she might go on like that all the way home. 'You won't die of it,' Liz snapped, and the child shut up.

Liz was unlocking the front door when the phone started ringing. Perhaps it meant company. She ran down the hall and lifted the receiver. 'Liz Knight,' she said.

'Mrs Knight? Hetherington here. I fear I owe you an apology.'

Her momentary panic faded; he couldn't know about the claw. 'Why's that?' she said.

'Because I'm afraid I let someone find out your number. Joanna Marlowe, the wife of the anthropologist who gave your husband the artefact. Your number was on my desk when she came to my office the other day, and I suspect she may phone you. Please make allowances for her – I expect you know her husband killed himself. You'll appreciate that she's still in a hysterical state.'

Liz knew at once that she'd already had the call – hers was the anonymous shrill voice; but she couldn't admit to it, she wanted time to think. 'Thank you for letting me know,' she said.

'I've been trying for some days. While we're speaking, perhaps I can ask you if there is any news of the artefact.'

'No,' she said at once. 'None at all.'

'Well, please do inform me if anything transpires.'

She put down the receiver and gazed at nothing. She couldn't think now, not until Anna was in bed. Anna had taken off her blouse and was waiting for Liz to notice her shoulder. The bruise was fading a little, which made the scratches more vivid. 'It doesn't look too bad,' Liz said, refusing to feel guilty; the child had asked for it. 'Just don't lie on it.'

'Oh, then can I swim tomorrow?'

'No, not yet. You said it was hurting. You mustn't go in the pool until it's better.' Liz couldn't help enjoying the way Anna had talked herself into that. 'And you must wear a blouse until it is.'

'I don't want to. It looks stupid.'

'Of course it doesn't. I don't, do I?' Why must all her conversations with Anna be so excruciatingly banal? 'Now, no arguments. You know what happened the last time you made me lose my temper.'

They had nothing to say to each other at dinner. If Anna wanted to be sullen, Liz decided she was best ignored. The silence intensified the sounds of eating, as though they both were trapped in a film whose soundtrack was turned up too high – the sea might have been the hiss of the soundtrack. Eating made her feel uncomfortable, as if she'd forgotten how to do it properly. The meat tasted overcooked. Perhaps it was.

Afterward Anna found an Enid Blyton to reread, which at least kept her quiet for a while. Nevertheless Liz couldn't think while the child was in the room; she might want to mumble to herself, she might give herself away somehow; she felt too confused to plan silently. The night closed in, the sea rumbled forward; Liz dozed and felt that the house was sinking into dark water, that she was sinking into a darkness within herself, where something raw was waiting. When she jerked awake and saw that Anna was nodding over the book, she sent her up to bed.

Being alone didn't help much. There were too many thoughts and feelings to deal with: Joanna Marlowe, who'd sounded like a spiteful villager but might have had a message for her after all; the way Liz had accused Alex, as if that would stop her feeling guilty herself; Jane and Georgie and Alan and Anna and, thank God, Jimmy; the claw . . . but whenever she thought of the claw her thoughts slipped awry, and she had to start again.

For some time she dozed. When she woke, she was convinced that she'd made Jane kill Georgie so that she could steal back the claw. The idea had the internal logic of a dream, but was more difficult to shake off than that; she couldn't help feeling that it contained some distorted inkling of the truth. She forced her eyes open, and at once her heart was pounding. Anna was in the doorway, staring fearfully at her.

Why was she looking like that? Liz would give her a reason – she was scared of the claw. She struggled to control her feelings, to wake herself up. 'What's the matter?' she demanded. 'What are you doing downstairs?'

'I don't want to be up there by myself.' She sounded as if asking Liz to come upstairs was very much the lesser of two evils. 'I'm scared. There's someone up there.'

Liz knew she'd bolted the front and back doors; nobody could have got in. Anna was starting all over again; she'd learned nothing. As Liz sprang to her feet, the house seemed to darken about her. Anna flinched back, but that wasn't enough for Liz any more.

'Just you remember what happened to Georgie,' she said.

Thirty-eight

When she heard what she was saying, Liz sat down at once. She couldn't have been properly awake, otherwise she'd never have said such a terrible thing. She wanted to go to Anna, but she made herself stay in the chair; Anna was safer that way. In any case, Liz couldn't look at her, couldn't look up while the room was so dark. 'I've changed, haven't I?' she said at last.

Anna said nothing. Perhaps she was afraid to speak, or agreed too deeply to be able to reply. 'I'm sorry. So much has been happening to me,' Liz said, and stopped herself in case she went into details. 'Do you think you should go away for a while?'

Still no response. When Liz looked up, Anna was gazing sullenly at her. She could hardly be blamed if she no longer trusted Liz, no longer knew how to take her. 'I mean it,' Liz said. 'Would you like to stay in the Lakes for a while?'

'Yes.' Anna's voice was small and miserable, as if she wanted Liz to know that she felt rejected. There was nothing Liz could do about that; there wasn't time for love to get in the way; she had to make sure while she could that the child would be safe. Just now she felt that she mustn't touch Anna – even when the child flinched as Liz went into the hall and picked up the phone.

The darkness was all around her, oppressive and prickly as fever; it felt like the threat of a total loss of control. She mustn't dawdle, she had to make the call before she began to have second thoughts. She carried the phone into the long room and sat down, or fell down. 'I'll get you there,' she promised.

She dialled as quickly as she could. The bell sounded distant and hollow, the way calls sounded when Alan picked up one of the extensions while she was on the phone. For a moment she thought someone upstairs was listening in, until she made herself wake. The darkness lingered, prickling. Suddenly the ringing ceased. 'Hello, who's this?' her father said.

He sounded more like his old self than the last time she had called. 'It's Liz,' she said.

'Well, that's always good news. How are you?'

'More to the point, how are you?'

'Oh, pretty well. You'd never know the old machine had been in for repairs. Just a bit sick of sitting around at home, that's all.'

'Would you like a little visitor to cheer you up?'

'She's always welcome, you know that.' But there was a slight hesitation in his voice, as if he regretted having made light of his condition quite so much. 'It's just that your mother has rather a lot to do while I'm convalescing.'

'She won't be any trouble. Will you?' She glanced sharply at Anna; she didn't mind if the child was scared, so long as she did as she was told. 'I really think she needs a change, and to be honest, so do I.'

'Well, let's see how things are in a couple of weeks.'

'I was wondering if she might be able to come sooner.' The darkness was closer, the prickling was worse. Why hadn't she thought out what to say before she phoned? 'You see,' she said desperately, 'something very tragic happened to one of our friends. It's affecting us both rather badly. Our friend killed her baby, you see. I've got to do what I can for her, and with Alan away, there's nobody to look after Anna.'

She'd turned away from the child; Anna must know she was lying. Or *had* Anna been affected by the news of Georgie's death? It was difficult to tell when she was so withdrawn. Liz closed her eyes; at least the dark in there was less unnatural, though it seemed darker in there than it ought to be.

'Well,' her father said eventually, 'that is a bad situation. Very bad.' He must be tapping the mouthpiece of the phone; the scrape of fingernails on plastic was very loud. 'I don't see how we can refuse. When would you want us to have her?'

'Would tomorrow be too soon?'

'Tomorrow?' He sounded taken aback. 'Just hold on while I have a word with your mother.'

She held onto the prickly receiver. Of course the plastic was smooth as ever; the prickling was in *her*, and so was the dark. She must have been mistaken about the sound of fingernails; it was continuing even now that her father had put down the phone. Apart from that sound there was a prolonged silence, until she heard his footsteps returning. Were they so slow because of his illness, or because he was about to disappoint her? She closed her eyes again, on prickly darkness.

'Are you there?' he said. 'Under the circumstances, we don't mind if she comes tomorrow.'

'Oh, fine. Great. Thanks ever so much.' She opened her eyes; she could stand the hovering darkness now. 'I'll run her to London and put her on the early train,' she said. As soon as they'd agreed on arrangements for meeting Anna at his end, Liz rang off. 'That'll be nice, won't it? Perhaps you can stay with them until daddy comes home.'

Certainly Anna seemed happier – relieved to be escaping, perhaps, but Liz couldn't brood about that just now. 'Shouldn't we pack?' Anna said, as if she needed to see that before she could believe her good luck.

'Yes, we should.' Packing might tire them both enough to sleep and by then Anna would have forgotten all her nonsense about there being someone upstairs. Perhaps not, however: for once they reached her bedroom she kept glancing nervously toward the wall. There was nothing beyond the posters – giant enlargements of flowers with a bee the size of Liz's head emerging from a rose – except Liz's workroom with its telephone extension. The darkness was lingering, but Liz could stand it now. As the huge flowers glowed through it, she was reminded of a jungle. Would Alan ever phone?

Anna fell asleep before she did. No doubt that showed how glad she was to be leaving. Liz lay and wondered about Joanna Marlowe. Was the woman crazy because of her husband's suicide? There were too many things Liz didn't understand, and trying to think about them made her prickly all over. Once Anna was out of the way, she'd be able to think.

She hushed the babel of her thoughts and tried to sleep. She still felt she was being watched in the dark. She could stand it for one more night – she knew she'd be rid of it once she was rid of Anna – but what on earth made her think that? It must be one of those thoughts that float on the edge of sleep, less thoughts than dreams. Soon she was asleep.

Anna woke her as soon as it was light. 'You said I was going to stay with granny and grandpa today.' She sounded afraid that Liz had changed her mind. 'So you are,' Liz said, hugging her and rolling out of bed. After last night's prickly darkness she felt full of sunshine, just like the house. It seemed the kind of day when nothing could go wrong.

At breakfast she grew wistful. 'You'll write to me, won't you? And I'll phone you now and then.' Anna promised to write, mumbling through a mouthful of cereal; she was obviously anxious to get away, and Liz couldn't blame her. She'd make it up to Anna when she came home, make up for the way she'd treated her. She only hoped that Anna would be willing to come back.

She left the dishes in the sink and carried Anna's case downstairs. It was really too small for her now: a toddler's case, plastered with souvenir stickers, its corners scuffed like the toes of a three-year-old's shoes. Liz remembered the first time Anna had carried the case – a sunny Cornish day, Alan squeezing her arm as the pair of them watched Anna trotting proudly ahead. Suddenly she felt her eyes grow moist. She locked the front door quickly and dropped the case outside the garage. She heaved at the garage door, which flew up, rattling. She had to stoop again for the case, and so she caught sight of the pool of brake fluid at once.

As she bent lower to peer under the car, the prickly darkness closed in. She could see at once that the brakes would be useless. She hadn't used the car since Rebecca had told her about Jane, and now she remembered driving furiously home from The Stone Shop, too angry and distressed even to look at Anna. Had she driven over a bump in the road too violently? If so, it was a miracle they hadn't had an accident on the way home.

Anna was gazing at the pool of fluid, and the corners of her mouth began to droop. This was her fault too, Liz thought – not that that was any help. 'Does that mean I can't go?' Anna said miserably.

'Not at all. We'll get you there.' Liz was thinking fast: she'd intended to drive Anna to London and put her on the direct train from Euston; now they'd have to take the train from the village to Norwich, then another from Norwich to Euston. Good God, she'd be away all day. She slammed the garage door into its groove and grabbed the suitcase. 'We'll have to hurry,' she said.

By the time they were halfway to the village, she was panting. Anna kept running ahead to the next curve, glancing back. 'Go on,' Liz cried. The day was already hot; the hedges looked dusty as her throat was becoming; the baking air seemed to cling to her, an additional weight that was imperceptible but enervating. A couple of families passed her on their way to the beach; the adults smiled sympathetically, the children stared. What time was the train? At least she hadn't heard it. Surely that meant it hadn't gone.

The village was crowded. Old folk ambled, fanning themselves with hats or newspapers, slowing down their progress. Birds fluttered back and forth under the roof of the bus shed, cottages blazed like sheets in a detergent ad. At least there was no train at the station. The tiny booking hall was deserted; the ticket window was a frame from which the painting had been removed, glass over brown board; the hall smelled like an attic, dust and old wood. Perhaps you had to pay on the train. If not, they could pay at Norwich.

She sat and watched the crowds and tried not to think how long she'd be away while Alan might be trying to contact her. His faded display had gone from the window of the post office, someone else's bright new books had moved in. Now and then she heard an engine, but it was always a barge on the waterways. Shouldn't she accompany Anna all the way, rather than putting her on the train at Euston? It was a long way for a six-year-old to travel on her own.

Anna was growing restless, marching up and down the platform. 'Isn't it coming yet? How long will it be?' She sounded afraid that Liz would change her mind and take her back home. There was chugging in the distance, along the brownish railway lines – but it must have been another barge, because the sound was drifting away. Liz was growing as fidgety as Anna; she didn't like being away from the phone for so long. She was beginning to wonder if it was such a good idea to send Anna away after all.

Anna was plucking at the long sleeves of her blouse. 'I'm so hot, mummy. Can I go and get a drink?'

'Better not, in case the train comes.' The nearest shop for lemonade was the post office, and all at once she was afraid of losing Anna in the crowd. Passers-by were gazing at her as if she were some kind of tourist attraction, a wax figure on a disused station. She felt like wax – melting wax. Three youths in denim stared at her for a while before swaggering toward the beach. 'Don't miss your bus,' one shouted, which she thought especially pointless.

She went to the end of the platform and stared along the tracks. She'd never seen them looking so disused. Surely the train ought to be here by now. Suppose it had been cancelled? These trains sometimes were. If only there were someone to ask . . . Then she heard footsteps in the booking hall, three steps on the hollow boards; three were all it took to cross the hall. She turned as he emerged onto the sunlit platform. It was Jimmy.

'What do you think you're waiting for?' he said.

'Would a train be too much to hope for?'

'I'm afraid it would,' he said, and her innards lurched. 'Surely you heard? There's an unofficial strike to try and stop them closing the line. No trains until further notice.'

'Oh no,' Liz said, more for Anna's sake than because of any disappointment of her own.

'Where were you wanting to go?'

'I wasn't going anywhere. I was sending Anna to stay with my parents,' Liz said, hugging the child in a bid to console her. 'We'd been getting on each other's nerves, hadn't we, Anna? Something had to be done. We'll just have to get on with each other, that's all.'

It sounded false even to her, especially since Anna had pulled away. 'What brings you to the village?' Liz said, for the sake of something to say.

'Mostly keeping out of the way. Mrs Marshall's in a foul mood. She's had a cancellation for the next seven days, and she's got no chance of filling it now.'

'Perhaps I'll call in and commiserate later.' For a moment, until she realized what she was thinking, Liz thought of taking up the cancelled booking, just to get them out of the house. Was she mad? No – she was letting Anna confuse her again, that was all. It was Anna's fault, just like everything else. Why had she let the child get to her so badly? What tales would Anna have told her parents about her? Anna could just stay with her, where she belonged – and she'd better behave herself; she'd made Liz waste enough time as it was. Liz took Anna's elbow and the case, and strode toward the road. She wasn't going to be distracted again. She still had to decide how to retrieve the claw.

Thirty-nine

The jeep lurched to a stop. The forest was closing in, and so was the thick moist green twilight beneath the trees. 'We shall have to walk from here,' Isaac said.

Alan stared about him in the desperate hope that the lurch of the jeep might have woken him up. Of course it was an absurd hope. He was already wide awake, and neurotically alert. He wasn't dreaming, though the forest resembled a dream. It resembled the forest he had dreamed of, which suggested that he was close to the dreadful thing he had been told he must do.

How could he distinguish this place from any other part of the forest? He and Isaac had been in here for so long that it seemed strange to think of the open sky, of any sky that wasn't composed of countless overlays of green. Nothing distinguished this place: great sweaty limbs of trees reached up through the green twilight to the green ceiling, young trees grew in the spaces between them, thin stalks tipped with a few pale leaves. Yet he felt as if this place led to his dream, as if one of the paths between the trees led there – as if this place had been the start of his dream, which he couldn't remember. As he sat there in the passenger seat his body was stiffening, his innards felt like bile.

Isaac took the pistol from under the dashboard and thrust it into his belt, then he came round the jeep to Alan. His eyes were sympathetic and encouraging. 'Come on,' he said, clasping Alan's shoulder for a moment. 'Perhaps we haven't far to go now.'

Of course that was what Alan feared. Isaac laid one hand on the pistol. 'I will help you all I can.'

Even if he was undertaking to kill the Leopard Man,

that still left the worst for Alan. Perhaps the chief in the village of beehive huts had been wrong after all, yet it seemed horribly logical: cannibals ate their victims in order to ingest their power, therefore in order to consume the power of a cannibal cult for ever one would have to . . . He swallowed, choking, desperate to believe he was dreaming, but the last time he'd slept was last night in the jeep, baboons swinging down from the dark overhead to scratch and scream at the windows, huge shadows lumbering past beyond the reach of the headlights. It wasn't a dream, nor could he tame what was happening to him by thinking how he might write about it one day; that no longer worked. It was happening now, and it was all he could do for Liz and Anna. Though his legs felt heavy as concrete, he climbed out of the jeep. 'All right,' he said through his stiff cumbersome lips.

He strode out at once. If he had hesitated now, he would never have been able to go on. The ground between the trees was springy with leaf-mould; it yielded underfoot, an oddly intimate sensation – he felt as if the forest were accepting him. He was striding so determinedly that Isaac had to hurry to catch up. 'This way, you think?' Isaac said, and it was only then that Alan realized that he was acting as if he knew.

He glared about. He couldn't know, there was nothing to recognize, it was all the same: the moist green velvet light, the looming juicy green of vegetation, screams and leaping overhead, snakes like liberated vines. Fruit bats dangled, furry blotches in the dimness; they hadn't been in his dreams. He was walking in the direction the jeep had been going, that was all. 'It's as good a way as any,' he muttered. He mustn't stop, he mustn't falter; above all, he mustn't think about what he'd done in his dream.

The trees went on for ever. The world had turned into forest. The darkening path felt warm and soft as fur. A whirring overhead made him glance up. He'd thought it was a flock of bats, but it was a helicopter, invisible above the mass of foliage. It seemed a promise of help, until he realized that it could never land in the forest. The sound was already fading away to his left, away from the path he had to follow.

He couldn't know that; there was nothing to show that it was. His dream meant nothing, he mustn't trust a dream. But there was one thing he couldn't ignore: that long before his meeting with the chief, he'd already dreamed of doing what the chief had told him he must do. His innards were struggling now, rebelling. Just because the path was darkening, that didn't necessarily mean he was near his goal – but he would be there eventually, he had no choice but to act out his dream. He felt as if he weren't so much walking now as stumbling forward under the weight of that thought.

Isaac halted him. The translator was gazing about, holding up one hand for quiet. He stood for a while, then he shook his head. It had only been the helicopter. 'We should be stealthy now,' he whispered, 'in case we are near.'

Alan found his own voice was too shaky to control. 'Do you think we are?'

'I don't know. But we ought to be careful.' Isaac was gazing at him as if to discover how Alan would face what lay ahead. 'I told you that they may hunt in packs – if they are the last traces of the original Ju-Ju.'

But now it was Alan who was gesturing for silence. He'd been staring ahead between the trees, where the path darkened progressively. Now he saw why. A quarter of a mile or so further on, the foliage closed in, a tangle of young trees and creepers and vines. There was no longer a path.

He knew what that meant. In these last days in the forest, such places had been the only signs of humanity they had found: deserted native farms, cleared areas where plants and small trees had taken over. Why did the sight of this latest one make his throat grow dry and burning?

He was stumbling forward before he knew it, hardly aware of the leaf-mould beneath his feet, hushing his footsteps. As he approached the tangle of vegetation, not only dimness but silence closed in, as if the green wall could soak up sound as well as light. After the incessant clamour of monkeys and birds, the silence was suffocating. He could hear his heart, which sounded large, juicy, very soft. He felt intensely vulnerable and, despite Isaac, quite alone.

But the faint track was turning. It bypassed the impenetrable confusion of trees and undergrowth. For a moment he felt as if he'd been reprieved, as if he wouldn't have to do what his dreams and the chief and Isaac had all told him he must. He glimpsed dim conical shapes through chinks in the foliage.

'It's just another deserted village,' Isaac said.

Did he sound relieved? Nevertheless he was still whispering. 'Abandoned,' Alan corrected him, and halted, legs suddenly trembling. He had seen a gap in the tangle, a way through.

It took him a long time to step forward. He could see that it was the hidden entrance to a path. It had been made since the perimeter of the village had become overgrown – since the village had been abandoned. The place was not deserted.

As he took one stumbling step forward, more to keep his balance than out of any wish to go on, a fragment of the undergrowth scuttled away from him. It was a chameleon that was turning into jungle. The shock brought him back to himself: he no longer felt he was sleepwalking. Isaac was fully aware of what he was doing, coming all this way for Alan, away from his wife and his bright-eyed daughters. If he could do so much for Alan, surely Alan could do what he must for his own family? Perhaps he could if he didn't think about it. He stepped forward and squeezed between the fat moist trunks of the trees that formed the gap.

They felt like sweaty flesh. Thick rubbery leaves stroked him, cold wet caresses. A mass of flies buzzed out of the knee-high undergrowth and crawled over his face and arms. Though the path was short, he was ready to tear his way through before he'd struggled to the end, to splinter the trees, anything to fight the silence, the congealing dimness, the flies that he hadn't room to beat off. By the time he reached the end of the path he was so desperate for freedom that he almost fell.

It was even dimmer here, and more oppressive. Though the trees and the undergrowth had been cut back, branches and dense foliage stooped overhead. He had to stand on the squelching grass while his eyes adjusted, and then he stood gazing. If he let himself feel anything, it would be relief. Thank God, this wasn't like his dream at all.

There were perhaps a dozen huts in the clearing, squat conical buildings, little more than a roof and a circular wall with an open doorway that faced into the compound. Some of the roofs had collapsed. As the huts took shape from the dimness they made him think of giant mushrooms, swollen by the climate, or by magic. They were grey with dimness and moisture, and seemed to glisten like snails. They looked as if they hadn't been lived in for years.

In that case, why was he afraid to go forward? It was only a primitive village, the trees were nothing but trees . . . Yet he already felt as if they were creeping forward to surround him. What was that clutter of thin whitish sticks in one hut? Were they bones? If he stepped forward he might see, but he felt as if something was waiting for him to move.

He mustn't be afraid, not now. There wasn't even a reason for him to be. Good God, what would he be like when there was? Fury made him step forward, a fury that left no room for thought. He stopped halfway between the huts and the way through the trees, his head twisting back and forth as if he were a beast in a cage.

He was still trying to decide what the whitish sticks were when a sound behind him made him swing round, his empty hand snatching at the air as he realized that he had no weapon. The sound had only been Isaac, but as Alan turned, he saw what was wrong with the trees. A red shape had been painted on the trunk on each side of the gap.

He had to peer before he could make it out, and yet he felt as if he knew it. It was a thin crouching shape, the shape of a man – or almost a man. It had been painted in blood, which looked fresh. A man composed of blood, or covered in it – where had he encountered that before? He was struggling to think when Isaac whispered 'That's it. That is what they believed would hunt with them.'

Alan couldn't think. His inability to think, combined with the thickening gloom, maddened him. As he peered at one of the bloody paintings, he realized that the crouching shape was stirring, ready to leap at him. No, a mass of flies was crawling on it; that was why its limbs were squirming. He turned to Isaac to ask him to explain what he'd said. But Isaac was gazing beyond the huts. He was gazing as if he couldn't look away.

As he followed Isaac's gaze, Alan felt the nightmare closing in. He was scarcely aware that he was moving forward, and he couldn't have halted himself; there is no controlling a nightmare. He'd moved before he could even see what Isaac saw.

The first thing he saw through a gap between the huts was a cooking pot, a grey bulge in the dimness. It took him a few moments to realize what it was, from the pinkish glow of the fire smouldering beneath it. As he peered at the glow, a shape loomed at the edge of his vision, a thin shape against the trees at the far side of the clearing. He looked up and met the eyes that were watching him.

The dream had him now – the dream in which time was suspended, and from which he would never wake. He had seen that figure before, the thin crouching figure wrapped in its own limbs like a dried-up spider. Now he saw that its head was disproportionately small, which made it look even less human. The air about it seemed darker, swarming, and he thought of flies.

He was only peripherally aware of all this. All he could see were the eyes. If the body looked almost wasted away, the eyes were unnaturally bright with a kind of insane senile brightness. He could read their dreadful hunger all the way across the clearing. They were insatiable, and they were waiting for him.

He had forgotten Isaac until the translator took hold of his arm. 'He's alone,' Isaac murmured, as if that mattered. 'The others must be hunting. Stay here.'

He stepped forward, drawing the pistol. Perhaps he meant to give himself no time for second thoughts about what he had to do, but then it would be Alan's turn. At least the spidery eyes were watching Isaac now. That might give Alan a chance to prepare himself, but that thought was appalling too.

Now he could see more of the dried-up figure that was squatting amid its tangle of limbs. Its skin was like a mummy's, leathery and ancient; its mouth was a skull's mouth – too large for the head. It looked as if it had no right to be alive, and yet the eyes looked older than the body, the life in them did.

Isaac was moving more slowly. Perhaps he'd seen exactly what he was approaching. Alan had a sudden inkling that Isaac couldn't stop himself. The silence was a stagnant fluid in which they were drowning. It dragged at their limbs, it suffocated time. Isaac might take forever to reach the thing that was watching them – and then Alan realized that Isaac had found he couldn't shoot. Now that it came to the moment, he couldn't kill another human being, however nominal its humanity was, in cold blood.

Alan was suddenly afraid for him. He opened his mouth to call him back, but sourness choked his throat. He went after Isaac just as the crouching figure opened its enormous mouth, baring pointed brownish teeth. Even at that distance Alan could smell its breath, which stank of stale blood.

He made a grab for Isaac, but wasn't quick enough. Isaac must have seen what was coming, for he halted. Nevertheless neither of them could have believed that anything so old and withered could move with such speed.

Before Alan could reach Isaac, or Isaac could step back, the fleshless creature sprang from its crouch and came scuttling at Isaac on all fours.

Isaac stumbled backward, almost tripping himself. It wasn't enough. The dried-up man had the swiftness of a spider, and the method too. Before Isaac could kick out or retreat further the creature seized him, grabbing his ankles and swarming up him, wrapping its legs around his. As Isaac struggled desperately to free himself from the thing that was grinning mirthlessly up at him, he lost his balance and fell on his back in the squelching grass.

His arms were flailing helplessly. All the breath had been knocked out of him. The pistol had jerked from his hand and was trapped under his body. As he screamed, the fleshless man climbed onto his chest and crouched there, the wizened head darting to his throat.

Alan rushed at the creature to drag it away from Isaac, but the long brownish claws were already at Isaac's throat. They ripped open the jugular vein, releasing an appalling rush of blood. Isaac's convulsion uncovered the gun, and Alan snatched it up. Before he could use it Isaac's screams had choked off as the enormous mouth fastened on him and tore out a mouthful of his throat.

Isaac's outstretched hands clawed at the muddy earth, then they relaxed. He was dead. Alan's only thought was that he had brought Isaac here to his death. He was staring, dazed and unable to move, at Isaac's inverted face and blank eyes when the scrawny thing on Isaac's chest looked up, exposing the raw ruin of Isaac's throat. The ancient eyes gazed brightly at him until he understood what their expression meant. It was an invitation – an invitation to feast. He lifted the gun with a hand that was all at once steady and fired once, twice, blowing out those unbearable eyes.

Forty

Alan leaned against a tree at the edge of the clearing. He was afraid that he was going to fall. As soon as the eyeless figure had jerked and fallen back, his fury had left him. He felt drained, giddy, weak as a convalescent. The silence seemed empty now, no longer ominous, but his thoughts were deafening. He was thinking of what he still had to do.

It made his guts squirm. How could he ever have believed himself capable of such a thing? He was just an ordinary civilized human being, alone and far from home. True, he'd left behind everything he knew and loved; but that didn't mean that he could leave himself behind. There was nobody to see what he did except himself, but that was enough to prevent him. Perhaps if Isaac had still been alive to encourage him he might have forced himself, for Anna's sake.

Isaac had died in bringing him here. Isaac had as good as died for him. That thought rekindled his fury, briefly. However dreadful his task might be, considerably less than his life was required of him. It would be a kind of revenge for Isaac, and that was the least Isaac deserved. He made himself step forward while that was clear in his mind, and used one foot to lever the withered corpse off Isaac's body.

Averting his eyes from the wound that had been Isaac's throat, he reached inside Isaac's jacket and found the knife. His innards clenched again. He must have been hoping it wouldn't be there. He'd known it was, known that Isaac had been keeping it out of sight so as not to remind him before it was necessary. He grasped the sheath and drew it out, making sure he didn't touch the blade. He knew how sharp it was.

The glade was growing dim. Did that mean it would

soon be dark, or was it just his eyes? Perhaps the Leopard Man's companions were on their way back. At least that gave him a reason to hurry. He stuck the sheathed knife in his belt and stooped quickly to the old man's wrists. He wanted no time to think.

He began to drag the corpse along, its buttocks bumping over the ground. Its trail on the grass looked more like an insect's juices than blood; very little had leaked out of its leathery face. When he'd dragged the corpse almost to the fire, he dropped the wrists and went to look in the pot.

Except for a few inches of steaming water, it was empty. He poked at the embers beneath it with a stick. In a moment they reddened and flared up, and before long the water was bubbling. It was churning, and so were his guts. How could he go through with this horrible farce? But it was the only way he could think of to attempt what he had to do.

He pulled out the knife and stood over the corpse. By God, there wasn't much of it. He was grinning savagely, hysterically. To come all this way, through so much, only to be thwarted because there was no meat on his adversary's body! He turned it over with his foot, then he had to close his eyes, he was so sickened by his plan. There was no alternative. He stooped, and with two inexpert slices hacked off the corpse's scrawny buttocks.

He had to close his eyes again before he could pick up the pieces of meat. He would have carried them between finger and thumb, except that they were too slippery. He dug his long nails into them and stumbled to the cooking pot, almost running. Rump steak, his mind was babbling, rump steak. When he threw in the meat, drops of hot water stung his hands like needles.

He began to pace slowly around the clearing. If he walked fast he was too aware of trying to distract himself. It still wasn't dark; the general gloom seemed not to have deepened – perhaps he'd been trying to believe it was later than it was in order to give himself an excuse to flee. In the silence he could hear the pot bubbling. His stomach tightened, his throat writhed. He remembered Isaac's words: *By devouring your enemy you gain his power, conquer it – there is no other way to conquer the power of the Leopard Men, of the claw.* He'd been eating dead flesh all his life, that was what meat was; he just hadn't butchered it himself before. Butchery was the old man's corpse face down on the grass, the glimpse of reddened bone poking through the raw flat patches where the buttocks had been. Alan had to turn away quickly, choking.

Time was passing. The water in the pot must be boiling now. As the steam drifted toward him, it seemed to bring with it a faint smell of meat. Every moment made his throat tighter, made him shrink further into himself, more and more aware of what he was proposing to do. By God, he'd go through with it; it must be the worst thing you could do to a Leopard Man – that at least would be some revenge for Isaac. All at once, while his fury was uppermost, he strode to the pot.

There wasn't much meat to be seen through the greasy bubbles. The two slices looked greyish and shrunken. At this rate there'd soon be no meat left. He plunged the knife into the boiling water and speared one slice. When he held it up, steaming, he could almost believe it was just meat – dark chicken meat, perhaps. As soon as it seemed cool enough, he sawed off a piece. Holding the rest in his left hand, he lifted the piece to his mouth on the point of the knife.

He'd hoped that it was small enough to swallow without chewing, but his throat had closed tight and his mouth was dry. He had to chew the stringy meat, chew and keep chewing. He was holding his breath, with the vague idea that to do so would prevent him from tasting, but there was a taste like greasy pork in his mouth now – not quite enough like pork. Though he had his back to it, he was intensely, almost feverishly, aware of the mutilated corpse. He swallowed at last, and stood there, eyes closed, stomach writhing, body trembling.

The portion he'd swallowed might not be enough,

assuming that mattered. He sawed off another small piece and managed to down that, then he stuffed the rest of the slice into his mouth, chewing desperately, eager to be finished. That was a mistake. His stomach rebelled. He had to keep the meat down, whatever he did; whatever happened, he mustn't open his mouth. He was chewing violently, but his mouth was dry. His thoughts were babbling, trying to take his mind off what he was doing: rump steak, think of Anna, finish here and then he could go home, do it for Anna and Liz, they need never know, they must never know, one look at his face and they would know, if they recognized him at all, the butcher, the baker, the cannibal maker, my husband the cannibal . . .

All at once his whole body convulsed and he vomited uncontrollably, straight into the pot. He felt as if he was trying to vomit the depths of himself, give back the part of himself he couldn't bear.

He groped his way blindly to the trees and leaned against them. He was shivering as if he would never stop. He felt purged, empty, hardly there at all. Sounds of the jungle, faint but clear, surrounded him. Soon it would be dark. He felt that the moment he left the support of the trees he'd fall and never be able to move. Yet he *had* to move: suppose the old man's companions came back while he was here? He had to go into the darkening jungle. There was only one thing he could think of to do.

Forty-one

Liz stood in her darkening bedroom and gazed down at Anna. Beyond the curtains, night had already swallowed the sea. Darkness was softening the shape of the bedroom furniture, settling on Anna's face, smoothing out the frown that was like a deep scratch between her eyebrows. Incredibly, the house was silent except for the rushing of the sea. It seemed impossible that Anna was quiet at last.

Since the day before yesterday she'd been intolerable, worse than a baby, far worse. 'You *said* I could go to the Lakes. When *can* I go?' Liz had begun to feel as if these were the only words the child knew, that she'd learned them like a parrot – a parrot that could follow Liz from room to room, pestering and whining. No, nothing so intelligent as a parrot: a worn-out mechanical toy that could no longer do what it had been built to do, a toy that could only wander aimlessly about, squawking its two sentences over and over. A toy would have run down eventually, but Anna would undoubtedly start up all over again in the morning. Long before dark, Liz felt she was ready to do anything to get rid of the child.

There was nothing she could do. Even when the car was repaired – the repairman was collecting it tomorrow, they took their time hereabouts – she was damned if she'd put her parents to any further trouble. She didn't blame her father for being disgruntled when she'd cancelled Anna's visit. To have inconvenienced her parents so much for nothing, when her father was convalescing, and all because Anna had made her lose her temper – she couldn't understand why she'd felt the need to send Anna away at all. It wasn't as if she'd said anything to the child that a normal person wouldn't have said under all the circumstances. Anna was lucky that Liz had managed to confine her anger to words.

She turned away from the bed, for the sight of Anna was only making her angry. Besides, she had more important problems than Anna to deal with. As she went downstairs, the sound of her footsteps reminded her how empty the house was, how far away Alan was. She wished desperately that he would come home. Apart from anything else, she'd be able to talk to him about the claw.

She couldn't talk to Jane. She ought to have done so when she'd had the chance; she ought to have gone with Rebecca and Gail, and found an excuse to speak to Jane alone. She would have been able to but for Anna, but for being unable either to leave the child with anyone or to take her with her. Now it was too late; Gail had returned from her visit yesterday almost in tears, saying that now Jane was refusing to be visited. It wasn't only the refusal that had upset her, it was Jane's reason for refusing. Apparently she was claiming that someone she'd trusted had made her kill Georgie.

It couldn't be Alex; even Jane couldn't have trusted her. Could she have meant Anna? There was no doubt in Liz's mind that if it hadn't been for Anna and all she'd done that day, she would have been in time to prevent Jane from harming Georgie. Anna was as responsible for the baby's death as Jane was – more so, for Jane couldn't have been able to help herself.

Liz shook her head dully. It was no use brooding about it, but what else could she do? She couldn't find a pretext to visit Derek at home, because he wasn't there; he couldn't bear to stay alone in the house. Why couldn't she ask him or the police to search the house for the claw? Somehow she didn't want anyone to know how important it was to her, perhaps because it seemed shamefully trivial in the context of Jane's tragedy. Could she break into Jane's house? She couldn't imagine herself doing so. She seemed unable to think clearly on the subject of the claw.

She went downstairs – the glimpse of red in the hall was

the phone, of course, though for a moment it made her feel
inexplicably nervous – and sat for a while in the long room,
her back to the sea. Beyond the dormant television, the
last gold in the sky was tarnishing. She watched the sky
turn blue, dark yet luminous. It looked infinitely deep and
peaceful, but its peace couldn't reach her, even now that
Anna was laid to rest. She felt helpless and frustrated,
without a thought in her head.

She picked up the remote control of the television, for
company. Soon she was switching channels. An audience
was laughing at a joke she'd missed; a pair of politicians
were arguing like talking busts; forgotten British actors of
twenty years ago were trying not to make their progress
through a studio jungle look too easy. Wasn't this the kind
of film in which Alex had made her thirty-second début as
a child? All the more reason not to watch it. Still, the
pathetic jungle had reminded her what she could watch –
the one thing that might make her feel closer to Alan. She
found the African videocassette and fitted it into the
videorecorder.

Camels sneered and lurched to their feet, crocodiles
yawned like man-traps. Here was the mosque yet again,
the worshippers crowding in, and she remembered that
time with Alan running the tape back and forth, and Isobel
treating her as if she were mad. She was secretly hoping
that by some magic coincidence, Alan might phone while
she was watching the tape. Surely he must call soon – it
had been so long. Surely he must realize that she was
desperate to hear from him? If he called, she'd somehow
persuade him to come home. That would solve her
problems. She wouldn't have to deal with Anna by herself.

Before the tape had finished, she was dozing. Night had
closed over all the windows now, wind rushed the sound
of the sea past the house, a dark flood. She kept jerking
awake and glimpsing the telephone, glimpsing red. She
was hoping so intensely that the phone would ring that she
kept hearing a single note of the bell. She'd be happy to
hear from anyone, so long as it wasn't Joanna Marlowe.

What *had* that woman meant? Nothing that made any sense to Liz.

She turned off the cassette – no point in running it if she was going to doze – only to feel more awake, or at least on the edge of wakefulness. She couldn't tell if she was about to sleep or to awaken. The sound of the sea made her feel as if her paintings on the wall had come to life. She started the tape again. Here came the mosque, the crowds trooping in. Shouldn't that remind her of something? Perhaps it would have, except that she was nodding off, wearied by Anna, lulled by the sound of the waves.

They sounded like breathing. She was almost asleep. The breathing was in the room with her, but she didn't mind; it must be Alan. She was dozing while he watched the cassette. What was he looking for? What did he want her to see? All at once she remembered why he'd replayed that cassette, remembered what it was he thought he'd seen there. Her eyes opened wide, and then she cried out. The crowds were flocking out of the mosque, and the first to emerge into the sunlight was a thin figure covered with blood. It was coming straight toward her, baring its gory teeth in a grin.

It was only a glimpse. The next moment she'd switched off the recorder, so violently that she dropped the remote control. She was trembling, because now she thought she knew why her glimpse of red in the hall on her way downstairs had made her so nervous. Hadn't it seemed to glisten like a skinned tomato? Had she been too ready to tell herself without even looking that it was the phone?

She had to prove there was nothing, she had to look in the hall. She got up like an old woman, slowly and shakily. The moist regular sounds of the waves seemed very close to her, behind her and beyond the door as well. She was reaching for the doorknob when the telephone rang.

She froze. She didn't know what else might be in the hall. If she'd been able to take her time she could have coaxed herself out there, but the phone wasn't giving her a chance. It was counting the moments while she sum-

moned up the courage to open the door. Five rings, six . . .
It couldn't be much longer before the caller gave up. She
threw open the door – the doorknob banged against the
wall – and grabbed the phone. The hall was empty. There
was nothing else that was red. 'Hello?' she cried.

The phone was full of static that sounded distant, as if
one of the extensions had been lifted. As she pressed the
receiver against herself, so hard that her ear ached, she
made out a faint unsteady voice. 'Liz,' it said.

'Alan!' It didn't sound much like him – the bad line
must be making his voice thick – but she knew that it was.
Nothing else mattered, certainly not her hallucinations in
front of the videorecorder or in the hall. 'I can hardly hear
you. Where are you?'

His voice was intermittent, as if he had little control
over it – the line must be breaking it. 'I'm still here.'

That meant Nigeria; she'd already deduced as much
from the terrible line. 'You're coming home now, aren't
you? You mustn't stay away any longer. I can't cope by
myself. You must come back.'

It seemed a long time before his voice came drifting to
her. 'I need you,' he said.

'*I* need *you*.' She was wondering how much he'd heard
of her pleas. 'Can you hear me?'

'Yes.' Perhaps it was the faintness of his voice that made
the word sound so despairing.

'I need you more than ever. We both do.'

'No.' All at once he sounded savage. '*She* doesn't.'

Was this Anna's fault, too – that he felt rejected, cast
out? Was there no end to the trouble the child could cause?
Liz was suddenly afraid that he would ring off before she
had persuaded him to return. There was something she
had to tell him, something that would bring him back, and
she couldn't recall what it was. She could have wept with
frustration, except that it would have wasted time. 'Look,
never mind how she behaved,' she pleaded. 'I'm desperate,
Alan. I'm not exaggerating. You must come back.'

When at last he spoke, she could only assume that he hadn't heard. 'I just wanted to talk to you.'

Did that mean he'd said all he had to say? She was thinking desperately – something she must tell him, something crucial – but her ear was throbbing, making it even more difficult for her to think. 'Wait,' she cried, but now everything that had happened since he'd gone away was crowding her mind: Anna's unforgivable behaviour, Georgie's death . . . Of course, Jane's theft of the claw. How could she have forgotten? Thank God she'd remembered in time! 'Alan, you must come home,' she said, 'and I'll tell you why. I know where the claw is. It's safe.'

She heard him draw in his breath sharply. At last he was responding. She wanted to follow up her advantage, but it was best not to interrupt his thoughts. She had him now. She was waiting for him to admit as much when the line went dead.

She stood for a while, hoping that it was a temporary fault. The line was so silent: not even static, just a hollow silence that made her feel overheard. Eventually she replaced the receiver. The phones ringing on each floor must have awakened Anna, for she could hear bare feet padding overhead. At least she could now tell the child that daddy was coming home. Surely that was what his gasp had meant.

But when Liz looked into the bedroom, Anna appeared to be asleep. Her side of the double bed was tousled, and she was lying in the tangle like a china figure in tissue-paper wrapping. Why was she pretending? Perhaps she thought Liz would be angry with her for trying to overhear. 'Who do you think that was on the phone?' Liz said.

The child didn't speak or move. That annoyed Liz, who went forward. Her own shadow on the bed made her falter momentarily: it looked as if she were carrying the claw, until she realized that it was only her hand with its long nails. 'Anna, I know you're awake. Don't you want to know who that was?'

Still the child didn't stir. Did she think that Liz hadn't

heard her padding about? Liz bent to shake her out of her pretence; if her nails touched the child, *that* ought to make her stop pretending . . . But then she faltered. Was she really sure enough of Alan to say that he was coming home? She didn't want to raise yet more false hopes. Perhaps Anna's pretence had become reality by now. In any case, she could lie there while Liz tried to call Alan back. It was a long shot, but he might have been calling from his usual hotel in Lagos. The number was somewhere in his workroom.

When she reached the top floor she glimpsed the sea, a huge dim restlessness. Alan's room smelled musty with disuse; a pile of letters for him had toppled toward the edge of the desk, a cobweb bellied from a corner of the ceiling. The room felt as if it had reverted to being an attic. Eventually she found his address book underneath the typewriter. She knew the hotel was listed there, but she couldn't recall its name. Was Anna roaming downstairs again? As soon as she'd made this call, Liz would find out why she was padding around.

She recognized the hotel and its number at last, scribbled beneath Teddy Shaw's name, presumably because it was Teddy who saw to the reservations. The wind made the window shudder as she picked up the receiver and whispered a brief almost wordless prayer. She hardly noticed how sticky the receiver was, for as she put it to her ear she heard an unmistakable sound. One of the extensions had been lifted.

It must have been Anna all the time. 'Anna, if you don't put that down at once I'll come downstairs to you, and you won't like it one little bit if I do.'

After a moment she heard what might have been a response, but in that brief interval she'd also noticed something else: there was no dialling tone – there was no telephonic sound at all. It wasn't only Alan's call that had been cut off; the phone was dead. There was no sound except the breathing on the extension. Her hand tightened convulsively on the receiver, the earpiece jerked against her face. It wasn't Anna's breathing.

She had thought it was, several times before. She'd thought it was Anna, snuffling in her sleep or from grief. She couldn't make that mistake now, not with the moist thick snuffling pressed up against her face. It was as if she'd gone blind, unable to see what had overpowered her. She flung the receiver away from her as though it were rotten, and backed toward the door.

She couldn't go out there. The intruder was on one of the lower floors. It had her trapped. It had been up here too, listening to her and Alan; that was clear from the mark the receiver had left on her hand – a smear of brownish blood. She wiped it frantically on a piece of waste paper, and threw the crumpled paper as far away as she could.

She had to go down. She couldn't phone for help. And it was pointless screaming for help from the open window, nobody lived close enough to hear. She couldn't simply take a chance that someone might be passing – the delay would give the intruder time to come up to her. At least it was still by the extension, whichever extension it was; she could still hear the snuffling over the phone. It sounded hungry. She *had* to steal out of the house before it started prowling again.

As soon as she reached the open door, she smelled blood. The stench, and the prospect of all those stairs to be crept down, made her faint. It wasn't even as if she'd be able to sneak away – not with Anna. She'd almost forgotten that the child was down there, closer to the intruder than she was. However could she wake Anna without being over-heard? But she couldn't leave Anna, however tempting the notion was, however just it seemed. If only she had the claw! She'd have been able to take care of herself then, she knew she would.

She crept down toward the stink of blood. Two steps, and the staircase seemed to melt like jelly; she had to grip the banister with both hands. The house smelled just like the pillbox, that day she'd gone in. She knew what was waiting downstairs for her; she'd known as soon as she'd heard the snuffling and seen the smear of blood.

The banister was growing soft now, squirming beneath her hands as if she'd grabbed hold of an enormous maggot. Her senses were receding. In a moment she'd lose consciousness. If she fell downstairs, at least she would be unaware of what happened then.

She was dangling there near the top of the stairs, held up only by her hands – the banister felt more like water now, she was about to lose her grip – when she heard the intruder. How could she have mistaken that padding for Anna's? It was too deliberate, and certainly too large. Clearly it no longer mattered that she could hear, since she was trapped. The intruder was coming up to her.

That moment of hopeless terror gave her strength. Since she was trapped, it no longer mattered what she did. All at once she was descending the stairs, swiftly and silently. She reached the middle landing and thought for an instant of carrying on down and out of the house, while the intruder was still on this floor. But the next moment she'd dodged into her room, switching on the light and closing the door, leaving it less than an inch ajar.

The light woke Anna. She sat up violently, snatching the edges of sheets from beneath the mattress. Her eyes were bulging, her mouth was opening; she was about to scream. Liz ran forward and clapped one hand over the child's mouth. 'Listen, Anna. Be quiet and listen. We have to get out of the house. Now, without any noise.'

Anna was struggling, though she was awake. Her lips were writhing under Liz's hand, which she was trying to pull away from her mouth. People weren't supposed to behave like that – they never did in films. It took Liz a while to realize that the child was gazing terrified at her other long-nailed hand, which was hovering defensively. 'Don't start being stupid, Anna. That isn't for you. Not this time.'

Why had she added that? Because she was distracted? Because she was wasting time when the intruder was on the prowl? Was the stench of blood approaching? If she took her hand away from Anna's mouth the child would scream; Liz could see it in her eyes. By God, she ought to leave her here. It would solve everything. But she no longer knew quite what she meant by that; the moment when she'd known was past. She turned her free hand palm upward, and felt utterly defenceless. 'I hope you're satisfied. Now get out of bed and don't you dare make a sound. One sound, and you won't make another, I promise you.'

When Liz took her hand away from Anna's mouth – the hand hovering a couple of inches away, more like a claw than the other had been – the child made no sound. Liz dragged her out of bed and stood over her while she got dressed. Anna followed her like a sleepwalker, her arm limp in Liz's grasp. They were at the door when Liz realized that she could no longer hear the sound of padding.

She'd lost track of it while she was dealing with Anna. Perhaps the intruder was outside the door now, grinning bloodily. She threw the door open, catching it before it could strike the wall. The landing was deserted, but the stench of blood was as strong as ever.

The intruder might be waiting downstairs to pounce. Wasn't the stench even stronger down there? And it wasn't just blood, it was the fetor of a beast, or something worse. She was trying to tiptoe down and at the same time keep hold of Anna, who seemed determined to stumble. By God, if Anna could make a situation worse in any way, she would.

Liz stepped over the bottom stair, which always creaked. She grimaced for Anna to step over it too, but the child trod on it before Liz could wrench her arm. To think she'd once been delighted to have such a big house, such a long hall! The doors were closed, but did that mean the rooms were empty? Wasn't there a dark smear on the doorknob of the long room? Liz ran, dragging Anna, their footsteps thundering; stealth would take too long. The lock of the front door was stiff, and she heard padding behind her – she couldn't tell how far off, or even if it was real. She heaved the door open and almost fell out of the house.

She slammed the door at once, even though it cut off the light from the hall, and ran into the dark, still hauling Anna behind her. Because she knew where the road was, she could just make it out; a strip of fractionally lighter darkness, blurred at its verges. Beyond that, she could see nothing. She mustn't think that the thing in her house was necessarily better at seeing in the dark than she was, or swifter. She could only run past Seaview and the turn-off to the village, running faster when Anna tried to lag behind, dragging the child until she had no option but to keep up. Anna was sobbing with fear, but somehow Liz felt less afraid now. She knew where she was going, if she could only think. She wasn't fleeing to the hotel, she was going somewhere that would keep her safe.

She managed to hold her breath as she ran. 'Shut up, Anna,' she hissed. Couldn't the child stop her row for even a moment? How could she have enough breath to sob and to run? Liz could hear no sound of pursuit, but those bare feet would make little noise out here. If only she had time to reach where she was going – but she hadn't even had time to think what use Jane's house might be, when a car rounded a bend ahead and trapped her and Anna in its headlights.

She stood there while it drew to a halt. She knew the puzzled frowning face that leaned out of the driver's window, if only she could think. 'A bit late to be out walking,' he said. 'Can I give you a lift somewhere?'

Of course, he was staying at the Hotel Britannia. There was his wife, staring dubiously at Liz through the windscreen, then rearranging her features hastily into a smile. The hotel was all that Liz could think of now. 'Yes, thank you, to the hotel,' she said, shoving Anna into the back of the car and giving her arm a warning squeeze as she climbed in beside her. God help the child if she made these people think worse of Liz. She was already regretting having accepted the lift. Going to the hotel wouldn't solve anything, but she was afraid to think what would.

Forty-two

Liz woke feeling feverish. The room was too hot, the cries of children sounded as if they were just outside the window; even the bed didn't feel like hers. She reached out drowsily to find a cool patch under the oppressive blankets, and realized she was alone. Anna was gone. It was all over, thank God.

A movement in the room made her open her eyes, her stomach fluttering. The movement was Anna; nothing at all was solved. That much was clear from the way Anna was gazing at her, as if her mother were some kind of monster she'd been trying not to wake. What the devil had she to be scared of? Was she still blaming Liz for last night? You'd think Liz had dragged her out of bed for no reason. Maybe she should have left her there to find out for herself, instead of bringing her to the hotel. That would have taught her.

She'd made it as difficult as possible for Liz to take refuge here last night. Liz was awakening now, and remembering. Gail hadn't looked exactly welcoming when they'd appeared in the foyer, especially when Liz had told her they wanted to stay the night. She'd turned sympathetic, though dubious, when she'd realized how desperate Liz was – sympathetic enough to ask no questions for the time being. But just then Anna had to go and plead for a separate room. One look from Liz had silenced her, but the damage had been done. The child could hardly have made it clearer to Gail that she was terrified to be alone with her mother.

It was all Liz's fault, of course. What a monster she was, to have saved Anna from the thing that had got into the house! In the bathroom adjoining her hotel room she'd scrubbed her horribly sticky hand in water that was as hot as she could bear, and had felt almost safe. Thank God, she didn't need to think what she'd left prowling her home; she *mustn't* think about it. She'd escaped, that was all she need remember. Eventually she'd slept, one arm round Anna to make sure she didn't sneak away, though the child had tried to struggle out of her grasp. While she slept she hadn't felt nervous at all.

But she was nervous now. Anna was making her nervous, watching her as she might have watched a dangerous animal escaping from its cage, shrinking back when Liz came near.

'Listen to me, young lady,' Liz said, grabbing her arm. 'If you behave like that in public, you'll be very sorry.' She could hear children scampering in the room above; had she been overheard? It didn't matter – she wasn't saying anything that a million other parents wouldn't say. She gave Anna a shake and let her go, and went into the bathroom.

As soon as she was dressed, she hurried the child downstairs. She wanted to clear up the situation with Gail. She'd had one bad moment in the bathroom, turning sick as something red loomed outside the frosted glass, but it must have been a kite above the cliff. Was she going to be as nervous as this for the rest of their stay? Perhaps it would help if she felt more welcome.

Gail was in the office behind the desk, typing out the lunch menus. She didn't look encouraging. Liz ignored that. 'Gail, is it all right if we keep that room for a few days? I'll pay you, obviously.'

Gail frowned at her typing, but not only at her typing. 'That depends how long you mean to stay.'

'Just until Alan comes home.'

'Why, is he on his way?'

'I think so.' That sounded like a lie. 'Yes, he is,' Liz said.

'Oh, I'm so glad. I know it's been hard on you with Alan away, on top of everything else.' She was smiling now –

because Liz wouldn't be staying long? 'Will he know you're here?'

'Yes, I'm sure he will.'

'Well, then you wait here for him if it'll make you feel better. We'll work something out when you leave. You understand, it can only be for a few days, though.'

Liz had to be thankful for whatever she could get. She strode outside, feeling reprieved. The sky was so bright that it hurt her eyes, or perhaps they were burning with lack of sleep. The heat clamped on her forehead at once. Yes, the red on the cliff was a kite, and the other glimpse by the pool was a red swimsuit. The snuffling behind her – she turned sharply to peer into the foyer, which was blotchy with after-images – turned out to be a child with hay fever. She closed her eyes to give her vision time to settle down, but she was afraid to close them for long.

'Is daddy really coming home?' Anna said.

Liz reached for her through the blotchy orange blindness and squeezed her arm, or tried to; she felt the child stiffen, steel herself for another bruise. 'Yes, he is. That's one reason I was trying to wake you last night,' Liz said. But that reminded her of the other reason. She could tell that Anna didn't believe her, not after the way she'd treated her last night. 'I think you can stay in the nursery,' Liz said.

Toddlers were playing hide-and-seek in and out of the sand-pit; two little girls were cooking pebbles on a Fisher-Price cooker. The nursery girls came to meet Liz at the gate. 'Are you going to leave Anna?' Maggie said.

'I was meaning to stay too.' Something in Maggie's voice made Liz tighten inside herself. 'I thought you might need some help.'

'Thanks very much, but we can manage.'

'Oh, I see.' So they'd had their instructions, had they? Several parents, some of whom had overheard her row with Alex earlier, were watching her to see what she'd do. Liz opened the gate, and the girls stepped back. 'I'm sure you won't mind if I keep an eye on Anna,' she said, as she pushed by them.

She dragged one of the canvas sun-beds into the meagre shade of the hedge at the seaward limit of the playground and lay there defiantly, watching. Let them try to move her, by God, and there'd be such a scene! Parents kept glancing at her; so did Anna, as she played morosely on the slide and the largest swing. Trust Anna to let everyone see that she was nervous of her mother! No wonder they were all watching Liz. Perhaps there was another reason: the couple who'd given her the lift last night must have passed the word to the other parents. No wonder they didn't want to trust her with their children. Still, Anna was quite enough for her to cope with.

Really, she ought to be glad that she was being watched. Surely it meant that nothing could come to her? Out here in the sunlight she was safe from what had been in her house last night. Or was she? If she truly believed in it, mustn't she believe that it had not only been in the pillbox and her house, but on the television screen as well? No – she would rather believe that her glimpses had been caused by her nerves, that the sounds she'd heard in the house had been Anna, after all. Somehow it was easier to believe that now, especially since it was Anna who'd got her into such a state.

Yet she was still afraid to go home until Alan returned. Surely he must be on his way by now. The red beyond the hedge was a kite, a kite, but still she didn't like its swoops. The glimpse of red through the fence around the pool was the child's swimsuit, but every minute Liz was more on edge. Even the swings troubled her, dark shapes jerking up at the limit of her vision. Thank God the bar would be open soon, then she could leave Anna with the nursery girls; that was what they were here for. Besides, Anna had struck up a conversation with a young girl who'd been swimming in the pool.

It was almost time for the bar to open when Anna and her new friend headed for the gate. 'Where are you going,

Anna?' Liz called, and all the parents glanced at her. She couldn't speak to her own child now without being made to feel like a leper.

'Just up to her room.' There was a hint of a whine in Anna's voice which embarrassed Liz. How could she once have thought so much of her? 'Well, be quick.'

Five minutes later she heard the rattling as Jimmy raised the grille above the bar. Several parents stood up eagerly. Liz was glad. That meant they wouldn't be out here spying on her when she dealt with Anna for dawdling upstairs, for making her even more nervous. She should never have let the child out of her sight. Now the remaining parents had taken their children into the nursery building for lunch, and Liz was alone. The sunlight and the open landscape seemed suddenly deceptive, isolating her and yet surrounding her with hiding-places. She rose quickly – the red blur that came swooping towards her as if it had been lying in wait was a kite, just a kite – and headed for the bar. It was one way into the hotel. Perhaps Anna might even be in there, talking to Jimmy.

She was, and she turned guiltily when Liz came in. Did she look so guilty because she thought Liz might have overheard what she'd been saying to Jimmy? Or was it because of the way she was dressed? She'd borrowed her new friend's swimsuit, which displayed her bruises for all to see. 'Go upstairs at once and get dressed,' Liz said.

'I want to swim.' With so many people to hear, the child was defiant. She dodged out of Liz's reach and marched out through the open windows.

Liz felt as if everyone in the bar was watching her. They must all know why she wanted to cover up the marks on Anna's body. What did they know about it? More to the point, what could they do? Anna was her child, Liz was the one who had to deal with her. Let them try to stop her if they dared.

She went after her, feeling light on her feet, swift without having to run. Anna was struggling to unlatch the gate to the pool, but Liz would be on her before she could escape. Her nails felt electric, more alive than any other part of her. By the time Anna turned and saw her, it was too late. The way the child's eyes widened made Liz feel grimly pleased, so much so that it took her a few moments to realize that the child was staring beyond her, not at her at all.

Liz whirled round. Mr Mullen, Joseph's father, had come up silently behind her on the grass. In his red half-cooked stubbly face, his eyes looked like glass. He held her gaze for what seemed minutes before he spoke. 'Yes, that's right,' he said fiercely. 'I'm watching you. Just remember that.'

The wire gate slammed at her back. When at last he turned away and she was able to turn, she was just in time to see Anna diving into the pool. The long legs parted as the pale blue water took her, like an obscene gesture at Liz. Liz's fingernails were tingling, her nerves crawling with frustration. Some of the parents had come out to sit at one of the tables on the grass. Anna had escaped for now. Maybe she thought that here at the hotel she was safe from Liz – but the way Liz felt now, it would only make things worse for the child in the end.

Forty-three

The fog closed in overnight. It was at the open window when Anna woke next morning, and in her mouth, a horrible taste like being very ill. It made the sheets feel as if she'd wet the bed. She struggled out of them and ran to the bathroom, away from mummy, who was at the dressing-table and watching her in the mirror, watching her as if the mirror was a glassed-in cage. 'Don't close the door,' mummy said, in a voice so cold that it made Anna shiver.

Anna washed hastily and put on the clothes she'd worn yesterday, the only clothes she had at the hotel. They made her feel grubby, but she dared not say anything to mummy. She was hurrying so that they could go down to breakfast, so that she wouldn't be alone with mummy. She was frightened to be alone with her. She wished someone would take her away until mummy was better, until she turned back into mummy again. She wished as she'd never wished anything else that there was someone she could ask — someone she could tell about mummy. Whatever had happened to daddy was happening to mummy too.

It wasn't just that she'd dragged Anna out of bed in the middle of the night and into the dark. It wasn't that she'd looked ready to kill her when she'd worn her new friend's swimsuit, so much so that Anna had jumped in the pool to escape. It wasn't even that since then mummy had seemed ready to attack her at any moment, for any reason. These things were only tiny parts of what was happening. Mummy was nobody she knew, that was the horrible truth — she was a stranger who'd taken her place and who hated Anna for no reason. She was worse than daddy had been just before he'd gone away. Anna couldn't help remembering that now. If he really was coming home, that frightened her too.

Mummy unlocked the door of the room as soon as Anna came out of the bathroom. She didn't say a word, but her look was enough: her eyes said that she'd know everything Anna did, know if Anna said anything to anyone. Had she heard Anna's thoughts? Sometimes in the past, when mummy had been mummy, they'd been able to know what each other was thinking, and perhaps this stranger who looked like mummy could. She'd seemed to know yesterday, when Anna had been struggling to tell Jimmy a little of all that was wrong. All the way downstairs to breakfast Anna felt mummy's gaze on the back of her head, glaring at her thoughts.

The dining-room was full of children and their parents, having breakfast. Grown-ups said 'Good morning' to mummy as she passed, and all of them watched her. Some were frowning. The waitress looked surprised when she came to their table, but before she could speak, mummy said sharply, 'Mrs Marshall knows we're here.' The kitchen door swung open and shut, open and shut, and Anna saw the waitresses chattering beyond it, gazing towards their table. Mummy saw them too, and Anna felt her growing more tense. They were making her even more dangerous.

The parents had turned away now. Couldn't they see how frightened Anna was? But no – they were parents; they'd think mummy was right whatever she did – grown-ups always stuck together like that where children were concerned. Anna stared out of the window; she couldn't bear to look at mummy, but because of the fog there was nothing else to look at. The grass looked like an old worn carpet, faded and ragged; the horizon was pressing against the cliff. The fog made her feel trapped, especially when she heard grown-ups saying that these Norfolk fogs could last for days.

She didn't feel like eating breakfast. Her hands flinched from the hot plate as she cut her bacon into pieces, smaller and smaller. Eventually she put a piece into her mouth, but it wouldn't go down. When mummy reached over to push the plate closer to her, Anna was afraid she meant to burn her with it. 'Eat up, Anna. You want more than that,' the stranger who was pretending to be mummy said. All the grown-ups must believe she was who she sounded like. They'd trapped Anna even more than the fog had.

Eventually the waitress cleared away Anna's plateful of cold bacon. The grown-ups were already packing their cars in the hope of driving beyond the fog. The hotel would be empty, and Anna wouldn't even be able to go outside, away from mummy. All at once the hotel seemed very small – another small dark grubby place that was locking her in.

She brushed her teeth in the bathroom. She would have to play in the hotel. Suddenly she realized what that could mean. Jimmy the barman would play with her, she could talk to him while mummy wasn't there – mummy wouldn't want to watch her play. It made her miserable to think of telling on mummy, but now, seeing her watching her in the mirror, she was too frightened to stay silent. 'Can I go to the games room?' she said.

'*Please* may I go to the games room?' Mummy was pretending that she was still mummy, except that correcting her seemed to make her hate Anna even more. As she did her hair she was getting more and more angry with its tangles. Please let her take a few minutes, please let her say that Anna could go down! 'Go on then,' mummy said at last, as if she were glad to get rid of her, 'but don't you dare go out of the hotel.'

As soon as Anna was out of the room, she began to run. Mummy might hurry after her to keep an eye on her before she had a chance to talk to Jimmy. She ran down two floors and through the foyer, past the goldfish that were swimming round and round as if they couldn't stop. Gail was at the desk, and said, 'Hello, Anna' as though she wanted to talk to her. Should she tell Gail? But Gail was mummy's friend; she couldn't. Even telling Jimmy would be hard enough. She gasped 'Hello' and ran on, to the bar. It was empty.

For a moment she didn't know what to do. He was the barman – she'd been sure he would be in the bar. She could ask Gail where he was, but now she was frightened to go back into the foyer in case she met mummy coming downstairs, so frightened that cramps started in her stomach. While she still could, she dashed across the foyer into the corridor opposite without speaking to Gail – if she asked her where Jimmy was, Gail would be able to tell mummy that Anna was with him.

He was in the lounge opposite the games room. She had almost run past the doorway before she saw him in a chair by the window, peering at a newspaper by the foggy light that hung above the shrinking lawn. He didn't look as if he was actually reading. Perhaps he just wanted to be by himself, for his smile at her was quick and dismissive. 'Going out?' he said.

'Mummy says I have to stay in.'

'I expect she knows best.' He lowered his head to the newspaper until she couldn't see his face. 'Well, I'll see you around,' he said.

He didn't understand, he hadn't seen how desperate she was. She was shifting from one foot to the other; she felt as if she was going to wet her pants. She couldn't think what to say about mummy, she couldn't bring herself to say anything – and mummy might come downstairs at any minute. If she got him out of the chair and away from the newspaper, she might be able to tell him. 'Will you play table tennis with me?' she blurted.

'All right, I'll give you a game later.' He turned a page, but she was sure now he wasn't reading. 'Before I open up.'

She was going to wet herself from fear. She pressed her legs together, bit her lip viciously. 'Will you now?' she pleaded.

He let the newspaper droop away from him and gazed at

her. 'All right,' he said at last, 'if you're that desperate. It isn't as though I've anything better to do.'

All the same, he peered at the newspaper for a while before he stood up. He must have been trying to read after all. He strolled across to the games room, while she pleaded silently with him to hurry up before mummy found her. She couldn't say anything until they started playing – she didn't know why.

He took the bats and ball from their cupboard by the snooker table. 'Come on, then,' he said, seeing her hesitating in the doorway.

In fact she was desperately trying to think what to say. She wished she hadn't asked him to play table tennis now. It had been the first thing she'd thought of to get him out from behind the newspaper, but she was no good at the game. She was struggling to hit the ball when she ought to be telling him about mummy. He was sending her easy ones to hit, he was letting her return ones that didn't bounce on his side of the table, but all she wanted was to get rid of the ball and give herself a chance to talk. She slashed wildly at the ball with the edge of the bat, and the ball bounced under the snooker table.

She was crawling to retrieve it when she realized this was her chance. She'd start telling him as soon as she stood up; she wouldn't play any more. She scrambled to her feet with the ball in her hand, and then she realized something that made her stomach feel like a stone: she *couldn't* say anything about mummy. She couldn't even open her mouth.

'Your serve,' Jimmy said, but all she could do was bounce the ball and try to hit it over the net. It took her three tries before it went over. She couldn't tell anyone about mummy, it was too horrible a thing to say, so much so that it paralyzed her mouth. The more she tried to say it, the less able she was. She tried to hit the ball and felt as if she'd turned into a machine. She was trapped inside herself.

Someone was coming along the corridor from the foyer.

It sounded like Gail; she must want Jimmy for something. Suddenly Anna was praying that she'd take him away for just a little while, just long enough for her to get ready to tell him about mummy. She had to tell him, however much it hurt, because the thought of being alone with mummy for another night was even worse. She turned as Gail reached the doorway. Perhaps she could tell both of them. But it wasn't Gail in the corridor, it was mummy.

Anna turned away at once, terrified that mummy would see in her face what she'd been about to do. Perhaps mummy already had, for she went to sit in the lounge where she could watch them. 'Just keeping her out of mischief,' Jimmy called to her. Anna knew that mummy didn't want to watch the game, she was making sure that Anna couldn't tell.

The next time Anna had to scramble after the ball, she risked a glance at mummy. Mummy was watching her as if she was an insect that had got into the hotel, and mummy was just waiting for her to come close enough to squash. Anna hit the ball blindly, missed the return. How could she make mummy go away so that she could tell? Maybe she could say that she wanted a drink or that Gail had been looking for mummy – but they were desperate ideas, not even worth trying. She hacked at the ball, which bounced along the snooker table and rolled into a pocket. By now she was playing because she was afraid to stop.

While Jimmy was finding another ball she heard footsteps in the corridor. Could it be someone for mummy? Would whoever it was come and take her away? The slow footsteps halted between the doorways, and a man looked both ways as if it were a crossroads. He was Joseph's father, Mr Mullen, the gardener. He stared at mummy and then at Jimmy, and seemed not to like either of them. After a while he tramped away down the corridor, and Anna turned away, frightened by mummy's eyes.

She missed the next ball, which rolled toward the lounge. She managed to grab it before it went in. As she stood up, Mr Mullen came back, wearing gloves now and carrying a pair of shears. He was going to do some work on the gardens while the fog kept people out of his way. He halted between the doorways and stared at her. His eyes were shiny and blank, and she could smell something funny on his breath. After a while he said, 'You want to stay away from him.'

His fierceness made her unable to move, though she wanted to flee into the games room. 'Why?' she blurted out.

'You ask him. Ask him what happens to his girlfriends.'

He wasn't really talking to her, he was talking to Jimmy. Realizing that, she backed away into the games room and threw the ball to Jimmy before it could crack in her fist. He bounced it on the table, kept bouncing it, for Mr Mullen hadn't gone away. 'Go on, you ask him about his girlfriends,' Mr Mullen said. 'God help them.'

Jimmy slapped the ball down viciously with his bat. He was trying to ignore Mr Mullen, but failing. 'What's that supposed to mean?'

'*What's that supposed to mean?*' Mr Mullen was putting on an idiot's voice. 'We all know about your girlfriend,' he said in his usual voice. 'Dope's the word, isn't it? The word for her and what she uses. I suppose you use it as well.'

Jimmy threw the bat on the table; the crack made Anna jump. 'Yes I do, as a matter of fact. It does nobody any harm.'

'A pair of damned fools. I'll bet you live together as well. What are you going to do if you get her pregnant, son? Get rid of it? It'd be better off dead than living with you two.' He was spitting with sudden fury. 'By God, my boy Joseph's supposed to be an idiot, but he's – he's a genius compared with you and your girlfriend. And they're going to let you teach youngsters, are they? My God, what are you going to do to them?'

'Undo the harm their parents have done to some of them, I hope. The absolute authority of parents is fascism in the home. Hardly anyone cares, even when they know what's going on.'

Their fury terrified Anna. She wished she could run to mummy, but mummy was the last person she could turn to. All she'd wanted was to talk to Jimmy, but he no longer seemed to realize she was there. Could she plead with mummy to get Gail? Might mummy even take Mr Mullen away?

Mr Mullen was jeering at Jimmy, who lost his temper completely. 'You didn't seem to do your own son much good,' he said.

Mr Mullen's face seemed to darken and swell, and Anna retreated behind Jimmy. Why was mummy still sitting and watching? Why didn't she *stop* them? 'Look, I'm sorry I said that,' Jimmy said, sounding ashamed. 'Let's both forget everything we said, all right?'

'Yes, you'd like to forget what I said, wouldn't you? I haven't said the half of it.' He waved the shears as he tried to think what else he had to say. 'Not much chance of you two having children, anyway. I don't suppose you even have your girlfriend in the normal way.'

Jimmy sounded bored and disgusted. 'Oh, go away.'

'Don't you tell me to go away. Don't you tell me what to do. I've been here since before you were born. I'll teach you to tell me to go away.' Waving the shears more dangerously, he lurched into the room. As Jimmy stepped in front of Anna, Mr Mullen kept coming, brandishing the shears. 'Go away – don't be bloody stupid,' Jimmy said, with an edge to his voice. He stepped back toward Anna, then he halted, blocking Mr Mullen's way. As Mr Mullen raised the shears above his head, Jimmy punched him in the face.

Just as Mr Mullen fell on his back, blood pouring from his nose, Gail appeared in the doorway. She must have come to see what the shouting was. She gave the situation one glance and turned on Jimmy. 'That's it. You've caused enough trouble. Go and pack your things right now.'

Mummy jumped up. 'Gail, listen to me. It wasn't

Jimmy's fault. He's the one who's been causing trouble.' She pointed at Mr Mullen, who was struggling theatrically to his feet, a reddening handkerchief clasped to his nose. 'Do you know what he said to me yesterday? He came up to me for no reason at all and said he was watching me.'

'Don't interfere.' Gail wasn't even looking at her. 'You wouldn't be staying either, if it wasn't for Anna's sake.'

'What do you mean?' Mummy's voice was suddenly squeaky as chalk on a blackboard. 'What do you mean, for Anna's sake?'

Gail looked sadly into her eyes. 'Just don't ask, Liz.'

Jimmy was striding away down the corridor, his shoulders hunched up. Even if Anna ran after him, he wouldn't help her now. She'd lost her chance. But there was something worse: Gail knew how mummy had changed, and yet she wasn't going to help Anna. Anna's legs were shuddering, once more she felt as if she was about to wet herself. Gail had made mummy angrier, but she wouldn't save Anna. Nobody would.

Forty-four

'Just don't ask, Liz,' Gail said – and all at once Liz didn't need to. She remembered her saying, *'People who hate their children need help,'* and then she knew why Gail had let her stay. Gail was keeping her where she could see her, watching and waiting until Liz did something she could report to the police, the social workers, Isobel. She glared at Gail until her eyes burned, then she dragged Anna upstairs to the room. No doubt Gail could see how she was squeezing the child's arm. Let her try to interfere if she dared.

She gave the bedroom door a slam that must have resounded through the hotel, and pushed Anna into the room so violently that the child fell on the bed. Anna huddled there and watched Liz fearfully. She'd better be afraid – if it hadn't been for her Jimmy wouldn't have been sacked – Jimmy, the only person Liz had felt at ease with in the hotel. By God, if Anna could make things worse, she would. Everything that had gone wrong for Liz in the last few months, everything Anna had done, seemed to be gathering in Liz's skull, an unbearable weight that was growing like a tumour, crushing her mind. There was something she could do to lift that weight, if only she could think – something she *must* do before her mind burst. Perhaps she could do it without thinking.

That idea seemed promising, but it didn't tell her what to do. She couldn't go home, in case the thing that had driven her out was still there. There was nobody she could consult or take refuge with; there was nowhere she could go, especially in this fog. She was trapped where Gail could spy on her, with the pressure in her head growing steadily worse, impossible to disobey but equally impossible to interpret. She felt sticky, crawling with heat. At least there was something to do, then. 'Take your clothes off,' she said.

Anna stared fearfully at her, almost cowering. 'Do as I say,' Liz cried. 'All of them.'

She glared at the child until Anna began to unbutton her blouse, sobbing dryly and trembling. Anna made it look as if she was no longer capable of manipulating the buttons, as if she weren't old enough to know how to handle them. Liz watched her, loathing her babyishness. How could she once have loved and been proud of this child?

Eventually Anna had almost finished. She pulled off her socks and sat shivering in her pants. 'Those as well,' Liz said, and when she didn't stand up, moved towards her. Anna dragged them off for fear that Liz was going to, and sat quickly on the bed again, trying to hide herself behind her limbs. 'Give them here,' Liz said.

Anna gathered her clothes from the bed and passed them over, almost dropping them rather than touch her mother. When she tried to give Liz her shoes as well, Liz said, 'Don't be stupid. I can't wash them, can I?' Then she undressed swiftly and washed all the clothes in the bathroom.

As she hung them over the bath, she realized that Anna must have thought Liz was making her undress so that she couldn't run away. It wasn't such a bad idea at that, except that she wouldn't put it past the child to run out naked – one more thing for everyone to blame Liz for. What if she was planning to do so? But when Liz ran back into the bedroom, Anna was lying on the bed, clenched foetally about herself. Perhaps she'd only just adopted that pose, in order to disguise her intentions. Liz shoved a chair against the outer door and sat there. Anna needn't think of getting past her now.

In time the dripping of clothes in the bathroom slowed, grew less rhythmic. Liz sat and couldn't think for the pressure in her head. It seemed to have stabilized now, almost as if it were waiting. The corridors were silent, the chambermaids had finished hours ago. She was alone up here, alone as the mad wife in the Victorian novel who'd been locked in the topmost room.

Sitting idly was making her tired, and she was nodding. It didn't matter if she dozed, Anna couldn't move her. She was almost sleepy enough to realize what Anna looked like, what the sight of the naked body lying on a white surface reminded her of: an altar? A butcher's? Now and then, as she jerked awake, she realized she was naked too and felt as if she were being watched. But only the fog was nuzzling the window. Surely this was one place where they couldn't spy on her.

She jerked awake, thinking she'd heard stealthy footsteps outside the door. She strained her ears, but could hear nothing. Was somebody standing out there, trying to overhear what she might be doing to Anna? Let them try. A harsh smell was seeping into the room, but that must be the fog. Her nostrils wrinkled at the smell as her head sank again, drawn down into sleep.

It was her own smell. She could tell that from the way people drew back from her as she padded through the hotel. The hotel was much larger and older – the pillars in the dining-room were so tall that the ceiling was lost in darkness – but that wouldn't prevent her from finding Anna: there was nowhere in the world the child could hide from her. Diners peered at her from their islands of light, but the candles on the tables were guttering; now she could see only the glint of eyes and teeth. For a moment she thought she'd lost Anna after all, until she realized that she wasn't alone in the hunt. One of the Labradors from Gail's party was running with her; she could hear it snuffling. A woman at one of the tables leaned forward confidentially just as all the candles went out, and said, 'I used to hear that too.' Liz knew she was Joanna Marlowe, but it seemed unimportant, for Anna was running towards her out of the dark now, and the snuffling was close at her heels. When Liz grabbed her she felt small, too small, and utterly helpless. She was a baby again. Liz was on the edge of remembering how it had felt to hold her baby when she woke.

The memory was gone at once, for she could see Anna, the real Anna, staring at her from the bed, staring as if she wished that Liz would never wake. How *dare* she look at her like that! Liz stumbled to her feet, and was satisfied to see the child cower back. Why were they both naked? When she remembered why, she found that she was shivering. The clothes were dry enough. She bunched Anna's in one hand and flung them at her. 'Get dressed,' she said.

Soon Liz was dressed, traces of damp making her clothes cling to her. She couldn't stand the child's look. 'What's wrong with you?' she cried.

The child looked afraid to open her mouth, but managed to mumble, 'I'm hungry, mummy.'

'Are you, mummy.' It enraged her that the child should dare to call her that now, after all that she'd done. Outside the window the fog was darkening; she hadn't realized she'd slept so long. 'Well, we shall go down,' she said, almost to herself, 'because *I'm* hungry, and I'm damned if I'll let them stop me from eating.'

She gave Anna a look to make sure she didn't try anything, then she unlocked the door. The corridors were deserted, the rooms were silent; on the second floor a child was beginning to wail. Gail was hurrying back to the reception desk after alerting the child's parents. She gazed at Liz, but said nothing. Liz strode past, ignoring her.

She faltered when she reached the dining-room. It was so dark in there – was dinner over already? She felt achingly ravenous all of a sudden; she didn't know what she'd do if she didn't get something to eat soon. Then she realized that there were people in the dark, that it wasn't quite dark after all. The Marshalls must have decided to take the guests' minds off the fog by having a candlelit dinner. It reminded her of her dream, but at least people wouldn't be able to spy on her any more. She made her way through the dim maze of tables and hovering faces, gripping Anna's shoulder in case she thought of slipping away in the dark.

The waitress seemed reluctant to serve them. Liz felt her long nails tingling. She was just preparing to say, 'If Mrs Marshall has told you not to serve us, you just bring her here to me' – *that* would stop all the whispering around her – when the girl took out her pad. How many of the nearby diners had realized what was going on? She couldn't make out the flickering faces, only their glinting eyes, all of which seemed to be watching her.

Anna wouldn't look at her. She stared at the jerky blur of herself in her plate. Liz wished she hadn't brought her downstairs; the child would only put her off her dinner. Most of the other children were in bed, except for one little girl proudly wearing her first evening dress. To think Anna had been like that once! Now Liz dreaded taking her anywhere, loathed the idea. If only they were at home, she could have locked the child in Alan's workroom.

She ate her prawn cocktail without tasting it, while Anna drank her orange juice. The surrounding conversations were so quiet that Liz could hear every sticky sound that Anna made. Her stomach was writhing. 'Make less noise, child,' she hissed, and the spying eyes glinted at her out of the dark.

The waitress served the main course and glided away. As Liz tasted the roast pork, she had the impression that the girl had been eager to be gone. What had they done to the meat that it tasted so wrong? She couldn't make out what it was, only that she couldn't eat it – she knew in advance that it would do nothing to satisfy her hunger. Perhaps she was meant to make a scene about it, so that they could throw her out of the hotel. She forced herself to do nothing, to wait while Anna ate most of her dinner, in between shooting fearful glances at her.

The waitress came back and Anna asked for ice cream; Liz ordered cheese and biscuits for herself, as much to prevent the waitress from remarking about her untouched meal as anything. She managed to eat the cheese, which put a dull weight in her belly. The swarm of candle-flames dazzled her, darkening the surrounding air; unstable faces mouthed and ate. What had they been eating in her dream? She had a vague feeling that if she did remember, she would wish she hadn't. The pressure in her skull was growing, aggravated by the flickering dimness, by the spying eyes, above all by Anna.

As the waitresses cleared away the last dishes, a dance band was setting up on the stage at the edge of the dance floor. That would be too much – people dancing to old favourites, while Liz's skull grew more and more like an open wound. 'Hurry up and finish that,' she said harshly to Anna, who was stirring the last of her ice cream with her spoon.

As soon as the child had finished scraping her dish, a sound worse than fingernails on slate, Liz stood up and took her arm. The band had begun a waltz, a guitar and snare drum turning it into something more primitive. Liz hurried the child out before the music could blot out her sense of direction in the maze.

The corridors looked flickery with after-images of flames, and yellowish with fog. At least the upper floors were quiet, except for the muffled sound of the band, drifting up from below. She unlocked the door and shoved the child into the dark room, shoving harder when the child baulked. She wasn't giving in to Anna's fears this time. There was nothing in the room except the harsh smell, which must be the fog.

Liz switched on the light and locked the door. Anna was staring nervously about. 'What's wrong with you now?' Liz demanded.

The child seemed to have to think. 'I'm tired,' she whined.

'Then go to bed and stay there.' Liz waited while Anna used the bathroom, then watched as she climbed shivering into the chilly bed. Liz switched off the room light; she could think of nothing else to do but go to bed, and she certainly wasn't leaving Anna up here if she couldn't lock her in. She went into the bathroom, leaving the door ajar.

She splashed cold water on her shiny face and brushed her teeth. She could hardly look at herself in the mirror, this pasty, dull-eyed mask, with hair like rusty rope. Halfway through rinsing out her mouth she suddenly stopped, for she thought she'd heard snuffling in the bedroom. She froze, choking down a mouthful of water and toothpaste, but there was no further sound. It must have been Anna feeling sorry for herself.

Liz left her clothes in the bathroom – she must cut her nails when she could find a pair of scissors, she was snagging them on her clothes – and eased open the bathroom door. Anna hadn't moved. Liz switched off the bathroom light and closed the door to shut off the gurgling monologue of the plumbing; then she groped toward the bed. She hadn't quite reached it – she'd misjudged her distance in the dark, and the fog blocked out any light from the window – when she smelled blood.

She would have backed away toward the bathroom, but she couldn't remember which way to go: not straight backwards, certainly. She reached out one shaking hand for the bed, through the darkness that stank of stale blood, and touched something soft. A blanket – Anna beneath a blanket? But then the soft object shifted under her hand, and her fingers touched its eyes, its encrusted sticky cheek, its teeth.

She recoiled, spastic with horror, and collided with the bed. Now she knew where she was; she could see the strip of light from the corridor at the foot of the outer door. She staggered towards it, wrenched at the handle. Then she remembered the bolt. In the strange room she couldn't locate the light-switch.

Her fingernails were in the way, she couldn't grasp the bolt. Then she had it, and the next moment the door was wide open. Light flooded in from the corridor – not enough light. She jerked the switch for the bedroom light, and Anna started screaming.

By God, she was screaming, not at the thing in the dark, but at Liz. Though Liz couldn't believe it, the room was empty. Nothing under the bed, nothing in the bathroom either, when she threw open the door. 'Stay there,' she snarled at Anna, who looked ready to run out of the room. The intruder had felt too solid to have been imaginary. Locked doors meant nothing; it could come to her whenever it was dark. Perhaps it was still watching her; someone was – her neck was prickling. She whirled round. Gail was staring at her from the corridor.

However must she look, naked and ranging about the room like an animal in its cage? Still, there was no need for Gail to watch her quite so disapprovingly. She must have come upstairs to spy on her, otherwise she couldn't have got here so quickly. She was trying to look as if little was wrong. 'Liz,' she said, 'I think it would be a good idea if I found you some room in the cottage.'

So that was it. She wanted an excuse to observe Liz more closely, to take Anna from her or call someone who would. 'No thank you,' Liz said, though she was shaking. 'We'll stay here for tonight.' Before Gail could protest, she'd closed the door in her face and slammed the bolt home.

There was silence in the corridor while Gail considered what to do. Eventually Liz heard her footsteps retreating. She grinned savagely, triumphantly. Behind her Anna whimpered, 'I don't want to stay here any more.'

Liz turned slowly, enjoying herself. When Anna saw her grin, she flinched against the pillows. 'You're going to get what you've asked for,' Liz said.

Forty-five

Anna lay in bed for hours before she dared to move. She could hear the band downstairs, but it sounded as if it was miles away. It might as well be, like everything else in the hotel. Nobody cared what mummy might do to her, not even Gail, who could see how mummy had changed. Nobody cared what happened to Anna; she was only a child. She began to sob, but managed to choke the sound back before it got out; it might wake mummy, who was sitting in the chair that she'd pushed against the locked door. The thought of waiting until she was sure that mummy was asleep made her eyes sting with a yearning for sleep, but she mustn't sleep, not yet. There was still one person who could save her, who would come and take her away.

The band fell silent at last. She heard people singing along with it: '*Good Night Ladies.*' Because of her lack of sleep she thought for a moment that they were singing to mummy and her, and perhaps mummy thought so too, for her nodding head jerked up from her chest, her eyes widening and glaring at Anna. Anna hid her shivering under the bedclothes and peered through her eyelashes, praying that mummy couldn't see her watching.

Car doors slammed, cars shrank into the fog. Grown-ups came upstairs, talking quietly. Mummy's eyes glinted slyly at the sound of the people; Anna saw her listening until they'd gone into their rooms. Now mummy's head was leaning sideways, lower and lower each time, eyelids drooping. Her hands plucked at her handbag, which she'd taken off the chair to make room for her, then they relaxed. She was asleep.

More than anything else, Anna wanted to sleep too. She

sobbed with her hand over her mouth; she didn't dare go to sleep – she didn't know what mummy might do to her if she did. What had mummy meant to do before? Anna had heard someone creeping toward her in the dark, and then mummy had thrown open the bedroom door and switched on the light, because Gail had been outside. It must have been mummy who'd been creeping up on her, but she hadn't been able to do what she'd meant to do, because of Gail. But then she'd locked Gail out, and Gail had gone away and left Anna all alone with the stranger Gail thought was mummy. Gail didn't really care what happened to Anna.

Someone did. Auntie Barbara might have, which was why mummy had stopped her from coming to stay. Daddy might, Anna was no longer sure, but he seemed to have gone away for ever. Rebecca did, but mummy had made sure that Rebecca didn't know what she was doing to Anna. But there was someone who knew, or at least suspected, and cared. No wonder mummy didn't like her. If Anna could let Granny Knight know what was happening, she'd come at once.

But now that it came to letting her know, Anna was terrified to move. If she tried to phone, mummy would wake, mummy would see what she was trying to do. Couldn't she just lie here while mummy was asleep, and hope that everything would have changed when the sun came up in the morning? But the thought of lying there all night terrified her too, for she was so tired that she might fall asleep, might be asleep when mummy woke.

Just then one of mummy's hands moved sleepily, its long nails scraping the air. Anna shuddered, imagining what those nails might do when mummy woke. That was enough to start her inching across the bed toward the phone.

It was on mummy's side of the bed, and it seemed hours away. Anna edged across under the bedclothes, holding herself and her breath still after each tiny movement. Each time she moved, the chill of the new patch of sheet made her shiver. Once the bed creaked, and she froze, biting her tongue so hard that she almost cried out. But mummy hadn't stirred, and so eventually Anna moved again, still sobbing silently.

When she reached the far side of the bed at last, she inched herself into a sitting position against the pillow. Now she could stretch out her arm for the phone. She *had* to do it; but how much noise would the phone make? It would ring and wake mummy; she knew it would. She was back in the small dark grubby place again – she'd never left it really – and the phone was beyond it, out of her reach. Whether she just lay there or lifted the phone, it all came to the same thing: mummy would hurt her, hurt her terribly, far more than the bruises that were stinging her arms.

The pain and the hopelessness made her reach out suddenly for the phone. After all, if it came to the same thing in the end, it didn't matter what she did. She reached out more quickly than she meant to, and the bed creaked loudly. She buried her face in the pillow; she could already feel mummy's nails raking her back. It was a long time before she could look.

Mummy hadn't moved. Anna reached out again, this time more stealthily. Her fingers stretched further and further, over the Bible on the bedside table. She had to lean out of the bed, and she was terrified in case it creaked again. Then, at last, her hand closed on the receiver.

She held onto it for a very long time, telling herself that she was making sure she wouldn't drop it, while her skin prickled, her armpits turned clammy, uncomfortable, unbearable. She had to move her arm, to pull away the sticky patch of pyjama from her armpit. She lifted the receiver, and the phone rang.

It was only one note, but it was as loud as the telephone ringing. She froze, clinging to the receiver, waiting for mummy's eyes to open and see what she'd been trying to do. But mummy's eyes were still closed – or were they open just a slit, watching to see what she'd do next? She couldn't replace the receiver in case the phone rang, and yet she couldn't bring it toward her face either. It took forever, but at last she managed to persuade herself that mummy couldn't see her after all.

She inched the receiver towards her and pressed it against her ear, slipping under the sheets to hide from mummy. Then, immediately, she shoved herself up again, terrified of not being able to see what mummy was doing, and of pulling the phone off the bedside table. She held her breath and waited. Gail would answer in a moment. Anna didn't know Granny Knight's number, but Gail would. If she didn't, she could look it up.

She pulled her pyjama away from her armpit with her free hand and pressed her legs together for fear of wetting the bed. Could she keep her voice low enough for mummy not to hear and still manage to be heard by Gail? Her heart was thumping so loud that she was afraid it would wake mummy. 'Hello,' she whispered; she could hardly hear herself. Perhaps her voice was so tiny because she'd realized at last that there was nobody at the switchboard.

There was a number you could dial if you needed someone in the night, the number of one of the rooms, but Anna couldn't think what it was. Wasn't it on a notice somewhere in the room? Yes, of course: the notice was on the inside of the door – the door against which mummy was sitting. The notice was hidden behind her chair. Anna let out a loud sobbing sigh. She didn't care if mummy heard now.

Mummy had, in her sleep. She stirred, and her handbag slid off her knees, catching its strap on the arm of the chair and dangling there. Mummy's hands groped blindly about for it. Anna was praying frantically – she *did* care if mummy woke after all; *please* don't let her wake, *please* don't let her see Anna with the phone . . . Mummy's nails seemed to be searching wakefully for something to claw, her eyes looked as if they were about to open. At last her hands were still, and the rest of her.

Anna laid the receiver on top of the Bible, as gently as

she could. She didn't dare replace it in case the phone rang again and woke mummy before she could hide under the sheets. She drew in her arm and lay there, propped up on the pillow. She was shivering again, afraid of what she'd realized she could do, what the sight of mummy's handbag on the arm of the chair was telling her she could do. Mummy's address book was in there. Granny Knight's phone number was.

There might just as well have been a blazing fire between her and that little book. How could Anna try to get it when it would mean going close to mummy, within reach of her nails? But equally, how could she lie there, knowing that the phone number was there, and that all she had to do was creep over and get it? She was sobbing again, stuffing the bedclothes into her mouth. She wanted to scream, wake mummy and get it all over with.

Before she knew it, she was slipping out of bed. She didn't want to, but she couldn't stop herself. She put first one bare foot on the chilly carpet, and then the other, easing herself off the bed to make sure it didn't creak, holding her breath as if that would help, sobbing inside herself. She was a few inches closer to mummy, and that terrified her. She dropped on all fours, out of sight beside the bed.

Now she couldn't see mummy, couldn't see if she woke. She began to crawl alongside the bed, and found she'd almost forgotten how to crawl. Even before she could see mummy, she was panicking. The coverlet hung down to the floor, so that she couldn't see under the bed, and she felt that something was crouching beyond the far side of the bed, waiting. Was it the man who'd spied on her at home, the man she could never quite see? She crawled hastily to the foot of the bed, and was almost in mummy's reach.

She faltered there, shivering. Her arms and legs felt numb and twisted, her pyjamas were glued to her. She couldn't go on, not now that she was close enough to see mummy's face. Mummy's mouth was drooping open, a cruel curve that showed her glistening teeth. Anna thought it was the most horrible expression she had ever seen. The stranger who pretended to be mummy was made up of teeth and nails; Anna could see nothing else. She couldn't stand up, she couldn't crawl backwards. She would be frozen there until mummy woke.

The thought terrified her so much that she found she was moving. She could only move forward. She was beyond the bed now, but she didn't dare look back to see if anything was crouching by it – she didn't dare take her eyes off mummy's face. Had mummy's breathing changed? Was she awake and waiting for Anna to crawl within reach? Was there a watchful glint behind her eyelashes? Even if there were, Anna couldn't stop herself. Her trembling limbs took her all too quickly to the chair. In a few moments she was squatting beside it on her aching legs, pressing them together, and within reach of mummy's bag.

She stared at it and struggled to reach for it, to be able to crawl away and hide. The bag looked impossibly real, the only real thing in the world, and she was staring at it out of the small dark grubby place. She couldn't just open it – the catch would make too much noise; she had to slide it off the arm of the chair and creep away with it, which meant first edging the strap from under mummy's nails. She couldn't do it, the thought of trying made her sob inside herself. But she had to move, for her legs were aching terribly; if she had to squat much longer, they'd hurt so much that she would stagger to her feet and straight into mummy's arms. The thought sent a shudder through her that almost overbalanced her, and she reached out a trembling hand to lift the strap of the bag. Her teeth were chattering, she couldn't keep them still, even by clenching them until they ached. Perhaps that was why, as Anna grasped the strap and began to slide it gently but shakily along the arm of the chair, mummy opened her eyes.

Forty-six

Mummy's eyes opened, and Anna tried to scream. If she managed to make a sound, she knew she'd scream until everyone in the hotel woke up, until they came to break the door down, to stop mummy before it was too late. But she couldn't scream; she couldn't move at all, not even to relieve the agony in her legs, which in any case she was too terrified to feel. As mummy realized what Anna had been doing, her eyes were growing brighter every second, more and more like a horrible stranger's. Once Anna had seen a rabbit frozen by the headlights of the car; now she knew how it had felt in that pitiless murderous glare.

Mummy's lips opened, baring her teeth. She leaned toward Anna. Could Anna scream now, before those nails seized her? If she waited until they did, it might be too late. But mummy was going to speak, and she couldn't scream while mummy was speaking, even if it was a stranger who was pretending to be mummy. Besides, she was too frightened of what mummy was going to say.

'Well then, you little thief,' mummy said. 'I've caught you, haven't I?'

Anna couldn't speak, she could only squat there, her thighs jerking like a broken wind-up doll. She couldn't make a sound, not when mummy's voice was so gentle. It wasn't that she no longer wanted to – it was that mummy's gentleness was so terrifying that it choked off her scream.

At last the horrible delight faded from mummy's eyes and they grew blank, gazing at Anna as if they were looking at nothing. When she spoke, she sounded almost indifferent. 'Get dressed,' she said. 'We're going now.'

Anna was shivering so much that she could hardly struggle into her clothes. She'd had her chance to scream for help, but now the moment was past; it almost seemed there was no reason to scream now, though she knew there was. All mummy had said was that they were going – she hadn't said anything about going home. Something in her eyes had said they were going somewhere else.

In a minute mummy was dressed, and waiting for her. When Anna made for the bathroom, her legs getting in her way, mummy said, 'Stay out of there.' She didn't want the bathroom noises waking anyone in the hotel. She didn't want anyone to know they were leaving. Anna must let someone know. But as mummy unbolted the door to the corridor she gave Anna a look that dared her to make a sound, a look that already knew she could not. Anna was a rabbit again, frozen in the moment before it was all over.

The corridor was deserted and chilly. The fog outside seemed to have dimmed the lights. There was no sound beyond any of the closed doors; everyone was asleep, whatever time of night it was. It felt cold and grey and empty, neither night nor morning. All the way along the corridor and down the stairs, Anna was praying that a door would open, that someone would appear so that she could run to them, plead with them not to let mummy take her away, plead to be taken to Granny Knight instead. But nothing moved except the fire doors they had passed through. She was alone, with mummy at her back and the aching of her bladder, the agony between her legs.

Nobody was at the reception desk. The potted plants looked dusty in the blurred yellowish light; the glass panels of the lobby doors seemed to have turned into fog. Mummy unbolted the doors quickly and quietly. Surely you weren't supposed to open them at night? Shouldn't that set off an alarm? But there was no sound in the hotel except the mousy squeak of the hinges. Nobody came. Anna was still waiting and praying when mummy pushed her out onto the steps and into the fog.

The fog wasn't quite dark, but it seemed to press close to her face, so close that she felt as if her eyes were closed. When mummy shoved her forward onto the gravel path at the bottom of the steps, her footfalls sounded trapped with her. The fog was her small, dark, grubby prison now. Even if she screamed, nobody would hear her through the fog.

It drifted in front of her as mummy hurried her forward, nipping Anna's bruised arm between her fingers, to the edge of the glistening road. As soon as she reached the verge, Anna couldn't restrain herself; she didn't care what mummy did. She squatted so desperately that mummy lost her grip on her. As Anna relieved herself, mummy stared down at her as if she were an animal soiling a carpet, and dragged her to her feet as soon as she'd finished. 'Come on,' she said in a voice that was colder than the fog.

The fog drew back along the road, which glistened like a giant snail's track. Drops of moisture clung like spawn to the spiky grass of the verges. Sometimes the verges heaved up, turned into spiny banks. If she could see all this, it must be morning; they must have left the hotel just before people began waking up, she must have spent all night trying to be stealthy. The thought made her sob hopelessly, until mummy glared at her.

The sun was breaking through now. Occasionally she saw herself and mummy silhouetted on the fog, a huge figure holding a small one, folded up like paper from their waists. Everything that loomed out of the fog and grew clear was uncomfortably intense, close as the photographs in her Viewmaster at home. Mummy and daddy had bought her that for her sixth birthday. She sobbed inside herself.

Mummy was walking faster now, as though by hurrying up she could break through the fog. Or was she trying to run away from something? For a moment, and then again, Anna felt that something was loping after them on all fours, just beyond the fog. It must be the man who hid from her, except that he wasn't a man.

They were passing the graveyard. Gravestones congealed out of the fog. The church drifted by, a dark vague meaningless bulk, and then there was nothing to be seen but dripping grass and slippery road. Far away in the village to her left she heard the intermittent hum of a milk-van, the clink of bottles. Mummy was almost running now, pinching Anna's bruised arm to make her keep up. But where was she running to? Not home, for suddenly they were passing their gate, and mummy wasn't turning in there.

They must be going to Jane's. Anna didn't like that idea very much, not when baby Georgie had died there. But there might be someone at Jane's. Now she thought about it, she felt there would be. Before she could try to think who, she was jerked to a halt; pain flared along her arm. Mummy was staring at their house.

At first Anna couldn't even see it. As the fog curled and uncurled, she squinted until she felt dizzy. Then suddenly the fog thinned enough for her to see the front of the house, and she realized what mummy had seen. There was a light on inside.

Was it daddy? She couldn't think who else it might be. If daddy had come home, she wasn't sure how she felt about it; she didn't know if she wanted to go to him, not when she remembered how she'd last seen him, changed like mummy. But she had no choice. Mummy jerked the gate open and hurried her along the path.

As soon as they reached the door, mummy rang the bell. After a while she rang again and began to search for her key. Anna was more afraid than ever: afraid that someone would open the door, afraid that nobody would. She might have run into the fog now that mummy had let go of her, but mummy was glaring at her as if she could read her mind. No doubt she could. She had her key now. She gripped Anna's shoulder as she opened the door, and sent her stumbling into the hall.

The fog was there already. The light looked smoky, burning out. For the first time, as far as she could remember, she couldn't hear the sea in the house. The silence made her skin prickle. It felt as if there were someone in the house, holding their breath. When mummy called 'Alan?', her voice seemed so loud that Anna cried out.

There was no reply. 'Alan?' mummy called again, shoving Anna along the hall. For a moment she sounded like mummy, but she was still behaving like the stranger. She called once more, this time sounding less like mummy. Anna sensed that she was growing angry and nervous – which meant dangerous. By now Anna was sure that daddy wasn't here.

Mummy opened the door of the long room. The room smelled musty as an attic, like the rest of the house. Mummy was staring about as if she recognized nothing, not the videorecorder with a cassette still in it, not even her paintings of the sea, which looked dusty and faded. When she caught sight of Anna's tortoise made of shells, her eyes gleamed. For a moment Anna thought she was going to smash it, or her.

Mummy dragged her across the hall to the playroom. The floor was covered with toys; Anna hadn't cleared up for a while, she didn't like clearing up. Mummy's hand was tightening on her shoulder at the sight of the room, her nails digging in until Anna was ready to scream. She was afraid to scream now, so far from anyone. She was afraid of what mummy might do to stop her screaming.

Mummy was lugging her to the kitchen now, so roughly that Anna's heels dragged over the carpet. Mummy was staring at knives in the rack on the kitchen wall, and Anna's stomach twisted violently as she wished she could twist herself free. But mummy was pulling her toward the stairs. '*Someone* put the light on,' she was muttering.

At once Anna realized that it had been mummy – that *she'd* left the light on the night they'd gone to the hotel. She didn't dare say so, but her fear and frustration made her speak. 'Daddy isn't here,' she complained. 'Why did we come home?'

Mummy stared at her as if she'd forgotten Anna could talk. 'Because you asked to.'

Her voice was cold and full of hate, the stranger's voice. 'I want to go back to the hotel,' Anna whimpered.

'You mean you don't want to stay here with me.' Mummy's eyes were brightening. 'That's the truth, isn't it? What a wise child.'

'What's wrong?' Anna couldn't help it, she was sobbing. 'You aren't like mummy.'

'Oh, don't I meet with your approval? It's all my fault, is it?' Mummy was hauling her upstairs, not stopping when Anna tripped and bruised her ankle on a stair. She must know by now that daddy wasn't here. What did she mean to do upstairs?

Fog shifted at the landing windows, as if the house were drowned and drifting under water. It didn't just smell musty, it smelled harsh; it made Anna think of a zoo. Mummy was dragging her from room to room, first her and daddy's bedroom, now Anna's, her hand pinching Anna's shoulder cruelly as she looked into the small untidy room. What was she looking for? Anna was afraid to think.

'Yes, of course,' mummy was muttering. 'There is one room.' She was making for the stairs again; she was dragging Anna up to daddy's workroom. Anna sobbed and struggled, but it was no use: mummy was stronger than she was – stronger than Anna had ever known her. Anna was on her knees as mummy dragged her up the last few stairs and across the landing, tugging her all the more roughly when Anna screamed. But before she'd reached daddy's workroom, they both heard a car draw up outside.

Mummy jerked her to her feet before Anna could resist. She must have meant to lock Anna in the workroom while she went to see who was out there, but then she decided that would waste time, for she dragged Anna to the landing window. Something red was out there on the road, reddening a patch of fog. It was a red car. Anna was praying that she knew whose it was, and it seemed her prayers were answered: Granny Knight was striding towards the house.

In the moment when mummy saw her too, Anna had

the chance to scream for help, to bang on the window; Granny Knight would have seen her. But already mummy was jerking her away, hurting her arm so much that Anna couldn't even cry out. She threw open the door and shoved Anna into daddy's workroom, where she fell on the floor just short of the desk.

Anna struggled to her feet, terrified of mummy's eyes. 'Are you going to make a sound?' mummy demanded, in her stranger's voice. Anna wanted to say no, to promise she'd be quiet so that mummy would lock her in and go downstairs, so that she could scream for help as soon as she heard mummy opening the front door. But mummy was reading her mind again. She stared into Anna's eyes, then she lashed out. Mummy's hand swinging at her face was the last thing Anna saw as she fell.

Forty-seven

Liz gazed down at Anna where she lay sprawled on the workroom floor. She was ready to hit the child again if she moved – she was ready to do whatever was needed to make sure that Anna couldn't cry out to Isobel. But Anna wasn't moving. Liz must have knocked her cold before she fell, otherwise she would have cried out when she hit the floor so awkwardly. Satisfied, Liz went swiftly out of the room and bolted the door.

Isobel was knocking at the front door. The sound reverberated through the house as if the entire building were made of wood. It didn't matter that it made her jump and curse Isobel; at least it couldn't rouse Anna. Isobel was ringing the bell, but Liz was calmer now; Isobel couldn't know she was in the house, she had only to wait up here until the interfering woman went away.

Isobel was knocking again and again. Let her knock – Liz hoped she went on until her hands were raw. What did the old bitch want, anyway? What was she doing here? Of course, she couldn't know that Liz was supposed to be at the hotel. Liz didn't even know what she was doing here herself, except that someone had left the light on in the house. Good God – of course, *she* had, the night she'd fled to the hotel. But she hadn't been going to the hotel that night, she'd been heading in the other direction . . . Only then those people in the car had interfered. She knew where she must go as soon as Isobel went away.

Isobel was knocking and ringing now. The knocking pounded inside Liz's skull, the ringing jangled her nerves. Stupid bitch, didn't Isobel realize she was only making it worse for Anna? Even now Liz was considering hitting

322

Anna again to make sure she kept quiet. But after one last thunderous knock, Isobel seemed to give up.

Liz listened to the silence and felt indescribably grateful. She was calm now, she didn't have to listen to Anna. Once she heard Isobel's car she would take Anna out. She could carry her, the child was light enough. Nobody would see them in the fog. She felt so calm it was as though she'd already done what she had to do, until she realized that she hadn't heard the car or even Isobel's footsteps receding. Isobel was still outside the house.

Liz risked a glance from the landing window and found that she was looking directly down on Isobel, a squashed dwarf whose most prominent feature was a pair of folded arms. For a moment Liz wished she could find something heavy, balance it on the sill, open the window stealthily – but there was nothing, and in any case, she felt unable to cope with complications. She had to get rid of Isobel as quickly as possible. That meant now, before Anna regained consciousness and began screaming.

Liz strode downstairs. Whatever happened, she wouldn't let Isobel in. Isobel was standing with her back to the house, but she turned and came forward as Liz opened the door. 'Where is Anna?' she demanded.

Her grim face made it clear that she didn't mean to be turned away. 'At the hotel,' Liz said at once.

Isobel peered suspiciously at her through the veils of misty breath that drifted between them. 'If she is, so much the better,' she said, stepping forward.

Liz found she couldn't close the door entirely; she'd let Isobel come too near. With barely controlled fury, she said 'Goodbye, Isobel.' The words sounded like a curse.

Isobel's eyes narrowed. 'Why are you so anxious to get rid of me?'

'Isobel, I'm tired. If you're so worried about Anna, why don't you go to the hotel?'

Surely that ought to get rid of Isobel – but Isobel stayed where she was. One good unexpected shove against the door would send her flying, but Liz controlled herself, though her hands were fists, and her fingernails were aching, aching. Shoving Isobel would hardly get rid of her. 'Isobel,' she said as calmly as she could, 'will you please let me close the door. I want to be alone.'

'I'm sure you do.' What did Isobel suspect, that she emphasized that so heavily? 'Not this time, Elizabeth, I'm afraid.'

Liz's fist began to tremble on the latch. Isobel would still be here when Anna regained consciousness. Liz's mind felt like her fists, hard and aching and unable to open, all the more so when Isobel looked beyond her and said, 'I thought you said Anna wasn't here.'

At that, Liz whirled round and strode blindly down the hall – anything to shut Anna up before she got to Isobel. But she'd taken only a couple of steps when she saw that the hall was empty. Of course it was; Anna couldn't have got out of the locked room. She turned to demand what Isobel was trying to do, and saw that Isobel had already done it. She was in the house.

As Liz watched, speechless with fury, Isobel closed the front door and stood with her back to it, arms folded. Liz was close enough to scratch her face and her hands were trembling to do so, but what good would it do? Eventually she said, in a voice she hardly recognized as hers: 'So you have to trick your way into my house now, do you?'

'If it wasn't Anna, I don't know what it was. It certainly wasn't tall enough for Alan.' Nevertheless something had undermined her certainty. 'He isn't here, is he?'

'No, he isn't,' Liz said fiercely, 'so there's no reason for you to stay.'

Isobel gave a shrug which dismissed that and Liz as well. 'Perhaps it was a shadow. Well, I'm not here to talk about shadows,' she said, and stepped around Liz into the long room.

Liz's nails were throbbing, her nails were going to puncture her palms. Shaking with rage and frustration, she went to the foot of the stairs to make sure that Anna hadn't got out after all, though she knew it was impossible. Upstairs all was silent, but for how long? Suppose Anna was already conscious, and plotting? Suppose the child tried to phone for help? Liz grinned savagely: the phone wasn't working. But she couldn't afford to feel secure, she couldn't take the chance of Isobel's hearing Anna. She strode into the long room. 'Isobel, will you please leave my house at once.'

'Is it just your house now?' Isobel shook her head sadly and sat back in her chair, as if to be more immovable. 'I thought it belonged to my son.'

'I've told you he isn't here, nor is Anna.' Liz's head felt raw. 'So what do you want here?'

'You'll find out.' For a moment Isobel looked almost sorry for her. 'You'll see soon enough.'

'Don't play games with me, Isobel.' Liz's voice was rising; soon she'd be screaming, loud enough to wake Anna. 'Can't you see I need to be alone? Will you please have the decency to leave!'

'Why are you here if Anna's at the hotel?'

Liz was trapped. Get out, you interfering bitch, you fucking dried-up cunt, she screamed. She had never expected to use language like that, and saying it out loud would be no use. Instead she said the first thing that came into her throbbing head – anything to get rid of Isobel before Anna heard her, or she heard Anna. 'Look, Isobel, I haven't been honest with you. Alan's coming home.'

'Indeed,' Isobel said, with an unreadable look.

'Yes, and I want to be alone with him. We haven't been together for so long. I have things I want to say to him as soon as he comes home. Surely you can understand that? If you care at all about our marriage, you'll leave now.'

'I can certainly see that you'd rather nobody was here when he comes home, but I'm sorry, Elizabeth, it's not to be.' She folded her arms again. 'He called you to say he was coming home, did he?'

'That's right. Why not?' Then Liz remembered that the phone was out of order. Well, that didn't matter; as far as Isobel knew, he could have phoned Liz at the hotel. Or had Isobel already called the hotel? Did she know Anna wasn't there – was that why she was insisting on staying? Liz's thoughts whirled about her throbbing skull; she couldn't get rid of Isobel without knowing what she'd come for, but she didn't dare find out in case that gave her away. By God, if she couldn't make Isobel leave, she'd render her incapable of interfering. Before she knew exactly what she meant to do, she was sneaking behind Isobel's chair; whatever it had to be, she was committed to it now – and serve Isobel right . . . Then Liz faltered; she'd seen that Isobel was listening.

Had Anna made a sound upstairs? So much the worse for her and Isobel. But Isobel wasn't looking upward, she was staring towards the fog where the road should be. Now Liz could hear what Isobel had been waiting for: the sound of a car approaching slowly through the fog, a car that was slowing to a stop outside the house. The ignition was switched off, and there was silence.

Isobel stood up. Liz stayed where she was; moving would be pointless now. She wanted to lash out at Isobel, but what was the use? She knew the police were out there. Isobel had called them and come here to wait for them. Liz could hear them, two sets of footsteps on the path.

Isobel strode into the hall. Liz followed her, though she wasn't sure why. Had she time to confront the police before Anna stirred, to persuade them that nothing was wrong except interfering Isobel, or could she still dodge upstairs and sneak Anna out of the house? She was wavering as Isobel went quickly to the front door and let in the fog.

Beyond the drift of fog, two men were advancing down the path. At first Liz couldn't see their faces, because she was staring past them in confusion. The vehicle beyond the gate wasn't a police car at all, it was a taxi. It must be the taxi-driver who was helping the other man along the path. Liz's feelings were chaotic, and she had to support herself against the wall. Then the men came forward into the light from the house, and she saw that the man whom the taxi-driver was supporting was Alan.

Forty-eight

At first, when Anna realized she wasn't in bed, she thought she was at the dentist's. That was why she'd come back to herself in such a strange place, that was why her head and her jaw were aching. When she opened her eyes mummy would be there, leaning down into her eyes, saying, 'It's all right now, mummy's here.'

Then she remembered, and her eyes sprang open in terror, in case mummy was. But daddy's workroom was deserted except for her. One arm of the cross that his chair swivelled on was digging into her thigh, which throbbed worse when she flinched away. As she stumbled to her feet, she realized that the rough weave of the carpet had left an imprint on her cheek.

Standing up made her headache worse: the room was tilting, and she was crying out with the pain. As she limped giddily to the door, she was only half-aware of what she was doing. She shook the door when it wouldn't open, until she heard the noise she was making, and then she stumbled, sobbing, away from the door and sat in daddy's chair in case she fell down. Mummy had locked her in. What would she do if she heard her trying to open the door? She'd already knocked her down when Granny Knight was here – what would she do when Granny Knight had gone?

Perhaps Granny Knight already had. Perhaps mummy was coming upstairs now, stealthy as a cat. Anna glimpsed her creeping upstairs on all fours, her claws ready. She spun round wildly on the chair, but that made her feel so dizzy and vulnerable that she grabbed the desk. The desk jerked, the phone jangled, and she sat shaking with the effort of trying to be still for minutes while she wondered if the phone had also rung downstairs.

She began to relax eventually, but also to sob. The phone had told her what to do, but she was afraid to. She'd tried to phone from the hotel room; how could she go through all that again? But if she didn't phone, the only alternative was to wait until mummy came upstairs to her. Perhaps the phones downstairs wouldn't ring when she picked up daddy's phone. Sometimes they all rang, but not always.

She stared out at the billowing fog until it made her so dizzy she had to close her tearful eyes. Then, while her eyes were closed and she couldn't see what she was doing, she reached out and grabbed the receiver. As she lifted it off the cradle the phone rang, so loudly that she couldn't hear if the others had. Could that sound be heard downstairs? She clutched the receiver, afraid to open her eyes.

But she had it now, and she must use it while she had the chance. All she had to do was to dial 999 if anything was seriously wrong – mummy had told her that once. But her hand was shaking so much that she couldn't lift the receiver to her face. She was afraid that if she did, she'd hear mummy saying, '*I heard you.*' She dragged the receiver through the air and pressed it against her ear, pressed it until her ear burned, until she realized why she wasn't dialling, why it was no use: you had to wait until you heard the buzzing, the dialling tone – mummy had told her that, too. There wasn't any buzzing. The phone wasn't working.

She laid the receiver on the desk and began to cry in earnest, hopelessly, her head and jaw throbbing with every sob. The fog surged at the window and drifted away, surged and retreated. She wished she could climb onto the sill and jump – she couldn't see the drop – but she wasn't brave enough. She could only wait for mummy to come to her. Wouldn't mummy hear her crying if she picked up the phone downstairs? It didn't matter, she didn't care. That made her cry harder. But then, suddenly, she hushed, swallowing and gulping. She'd thought she'd heard voices downstairs.

She made herself let go of the desk and crept to the door, pressing her ear against it. She was terrified that the door would open without warning, that mummy would be there – so terrified that she didn't realize how she was trying to hang onto the wall until she felt wallpaper gathering under her nails. That made her squirm, but she had to be still, because there was a voice downstairs that wasn't mummy's. She had to press her ear against the door until her blood sounded like the sea before she was sure that it was Granny Knight's voice.

She hadn't gone yet. Anna realized she'd been behaving as if Granny Knight already had. She wanted to scream, but suppose mummy heard her before Granny Knight did? Suppose mummy got to her first? Having Granny Knight still here only made her feel worse; she was sobbing loudly now, she didn't care who heard, she just wished someone would so that everything would be over. She didn't want to try and speak to Granny Knight. She didn't want to use the phone.

But she could, if she was lucky. If she jiggled the cradle of daddy's phone until it rang, it might ring downstairs as well. If Granny Knight picked up the phone, Anna could tell her everything – she'd have to. Could she take the risk of mummy hearing instead? But already she was stumbling back to the desk, sobbing as she sat down in daddy's wobbly chair, sobbing painfully as she picked up the receiver and began to move the cradle, jiggling it more and more violently as it rang and still nobody answered. It was ringing downstairs, she could hear that now, and she could hardly breathe for sobbing. Someone must answer – her bruised arm was already aching, her head and her jaw and her whole body were.

When she heard the click of the phone being lifted downstairs, loud in her ear as the closing of a trap, she almost dropped the receiver. She had to clutch it with both hands. She didn't dare speak. Then she heard the hollow shell-like sound of a hand cupped around the mouthpiece. 'Yes?' a low voice said.

It didn't sound like mummy. Nevertheless it seemed to take Anna forever before she could swallow and draw a shuddering breath and, risking everything so completely that she had to close her eyes, whisper, 'It's Anna.'

'Yes?'

The voice sounded even gentler. It couldn't be mummy; she wouldn't speak like that, not any more. That thought broke the dam of Anna's fear, and she began to babble into the phone. 'Oh, please come and get me. Mummy's locked me in daddy's room. She's going to hurt me, she wants to hurt me, she isn't like mummy.' Now she was sobbing not so much with fear as with having to say such things about mummy; her face was blazing with shame. 'Please don't go away, please come and let me out. Please don't let mummy get me . . .'

The silence didn't last long, it only seemed so. 'I'll be coming for you,' the low voice said, 'don't you worry,' and Anna replaced the receiver as quickly and quietly as she could. She sat hugging herself on daddy's chair and watched the door. Thank you, thank you, she said over and over, not knowing if she was speaking out loud, or to whom. Nobody but she could have heard the low voice on the phone.

Forty-nine

It was Isobel who draped Alan's arm round her shoulders and guided him into the long room, while Liz searched for money in her bag to pay for the taxi, which had come all the way from Norwich. Alan seemed scarcely to realize it had to be paid for; he seemed aware of very little except that he was home. 'I'm all right,' he kept murmuring hoarsely to Isobel, 'I can walk.' But even if he didn't need to be supported physically, he was obviously grateful for the contact, pitifully so. When they disappeared into the long room, Liz gave the taxi-driver more than she'd intended, then closed the front door on him and the fog rather than wait for change. She didn't want to leave Isobel alone with Alan. She mustn't give her a chance to talk.

Alan was sitting in his usual chair facing the television. Liz was reminded of the time he'd shown her the Nigerian cassette, which was still on the videorecorder. She remembered the bloody man stepping towards her out of the mosque. The memory made her tremble, and so did the sight of Alan. He looked pale, famished, shockingly aged. His eyes looked as if he were hiding in them, or trying to.

Both he and Isobel were gazing at her. His eyes were pleading with her, Isobel's growing more suspicious every moment as Liz didn't go to him. Liz could see as well as Isobel that he was pleading with her to hold him, talk to him, ask him nothing for the moment; but she was afraid to go to him. Suppose he read in her face what she'd done to Anna? She was sure he would if she went near.

Eventually she did, for Isobel was growing visibly readier to tell Alan all she knew, or thought she knew. Christ, couldn't she leave them alone? Liz's body felt like one long tearing scream at Isobel, but she could only squat next to Alan and stroke his hair, massage his shoulders. He felt dismayingly thin and stiff and unresponsive; he didn't feel like Alan at all. Just now, what with the shock of his return and everything else that had happened to her, she, too, seemed unable to react.

Isobel's face was wavering, trying to be calm for his sake, but then her feelings won. 'Oh, Alan, what have they done to you?'

He stretched out his hands to her in a gesture that was meant to be reassuring, but, as he lurched forward in the chair, Liz saw how long his nails were. 'Don't upset yourself,' he said. 'It's over now.'

He sounded as if he wasn't sure himself. His voice was cracked and uneven, as though he'd almost forgotten how to talk. No wonder Isobel said, 'You need a doctor. Stay where you are, Elizabeth, I'll phone.'

'The phone isn't working,' Liz said, searching desperately for a way to turn this to her advantage.

'I don't need a doctor.' Alan leaned back, trapping her arm behind his shoulders, and closed his eyes. 'Just let me be quiet.'

Liz saw how to get rid of Isobel. Once Isobel had gone she might be able to talk to Alan, tell him how she'd changed – perhaps he could help her sort out her feelings. 'Isobel's right,' she said, for the first time in her life. 'We ought to fetch a doctor. My car's off the road, Isobel. I'm afraid you'll have to go.'

Isobel's eyes narrowed. She must know that Liz had got the better of her; how could she refuse? Yet she seemed prepared to do so, for she wasn't standing up. Liz was just wondering if hysteria would help – perhaps if she pleaded with Isobel to get a doctor, it would work on Isobel's anxiety – when suddenly her body stiffened, her lips froze. Upstairs a door was rattling.

It was the door of Alan's workroom. Anna had come round. Liz couldn't move; she was sure that Alan and Isobel knew what the sound meant. Perhaps if she didn't move, everything would go away. In a sense it seemed to, because the rattling wasn't repeated; Isobel relaxed, stopped listening; she must have decided that it had been only a draught. Liz was about to turn on the hysteria, when Alan demanded, 'Where's Anna?'

For a moment Liz couldn't speak for panic; she thought he knew. She swallowed painfully. 'At the hotel.'

'Are you sure?'

'Of course I'm sure. Why else would I say it?' Fool, she screamed at herself, he knows you're lying now; you wouldn't have said that if you were telling the truth. And see the way Isobel's looking at you now. But Isobel was watching Alan, who had put his hands over his face, peering out eventually through the crack between his hands as if he didn't want to be seen. He seemed both relieved and deeply distressed.

Isobel couldn't bear it. 'What's wrong with you, Alan?' she cried.

All at once Liz didn't want to know, dreaded hearing what had happened to him or what he might have done while he had been away. She didn't need to know just yet, only the doctor did. Alan seemed to agree with her, for whatever reason. 'I've told you, don't upset yourself,' he said, evidently unaware how his whole body was visibly writhing. 'I don't want to talk about it just now.'

'In that case, I might as well not be here at all,' Isobel said. 'I wonder why you asked me to come.'

Alan took his hands reluctantly away from his face. 'Because I didn't want Liz to be on her own.'

How much did he know? As much as Isobel suspected? Both of them were gazing at her. She could feel their pressure in her brain, building up into a scream or a confession – she wouldn't know which until the pressure forced her mouth open. So Alan distrusted her too, did he? Everyone did. Her fury at that gave her back some control. She must get rid of them before they heard Anna; she still had time. Getting them out of the way was all that was important now. 'I don't know what's wrong with you, Alan,' she said, with a bitter delight in her ambiguity, 'but you must listen to Isobel. You need to see a doctor right now. It'll be quickest if she drives you to the village.'

Isobel nodded agreement. Of course – then she'd have a chance to be alone with him, to tell him all about Liz. Liz no longer cared what Isobel said, so long as she was rid of them both before they heard Anna. Isobel came and pulled him up by his armpits, as if he were a child again – he couldn't weigh much more than a child, by the look of him. Supporting him with one arm round his waist she gazed down at Liz, until Liz wondered what she was waiting for. Isobel pursed her lips impatiently. 'I take it you're coming too?'

That wasn't the idea at all. Liz couldn't leave Anna locked up; suppose the child escaped, or managed to attract someone from the road? She had to stay here with Anna, she had to deal with her once and for all. 'I'd better stay here,' she stammered, 'just in case . . .' But she couldn't think of another word.

'If I'm to drive, you'll have to sit with him,' Isobel said, almost furious. '*Both* of us will be needed.'

Liz stared up at her, her nails clawing her palms inside her fists. She was thinking of wilder and wilder excuses not to go with Isobel, but none of them was any use – Isobel would know that she was lying. She might even suspect the real reason. Liz could only stand up, cursing and screaming silently, enacting on the small bright screen of her mind all the things she wanted to do to Isobel. But just as she stepped forward to support Alan, the phone began to ring.

It took her a moment to realize how it could, and who it was. A sudden delight, terrible and glittering, grew in her mind. Isobel was supporting Alan – only she could answer the phone. 'They must have fixed it,' she said, and went quickly to the phone before they could realize that it wasn't ringing as it should. 'Yes?' she said quietly, enjoying herself so much that she had to restrain herself from showing her teeth.

There was a silence whose nervousness she could almost feel, then a small timid secretive voice said, 'It's Anna.'

Liz made her own voice even gentler, so that Anna wouldn't suspect it was her. 'Yes?'

The words came out in a rush – Liz thought of diarrhoea, they were just as disgusting. 'Oh, please come and get me. Mummy's locked me in daddy's room. She's going to hurt me, she wants to hurt me, she isn't like mummy. Please don't go away, please come and let me out. Please don't let mummy get me . . .'

Liz was smiling sweetly. She turned to the others so that they could see. 'I'll be coming for you, don't you worry,' she said low and gently, and replaced the receiver. 'That was Anna at the hotel,' she said, knowing exactly what to say now. 'I have to go and collect her. You go on ahead to the doctor's and we'll join you there. I have to pack some things for her before I go.'

Isobel looked defeated; she couldn't argue now. But Alan seemed doubtful, wondering if he should speak. If he suspected Liz, if he said anything that suggested he did, she'd get to Anna before they did, by God she would. Then he shook his head and turned away. She watched Isobel helping him along the path into the fog. By the time they reached the car and she closed the front door gently, she was grinning so much her face ached.

Fifty

Anna sat and waited in daddy's room. Her dizziness had almost gone now, except when she tried to watch the blurry dance of the fog. Her head still hurt, but she thought that was mostly because of waiting. She wouldn't have long to wait now; Granny Knight was coming for her. She didn't want to wait much longer. She didn't like it up here.

She used to like it, before daddy had gone away. She used to love sitting here at his desk, pretending she was daddy. He would even let her sit at his typewriter and switch it on. But now the room looked old and sad, as if daddy had left it for good. His books and papers and his desk were going grey; she thought there might be spiders among the books. If she let herself, if she stopped reminding herself that Granny Knight was coming, she could almost believe that there was something very much bigger than a spider somewhere near, watching her and waiting.

She stuffed her fist into her mouth. She wanted to cry out to Granny Knight to hurry up, but she mustn't in case mummy heard. She must be patient; Granny Knight was bound to have to wait until she could come upstairs without mummy noticing. She wouldn't be long now. Anna had been waiting for so long.

She got down from the chair. Its wobbling was only making her nervous. Granny Knight was coming for her, she'd said that she was, but Anna wanted to see if she could hear her. She pressed her ear against the locked door. Now she would hear as soon as Granny Knight came up.

At first she could hear nothing, except perhaps the sea.

Or was that the sound of blood in her ears? She oughtn't to press her ear against the door; it would only make it more difficult to hear. But she did, and almost cried out before she realized that the sudden loud noise was her heartbeat, which sounded as if it was resounding through the wood. She managed to lever herself away from the door a little, for fear that mummy would hear her heart or that she would deafen herself.

Why couldn't she hear voices downstairs? She held her breath. She wanted to hear Granny Knight, to be sure she was still in the house. Her head was ringing with the effort of holding her breath, and she was beginning to feel as if someone was laughing at her silently, someone who was crouched just the other side of the door, when she heard a sound at last. It was the slam of a car door.

It sounded close to the house. But it couldn't be – or if it was, it couldn't be Granny Knight's car. Anna mustn't cry out to her – that would spoil everything. Another door of the car slammed, and then the engine started. Anna was fighting not to cry out now, and only just succeeding. It couldn't be Granny Knight, she'd promised to come for her. She wouldn't go away, not when Anna had told her about mummy. It couldn't be Granny Knight's car that was moving away, fading into the fog . . .

Suddenly Anna's heart leapt, and she had to stifle another cry, this time of joy: she could hear someone on the stairs! It hadn't been Granny Knight's car, Anna had known that all the time really, it probably hadn't even been as near as it had sounded. She was already forgetting it. All that mattered was the sound of footsteps on the stairs.

They slowed at the first landing, then came on up. Granny Knight must have told mummy that she was going to the toilet, and now she was hurrying up to the top floor before mummy realized. Couldn't she make less noise? She was climbing fast, but all the same she ought to take more care that mummy didn't hear her.

Anna was hopping jerkily from foot to foot with nervousness. Why, Granny Knight wasn't trying to be quiet at all. *She'll hear you, she'll hear you*, Anna cried, in a whisper that was trapped in her throat. Mummy must have heard by now that Granny Knight was coming up to the top floor. Why wasn't she trying to stop her?

Then Anna knew. She felt as if someone had grabbed her by the throat. It hadn't been Granny Knight on the phone at all. It had been Granny Knight who'd driven away, and now it was too late to scream. It had been mummy on the phone, mummy who'd said she would come for her, who was coming for her now. Anna was shaking so badly that she couldn't run or hide, she couldn't even think. She was paralyzed by the knowledge that it was mummy on the stairs, her footsteps on the landing now, mummy at the door and standing there to listen or to enjoy the thought of what she was going to do to Anna, mummy who was slamming back the bolt.

As the door opened, Anna moved. She had to, otherwise it would have knocked her down. She dodged behind it, out of sight for the moment, and watched in helpless terror as mummy came into the room.

Mummy was smiling. Her smile was crueller even than her outstretched nails: it wanted Anna to know that she was trapped, that there was nobody to help her, especially not Granny Knight. It wanted Anna to realize what was going to happen to her now. It grew wider as mummy glanced around the room. 'Playing games, are we?' mummy said softly. 'I know you're here waiting to be rescued. I'll rescue you, you little maggot.' She was reaching behind her to close the door.

Anna tried to duck under mummy's arm, to dodge round the door before it closed, before mummy noticed where she was. But there wasn't room. Her head bumped mummy's arm, and Anna screamed. Everything seemed to slow down like a nightmare: mummy turning triumphantly on her, her smile widening and her eyes gleaming as she jerked the door towards her, trapping Anna between the door and herself. 'So there you are, you little insect,' she said, grabbing Anna with her other hand.

Anna wrenched herself out from between mummy and the door just as mummy's hand closed on her shoulder. Mummy's nails ripped her blouse and her skin, but Anna was free and running desperately out of the room. Mummy slammed the door to trap her in it, to squash her in the opening like the insect she'd said Anna was. She was a fraction too late. Anna was beyond the door and on the stairs, almost falling. She couldn't hear her own feet on the stairs for her screams.

The door of daddy's workroom slammed open before she was halfway down the first flight of stairs. She fell then, clutching wildly at the banister, managing to hold on just as her feet struck the edge of a stair. The impact hurt her ankles terribly, but her only hope was to run downstairs – otherwise she'd fall. She hadn't time to regain her balance, for mummy was already on the landing.

She ran limping and sobbing to the front door, and fumbled with the latch. Her fingers felt like someone else's, swollen and clumsy; she was terrified that any moment she'd forget how to open the door. As the latch clicked and she remembered to pull at the door, mummy came into the hall.

She wasn't smiling now, though she was showing her teeth. Anna remembered a dog she'd once seen, dribbling white froth. Mummy had hugged her and told her not to move until men in uniform had come in a van to take the dog away. Mummy looked like that dog now – her face did, as she came rushing down the hall at Anna, her long nails reaching for her.

How could Anna turn her back on her? But somehow she did, and fled screaming into the fog, which surged forward as if it were helping mummy, telling Anna that she was trapped, that there was no point in running. It made her feel that she wasn't running at all, just trying to struggle through the grey that hardly moved, while mummy overtook her easily, nails stretched out to drag her back. When she reached the gate and limped out onto the road, she felt she'd run almost as far as she could.

But she could hear a car, on or near the road to the village. Was it Granny Knight's car? It didn't matter who it was, surely they'd hear if she screamed loud enough for help? She ran along the slippery road, screaming at the top of her voice. Her throat felt scraped to shreds by her cries and the fog she was sucking in.

She hadn't reached the road to the village when she stumbled to a halt. She couldn't hear the car any longer. She began to sob, and then she held her breath, she tried to be completely still, not even to shiver. She couldn't hear mummy either. She didn't know where mummy was, how close she might be in the blinding fog.

She'd started to cough, and then to sob because she couldn't suppress her coughing, when she heard the car again. It was on the village road. She wanted to scream for help before it went away, but she made herself be quiet, even though her throat was burning with the urge to cough. In a few moments she was sure that the car was coming back.

Granny Knight must have heard her. She ran towards the village road, screaming Granny Knight's name. It took her so long to reach the road that she thought she'd run past it in the fog. But here it was at last – and here on the verge at the corner, a silent figure was standing. She was dodging away from the looming figure, screaming louder and more desperately, when the fog thinned and she saw that it was the signpost, its pointer dripping like a nose. How could she have thought it was mummy? But any looming shape in the dense fog could be; Anna still didn't know where mummy was.

She limped along the village road as fast as she could. Whenever she slipped on the glistening tarmac, shapes lurched at her out of the fog. She hadn't the breath to cry out now, even though the car was nearer. In a few minutes she saw its lights, steaming like ice. The light touched her and probed beyond her, picking out a crouching shape about to leap. The shape was a stile. The car had halted a few yards from her, and the door behind Granny Knight was opening. Once Anna was in the car, she would be safe.

Then the man who'd opened the door climbed out and came toward her, and she began to scream.

It was daddy, but all she could see were his nails. They were longer than mummy's, and they were reaching for her. As she stumbled backward away from him, she caught sight of his face. It looked worse than it had the night he'd gone away: it was white and hungry and desperate, the face of a stranger who was hardly even bothering to look like daddy. As he opened his mouth to speak, she shoved her hands over her ears and fled screaming, without the least idea of where she was going, back into the fog.

Fifty-one

Liz had almost reached the village road when she heard the car turn back. She ran until she came to the dripping signpost and halted there, clutching her chest, which felt raw, full of fog. She'd never catch Anna now, she could hear how far ahead the child was. As she clawed at the signpost, a splinter painful as a red-hot needle dug under one nail, frenzying her, but it was no use: Isobel had heard the child's screams and was coming to save her. She was welcome to the little bitch.

Liz paced forward, just to hear what they said about her. They'd never see her in the fog. Once she'd heard what Anna said, she would steal away into the fog, which she hoped would never lift. Anna had made her like this, forcing her to creep about in the fog, having to hide from Alan. By God, she wished she could give the little bitch what she deserved.

She stopped, because the car had. The only sound in the fog was the quick flat slap of Anna's footsteps on the road. Fog drifted about Liz's face, wiping out her sense of distance. She couldn't tell how far away Anna was, but if she could hear her running, she'd be able to hear what she said. When she put her hand over her mouth and nose so as not to cough, she felt as if she were clawing her own face in frustrated rage.

Then she strained forward like a runner at the start of a race. She could hardly believe what she was hearing. She stole forward almost before she even realized she was moving, and then she began to grin. Anna was screaming and running. She was running back towards Liz.

Liz crept forward swiftly, enjoying her stealth. Her speed felt effortless; she seemed fluid as the fog. She still couldn't judge how close Anna's limping footsteps were; they sounded flattened, and so did the muffled argument Alan was having with Isobel; running and voices merged into a single plane. Perhaps Anna thought she was fleeing towards their voices instead of away from them.

Then Isobel raised her voice. 'Oh, can't I make you understand? She locked the child up. Anna must have been upstairs all the time we were there. If you knew how she'd been treating the child since you went away, you wouldn't find it so hard to believe. That's only one of the things she's been doing.'

So Isobel knew everything, did she? So much the worse for Anna: there was no longer any reason for Liz to hide what she meant to do. Liz was loping silently towards Anna's limping footsteps; already her throbbing fingernails felt as if they were embedded in her flesh. By God, Anna would pay for betraying her to Isobel and Alan. She didn't care if they were so near; their presence only made her more eager to deal with Anna once and for all. The fog would help.

She faltered for a moment as the car started, then she ran faster. She was still making very little noise. The car would herd the child towards her. She ran a few steps, then she halted, for even her stealthy movements were making it difficult for her to hear. So was the car, and she had to strain her ears for a frustratingly long time before she was sure that she could no longer hear Anna.

Was the child standing still, waiting for the car to pass? Or was she tiptoeing? She might tiptoe past Liz in the fog. Liz stood in the middle of the road and glared around her. The child wouldn't escape her this time. Liz would have to dodge out of the way when she saw the car's lights, but they wouldn't see her. The car was approaching too slowly to take her unawares.

It was the fog that made it seem so. Suddenly the smouldering beams of the headlights found her, splayed past her, lit up a movement on the verge to her left. She spun round, lurching that way to give Anna no chance to escape. But it wasn't Anna, it was a protruding clump of hedge.

Her mistake, and her rage at it, blinded her for a moment. Suddenly she was slithering on the wet road, but she didn't realize how badly she'd lost her balance until she fell. The tarmac hit her like a mallet as big as she was. She tried to suck in a breath that would help her throw herself out of the path of the car, but the car was coming too fast. Liz couldn't believe what was happening. As she raised herself on her hands to hurl herself aside, the front of the car rammed into her chest, smashing her backward on the road.

Fog poured into her body, and she was somewhere else, high in the grey air or across the invisible fields, hearing the belated screech of the brakes, the distant slam of car doors, voices that ebbed and surged, clear then muffled, then clear again. 'Oh my God,' Isobel was saying over and over like an evangelical record that had got stuck. 'Oh my God.'

Liz wished she could see Isobel's face, because for the first time in her life Isobel sounded as if she cared about her. All the same, she was glad to be so far from her own body, otherwise she wouldn't have been able to bear the growing pain. The whole front of her body was turning into pain. Hands touched her, she didn't know whose. 'You'll have to get to a phone,' Alan said in his new voice. 'I don't feel up to driving.'

Isobel had regained control of herself. 'You can't leave her on the road, not in this weather.'

Silence, grey: perhaps Liz had drifted away. 'If we're going to move her at all,' Alan said, 'you might as well drive her to the hospital.'

Metal noises, the hatchback being lifted, the back seat folded down. Liz was floating – no, hands were lifting her. It felt as if her pain had made her soar into the air. When they laid her down, nothing beneath her felt solid. 'You're coming too,' Isobel said, suddenly alarmed and startlingly close.

'I must get Anna. There she is.' Footsteps were running away. When he shouted Anna's name, the footsteps quickened. 'She must be heading for Derek and Jane's,' he said.

'I can't let you go by yourself, not the way you are.'

'I'm all right. Just let me take care of myself for a change. You get Liz to the hospital,' he said more gently. 'I can deal with things here, don't worry.'

Liz heard him running after Anna, then Isobel's door slammed. She could imagine Isobel shaking her head sadly, blaming Liz for his stubbornness. It didn't matter: Liz was floating away from her pain, and she didn't want to come back. Wait – wasn't there a reason why Anna shouldn't go to Jane's cottage, why she oughtn't to be there with Alan? The car started gently, and her pain surged up. She couldn't have stayed even if she'd wanted to. She was floating away where there were no more thoughts.

Fifty-two

Anna closed her eyes, which were smarting with the fog, and clung to the signpost, though the wood oozed like a snail in her hand. The ground squelched under her feet, mud was seeping into her shoes. Fog drifted toward her and away, making her feel as if she were swaying. She wanted to run and never to stop, but she couldn't go on until her heart slowed down. Besides, she wasn't sure what she had just heard.

She couldn't think, she couldn't plan. Her heart felt as if it was thumping her to pieces. Daddy had almost caught her, and then mummy had. When the car with daddy in it – if he *was* still in it – had started after her, she'd taken to the grass verge, sobbing inside herself and shaking as she'd tried to creep along. She'd been abreast of mummy before she'd seen her; the fog had parted and shown her mummy a few steps away, glaring about, looking for her. Anna had wanted to scream and give up, but she hadn't been able to; her feet on their aching ankles were still moving, smuggling her past in the fog. The fog had closed before mummy had seen her, and she'd stumbled as far as the signpost and was clinging there when she'd heard the sound.

It had something to do with the car. She'd heard a thud, and the car had stopped. Now Granny Knight was crying, 'Oh my God,' over and over. Perhaps the car had gone off the road and crashed into something; perhaps that was what the voices were muttering about now – but Anna couldn't tell whose voices, or even how many. It wouldn't help her if the car had crashed; it would only mean that Granny Knight, who might still be on her side, would be left behind by mummy and daddy while they hunted Anna in the fog.

She heaved herself away from the spongy signpost and began to run. She was weeping as the glare of the fog stung her eyes, weeping with hopelessness. She couldn't head for the village, and it was too far to the hotel. She could only run toward Jane's.

They'd heard her. The muttering stopped, and daddy shouted her name. She ran faster, taking to the verge to make less noise. She could hear daddy running to the signpost, coming after her along the coast road. She could hear the car. It was heading for the village.

So Granny Knight didn't care what happened to her. Mummy and daddy must have said something to her, to make her believe they weren't going to hurt her. Anna had no breath left to scream, and in any case, Granny Knight wouldn't believe her screams. The car dwindled into the fog and then, suddenly, between two painful heartbeats, it was gone. All Anna could hear now were daddy's feet padding quickly after her.

She couldn't hear mummy. She fled along the verge, terrified in case mummy had sneaked ahead of her and was waiting to pounce. Dripping grass-blades slashed at her, fog oozed back along the slimy hedges; underfoot the grass was slippery as polish. Whenever she slipped, she felt as if she were at the edge of the cliff, falling toward the sea she couldn't hear.

Daddy had stopped shouting her name. The fog made it impossible for her to tell whether or not he was catching up with her; his footsteps sounded closer than her own. He'd stopped shouting so that he could hear her better. He was going to catch her. All he had to do was run faster than she was running, along the road.

She dodged, sobbing, off the grass verge, towards the edge of the cliff. She had no idea how close it was. She felt she must be near Jane's by now, but perhaps that was just wishful thinking. The fog dragged over the grass, which looked coated with it; blades nodded, as if the passing of the fog had forced them down. The road had vanished, and the fog seemed to be spinning around her now; there was nothing to hold her sense of direction. She shouldn't have left the road, because now she couldn't hear daddy any more – or anyone else who might be coming for her. Was someone watching her, just at the edge of her eye? When she turned there was nothing but a fading glimpse of red.

She stumbled through the unkempt grass, and felt as if her feet were sinking into the soggy ground; mustn't quicksand feel like this? She wasn't running so much as putting her feet forward to stop herself from falling. She hardly knew where she was, or what she was doing. When she finally reached a landmark she knew, she was almost in it before she remembered what it meant.

It was the blackberry thicket. That meant she wasn't far from Jane's, though she wasn't as near as she'd been praying. She could follow the path through the mounds to the field next to Jane's house. The blackberries would hide her. She limped between the first of the dark thorny mounds.

At once she wished she hadn't. The mounds and the fog made her feel closed in, unable to get out of the small dark grubby place that was growing darker and grubbier. As each mound swelled up out of the fog she thought that it was lying in wait for her, and then that something behind it was. She would have turned back, except that her sense of being followed was even stronger. That made her run wildly, flinching as each new mound loomed up, but now the blackberries were trying to catch her too, thorny tendrils fastening on her clothes. When they caught her they felt like claws, like mummy's or daddy's fingernails tearing at her flesh. Once, when she swung round to disentangle herself, there were no thorns at all, only a blur of red in the closing fog. The red must be berries – the tendrils must have let go and sprung back, but she had no time to be sure, she was too busy running and sobbing.

By the time she realized she'd strayed from the path between the mounds, she didn't dare turn back. Now she wondered if that flash of red really had been berries after all. She was struggling along a side path and praying it would take her out of the mounds, crawling as thorns closed overhead. When thorns clawed her shoulders, she felt as if someone had leaned down to scratch her, like a cat playing with a mouse. The blurred shapes that loomed over her seemed red more and more often now, but she couldn't raise her head to see.

She wormed her way between two mounds, sobbing because there was nothing left of her except the urge to sob. Sand squeezed under her nails, sand rubbed her sides; it felt like salt in a wound. What was it that kept looming over her and at her back besides the thorns? She struggled among the blackberry roots, so wildly that she dislodged part of one mound, uprooting part of the tangle overhead. The net of thorns was falling on her, it would hold her until daddy and mummy came with their nails that were worse than thorns. But she heaved herself out from between the roots with an effort that left her back a mass of scratches, and suddenly she was out of the thicket.

She plunged into the tall grass at once. She must be facing Jane's house. Now that she was in the grass she couldn't stop to think or get her bearings; the sound of the grass, loud as a flock of birds, drove her onward – and so did a growing notion that she wasn't alone in making the grass rustle. If something was running after her or with her, she'd never see it until it got to her; leaving aside the fog, the grass was almost as tall as she was. She longed to stop for a moment, for she was deafened by the grass, but the thought of slowing down even a fraction terrified her. She was almost blind with running when part of the fog loomed up, grew paler, more solid, turned into a white wall. But it wasn't Jane's cottage, it was the windmill.

She would have hidden in there if she had been able to open the door, but not only was it locked, the hinges as long as her arm were rusted solid. She huddled against the door, clammy flakes of old paint clinging to her smarting back, and tried to think which way she must be facing. You could just see this door from Jane's cottage when it wasn't foggy, if you leaned out of a window and looked to the left; that meant that the cottage must be to her right now, or was it to her left? If you looked in a mirror and raised your left hand your reflection raised its right hand, which was really your left – but how did that help? Her sobs were growing louder, she didn't care how loud. Then she pressed her hand against her mouth, because she felt that someone was just beyond the edge of the fog, invisible yet watching her. Was it only her own snuffling she could hear?

She fled into the fog again, heading left, but then she paused. Was that the direction she should follow? She veered to the right in case that was the way and because she had a vague idea of dodging whatever was out there in the fog. Suppose she couldn't get into the cottage? Baby Georgie was dead, and Jane had gone away; she wouldn't be able to get in unless Georgie's daddy Derek was there. Surely he would be – it was where he lived.

A patch of fog on her left stood too still for fog, and turned into stone, white stone; the windmill. She ought to have gone right after all, she was running in circles in the fog. She was limping away, her throat too clogged with fog even to sob, when she glimpsed a corner of the stone as it sank back into the grey. The windmill had no corners. As she peered at it, afraid to go closer in case it was another false hope, she made out the edge of the garden, the unkempt hedgeless garden that merged with the field. She'd found the house after all.

Now that she was so close, she could hardly move for fear that she wouldn't be able to get in. Jane had always left the back door unlocked so that anyone who came visiting could walk straight into her kitchen, but Jane had gone away. If she couldn't get in, where would she go? She'd have to run into the fog, on and on until she fell, until mummy and daddy came for her.

They were somewhere in the fog, their long cruel nails were. Perhaps they were very near. She limped toward the cottage, which came nodding at her as if it weren't much more solid than the fog. The ground oozed, soaking her feet; fog closed on the sides of the house, walling her in with the door. She had almost reached the door; she was lifting her hand to knock, although it was shaking with fear that nobody would be in, when she stopped and stared. Unless the fog was playing tricks, the door was ajar.

Had Jane come home? Anna hoped it was Jane: she didn't know Derek so well – she didn't know if she could tell him why she was running away. The fog surged toward her, an imaginary attacker which perhaps hid a real one. She could hear nothing but her own gulping breaths, couldn't hear where mummy and daddy were, how close they were to catching her. The door was open a crack, the fog hadn't deceived her. Someone was in the cottage, that was all that mattered. She stepped forward and pushed open the kitchen door.

Fifty-three

She didn't quite know why she was opening the kitchen
door so slowly. When it squeaked she wished she could
hide inside herself. Fog closed in on both sides of her. She
was shivering so badly that she almost let go of the handle.
As soon as the door was open wide enough, she slipped in
and eased it shut behind her, so that she could let go at
last.

It took her a long time to calm down enough to look
round the kitchen. At least she was in Jane's house. But
somehow the house had never felt like this before, too
empty yet not quite empty after all, darker than she'd ever
seen it, with the fog walling up the windows. It made her
think of an attic that nobody had been in for years, where
you knew that something was waiting to be fed in all the
corners. It was the small dark grubby place she had been
in for weeks, but at last it was real.

Now that she was able to look about, she felt less and
less safe. Unwashed plates spilled out of the sink, a kitchen
drawer lay on the linoleum, surrounded by fallen knives.
The stench of stale cooking fat hung thickly in the air. A
buzzing drew her reluctantly to the sink, where a large fly
was struggling in the grey water. She couldn't stay in the
kitchen with the dying fly, its fat glistening body rolling
about in the greasy water, wings blurring desperately. The
door off the kitchen was open wide enough for her to steal
into the dining-room.

But the dining-room made her more uneasy. A pan of
milk stood on the polished mahogany table; the skin on
the milk was greyish and pockmarked, it made her think
of things that had gone bad. Next to the pan one of baby
Georgie's feeding bottles had dribbled on the polish. On

the mantelpiece and on a chair she saw half-eaten sandwiches. A fly buzzed past in front of her eyes, and she
flinched back so violently that she almost lost her balance.

She didn't know why, but she was even more afraid now
that she was in the house. She was afraid to stay where she
was, afraid to go on, afraid to run out of the house. Just
now she wished she could run out, for the smell of staleness
was making her sick; it was closing around her, worse than
the fog. There was something about it that made her think
of animals, of the zoo. The sense of things hiding in the
corners, or somewhere near her in the grubby dimness,
was growing. If the door into the hall hadn't been ajar, she
might just have stood there, too afraid to move.

She managed to slip into the hall without making a
noise. If someone was here, shouldn't she want them to
come to her? The smell was even thicker and more
sickening in the hall. Fog and condensation crawled up the
front-door panes, the living-room door stood open just
beyond the foot of the stairs. On the hall table between the
two doors, the telephone was perched on top of a pile of
directories.

She hoped that Derek wasn't in the cottage, because the
phone was more reassuring. She could call the police.
They'd come and take her away – they had to when your
mummy and daddy were going to harm you. She limped
forward, making no noise on the crumby carpet but no
longer caring if she did. She was at the foot of the stairs, a
few paces from the phone, when she heard daddy opening
the kitchen door.

She began to shiver so badly it seemed her legs might
give way. She clung to the slippery post at the foot of the
banister as her body leaned forward as if it had somewhere
to go. She couldn't run, he was too close, but perhaps she
could keep out of his way. She could hide upstairs, if only
she could sneak up. There was a hiding place in Georgie's
room.

She'd hidden there before. She'd squeezed into the
cupboard full of toys and poked her head out to make baby

Georgie laugh. Daddy would never think of looking there, only mummy and Jane knew, and they weren't here to tell. Nobody was. Nobody could save her from him but herself – and she couldn't move.

Her mouth shook as she bit her lip to keep in her scream. She didn't realize she had wet herself until her scratched legs began to sting. The discomfort made her legs move before she could control them, and the movement frightened her so much that she dodged up three stairs. There she froze, terrified to go further. She had forgotten which stairs creaked.

She was clinging to the banister, shaking from head to foot because she'd realized that she shouldn't have dodged upstairs at all but out of the house to hide while she'd had the chance, when she heard a creak. It wasn't the stairs, it was below her. Perhaps he was already in the hall.

She remembered how he looked. Though she was shuddering with unvoiced sobs, she began to drag herself upstairs by the banister, clambering desperately upward before he could see her. Her wet thighs rubbed together, stinging. The discomfort and her shaking made it impossible for her to choose where she trod on the stairs.

There were fourteen stairs above her, and it seemed to take forever for her mind to count them as she climbed. The banister felt like a balloon that was leaking; the stairs were swaying, stairs in a fun house that was no fun at all. She didn't dare look down for fear that she would see daddy, his blank eyes gleaming, his nails reaching for her. The fourth stair from the top began to creak under her foot, and she heaved herself upward away from it so desperately that the banister creaked instead. Blind with terror, she dragged herself up to the landing, trying not to touch the last three stairs.

The fog and the stale fat seemed to have gathered up here; the light was yellowish, the smell that made her think of a zoo was stronger; she had to press both hands over her mouth to stop herself from coughing. Downstairs the hall floor creaked, and only the stinging of her thighs prevented her from running.

She was passing Jane's and Derek's bedroom now. It was even more of a mess than downstairs. The bedclothes looked like giant knots, the drawers of the dressing-table lay all over the floor; Jane's make-up was spilt on the carpet, smashed jars and bottles covered the floor under the grey swirling window. Jane must have made all this mess, she must have been looking for something. Anna hadn't time to wonder what that might have been, for now she'd reached the door of baby Georgie's room.

She had to go in. She couldn't stand here waiting to be found, she'd scream and never stop until daddy came up to her. The yellowish light was settling on her eyes, and she felt as if they were clouding over. She reached out one shaking hand and clutched the doorknob, but she couldn't turn it. She was sure that if she looked into the room she would see baby Georgie, who was dead.

The hall creaked. Even that couldn't make her open the door. Though she didn't know what had happened to Georgie, she knew it had been horrible from the way everyone had avoided talking about it in front of her. If she opened the door he would sit up in his cot. What would he look like now he was dead?

Something creaked below her. Perhaps daddy was on the stairs now, perhaps he had heard her up here. Her fear of him was even greater than her fear of Georgie's room. Her hand was prickly with sweat, it felt as if the doorknob was electric and she couldn't let go. When she turned the doorknob convulsively she wasn't so much opening the door as falling forward into the room.

Georgie wasn't in the cot. She saw that at once, for the cot was splintered against one wall. His toys were scattered everywhere, but he wasn't in the room. She could see now why it was so foggy upstairs; his bedroom window was open a few inches at the bottom. She'd reached her hiding place; there was nothing to be frightened of in the room – and yet she was.

It wasn't just the dimness of the room, which was the fault of the fog. It wasn't the smell, though the room smelled more like a zoo than the rest of the house – a zoo at feeding time, she thought, without knowing why. It was the feeling that what had happened here was still here, even if she couldn't see it: baby Georgie's death.

She spun round, almost falling, thinking she'd seen red. It couldn't have been at the window: how could a red face have looked in up here? It hadn't been the mobile of six silver birds, still turning in the air above where the cot had stood; it hadn't been any of the Fisher-Price toys, rattles and music-boxes and an activity centre, though there was red in some of those. She mustn't waste time looking, she had to get into the cupboard before daddy came upstairs. She was stooping to the cupboard when she caught sight of the patch of red above the cot.

She stared at it, and then she shuddered away. She didn't want to know what it was. It wasn't really red, it was more brownish – a splash of reddish-brown as wide as her chest, high up on the wall. It looked as if a large egg had been smashed there, an egg full of — . . . She didn't want to know, she hadn't time to think. She got down on her hands and knees, all her limbs threatening to give way, and pulled open the cupboard doors.

Derek had built the cupboard into one corner of the room, with doors full of slats like wooden Venetian blinds. It reached to the ceiling and opened to reveal several shelves, strips of wood resting on wooden brackets screwed into the walls, several strips to a shelf. Toys were piled on all the shelves – so many toys for just a baby: Anna had heard mummy say once that Jane kept buying toys to try and keep him quiet. There was just room beneath the bottom shelf for her to squeeze in; at least, there had been a few months ago.

The space was full of toys now. She dragged them out one by one and piled them on the shelves she could reach, afraid that if she took out more than one at a time she'd make too much noise. She stooped and stood up, stooped and stood up; her legs were aching terribly, her thighs rubbing together, raw as scraped knees. More than once a toy almost slipped between the gaps in a shelf. She stooped and stood up wildly, terrified that her gasps of panic had been heard downstairs.

At last the space was empty, and she crawled in as quickly as she could. Then she began to sob. She'd grown too much since last time; she could no longer turn round in the space. When she tried, her shoulders lifted the shelf above her. If she hadn't backed out the shelf would have come loose, the toys would all have fallen, daddy would have heard.

She crouched on all fours outside the cupboard, shivering uncontrollably. If she crawled in backward, she wouldn't be able to move. What else could she do? There was nowhere else to hide. She backed shakily into the space and drew the doors closed, her fingers between the slats. One hinge squealed faintly, then there was silence, except for her aching heart.

The silence was beginning to let her feel safe, when she remembered that she'd closed the bedroom door. She wouldn't be able to hear if daddy came upstairs until he opened the door. She began to shake again as she peered through the slats, though she really hadn't room to shake. She was going to fall over, she couldn't stop herself – she would dislodge the shelf above her. She managed to lean her left shoulder against the wall to support herself, and then she felt as if the wall were shaking.

She stared out helplessly at the room. The slats let her see most of the brownish splash on the wall, but the more she watched it, the more she wanted to look away. It was making her want to think about it, think what it must be, here in the small dark grubby place that smelled like a zoo at feeding time. She was afraid of seeing baby Georgie – the brownish splash made her so, and she mustn't think why. If she did she'd run screaming downstairs, into daddy's arms, into his claws.

She was going to have to move soon; she was beginning

to get cramp. All her limbs were aching. Any moment one or the other of them would move, whether or not she wanted it to. If she lay down on one side and curled up, would that be more comfortable? She had to try. She eased herself shakily onto her left side, but that was aching so much that she almost cried out. She jerked onto all fours again, too hastily. Her shoulders were lifting the shelf above her. Everything was going to fall.

It was a long time before she dared to move, to lower herself on her arms so that the shelf settled back onto its brackets. She was afraid that it would miss the brackets and collapse on her. But when she made herself crouch down, shaking, it fitted into place. Nothing would fall now, nothing; *please, nothing* . . .

But something moved above her – something reached down out of the dimness and clawed at her back.

As she twisted out of its way, only her breathlessness saved her from screaming. She was cowering against the wall and the shelf now, and the shelf was going to come loose again, but she could do nothing about it. The strips of wood above her shifted, and the object that had clawed her fell out of the widening gap.

It was the claw that daddy had brought home from Africa.

She didn't know what it was doing here, nor did she care. She only knew that it made her prison seem even smaller and grubbier and darker. Was it what Jane had been looking for, why she had made all the mess and the brownish splash on the wall? Anna didn't want to think about it – she *mustn't* think. She grabbed the claw and shoving the cupboard door open, flung it out as far as she could.

It clanged against the wall near the brownish splash and thudded on the carpet. She'd got rid of it, but had daddy heard the noise? Was he coming up now, unheard, to see who was in Georgie's room? She had to close the cupboard doors before he came into the room, but she couldn't reach from where she was crouching, she couldn't move forward for cramp.

She strained her whole body forward and managed to touch the left-hand door. Her fingertips fastened on the slats and pulled, but her fingers were slippery with fear. Her touch swung the door out of reach.

He couldn't have heard, he would be upstairs by now if he had. She would have heard him on the creaking stairs. Not if he was creeping – and that thought made her jerk forward, out of her cramp. Her shaking fingers grabbed the left-hand door so frantically that she broke one of the slats. But she had a grip on it, she could draw it toward her, and now it was closed. She leaned sideways to get hold of the right-hand door, to close it as she backed into her hiding place.

She had just pushed her fingers between two slats when the door of the room opened and daddy came in.

Fifty-four

At first all he could see was the claw. Its talons were upturned toward him, beckoning. When he looked up he saw Anna cowering among the toys. She must have flung the claw away from her, he realized. Perhaps something had made her throw it down in front of him, a challenge. He had yet to do what must be done.

First he had to get Anna out of the room, away from the claw. He mustn't give in to the temptation to hurl the talisman into the fog, even if that might persuade her to trust him. It had to stay here, where he knew where it was. But when he moved toward her and the claw she cowered back into the cupboard like an animal into its lair.

He mustn't do anything that might make her run into the fog. Somehow he didn't want to leave her for any length of time in the room with the claw. He stepped forward again, slowly so that she could see what he was doing, and kicked the claw into the furthest corner of the room, near the mark where something had been thrown at the wall.

His gesture seemed not to help. Anna looked ready to dodge around him and out of the door the first chance he gave her. He remembered how she'd done that once before. 'All right, Anna,' he said. 'All right, baby. I won't hurt you. I want to take you where you'll be safe.'

Her face made it clear how that sounded to her. He mustn't let that reach him now; there would be time enough to feel shame and guilt and grief. 'Mummy's hurt,' he said. 'Granny Knight's taken her to the hospital. She'll want to see you're all right. Come on.'

She was staring at him with a child's boundless contempt, as if she couldn't believe he expected that to take her in. How could he have thought she would want to see Liz? He'd hoped that the idea of her mother in hospital would move her, but things had obviously gone too far. There was only one way to make her obey him, dismaying though it was. 'You don't want to stay here with me, do you?' he said.

He had to steel himself against the sudden terror in her eyes. 'Well then, come downstairs where I can see you while I phone for a taxi,' he said. 'You can sit on the stairs.'

He stood back from the doorway, though that took him toward the claw, until at last she crawled out of the cupboard. It looked as if cramp was forcing her to emerge. All the way across the room she seemed ready to run, to slam the door in his face. When he took her arm as he closed the door he felt her give herself up for lost.

He sat her down a few stairs from the bottom and managed to find a taxi firm that was operating in the fog. 'Just a few minutes, sir,' the girl on the switchboard promised, but he still wondered if he'd made his need sound urgent enough. Now there was nothing to do but wait and feel the exhaustion of his journey out of Africa threatening to overcome him, remember burying Isaac's body and saying as much over the grave as he could think of before trudging blindly through the jungle until luck brought him back to the road, remember the immeasurable sad resignation in Mrs Banjo's eyes before he had spoken a word . . . How long would the taxi be now? How long could he expect Anna to sit there without plotting to escape? Was the taxi delayed by the fog or by the follower of the claw, the blood-caked deathless famished follower? Surely it must try to stop Alan if it realized what he meant to do.

The soft sounds outside the house, a murmur and a thud, made Anna's eyes brighten with fear. It wasn't until the front door thundered that Alan was sure they had been the sounds of a taxi. 'Taxi for Knight,' the red-faced driver said, sniffing.

'We're ready,' Alan said, trying to pretend that everything was normal. The doors of the dripping vehicle had child-proof locks, thank God. He locked Anna in the back and turned away from her desperate look. 'I won't be a moment,' he told the driver, and ran upstairs.

He had to be quick, in case Anna persuaded the driver to let her go. All the same, he faltered when he reached the door of Georgie's bedroom. Suppose the bloody man was there, waiting to be fed or to save the claw? But the room was deserted except for a faint metallic smell that made his stomach churn. He grabbed the claw and felt nothing: no compulsion, no fear. What he had done in Africa had neutralized its influence over him. He shoved it inside his jacket, then he ran down to the taxi and sat beside the driver. 'Norwich,' he said urgently.

The fog appeared to be thickening. The road was a winding tunnel whose walls were closing in. The middle-aged driver slowed down even more whenever he heard a car. Alan tried to avoid meeting Anna's eyes in the mirror, but when he stared through the windscreen he thought sometimes that a figure was pacing the vehicle, just the other side of the wall of fog. Whenever the fog drifted he expected to see the figure waiting, red as blood.

The fog fell back as it reached the streets of Norwich. Five minutes later the taxi drew up in front of the hospital. He ascertained which ward Liz was in and hurried Anna through the gleaming corridors. For a while it seemed the corridor would never end.

Liz was trussed up in a bed at the near end of the ward. Her chest was bandaged, her right leg was held in the air by cords; she tried her best to lift her head to see who had come to the ward. Anna stared at her from the doorway and wrung her hands, then she ran into the ward, crying, 'Mummy.'

Isobel got up to restrain her, and caught sight of Alan. 'I won't be long,' he said, striding away before she could stop him. Of course he didn't know how long he would be, he only hoped. At least the sight of her mother in hospital had swept away Anna's fear, and now he had to make sure there was nothing to be afraid of, had to make sure that the claw could harm nobody else. He could feel how hard it would be to break. He climbed into the waiting taxi. 'Liquid Gases,' he said.

They had to go back along the road toward the coast, a journey of several miles. He couldn't have gone straight there, couldn't have risked taking Anna. Even now the sight of the storage tanks, looming like huge balloons out of the fog, made his stomach tighten, made him grasp the claw inside his jacket until the talons scratched his chest. It wouldn't be long now.

The rear lights of the taxi dwindled, staining the fog red, as Alan picked up the phone at the gate. 'Alan Knight for Mr Rothwell.'

'I don't know if he's on site just now. If you'll come to Reception I'll find out.' The owner of the rich deep Norfolk voice, which reminded Alan suddenly and poignantly of Isaac, released the gates for him, and Alan hurried along the paved crooked path which led to Reception. Apart from a tanker, he could hear nothing near him in the fog.

'He shouldn't be more than a few minutes.' The young man behind the window at Reception gazed at him. 'You're the writer, aren't you? I read *The Cold Cold War*. Borrowed it, actually, I hope you don't mind. The scene when they turn the hose on the girl is the one Mr Rothwell helped you with, isn't it? There were a couple of things there I wanted to ask you about . . .'

Alan couldn't cope with this just now. 'Do you mind if I find myself a seat in his office? I've been doing quite a lot of walking.'

'I suppose not, seeing it's you.' The other didn't look suspicious, only disappointed. 'You know where it is.'

The upper floor seemed deserted. Nothing moved beyond the frosted glass partitions of the offices. Alan sat by the site manager's desk, which was spread with a flow chart, and hoped he wouldn't have to wait long. If the site manager wanted to know why he wanted a sample of liquid nitrogen, he need only say that he would like to see how it affected metal for himself. Ten minutes' immersion and the metal of the claw ought to be ready to snap.

Perhaps the floor wasn't entirely deserted. Someone must have come in through an exit to the site, for he could hear them snuffling. Colds were to be expected in this weather. He glanced along the corridor, but could see nobody. He might be better occupied in finding Rothwell, since the manager didn't know he was waiting. The sooner the claw was beyond anyone's reach, the better.

He hurried to the nearest exit and down the metal staircase on the outer wall. The tanker was still manoeuvring in the fog, quite close now. Gravel crunched under his feet as he made for the building that housed the compressors. What with the fog and the noise of the tanker, he couldn't be sure if anyone had followed him out of the office building, couldn't tell if they were snuffling.

As soon as he stepped over the threshold, all he could hear was the constant shriek of the compressors. He climbed the steps and hurried along the catwalk, past the shrieking barrels fat as railway engines. When he mouthed 'Rothwell' at a man wearing a hard hat and ear protectors, the man pointed him toward the building where the turbines were.

The fog was closer now. It felt like concrete walls, massive and chill. Had it been a tail-light that reddened the fog just as he emerged? It had gone now. He wanted very much to find Rothwell.

The turbine building was smaller, the noise level even higher. All the machines looked grey with fog. He walked through quickly, wishing he could stop his ears. Nothing moved but the machines. Perhaps Rothwell was at the tanks, where the tanker must be loading.

Alan hurried toward the tanks. The shriek of the turbines had just faded into the crunch of gravel, and he was straining his ears to make out whether another sound was moving with him in the fog, when he faltered, clapping his hand over his mouth. He shouldn't look for Rothwell or for anyone, since the only way for the power of the claw to survive was for it to be passed to someone else.

He mustn't involve Rothwell. He'd remembered that the site manager had children. The only safe course now would be to involve nobody. He made for the tanks, as quickly and quietly as he could.

When a rounded shape loomed out of the fog he ran to it, for in the muffled silence he was sure he could hear snuffling. By the time he was close enough to make out that the shape was a tanker filling up with liquid nitrogen, the driver had seen him. 'Looking for someone?' he said.

'Mr Rothwell.'

'He'll be along in a minute.' The driver, a burly humourless man, looked suspicious. As Alan took a step back toward the other tanks he said, 'What've you got there?'

'Nothing.'

It was the worst answer he could have given. He cursed it and himself as soon as it left his mouth. 'Nothing, is it?' the driver said. 'Let's have a look.'

'If anyone does that it'll be Mr Rothwell, not you.' Alan was saying the first thing that came into his head – anything to avoid handing over the claw. He had no chance now of getting to a tank unnoticed and turning liquid nitrogen on the claw. If he tried to sneak away the driver would be after him. He stood trying frantically to think of some way to deal with the claw before Rothwell came, as ice gathered on the pipe that was filling the tanker, melting ice rained down from the tank. He was still trying when he heard the crunch of gravel beyond the cab of the tanker.

It wasn't Rothwell. He knew that when he glimpsed red, moving just inside the fog. It was the follower of the claw, the man who had had it made and been possessed by it, waiting to be fed – waiting for Alan to be forced to pass on the claw. It knew he would have to. Alan felt despair, colder than the fog that was forming a crust on the pipe, and then he had a last desperate idea. 'What's that?' he said, pointing toward the snuffling. 'A dog, is it? Chewing your tyres.'

The driver listened to the snuffling, then he went grimly toward the front of the tanker. 'Don't go away,' he warned Alan.

Nothing was further from Alan's mind. As soon as the driver was out of sight he grabbed the pipe to unscrew the connection. It was more difficult than he'd hoped; ice had sealed it to the tanker. He wrenched desperately at it and heard the ice crack. He spun the heavy ring, spun it again when the pipe didn't budge, wrenched again at the pipe. This time it came free, and he leapt back barely in time as it spilled liquid nitrogen over the gravel.

He had no time to waste. He pulled out the claw and slipped it into the belly of the tanker, into a bath of liquid nitrogen that must already be several feet deep. He hefted the pipe, which felt capable of gluing his hands to itself with ice, and shoved the end into the aperture in the side of the tanker, had to adjust it before he could spin the ring and seal the connection. Then he stepped back and turned to face what he'd heard.

He'd heard the driver cry out and fall. Now he heard a scrabbling of gravel. It wasn't until the driver called 'Mr Rothwell, are you there? Can you come here for a minute?' in a strange pale voice that Alan realized he was struggling to his feet. It must have been shock that had made him lose his balance. Alan could guess what he'd seen even before it came out of the fog, toward him.

It looked starved and desperate. Its scrawny naked body glittered with dried blood and ice. Its face looked hardly human now, if indeed it ever had. As it clawed at the tanker and the pipe it looked feeble but determined. Perhaps it couldn't deal with the connection because it was nearly all animal now. It tried a last time to reach the claw its nails screeching on the side of the tanker, then it turned on Alan.

Its bare feet had stuck to the spilled nitrogen. It lurched at him, tearing itself loose, leaving skin and flesh behind on the gravel. If it could do that in its desperation, what might it do to him in an attempt to make him retrieve the claw? All the same, he stood his ground. Whatever the follower might do to him, the claw was safely out of reach.

He wouldn't have been able to hear the intense cold inside the tanker break the claw, but he saw when it happened. He saw the naked figure jerk to a halt a few feet away from him, jerk and contort like metal under intolerable stress. All at once the crust of blood broke open in a multitude of places, and then the scrawny flesh did as its own thin blood boiled out. The figure collapsed as if age and death and its aftermath had seized it all at once, yet for an instant Alan thought he saw a kind of relief, almost gratitude, in its eyes.

He moved away from the stain on the gravel as Rothwell and the driver ran up. 'What was it?' they demanded. 'Did you see?'

'Whatever it was, it's gone now,' Alan said, and didn't care that they stared at his audible relief. They glared about then, not quite believing him. 'I'll come back another time,' he told Rothwell, who was hardly listening.

He knew he never would come back. The fog felt clean on his skin as he headed for Reception to call a taxi to take him to the hospital. He was himself now, and he knew Liz must be herself again. The influence was destroyed for ever. The sooner he was at the hospital, the sooner they could guide Anna back to trusting them. Sunlight began to break through the fog, and it felt like a blaze of hope.